Italian Bones of Contentions

Tina Assanti

authorHOUSE®

AuthorHouse™
1663 Liberty Drive
Bloomington, IN 47403
www.authorhouse.com
Phone: 1 (800) 839-8640

Published by AuthorHouse 12/12/2016

ISBN: 978-1-5246-5192-3 (sc)
ISBN: 978-1-5246-5190-9 (hc)
ISBN: 978-1-5246-5191-6 (e)

Library of Congress Control Number: 2016919929

Print information available on the last page.

Chapter 1

THE MAN LEANED HEAVILY ON the sticky coat-check counter and looked up at her with a sly glint in his aqua-blue eyes. Stroking Anita's sleeve, leaving wide tracks in the plush fur of her coat, he asked in mock innocence, "Focka fur?" This guy, standing with a damned clone or something beside him, was totally zonked. He leaned in so close that the top of his sweaty bald head almost nestled into her furry padded shoulder. He smelled of garlic, tobacco and grappa, and Anita screwed up her nose as she cringed away.

Of course, she, too, had had a bit too much to drink. It never took much to get her sloshed. Tonight—this lousy night full of gossip and innuendo—there had been about five too many. Bile from all that homemade Italian wine rose to her grim-set mouth.

Anita blinked over the man's moist head at the large central water fountain of the club's marble lobby. The sound of its cascading, artistically lit waters practically drowned out the crazy tumultuous sounds of the New Year celebration back in the hall. She was mildly aware of the gilt-framed portraits—some painted, some photographed—of forty years' worth of former presidents of the Vindenza Italian Canadian Club. She felt their penetrating eyes follow her every move. All men, all robust, all dark and, of course, all Italian-born.

She was still a little shaky after having skated on the spike heels of her black satin shoes through the accumulated ice and snow left on the pink-veined marble floor. She had been on her way to retrieving her coat when these guys seemed to lunge at her from nowhere. She defiantly smacked the dark, heavily varnished oak counter with her palm. The man jumped back but kept grinning.

"Jesus Murphy," she muttered, swiping away at her blonde bangs. She gave up and corrected his comment about her coat. "No, fox!" she slurred. "Fox! F-o-x." She rounded the vowels and cut the consonants for him carefully. "Shadow mink with silver fox!"

The stupid little man's grin widened, which made his stubbly right cheek twitch. She realized stupidly that this smelly, drunken Italian was hitting on her. "*Si*, datsa what I say-a, focka fur," he indignantly repeated, and then the idiot laughed.

What was his name again? Anita struggled to remember. Oh, yes, Guido Giordani. His brother, Mario Giordani—also visiting from Calabria, Italy—stood there ogling her, his gaze starting at her black satin high-heeled shoes and moving up her black-stockinged legs to her low-cut evening gown and the cleavage shyly peeking through the plush fur coat. He didn't even have the decency to continue on to her gold-and-aquamarine pendant and pearl earrings.

"Nice," she muttered. "I've just been royally undressed."

He supposedly spoke "nada de English," but he knowingly snorted a dirty laugh and grinned like a lecher.

"I thought you didn't speak English!" she bleated at him.

He shrugged his rather narrow shoulders under a gaudy purple silk shirt and said, "Focka eeza focka—*Italiano*, *Inglesa*—ya know?"

Focka eeza focka. Wonderful. Clever. "Oh!" she cried, the meaning of the word finally dawning on her. "It is not a fock fur!"

Guido pretended to ignore her outcry, chuckling a little first before gleefully continuing on with his line of thought. "You *bastardo* husband-a, Jack, she buy-a you dis *cappotto*?" He turned to Mario and they laughed together. They were having far too much fun flirting with her to want to stop.

"You don't know Jack. You never met him. How dare you call him a bastard," she said haughtily. "And yes," she lowered her voice, "he bought me this coat." She suddenly smiled sweetly as she caressed the fur as if it was a lovely little pussycat.

Guido leaned in again. "You-a deserve-a more dan dat *bastardo*."

"Why do you keep saying that?"

Mario shrugged. "Adriana, she tell us. You-a husband leave-a you, so ..." He shrugged again, "She-a *bastardo*. An' you-a no-a need dose-a rings now?" He pointed to her wedding and engagement rings.

"*He* bastardo, not she! *He* is *him* in English, and *she* is a girl!" Anita corrected.

Guido frowned, still hanging onto her sleeve but now for balance.

Mario piped up. "Who is-a girl-a?" He shook his head and then looked down at the melting snow on the marble floor. It had made a lovely swirly design. He started studying it intently as he swayed.

Guido continued on for Mario. "But we see-a you *bastardo* Jack-a las' week-a. How you say-a, we see at-a—" Guido turned to Mario, with thick dark eyebrows raised and strong short arms shooting out like wings.

"*Aeroporto. Con Pietro,*" hiccuped Mario, still studying the swirl.

"Ah! *Si!*" Guido turned and looked back at Anita. "*Aeroporto,*" he said agreeably, looking at her expectantly.

"Wha …? Airport?" Anita frowned. "Oh, *si*, he was going to Italy."

"*Che? Italia?* No, no, no," Guido said emphatically. "Venezuela!" Guido turned to look at Mario but had to nudge the man for his attention. Mario shook awake and peered at his brother. "Venezuela, *si?*" Guido repeated.

Mario beamed and nodded. "*Si!*"

"That's wrong," Anita said, raising a well-manicured finger. "So he was with Peter at the airport?" She whipped her head around to peer back into the banquet hall. Peter Giordani was a cousin to these two lechers, and he was one of Jack's business partners. No Peter in sight. Couldn't see him through all that cigar smoke. She swayed on her heels and slowly turned back to these two Italian cockroaches. "Why Venezuela? He's doing egg cartons for someone in Sardinia!"

"No, no. No she-a go to *Italia.*"

"She who?"

"She no-a go, you-a say!"

"No, *he* no-a go!" Anita was now totally confused. She waved a hand at them and turned to face the door. In the meantime, Mario and Guido impatiently babbled in Italian for a moment, their English vocabulary used up.

Anita turned back and stared blankly at them but then decided they didn't know what the hell they were talking about anyway. Suddenly the large hallway seemed to sway. She burrowed her face into the soft collar of her "fock fur and shadow mink" (as if she didn't know what they were getting at!) and tossed out a nonchalant and arrogant

"Whatever! I'm going home. *Buonanotte!*" She swung around to reach for the large brass door handles, but one of her heels skidded through the same swirly slush Mario was so interested in, and she skated to the door, making an absolutely graceless exit, all arms, legs and "fock fur." Guido and Mario were able to catch her by the hem of her damn fur coat and steady her.

Maria, 11 years old and gawky as heck, breathlessly ran up to them from inside the sweltering ballroom, shouting, "Anita! Anita! Mom said not to go! You have to stay and wait!"

Anita turned delicately, as her head now felt rather loose. She tried to focus on Maria's angelic white oval face and large black eyes. She stood wavering for a moment, deciding how to respond to Andy's apparent royal command.

Guido piped up. "Adriana, she wan' you to stay, *si*? Stay-a. We dance!" Guido did a hip-sway mambo-style.

"Oh Guido, she hates 'Adriana.' How many times do we have to tell you that? It's 'Adey …'" Anita paused. "Audey …" That still didn't sound right. She cocked her head and frowned.

"Andy!" corrected Maria.

"Yes, that's it! Andrey." Anita blew away a persistent tendril of hair from her eyes.

"Mom said to come *now!*" warned Maria, stamping her foot and then standing as stiff as a soldier can in a pink dress with ruffles.

Anita suddenly felt her stomach leap, and she made a split decision: *I ain't goin' to hang around here no more.* She shook her head slowly, silently turned and stepped through the open door. She stood for a moment at the top of the snow-covered concrete steps and paused, sensing the door slowly closing on the noise and music of a frantic Italian Canadian New Year's Eve dinner and dance. She could barely hear the Italian accordionist in the band leading everyone in the countdown to midnight and a new year – 1983.

Slowly she became aware of the soft silence around her. It was quiet enough to hear the oversized snowflakes gently settling on her shoulders and head. She sighed, wishing it was just as easy to shut the door on all the rotten anxieties pestering her.

Oh Lord.

So. Good ol' Andy. *Can't she see I need my space, goddammit!? God, you'd think it was her own husband who seemed to have up and disappeared!*

Anita snorted out loud. "Oh no," she mumbled, "never her poor Stefano! He'd never disappear on her, God forbid. Not even for a day." She grumbled to herself, cursing Jack for the millionth time that night. "And they insist that *my* poor husband could actually leave me for a fat pig accountant!" she yelled at the deserted wintry street. "Whoever she may be. Well, they're wrong, all wrong," she muttered. She shut up and looked around, suddenly aware of how deep the snow was getting.

In fear of being deluged by more Andy minions, Anita quickly bent over and, clinging tightly to the ice-covered wrought-iron railing with both hands, descended the stairs, her leather gloves clearing about an inch of new snow all the way down. The bunching snow crawled up her sleeves and packed against the inside of her hot wrists, making her shiver. Finally, it fully dawned on her that the snow was coming down quite heavily. *Pretty*, she thought. "Pretty," she said to the snow and smiled. *My Jack, I love my Jack*, she was thinking. *Good Jack.*

She meandered gingerly through the packed parking lot full of cars that now looked like massive scoops of sushi rice. She and Jack loved to eat sushi. She shook her head again and stumbled on through the ankle-deep snow. By the time she reached her car in the farthest corner of the lot, the snow had soaked her hair and made her makeup run. She opened the door, and an avalanche of snow fell onto the driver's seat. She plonked herself right into the middle of the pile and yanked the door shut. Silence. Her breath soundlessly puffed into the still cold air. Her cocoon of car, snow and ice offered a safe haven for the moment.

All alone at last, she held up her left hand and took off her soaked glove. She tipped her ring hand and allowed herself to be mesmerized by the dancing rainbow lights reflected off the diamond in the filtered light from the street. Then she wrapped her "fock fur"-covered arms around herself and proceeded to cry.

Chapter 2

NEW YEAR'S DAY MORNING, THE world outside her windows was strangely serene, with large wet snowflakes still falling steadily. The muffled roar of a distant snow blower laced the edges of the otherwise silent room. The phone rang much too early, waking Anita, who had slept in the middle of the bed fully clothed and still in the comfort of her fur coat. She moaned and covered her head with a pillow.

That damn phone. It kept ringing.

She groaned with frustration this time and, with a grunt, rolled over and sat on the edge of the bed. Unfortunately, that meant she was facing herself in the mirror. "Oh Lord," she whispered in shock. Last night was a mistake. She shouldn't have gone to that stupid place. Everyone thought they knew why Jack wasn't there with her. Andy made sure of it. A hate campaign against her husband had been taken up by the town's entire Italian Canadian population. And why? Did they not have enough to do without making up nasty stories?

Yes, she knew that Italian husbands did not, repeat, *did not* leave their wives for their mistresses. A number-one rule. "But Jack's *Irish!*" she yelled. Her face crumpled in grief. "They're wrong," she whispered to the mirror.

Riiing. Riiing.

Omigod! *It's Jack.* She grabbed the phone and yelled, "Jack?"

"Jack's shit, and who freakin' told you you could go?" Andy quipped.

"Andy, quit it! I can go back to my own home whenever I want to," Anita snapped. "You're not the queen. I do have a home, you know."

"Listen, people end up slitting their wrists this time of year for lesser things than friggin' asshole lily-livered husbands leaving them. You don't wanna do that, and I'm not gonna clean up no bloody mess!"

"I'm not going to slit my wrists, Andy."

"Yeah, so you say." There was a pause, and then, "So, hear anything from that son of a bitch?" Pause. "A 'Happy New Year,' maybe?"

Anita sighed. "No. And he's not a son of a bitch!" She sat quietly as Andy continued to tongue-lash her husband into mush and then told her to wise up and get on with it. Tough love. Cruel Andy. Cruel Jack.

Suddenly, Anita snapped to and focussed on what Andy was telling her: "Best of all, Stefano's cousins are over from Italy—I think you met 'em, Guido an' Mario? I can tell 'em to find him and, you know, give him a hard time. They said so themselves, a fine Italian husband would never leave such a looker as you."

"Wait a minute! A 'hard time'?" asked Anita. "What do you mean, Andy, 'give him a hard time'?"

"He's screwin' you around. No, pardon me! He's screwin' around on you!"

"Andy, you don't know everything. You have no right to beat up on him like that."

"Listen. You know 'em, Guido an'—"

"Yeah, Laurel and Hardy. I met them, Andy. I met them and their stupid jokes. Why would they give Jack a hard time? What are you saying? No, better still, don't answer that." Jack—Anita's darling, clever, impressive, perfect Jack—had turned her world upside down. And for what? For work? Her heart absolutely ached, she missed him so much. Jack, once apparently a dear friend of Andy and Stefano, had now been declared their enemy. And why? Anita sighed and let her burning eyes focus on the wedding picture sitting in its polished brass frame on her chest of drawers. Out of habit, a smile formed at the edges of her mouth as she listened to Andy ramble on. The photo was beautiful— two happy people in love standing by a rickshaw, arms around each other, big broad bright smiles that said, *We're so so happy! So lucky to have each other!*

Her eyes misted over, and the knife that was in her chest turned a little more. He hadn't called in two weeks. What if Andy was right? Jumping out the window headfirst did come to mind. Knowing her luck, she'd only land on a deep snow bank. "Chicken," she said to the mirror with a shake of her tousled head.

"You talkin' to me?" Andy yelled. Anita looked over at the empty half of the bed. That did her in.

"Okay, okay. I'll …" She sighed. "I'll come over. But just for a day or so. Until Jack comes back."

"Well, he won't, but good. Get here quick, but be careful. You'd think we were living in the goddamn North Pole." And then Andy hung up, just like that.

Chapter 3

"**M**ARIA! GET DOWN THIS MINUTE! You deaf?" Andy stood at the bottom of the carpeted steps, waiting for an answer. "I know you're there!"

"Whaaaat?" Maria's voice was shaping up to be just as loud as her mother's.

Andy nodded to herself. There was comfort in routine, and though another parent wouldn't stand for such rudeness from a precocious child this was normal for Andy. Her kid yelled back, and she knew everything was okay in the world. Routine.

"Get your skinny ass down here and help!" she yelled. In the Giordani house, loud was normal, and normal was good.

Andy went back into the kitchen and tended to a pot of stewing "bones." The nostrils of her prominent nose twitched at the agreeable aroma wafting up from the pot. Behind her, she could sense Maria slinking into the kitchen and plopping herself sulkily at the breakfast table. Stefano was already seated at the table. Big-shouldered and paunchy, he sat hunched over his bowl of porridge with his broad fist holding a spoon in midair. His piercing aqua-blue eyes under bushy black eyebrows drilled a sinister warning into Maria's large black-brown ones. Then he smiled and winked. This was part of the routine as well.

Stefano hardly ever spoke. In fact, after almost fifteen years of marriage to Andy, he still couldn't speak fluent English. There was really no need to, as almost everyone in his life spoke Italian anyway (though Andy refused to lower herself to his level and insisted on responding and speaking in English with both him and Maria). Consequently, for those who couldn't understand Italian, a few words, grunts, facial expressions, shrugs and the occasional banging of a fist on a table—the latter being very effective—was all he needed to get his message across. This also applied to Andy and Maria.

Stefano tapped the side of his bowl with his spoon to get Maria's attention again.

"What?" she asked innocently.

Stefano pointed a sausage-like finger towards the kitchen. Maria scowled and got up. Slowly she slid her bare feet over the ceramic tiles—made and installed by an Italian friend down the road—and dragged herself to her mother.

"Empty the dishwasher, and I'll get your breakfast," said Andy without missing a beat. Maria opened the dishwasher and let the door bang down hard. The clean glasses and plates clattered loudly.

"Maria!" yelled Andy.

"What?" Maria yelled back.

Andy held up the ladle and threatened to hit her daughter. She paused with meaning. Then she lowered the ladle and quietly pointed it at the girl. "Don't give me no freakin' attitude about last night again."

"Ah, Mom, I *hate* going to stupid parties. I could've *died* when you made me dance with Zio Rocko. And all those old guys said really rude things to me."

Stefano grunted from the table. "What dey say?"

"They said I was like a broom with two tiny peas!" cried Maria.

Stefano stared at her for a moment and blinked. Instantly, his face turned crimson.

Andy jumped in. "They're old, Maria, and they're Italian. They can't help it." She threw a glance at Stefano.

"It was gross!" complained Maria.

"Deya no mean nothin'!" Stefano passionately blurted out. He then quickly turned his attention back to his bowl of porridge.

"And he's always wanting to dance that stupid chicken dance with me. I swear to *God* I hate that song." Maria took a wet bowl out of the dishwasher and shook it over the sink.

Andy looked at the back of her growing daughter and noted that she indeed was sprouting into a tall thin woman-child. *Maturing before her time*, she thought. Andy then lifted the ladle into the air and yelled, "What? You don't like the chicken dance?" she teased, and she started to dance, flapping her arms and singing, "Tahdahdatta-dadatah! Tahdahdatta-dadatah! Tahtatta-dada-dada-*dah-dah-dah-dah*!" Andy clapped the last four beats, beef broth dripping from the ladle. Even Stefano chuckled and shook his head, his gold tooth glinting in the ray of sunlight that suddenly poured in through the kitchen window behind him. He looked over his shoulder and saw blue sky. *Aaah*, he thought to himself, and shovelled the porridge in faster.

"Moooom, stop!" Maria whined.

"Look at me, Maria! I'm a freakin' chicken!" Andy continued. "Just like your father's stupid hens that wake me up every goddamn morning," she yelled, elbows flapping, "*Caaw, caaw.*" In response, Stefano's exotic Vietnamese hens outside by the back wall answered with their own caws. Maria suddenly guffawed, laughing so hard she had to bend over double.

Stefano grunted, wordlessly pointed at Andy with his spoon and scowled.

"I know, I know," Andy said. "Your goddamn feathered pests. We eat 'em. So we're supposed to freakin' like 'em? What's wrong with buying goddamn chicken breasts at Bruno's, Stefano?"

Stefano rubbed two fingers together for "money" and finally finished his porridge. His spoon clattered into the empty bowl and, with a thrust, he pushed back his chair and stood up, stretching. "I go to barn-a," he announced.

"Yeah, you 'go to barn-a,'" Andy mimicked. She watched his broad back as he stepped down into the family room and then through the basement door. She listened as he trudged down the basement stairs, and in her mind's eye she saw him grabbing his lumberjack jacket, putting on his Portuguese fisherman's cap, and slipping on his massive boots. Out to the barn. *Goddamn barn*, she thought. She leaned back against her stove for a moment and stared out the back window at the swaying, snow-covered tops of the pine trees out back and the now-brilliant blue sky.

"Well, happy freakin' New Year," she mumbled.

Chapter 4

LONG MELTING ICICLES GRACED THE length of the eaves trough, dripping brilliantly clear icy water onto the warming blacktop driveway. Tiny rivulets collected into the smoothed-out dips of the pavement created by years of supporting Stefano's truck. Big and mud-splattered, the truck stood there now with "Stefano Giordani & Sons Contractors" painted along both sides. Steam rose from collected puddles under the massive tires.

Anita pulled up behind it in her grey Taurus station wagon. A couple of hens cocked their heads at the newcomer from where they were scavenging beneath naked willow trees along the driveway. Anita got out and swung the door shut, catching it in the straps of her overnight bag. She struggled awkwardly to open the door again and pull the straps free.

The slam of the door echoed over the back property and was heard—although in muffled form—by Stefano out in his barn behind the house. He stopped throwing grain at his clucking hens and poked his rosy wet nose out the barn door. The sight of Anita usually brought a strange sense of peace to him, but this time he was caught unawares by her presence and his heart skipped a beat. He took a step back and watched as she made her way to the back door. He dropped the sack, wiped his brow with the sleeve of his lumberjack jacket and left the barn.

Upstairs, in the kitchen, Andy was warming up Italian buns for lunch and spreading out thinly cut Black Forest ham and tomatoes on a large plate. "What took you so long!" she yelled, as Anita dragged herself through the family room and into the kitchen. "I oughta whip your ass for driving on your own last night, blondie!"

Anita sighed as she slid into a chair. The pounding of what sounded like hooves from upstairs preceded a grinning Marie, who shot into the kitchen and screamed as she jumped on Anita's lap. "Anitaaaa!" Anita grunted loudly as Maria's arms and legs banged into her.

"Maria!" yelled Andy.

"What? I love it," said Anita. "It's okay. Right, you?" She tickled Maria on the side of her bony rib cage. Maria giggled and screeched, her long legs and big feet hitting the wall.

"Maria!"

Maria pouted and got off Anita but dragged over another chair right next to her and sat beside her, head lovingly leaning on Anita's shoulder. Anita reached over to pat the girl on the back. Andy mutely raised her eyebrows, sniffed and turned back to the oven.

"Ya missed the best part last night," she said casually.

"Why, what happened?" Anita was now messing up Maria's hair. Maria giggled.

Andy dropped her arms and sighed. "Are you listening?"

Anita and Maria tried to wipe away their smiles.

"You left, when?" Andy questioned. "Midnight?"

Anita was about to answer when she was distracted by Stefano lumbering into the family room from the hall. He mutely nodded at Anita with a big, dazzling smile, hair wet with perspiration and a glow in his cheeks. Andy silently watched him and waited as he stepped up into the kitchen and took his chair for the second time that day. The wood creaked loudly under his weight. His eyes shyly lingered on Anita's returning smile.

He leaned forward and poured a juice glass of red wine from the ever-present wine carafe in the middle of the table. He had a soft spot in his heart for Anita, and he did the only thing he knew how to do to comfort her: offer his own homemade wine. He leaned over and gave Anita the glass. To make her strong, he motioned, pounding his chest. Strength. Then he showed a bicep and pointed back to her. Anita laughed and took a sip of the pungent liquid, letting it burn its way down her throat. Stefano nodded approvingly as he filled another for himself.

Andy cleared her throat.

Maria whipped her head around and looked at her mother. Quietly, Andy pointed to Stefano.

Maria got off her chair, took her father's glass and went to the kitchen sink. She turned on the tap, filled the glass halfway, carried it back to the table and handed the glass back to her father. Stefano frowned, added wine to the water and took a sip. He made a face and then looked at Anita with a shrug.

"Where were we?" Andy muttered, turning back to the stove.

Anita leaned over to Stefano and whispered, "For your heart?"

Stefano blushed and nodded. "*Si.*" Then he motioned for Anita to go ahead and drink her wine.

"Oh yeah," Andy said. She turned her head and saw Anita bent towards Stefano. "Are you listenin'?"

Anita gulped at her wine and quickly turned around in her seat. "Um, no, yeah, midnight."

Andy stepped over to the sink and peered at Anita under the hanging cupboard. "Well, you missed all the excitement! Antonia went to get her mink coat, see, at the coat rack—it's not mink, by the way, it's rabbit, but we pretend we don't know that like we're a bunch of idiots or somethin'—and she saw her Tony's shoes sticking out from under the coats. You know how Tony loves his expensive shoes from Italy, and they usually have these printed patterns in the leather and all that shit."

Stefano grunted and shook his head at the word *shit*.

"Okay, *kaka*," Andy said to Stefano, and then she turned back to Anita. "She thought maybe Tony took his shoes off 'cause she knew they hurt his corns, and now that he's diabetic ... well, you know. So she went over and bent down to get 'em for him when she notices a pair of kneecaps behind the shoes. And at the end of those kneecaps were legs, and at the end of those goddamn legs were feet in pink sling-back fucking shoes, and you can guess what that meant: Celina was giving Tony a ..."

"Andy," Stefano yelled, slamming his fist on the table and pointing to Maria.

But Maria ignored her father entirely and piped up, "What did Zia Celina give Zio Tony?"

"You're not supposed to be listenin' to no gossip, young lady!" warned Andy. She continued anyway. "Well, Antonia screamed like a banshee and everyone heard it, even over that freakin' loud accordion! He was back to his old tricks, see. Remember when he was doin' the same thing with you know who?"

"Who?" asked Maria and Anita in unison.

"Theresa," said Andy before Stefano could stop her.

Stefano banged the table again. "You no-a know dat, Andy!" he yelled.

"Yeah, I do-a know dat!" she retorted. "He makes a meal out of it with anyone at the drop of a hat! And he boasts to you guys!"

Stefano stared menacingly at Andy, the large nostrils of his equally large nose flaring. "Las' night-a, you no know dat."

"Oh no? Anyhow, we all know which chiquita wears pink around here!"

Maria piped up, "Mrs. Carlesi wears pink too!"

"Roberta?" Andy thought for a moment and then shook her head. "Nah. Roberta's at least got some friggin' class. She'd never lower herself to wear pink shoes. Just goddamn pink minks. Besides, can you imagine Roberta doin' such a thing?" Andy said, giggling.

"Do what thing, Mom?" coaxed the not-so-innocent Maria.

"Well," Andy continued, ignoring Maria, "Antonia told me if she'd had a gun she would've shot her! She screamed bloody murder, and she went to pick up that metal garbage pail that's behind the counter, you know? The one with that stupid print of the stupid Acropolis—as if we were freakin' Greek—and then she went to smash it into Celina's teased-up bleach-blonde head (you know she's not a real blonde, not like you, Anita), but all those goddamn coats got in the freakin' way. So somehow Celina manages to get out the back door of the coat room and run through the dance hall and out the kitchen doors! And guess what?"

Anita, Maria and Stefano said, "What?"

Andy tapped the side of that beak nose of hers and nodded. "No one's telling Bruno," and to Anita, "You know, the butcher?" Anita nodded, open-mouthed. "That's Celina's husband. Anyway, Bruno can't know about it, because not only will he kill Celina if he knows, he'll also kill Tony, and Antonia wouldn't like that too good, so she let it drop."

Everyone pondered deeply the perplexities of Italian Canadian domestic politics for a moment or two.

"Oh, by the way," Andy chirped. "You and me are going to a crystal party at Sandra's Sunday. And I'm not takin' a no from you, kid."

"Ah, Mom," Maria moaned.

"Not you, kid. Anita!"

"Andy, I've been to two already!" Anita protested. "I really don't need more crystal."

Andy brought over the hot crispy buns, the platter of meat and bottles of wine vinegar and olive oil. "Listen, I don't care how many times you go. You're going to every goddamn baby shower, wedding shower, wedding, christening, birthday, retirement … here, dip your bread into this." She stood back and continued marking the events off on her fingers: "Winemaking, cheese-making, sausage-making, fundraising, dances, funerals, birthing lambs, butchering lambs, canning tomatoes, grilling peppers, Tupperware parties, jewellery parties, packing radicchios, making gnocchi, making noodles and goddamn crystal parties!"

"Andy, please," Anita argued.

"And you're goin' with me to the hairdresser, dressmaker, butcher, baker, priest, barber, doctor, dentist, bank—more precisely, Italian Canadian Credit Union—and church, whether you're a goddamn Roman Catholic or not!" Andy plunked down in her own chair and poured olive oil and vinegar onto a small plate. She then broke a crusty bun and dabbed it into the vinegar and oil. "Oh, and by the way, you're helping me on Wednesday. It's my turn to polish the pews this week, and you're vacuuming."

"I'm sorry?" said Anita.

"You're welcome." And Andy flashed a grin.

Chapter 5

ANDY BENT OVER AND PICKED up a crumpled tissue from the plush red carpet underneath one of the pews. Stuck to the underside of that pew were small fossilized mounds of old gum, and she shivered in disgust. She let go of the half-filled garbage bag she was dragging behind her between the rows and straightened up, her back cracking. She kicked off her high heels and plopped into the pew with a groan.

"Cripes, some people are goddamn pigs," she said. Andy was about ten rows up from the front of the church. The ceiling was vaulted and looked more like a chalet than a traditional Catholic church. In fact, it resembled a Shakespearean theatre-in-the-round with rows of pews curved away from a large raised platform. In the middle stood a simple altar beneath a very large suspended metal cross, flanked on both sides by long stained glass windows. Earlier that day, there had been a funeral service, and on the floor were scattered used tissues, funeral pamphlets and the odd hymn book. Up at the altar there was an avalanche of flowers on and surrounding a very large, cream-coloured, brass-detailed coffin. Anita's frazzled head popped up from behind it.

"Andy! Shhh! You're always swearing!" she hissed, pointing up at the cross.

Andy crossed herself begrudgingly and rolled her eyes.

Anita looked around nervously. She had been searching for a plug in the floor for the vacuum cleaner but had trouble ignoring the coffin in front of her. She jumped and squealed as a crumpled-up paper missile hit her head. "Shit, Andy! Don't *do* that!"

Andy snorted a laugh. "Got ya! Wuss!"

Anita eyed the coffin. "Andy," she whispered. "Can't we come back later?" She tentatively touched the smooth and highly polished lid of the ivory-coloured casket.

"No, we can't come back later!" Andy yelled. "Anyway, the funeral home'll come back for it pretty soon." She looked at her watch. "They're probably on their way now. And there's no need to whisper, by the way. There's only me, you, God, and that stiff there, and we know he can't hear anything."

"God's house and all," muttered Anita.

Andy searched in a pocket and found a stick of gum. She peeled it and dropped the tiny pieces of foil in the direction of the garbage bag. She missed it entirely.

Anita searched through the flowers. She stopped and touched a salmon-coloured rosebud. "These flowers are beautiful," Anita said quietly.

"Yeah, they're beauts," Andy mumbled as she leaned back, stuck the gum in her mouth, and let her nose point itself up towards the cathedral ceiling. She noticed dust-covered spiderwebs floating from the girders. "Shit," she mumbled to herself, chewing loudly.

"What happens to them afterwards, Andy? They're far too good to throw away." Anita bent over a mound of pink carnations around the side of the coffin. She thought about her wedding day and the pink carnations she wore in her hair. Suddenly she panicked and broke out in a cold sweat. It was coming up on three weeks now, and still no Jack. She felt nauseous and clasped her stomach.

"They're from Peter's funeral parlour across the road." Andy's nose turned towards the stained glass windows overlooking the main thoroughfare, and she listened to the gentle sounds of traffic going by. She focussed on the windows, and her own stomach turned at the thought of having to wash them. "You met Peter, my brother-in-law?"

Anita had straightened up and now fingered a pristine white rose. "I know him, Andy. He's the one who sent Jack on his business trip."

"You believe that crap?"

"Andy, stop."

"So, you saw him and Sandra at New Year's. Filthy rich. Started off as mostly Sandra's dough, but now ... "She waved a hand towards the wall facing the road.

Anita begrudgingly resumed her search for an outlet and found one under the carnations. She plugged in the vacuum cleaner and stood up. "Of course I know her. She arranged a trip to Hawaii for ... Jack and me. Nice lady."

"Yeah, well. You know she was desperate to find a guy. She snapped Peter up just like that," she snapped her fingers, "as soon as he got off that plane from Italy."

Anita turned on the vacuum cleaner and continued vacuuming in front of the altar. Andy raised her voice over the noise.

"We sponsored him, you know, Stefano an' me! Did ya know that? Yeah, he did well, I tell ya!"

Anita turned off the vacuum cleaner to pick up some fallen blossoms, and Andy lowered her voice while picking at lint on her fine woollen skirt. "He got into a few things ... the business with your idiot of a husband, of course. What was it supposed to be?"

"Fertilizer," said Anita.

"Uh-huh ... that funeral parlour, florist shop on the corner down here, a beauty salon, Sandra and her travel agency, of course. They get it comin' and goin'. Somebody drops dead, and everyone in this goddamn town has to outdo everybody else buying the biggest and most expensive bunch of flowers. There's usually enough to drown the coffin and have a freakin' Niagara Falls on both sides down to the floor! Weddings, too. Birthdays, Mother's Day, Valentine's Day, little Suzie's freakin' piano recital, Holy Communion ..." Andy studied her fingernails. "So he sells flowers for a funeral, but they're still fresh when the funeral is over, you see, so he comes over and takes them back when he picks up the coffin, and then he puts them right back into the shop and sells them the next day for a wedding or a birthday. If they start to die, he donates them to the church and gets a tax receipt for 'em." She poked the air with a finger to make a point. "But Peter has a way of keeping 'em fresh." She stopped as she realized that Anita was staring at her with the vacuum hose in her hand held straight up in the air. "What?" she asked irritably, chewing away.

"What are you saying, Andy?" whispered Anita, appalled. "He sells the same flowers over and over again?"

"Shit. Did I say that?" Andy kidded, her voice loud and clear. She chuckled, and the sound was still echoing off the vaulted ceiling when the back doors opened with a soft bang and hiss and Father Carl Carloni briskly walked through and down the aisle. His dark beard was well trimmed, and he had a sophisticated touch of white at the temples. His face, though lined and worn, was ruggedly handsome and had soft-hearted undertones, giving him a welcoming and friendly aura.

"Oh, hello Adriana," he said. "I thought I heard your dulcet tones from the parking lot."

"Yeah, right. Hi, Carl. Whatya doin' here?" Andy brightened up and then swallowed her gum by accident.

"I work here, remember?" he said, smiling, as he continued down the aisle.

"Oh really?" she choked. "Hey, I see you got your flea collar on today."

Father Carloni touched the white plastic collar at his throat. "Yes, I finally had it dry-cleaned," he joked. Andy laughed loudly, almost choked again and coughed.

When Father Carloni glanced over at Anita, his heart seemed to stop for a moment. He stood with his mouth agape for a second before he caught himself. Anita was a blonde-haired version of a young Scottish woman he'd known once in Liverpool, England. His mind instantly flew back to 1963 and the Roman Catholic sanitarium he volunteered at. Her name was Dorothy, and she was married to a young Irishman who had run off with another young woman. It apparently tore her heart apart. She was a devout Roman Catholic and believed she had been doomed to never be able to remarry again. Her grief threw her into an abyss of physical pain and emotional turmoil, which directly or indirectly put her into the tuberculosis ward of the sanitarium.

Father Carloni had been called to her bedside to see if he could counsel her and bring her some hope for the future. She was the most amazing looking human being he had ever had the pleasure to rest his eyes upon. Dorothy looked like an angel. Light glowed from her head of long black tendrils, and her eyes shone with heavenly blue. It caught him off guard. It was the closest he had ever come to walking away from his sacred vows. Yet she had never had an inkling of how he felt. He wondered to this day if she was still alive, and if she ever thought back on the young priest who stuttered.

He was startled back to reality when Andy finally cleared her throat and said, "Listen, Carl, I want you to meet a good friend of mine, Anita. Anita, this is Father Carloni."

Anita dropped the vacuum hose and hurried up the aisle, hand outstretched. "Nice to meet you, Father."

Father Carl slowly held out his shaking hand. "Please," he gulped, "call me Carl." He shook her hand and looked down at it. Reverently, he laid his other hand on top of their clasped hands.

Anita smiled as she very carefully pulled her hand free. "Carl Carloni?"

"No, it's really Joseph Maria Carloni, but everyone calls me Carl for short. Right, Andy?" he finally said, looking over at Andy with his laughing, dark eyes. Those eyes swivelled immediately back to Anita.

"Behind your back, they call you other things," Andy teased. "Carl is just to your face."

"Oh, yeah? So what nasty things do they call me behind my back?" he quipped without taking his eyes off Anita. Anita blushed.

"*Mio Cara* Carl!" Andy flippantly threw at the cathedral ceiling. "And *Bellisimo!*" Carl and Andy laughed as Anita looked on. "And if you believe that, I've got some property to sell ya in Florida. What a waste, huh?" she said to Anita.

"Andy!" Anita muttered, turning a further crimson red. Father Carloni saw her blush and grinned like a little schoolboy.

"A fair maiden, thou doth blush so," he said. Anita smiled sheepishly. "What's your connection with this wayward soul, *bella* Anita?"

Anita first looked at Andy. "Well, my husband works with Andy's brother-in-law, Peter."

"Oh, your husband?" He finally drew himself up to full stature. "What's his name? I might know him."

"Jack. Jack Taylor?" Anita seemed to shrink.

He caught that and cocked his head, still smiling. Then as he remembered Jack. He frowned for a fleeting moment but then quickly resumed his benign smile. Anita caught the change. She cocked her own head to the opposite side of Carl's. She looked at him questioningly.

Andy jumped in. "Well, I guess we better get on with this." Andy saw something she thought she'd better cut off at the pass.

"Father Carl, I wonder if you could help me," Anita whispered.

Father Carl stepped forward and leaned towards her. "Of course, if I can." His heart skipped a beat. *I'll punish myself after*, he thought.

"Sorry, Carl, you can't help with this," Andy chimed in.

Anita turned to face her. "Andy! Please!"

Andy sighed deeply and plunked onto the nearest pew. She sighed loudly a second time just for effect.

"Carl. May I call you Carl?"

Father Carl swivelled his head amiably, held out both palms and then clasped his hands together. He smiled and nodded.

"My husband left on a business trip the third week in December." Anita started to become teary-eye and stopped to regain control.

Father Carl frowned in romantic concern and made a move to comfort her, but he quickly thought better of it. He reclasped his hands and kept the extremely concerned frown on his face. He hoped that did the trick.

Andy caught it and groaned under her breath. She shook her head and chuckled to herself. "Anita, don't waste his time," she admonished.

"Andy, nothing that comes across my path by the good Lord and our heavenly Mother of God could be a waste of my time. I am *here* for *exactly* …" he motioned up and down towards Anita, "*this!*" He turned to Anita and asked, "Would you like to step into my office?" Anita nodded silently and let him lead her through a door just to the side of the altar. Before closing the door after Anita, Father Carl poked his head out and said, "Excuse us, Adriana. You'll have Anita back shortly."

Andy shrugged and waved her hand. "Yeah, whatever." She settled back in the pew and sighed as she studied the spiderwebs on the ceiling once again.

In the office, Father Carl kindly motioned for Anita to sit in front of his old, scratched-up desk. Sun poured through a grime-covered window behind where he was seated. On the water-stained sill stood a single pot containing a dead, dried-up plant, species unknown.

The priest leaned in towards Anita. He reached out his hands and invited her to place her hands in his, which she did. He grinned happily and shifted his weight in his chair. He posed with his chin slightly up in the air, and then he sighed as he feasted on her with his eyes. "Now," he said quietly, his bottom lip quivering with emotion, "how can I help you?"

Finally, someone who will listen, thought Anita. *And he seems to like me.* Anita suddenly dropped her head, and her blonde hair fell over their clasped hands.

Father Carl whimpered. He saw she was starting to cry softly. He immediately let go of the right hand and reached for a dented tissue box in one of his creaky drawers. He slid it gently towards Anita, but it got stuck on a slightly sticky spot on the old wood. He picked it up after haltingly letting go of her hand, rubbed the heavily marked surface of the wood and placed the box neatly close to her head. She looked up and took a few tissues out, and he held the box tightly as she did. She wiped the tears away and started to wring the tissues nervously in her hands.

"I'm afraid something has happened to my husband. It's been three weeks since we spoke." She looked up at him, her eyes large and soppy.

"He's on a business trip, you said earlier?" Father Carl asked, falling into those large, soppy eyes.

Anita nodded. "Yes." Anita took a deep and quivering breath. "He was to fly to Italy first and arrange for a delivery of egg cartons to a new client. It's … it's part of our business. He was only going to be gone for five days, and he told me not to worry if I didn't hear from him. You know how difficult it could be to phone … from …"

Father Carl nodded vigourously. "Oh yes, I know veeery well." He thought back on his last trip to the western portion of Sardinia and remembered how it felt as if he'd stepped back into the Dark Ages. He had done a mild exorcism there of a young boy. He remembered something about cheese. He had vowed never to go back. *Perhaps I'll write a movie script about it one day*, he suddenly thought.

"Yes, of course, you probably … would …" continued Anita.

Father Carl shook the strange memory from his mind. "And no word from him since the day he left?" He sat back in his chair and posed with his fingertips together. *Do I look like a writer?* he wondered. "Well …"

They stared at each other—she for one reason, he for another. Finally he asked, "And you called the police?" He straightened up, shook off the memories good and bad, and reminded himself that he was actually a very good shepherd. He pursed his lips. He loved his congregation. And he was a good counsellor.

Anita nodded slowly.

He cleared his throat. "No help from them?"

Anita slowly shook her head.

"And you confirmed with the airline he actually flew to Italy?"

Anita nodded. "Yes."

He shrugged and sat back to think. "I don't—"

"They say he's left me for another woman!" she blurted suddenly.

Father Carl looked nonplussed. "Who says?"

"People. I heard rumours at New Year's. I was at the club and several people talked about it. It was very upsetting."

"Of course it would be," he said authoritatively. "What exactly do they say he did?"

"They say he flew to Italy with a redhead! Some accountant! And the longer he's gone, the more I tend to think that maybe they're right. Oh, why does he let me suffer like this?" She cried freely for a moment and then covered her face with the moist tissues.

Father Carl looked on and then played with the tissue box on his desk. "I see." He leaned forward and placed his hands on the desk. "I'll see if I can find out what happened to your Jack. It seems that us priests have a way of getting people to talk."

Anita looked up at him and for a moment, her eyes questioned him. They had a humorous sparkle in them. Almost impish. Like Dorothy so long ago.

"I mean, of course, we have a way of making people feel *comfortable* enough to talk." He closed his eyes as he secretly chastised himself. *That sounded like the Godfather, you dummy*, he thought.

As if she heard his thoughts, she grinned.

Father Carl sat up and fussed. "But these days, we don't torture people to get it!" He laughed.

Anita laughed too and stood up. She held out her hand, looked at it, wiped it on her skirt and then offered it again. Father Carl took her hand, shook it and laughed. He opened the middle drawer and took out a pen and pad. "Here, why don't you write down your phone number so that I can give you a call." He rolled his eyes to the side. "For business, of course." He motioned to the desk. "This business."

Anita nodded, quickly wrote down her number and then Andy's and then slid the paper back towards him. "Her royal highness insists I stay at her place because she thinks I'm going to slit my wrists if left on my own, so you can call me there as well."

Father Carl laughed and nodded. "Say no more." He stepped around the desk and gallantly opened the door for her. "And I'll pray for you," he said, smiling adoringly at her. He then cleared his throat, " ...and for your husband, of course."

Anita smiled. "Thank you."

They both stepped back out into the main church. Anita brushed her hair back behind her left ear as she carefully stepped around the cascades of flowers, making her way back to the vacuum cleaner.

"'Wondered what you two were up to," yelled Andy, still in the same position in the same pew.

"Andy!" Anita cried, looking wide-eyed at Father Carl. "That's not nice!" she hissed.

"Not to worry. I'm used to it," quipped Father Carl. Anita looked at him, and he motioned to Andy. "I'm used to her and this, I mean."

"Anita's staying with us for a few days," Andy explained needlessly.

"Yes, I know. Always the mother hen," he said, bowing slightly in her direction.

"With her, I have too!" Andy scratched under her chin. "I guess you know by now that her asshole of a husband took off with some goddamn …" Andy caught Anita's pointed glare at her. "With another …" she stumbled.

Father Carloni raised an eyebrow. "Another … woman? Yes, I've heard that there are rumours." He exchanged looks with Anita.

Andy rambled on. "She thinks he's comin' back. I tell her, forget about it! I mean, look at her, she ain't exactly a spring chicken anymore, if you know what I mean," Andy said, tapping the side of her nose with a forefinger.

"Gee, thanks, Andy," Anita grumbled. Her eyes drilled into her friend's.

Father Carloni looked at Andy askance. "Now, Adriana, you know very well we don't encourage giving up on a marriage so easily. Anita's right to stay hopeful." He looked over and smiled at Anita.

"Oh yeah, I forgot—we're still in the Middle Ages. No offence." Andy threw up her hands.

"I'll try not to take any," he said.

"Hey, the guy's not Italian and he's not Catholic, so no loss, right?" Andy reasoned.

"I'm sorry?" asked Father Carloni and Anita in unison.

"He's Catholic and he's Irish," Father Carloni said, making a stand by Anita. He looked over to exchange looks again with Anita, but she was staring at him questioningly.

"How'd you know *that*?" she asked.

Father Carloni shrugged. "I know lots of Irish Catholics. Just because I'm Italian doesn't mean I should neglect the other sheep." He motioned around himself. "Everyone knows everyone in Vindenza, Catholic or not Catholic. I know he's Irish!"

"Well, no wonder he's straying, Carl. He ain't a good ol' wop. Now, you take Italian husbands, Anita, right?" Andy went on, ignoring their looks of surprise. "They might stray now and then—let's face it, men are men," she shrugged.

Father Carloni opened his mouth to say something in retaliation but then closed it and instead cleared his throat loudly.

"Present company excluded, of course," Andy added quickly, nodding to Father Carl. "But they never, ever, *ever* leave their wives," she said, wagging her finger. She leaned forward in the pew, this being her favourite topic. "Never! But I tell ya, if I ever find out that Stefano strayed—you know?—he better run and hide from me, because I would cut off his *testicoli* and then I'd kill him!" She thought for a second and added, "Him *and* whoever the tramp would be!" She grinned and sat back. "Not that it would happen, of course. I know Stefano." With a laugh, she added, "He doesn't have it in him. He's a homegrown version. They're the most devoted." She made a funny motion with her head.

Father Carloni turned to Anita and pointed back at Andy. "She one clazy rady, huh?"

Andy quipped, "And you ain't no slouch either, Carl!" She laughed heartily.

"That's my exit line," said the priest. "Save the rest of your sinful thoughts for confession."

"Can't wait!"

"I have a christening to prepare for." He took Anita's hand. "It was a pleasure meeting you, Dorothy ... er, I mean, Anita. Call me if you need to speak to anyone. As I hope you found out, I'm a good listener." He looked sideways at Andy and then back to Anita. "I mean it. Call on me anytime." He tried to look truly professional. He patted her hand and turned to go.

Anita watched him cross in front of the altar and noticed that he dragged a finger gently along the lid of the coffin as he passed. He looked at his fingertip, and then he disappeared back into his office, gently closing the door after himself.

"Yummy, isn't he?" whispered Andy.

"Oh God! He's a priest, for crying out loud, Andy!"

"So? Didn't you see how he looked at you?" winked Andy.

"Andy!" yelled Anita.

Andy laughed and threw a crumpled paper at Anita, who picked it up and immediately threw it back at her, hitting her in the middle of her forehead. "Hey," Andy warned, "watch the nose!"

Back in his office, Father Carl heard the women's banter but did not listen. Anita's presence had shaken him, and memories had rushed in so quickly that it made him feel queasy—queasy and uncomfortable, because they were carnal memories, a reminder of his weaknesses and days laced with remorse. Her eyes were what unsettled him the most. He clasped his hands and whispered, "Please, God, forgive me these thoughts." He mentally tried to redirect his focus onto a level more holy than the misty, ignorant planes humans typically lived on.

He straightened in his chair. *God must understand*, he thought hopefully. He raised his eyes to the ceiling and as he did, the familiar and comforting touch of a celestial hand rested on his left shoulder. His body shuddered involuntarily. Slowly he raised his right hand to tenderly touch the ghostly presence. Somehow he knew he had been forgiven, and a familiar rush of intense love coursed through his midriff. He closed his eyes, smiled and decided that there was no room for guilt in this life.

He thanked God for the privilege of having loved an angel in his life, and he recognized that the happiness such memories brought was in itself a gift and a blessing. He said a little prayer on behalf of Anita and then on behalf of the love he once knew.

He opened his moistened eyes, wiped away the tears and picked up the slip of paper with Anita's number on it. He looked at it closely. Now somewhat sobered, he thought of the two men who had disappeared without a trace a few years back and of the accompanying rumours. He searched his mind for contacts he may have had that could possibly lead to information about Jack and his whereabouts. Somehow he sensed there was an urgency.

He opened his top left-hand drawer and pulled out a black, tattered address book. He flipped through the pages but, frustrated, he stopped and hung his head. Who was he kidding? He always felt helpless in the face of disappearing members of his flock. He always hit dead ends no matter how hard he tried. With reverence, he surrendered to the only tool he had at hand and clasped his hands in prayer.

Out in the main church, the back doors slammed open suddenly with a large bang. Andy and Anita looked up to see Peter Giordani rushing through.

"Speak of the devil," yelled Andy.

"Adriana! How is my favourite sister-in-law, huh?" said Peter. Dapper in a grey silk suit, white-on-white dress shirt with gold cufflinks and a dark blue tie, Peter was a walking billboard for "clothes make the man."

"I'm your only sister-in-law, you twerp. And stop calling me Adriana!" complained Andy before she motioned to Anita. "Hey, a broken-hearted angel here."

Peter walked down, reached for Anita's raised hand and kissed it. "*Si*," he smiled and eyed her appreciatively. "Charmed as always."

"Still no word?" Anita asked beseechingly.

"No. But I gotta tell you, 'Nita, it's quite possible he's just held up. You know, entertaining the customer, invited to their villa with no phone, testing out the wines—"

"Trying out the women," Andy added.

"Isn't there anything more you can tell me, Peter? A name of someone? A business?"

"Now listen, Anita. It's kind of in the boondocks there. He may be racking up the orders and too busy to look for a way to call or write."

Andy snorted.

"No, I mean it. It's wicked out there. Who knows what great leads he's come up with now? A sucker for our new plastic moulded egg cartons, or a new disposable container for Leo Mangiano the Pizza King in Siderno, Calabria. Who knows?"

"Aaahhhhh! Our fock-a fur lady!" someone called from the doorway as two men in suits came crashing through with a large gurney. Anita, appalled, turned around and immediately recognized the two goons she had met at New Year's—Guido and Mario. They waved at her in unison.

"Oh Lord," Anita cringed, casting a glance over to the door behind the altar. She lifted a finger to her lips. "Shhh!"

"Yeah, guys. Smarten up. We're in church already!" Andy snapped, her voice echoing. And to Anita, "What's this 'fock fur' thing they're talkin' about?"

Anita rolled her eyes. "It's a long story." She put her hands into her skirt pockets. "I'll tell you later."

Peter motioned to the guys to keep moving and joined them by the casket. Then he motioned to Anita and Andy to come closer to him.

"I have a little joke for you," Peter said, glancing over his shoulders and dropping his voice. "A man is-a walking home at night, and he hears *a'bump-a'bump-a'bump-a* behind him. So he walks faster but looks back and makes out a coffin banging its way down the street after him, *a'bump-a'bump-a'bump-a*. The man, he starts to run to his house, see, and the coffin bounces after him even faster, *a'bump-a'bump-a'bump-a*. He runs up to his door, looks for his keys, opens the door and locks it behind him—and the coffin crashes right through the door! The coffin starts to open, still bumping up to him. The man, he runs to the bathroom and locks the door, his heart-a pounding, and *crash!* The coffin breaks down the door, still coming at him. The man screams and then grabs something, anything! So he finds a box of cough drops and throws them at the coffin ... and the coffin' stops." He grinned.

Andy smacked him on the shoulder. It took a second longer for Anita to get it, and she groaned. "Oh, that's awful!" she cried.

Mario and Guido sneered and chuckled from where they were standing. They had moved some of the flowers to the side and now grunted as they struggled with sliding the coffin onto the gurney. Suddenly, the coffin slipped out of their grasp and crashed to the floor, knocking off the lid. The body of a portly elderly man rolled out and fell face down on the plush carpet. Guido and Mario each screamed in soprano.

Peter yelled *"Merde!"*

Andy yelled, "Fuck!"

Father Carl ran out of his office, saw the body, put his hands to his face—which turned ashen—and fainted.

Anita almost peed her pants and ran to Father Carl while Peter, Mario and Guido—all throwing out undecipherable Italian expletives—grunted as they placed the coffin on the floor. At the count of *uno, due, tre,* they lifted up the corpse and plunked it back into the coffin. They slammed the lid shut, and all three sat on it to catch their breath.

"Holy fuck!" Andy yelled again.

Father Carl stirred awake, his sunken eyes riveted on the coffin. Anita helped him up, and the two of them joined the three stooges in lifting the coffin back onto the gurney. After a pause, Andy sprang forward as well and desperately tried to steady the rolling gurney into place for them. With a clatter, the coffin finally balanced on top.

Stunned, all five stood back and froze in place with their hands over their mouths. After a moment, Peter was the first to stir.

"Well, that was fun, wasn't it guys? He-he." He straightened out his thousand-dollar suit and slicked his hair back with a quivering hand.

"You should've given it cough drops," said the breathless Father Carl.

Andy snorted loudly and Peter guffawed, pointing at Father Carl. "Very good, Father, very good. Yep."

Father Carl put his hands up and stepped backwards towards his office. "Everything sorted out here now? Yes? Okay. Excuse me, I'll get back to, uh, what I was doing, if that's okay." He almost tripped over the vacuum cleaner but fell in step again. He felt behind him for the doorknob and quietly turned and stepped into his office, closing the door gently behind him.

"Holy shit," Andy muttered, unusually speechless.

Peter adjusted his sleeves with a jerk and tapped on the top of the coffin lid. He whispered, "Hey. I wanna show you something." He turned to Anita. "Have you ever seen a corpse ..." he made the sign of the cross silently and quickly "... as beautiful as this guy?"

Anita licked her dry lips. "Actually, I, uh, didn't get a good look." She turned to Andy wide-eyed. Andy shrugged, frowning.

"No, no, no. Don't worry," Peter said. "I ask you as a professional mortician."

"Doesn't a mortician have to be a professional?" asked Andy. "Either that, or you're psychotic."

"Wait. I'm very proud of the work I do here, and I'm sharing this with you because I want you to see how dignified this work can be.

Please, here … "He opened the top half of the coffin, exposing the elderly man once more. Andy and Anita leaned forward. The corpse's face was colourfully made up, his silver hair blown into a bouffant and looking …

"Peter, you made him look like he's in drag," Andy said. "Either that, or 'she's' a butch."

Peter ignored her and carefully straightened out the corpse's tie. Tenderly, he patted the corpse's chest. "There. Look at that. There, my dear ladies and gentlemen, is a masterpiece. That takes talent!"

Anita silently looked over at Andy, who snorted once again.

Suddenly, Anita felt sick. "Um, can we finish up here, Andy?"

"Yeah, no rest for the wicked, not like the dead, right?" Andy quipped. She went up the aisle and retrieved her green garbage bag while Anita quickly turned on the vacuum cleaner and vacuumed as far away from the coffin as possible.

Over the noise, Peter yelled, "Don't forget Saturday, it's your godson's birthday. And bring Anita along."

"Yeah, we'll bring some flowers. I might as well buy some off that coffin now, Mr. Swift. It'll save you having to put them back in your storefront window!"

Peter pretended he didn't hear and walked out with his arms loaded with flower arrangements. The two cousins, grinning lecherously at Anita, followed behind him, rolling out the heavy casket with the rest of the flower arrangements carefully balanced on top. In their wake, they scattered a long line of dead flowers.

"Oh, for fuck's sake," Andy muttered as she grabbed her garbage bag and went over to clean up the carpet once again.

Chapter 6

ANITA LISTENED INTENTLY AS SHE held the phone to her ear while leaning against the wall in the hallway. Andy came stomping down from upstairs carrying a massive straw basket overflowing with dirty laundry.

"Maria's asleep?" whispered Anita.

Andy nodded. "Who ya callin'?" she demanded.

"I'm listening to my messages," said Anita sadly. She listened for another few seconds and then silently hung up.

"No message from him, right? I tell ya, forget that asshole!" Andy insisted. "Would ya look at what he ran off with? She's nothin' but a whore! You care about a man with taste like that?" And thinking it would cheer her up, she pinched Anita's burning cheek and said, "You know every single guy at the social club would gladly push Jack's *cojones* up his ass for you. They think he's nuts for leaving you. Every male drools over you, and I don't mean the babies!"

"Andy, most of them drool anyhow, they're so old," said Anita.

Andy laughed. "You're right there! A bunch of toothless, dirty old men!" But Anita wasn't laughing. Andy sighed. "What's wrong?"

"Well, it's just rumours, Andy. I mean, have you actually, with your own eyes, seen him with this redhead?"

"You know what? I don't need to. Others have, and what they say is good enough for me. Besides, all men would do the same thing given half the chance. Except for—"

"Yeah, I know. Except for Italian husbands."

Andy balanced the slipping basket on her left hip and scratched behind her right ear. "Besides which, I've known him longer than you have, and believe me, he ain't no saint. He only started to be nice after he met you. I guess he got bored doing the right thing."

A dark cloud passed over Anita's brow. Andy pretended not to notice. She looked at her nails and pretended to study them in the dark. "You deserve better."

"Andy, you don't know him like I do!" Anita threw up her hands. "This is driving me crazy not getting a hold of him. And no, Andy, I'm not going to give up. If anything, I don't deserve *him*!" Anita stepped away from the wall and into the dark kitchen. "I know in my mind that the world has to keep on turning. I feel like it's the end, and yet the birds keep on chirping, the sun keeps going up and down, but all the time I'm dying inside!" Anita stopped near the kitchen table. She covered her face with her hands. "I miss him so," she murmured through her fingers.

Andy stepped over to Anita and put the basket down. She tried to pry a few of Anita's fingers apart as she bent over to peek through them.

"Knock, knock," she said.

Anita dropped her hands and wiped her face. "Who's there?"

"Otch."

"Otch who?"

"God bless you!" laughed Andy.

Anita tried to smile, but she couldn't. She took a tissue out of her pocket and blew her nose. She shook her head. "That wasn't funny."

"No, you're right, it wasn't funny."

"Andy, this is no good. I have to go home. Besides, you don't want me underfoot. I'm just in the way."

"No you're not, Anita."

"Yeah, and Stefano …"

"Hey, it was Stefano"s idea we keep you hangin' around."

Anita fell quiet and searched Andy's eyes. "Stefano? Now why would he care about me?"

"Because we Italians look out for one another, girl."

"I'm not Italian."

"I know, but we are," said Andy.

"Do you realize that's the first time I heard you acknowledge being Italian?"

"Well, I'll only admit to what little is good in being Italian."

Anita fell into a chair at the table. She looked down and fiddled with her tissues. "Well, I'm grateful for all you've done, Andy, but I can't be a weight around your neck like this. And I can't take any more time off work. And Jack …" Her voice broke, and she paused a moment. "I have to … I have to do something about this, you know? And not grieve like he's dead or something." She blew her nose. "I mean, really, he's only been gone—what?"

Andy dropped the heavy basket on the table. "Hellooo? Almost a month! And how long did he say he'd be gone?"

"Five days, maybe a week."

Andy looked up at the ceiling and then down at her slippers. "Okay," she shrugged. "Tell you what. You go home, but come back Friday night. Okay? Stay for the weekend and we'll do the crystal party thing on Saturday afternoon and then Stefano's godsons' birthday thing that night. Whadya think?"

Anita nodded. "Yeah. I can do that. Okay."

"Okay," Andy said. She hoisted the basket. "Time to hook up my chain to the washing machine. You know the way out! But don't lock the door behind you, 'Nita, 'cause Stefano's still in that friggin' barn. He's got this friggin' new exotic Japanese long-tail rooster or whatever it's called. It cost a shitload of money. It's supposed to be frigging horny all the time. But then who gives a shit anyway, right?" She walked down the few steps to the dark family room and on to the basement stairs. "At least someone's getting some tail. No one around here, ain't that right, Anita?"

Chapter 7

AND SO, AS MUCH AS Andy hated to let her go, Anita finally went home that night—all of fifteen minutes away. She spent the night tossing and turning, coming up with a dozen different reasons for Jack's silence, if not disappearance. Early the next morning, she made another one of many calls to the factory—a plastic moulding company owned by Jack and a consortium of silent partners. Jack had one rule: never call the factory, as it was a madhouse, and it was better to reach him on his car phone than to bother his overburdened receptionist, Nancy. Of course, Anita had been breaking that rule since the day before Christmas, when he should've been home. But during the night, there seemed something sinister about that rule. Doubt plagued her, and she began to think that Jack might have had something to hide. Goddamn that man! She picked up the phone and dialled the factory.

Nancy answered the phone. "Happy New Year! J & P Plastics Inc. May I help you?"

"Hi, Nancy. Happy New Year."

Nancy was usually crisp and businesslike, but as the weeks went by, she had warmed to Anita and was most concerned. Today, she sounded agitated. "Anita! What a coincidence! I was about to call you!"

Anita's heart jumped. "What?"

"Well, I just opened up the office, and there was something in the fax machine from Italy."

Omigod! Anita thought. "Omigod!" she cried.

But Nancy was distraught. "Yes, a fax from Calabria, Italy ... um." Nancy paused.

"Nancy, talk to me!!"

"Anita, it's a fax confirming a reservation at a hotel for a Mr. and Mrs. Jack Smith."

"Jack Smith?" Anita was perplexed. Her heart sank. "Mrs.? Why Smith?"

"I'm so sorry," said Nancy. Anita ignored what the woman was implying.

"Nancy, give me the information, please."

Nancy obviously was torn. Jack was her boss, and Anita knew Nancy had conflicting loyalties here. Should she keep to business and be loyal to her employer, or should she help Anita find her missing husband?

"Well, hang on. Maybe I've got this wrong now. Hang on a moment, Anita."

Anita's heart sank. Nancy was no longer going to help her. *That's the last time I'll be nice to her*, she thought. Assuming that life would get back to normal, ever.

"Anita?" asked Nancy. "You there?"

"I'm here."

"This obviously came in during the holidays. It's dated last week in December, which makes sense."

"How does it make sense?"

"Well, you remember, surely, that initially you were to go with him and make a nice second honeymoon out of it?"

Anita was stumped.

"Anita? Remember? Jack decided not to make it a personal trip, something about Christmas not being the same if not at home?"

"You're kidding, right?"

"Uh, listen, it's starting to get pretty busy here, so I better go. I know this fax doesn't explain any more than what we know. I'm really sorry I gave the false alarm."

"Nancy, I had no idea that Jack thought we might make it a nice trip for us. I would've jumped at the chance."

"Oops," said Nancy.

"Yep. Oops."

She didn't even know she was going to do it, but Anita hung up on Nancy—furious at Nancy and even more furious at Jack. Plus, she was furious at Peter for hiding something, and furious at Andy because she was probably right about everything. And she was furious at the world,

"Because this ain't supposed to happen to me!" she yelled at the walls. She covered her face and cried.

Two minutes later, she stopped sobbing. She sniffed, wiped her eyes and blew her nose. Nancy had at least given her some kind of information—even if it wasn't something she wanted to hear. She picked up the phone and dialled again. This time it rang a dozen times before it was answered.

"Good morning and Happy New Year. Thank you for calling—will you hold?" And Nancy left her dangling. As she waited through lounge music over the phone, Anita had a few moments to gather her thoughts together. She had to be sly, she thought. Quiet, sly and smart.

"Thank you for waiting. Nancy sp—"

"Oh, Nancy, I'm so, *so* sorry. We were cut off somehow, and I've been trying to get back to you. I know you're busy, but I have one more question."

"Sure, anything." Nancy was once again businesslike.

"Jack mentioned he might drum up some business with the Pizza King in Sardinia, Calabria. I don't know why I hadn't thought of it. I saw Peter the other day, and he happened to mention this guy. Can you please give me the address and phone number?"

Nancy seemed to mull it over before she spoke again. "Yeah, sure, Anita. Just one moment."

Anita was put on hold for a moment, but she quietly gave herself a pat on the back while she waited. *Sly as a fox but strong as an eagle*, she thought. Geez, that sounded great. It managed to offer a little strength.

"Anita? Yeah, um, there is a note pertaining to a Pizza King in Sardinia, Calabria, but the contact number seems to be in Georgia."

"Georgia? In the states?"

"Yeah, no specific address, but it does imply that the head office is in … let's see … looks like Darien." Nancy rustled some papers. "Yes, a Mr. Man—"

"Mangiano."

"That's right. As a matter of fact, Anita, a Mr. Mangiano called just after Peter left for Italy. I asked for a message, but the guy hung up on me."

"Well, thanks, Nancy. It isn't much, but it's something."

"Um, Anita. I'm sorry but I …"

"Oh, sorry. I'll let you go."

"No, that's not what I meant. I owe it to you to tell you a couple of things."

"Yeah?" Anita's heart skipped a beat.

"Well, first of all—and you're going to hate me for having kept this from you, but I didn't know what to do ..."

"I know. What is it?"

Nancy sighed. "Jack went and bought two round-trip tickets to Italy. He ordered them, I didn't. I just happened to see the itinerary on his desk."

Two tickets? Anita couldn't breathe.

"But also? He's supposed to be meeting with the bank tomorrow morning. It has nothing to do with work. It's with the bank you deal with. They've been calling him consistently since Thanksgiving. I think you should know that. Have you gotten any calls?"

Anita felt the blood drain from her face. "No. I haven't. Which bank?"

"Cooper Century Bank."

Anita froze. All was lost. All was lost.

"Anita, I have to go."

"Yeah, you go. Thanks very much."

"You hang in there now. And I'm sorry."

Anita slowly hung up. Their mortgage was held by Cooper Century Bank.

Anita looked at her watch. "Holy shit!" she yelled. She was late for her first day of work in the new year. She jumped up and ran into the bathroom.

The phone rang. She poked her head out of the bathroom, looked at the phone and then jumped to grab it.

"Hello?"

"Anita? It's Tricia, honey."

"Tricia? Tricia!" Tricia was one of thirty women who worked on the assembly line in the shop.

"Yeah, honey. I's heard. Now, I don't have time to talk too much, as I'm not supposed ta get off da floor, but I wanted to tell ya somethin'. There's somethin' wrong wid Jack, honey. S'not hisself."

"Don't I know it, Tricia. Have you heard from him?"

"No, should I have?"

"Tricia, I haven't heard from him since before Christmas!"

"Oh no, love. I didn't know that. No, I's wanted to tell ya that your Jack ain't right."

"You can say that again."

"Well, we do have a slight problem here on da floor."

"Wha ... what do you mean?"

"Well, everything's fallin' apart here. In fact, some of us girls said we'd quit 'cause of the way he was with us."

"He's ... what?" coaxed Anita, dreading to hear more.

"Well, he hasn't been hisself. He's been acting really irritable lately. You won't believe this—he told Sam to 'F— off !'"

Anita gasped. This was crazy. Sam had been plant manager since the first day they had to expand the business and moved from a suite of three offices to their own factory. In fact, it was Sam who had eased the business through its expansion phase. He was worth his weight in gold, Jack always said. The worst of it? Sam was a Baptist. Very prim and very proper—never drank, never swore. Poor soft-spoken Sam. "Oh my gosh."

"What should we do, Anita?" Tricia asked. Anita could hear the hustle and bustle of the plant in the background.

Anita bit her lip. "I don't know. I've already called the police, and they said there's nothing they could do. That ... that it was perhaps a case of a husband running off with another woman. They even asked if we had marital problems, for crying out loud. Listen, if, and when, *any* of you hear anything about him, could you please ..." Anita stumbled.

"I'm sure he's okay, honey. He can never leave such a fine woman. You'll see, he'll come back. And, yes, honey, if I's hear anythin', I'll let you know right away!"

Anita nodded to the phone. "Thanks, Tricia. You have no idea. Thanks so very, very much." She hung up and remained lying on the bed, staring at the ceiling.

She had already missed a few days at the station. She was a reporter with the local AM radio, reading the news and putting together special reports, a good deal of it live-on-air stuff. *Oh my God, can I really focus on work?* she fretted. She took a deep breath and exhaled slowly. Tricia's voice and kindness gave her solace, but the woman's story left her even more confused. *Well, tomorrow is indeed another day*, she reminded herself. *And tomorrow I just might hear from Jack!* For some odd reason, that thought made her feel a heck of a lot better. But she wasn't ready to go to work. *They're going to hate this*, she said to herself.

She dialled the station.

Chapter 8

THE CALL BROUGHT MORE SOLACE. She explained the situation and her boss was concerned, telling her she could have all the time she needed. She thanked him and insisted it was just for one more day. Feeling amazingly free, she threw on a track suit and fussed over the house, cleaning it from top to bottom, paying special attention to Jack's study. It occurred to her that Jack hadn't taken anything more than what he normally would've taken on a business trip. A good sign? It had to be.

The perplexity of hope, she marvelled. The more she became aware of how truly little he had taken with him, the more she chastised herself for having been so upset. How could he leave his files and his favourite CDs? His workout clothes and his suits? Of course he was coming back! If she looked hard enough, the signs were all right there under her nose. And he'd see that she never doubted him for one moment.

"Oh, blessed relief!" she yelled at the ceiling in the living room. She did a little jig on the Berber carpet and clicked her heels. "Right on, baby!" And with a whoop and holler, she spent the rest of the day and night with a blessedly lighter heart.

The next morning, though, her bubble burst. As she was getting ready to go to work, Anita opened the automatic garage door to find two gentlemen waiting on the driveway.

The taller of the two spoke. "Mrs. Taylor?"

"Yes."

"I'm sorry, ma'am, but we're repossessing the car. Can we have the keys?"

Anita froze with her bag slung over her shoulder and the car keys in her hands. "For my car?"

"Yes, ma'am. Here's your court order. There's also information in there explaining how you can get your car back, but for now, we're going to have to take it away."

Anita's thoughts were scrambled. She couldn't think rationally. "I don't understand. I'm sure we're up-to-date on our payments."

"Well, according to the bank, you aren't." He held out his hand. "Please, may I have the keys, or should we tow it?"

She silently held out the keys. The man took them. The taller man got into her car while the other man started the car they arrived in.

"Wait!" she yelled. "I have to go to work!"

"Sorry, ma'am. We can't help you." The man started backing out of the garage. She ran and hit the hood.

"Wait! My stuff! I have stuff in there!"

The man stopped the car and got out. She went through the car and found and took her things, her hands shaking—from under the seats, trunk, glove compartment, behind the sun visors, in the CD player, everywhere she could think of, even her garbage. Then the man got back in the car and drove away, leaving her standing in the middle of the garage with all her junk scattered on the cement floor around her.

She did not go to work that day.

❧

About a hundred miles south of Savannah, Georgia, a huge rust-bucket of a shrimp boat puffed noisily as it made its way up a marshy creek from Sapelo Sound and headed home to Darien. The air was warm and muggy, and the sky was a brilliant blue, with large white cumulus clouds. As it slowed down, a mass of seagulls caught up to its stern. Their wet beaks flashed as they dipped and careened at the nets teeming with shrimp.

The day had been a good one, and not just in the haul. More importantly, the day was not too humid, not too hot—perfect weather for short-sleeved T-shirts, while those poor suckers in the North suffered the wind and snow. Here, in a small parish called Shellman's

Bluff, there was as yet little activity in the biting-insect category, though the cockroaches were big enough to keep as pets. But, hey, *c'est la vie.*

The boat nudged onto a well-worn floating dock as a lanky young man jumped barefooted onto the bleached hot boards with a bowline in his hand. He quickly wrapped it around a cleat while the portly skipper let go of the wheel in the wheelhouse and huffed along the deck to the stern line. He threw it deftly to his young first mate to tie onto another cleat. He then straightened up and stretched, cracking his back and his shoulder joints. Years of heavy lifting and a good-sized gut consistently caused pressure on his spine, but a healthy dose of grappa and a hard woman always helped numb the pain.

Chewing on a cigar, Leo Mangiano took off his Portuguese captain's hat and scratched his head. He looked around at the shore and the massive live oaks covered in brooding Spanish moss hanging from every branch and limb. Here, Georgia was at its strangest, like another universe, with a history of cotton plantations, sugar cane, indigo and rice; of songs written for every little chore there was; of alligators and wild boars, possums and armadillos; of gumbo, grits and okra and grouper, scallops and crab. A faraway land so different from his homeland in Calabria that if it wasn't for his bimonthly sojourn to Little Italy in New York, he would've eventually forgotten he was Italian—God forbid.

"Here, Willie, you take over," he said as he threw his first mate a spring line. Willie—tall, dark and sinewy, looking much older than his seventeen years—grabbed the line and readjusted the position of the boat. It was a pretty rough-looking shrimp boat. Built in 1937 and shipped up from Galveston, Texas, years earlier, it was all rusty stanchions. The name, *Santa Maria*, was half-faded on the stern, but it didn't leak, and it had enough room in the pilot house for Leo to stay out of the sun and to keep his own personal statue of Santa Maria in her own little niche by the wheel.

Better still, it had half the usual holding tank for fresh water. The other half was used for smuggling. Smuggling was Leo's specialty, and he smuggled whatever was the latest fad: drugs, pornography, booze, counterfeit money, people and even Cuban cigars. However, this kind of smuggling was just to keep his hand in something tangible. It was fish bait compared to what he really did. The hard stuff was in Venezuela, where he had another partner working in his stead. He was't too keen about his quarterly visits that far south, but it was the most lucrative part of his business, and he considered himself to be quite clever and ruthless.

Young Willie tried not to know or see too much. He was lucky to have a paying job, and although his mother always asked what it was that they were *really* doing out there with that "sardine can," he could always simply say, "shrimpin'," which was at least part of the truth.

"Willie!" she'd yell. "You know better than to turn a blind eye with someone like that Italian devil!"

Willie's mom, Yvonne, was cook at the Navy Café along Rum Alley by the wharf and liked to frequent the Darien Baptist Church two blocks over. She always volunteered to run Saturday's movie night at the church, because she had fashioned herself to be as close as you can get to being a movie star in this tiny community.

In her younger days, a hundred pounds lighter, she'd had a walk-on part on the James Bond movie *Live and Let Die* that was filmed in New Orleans in 1973. It paid her for the twelve hours that she had to wait to do her thirty-second one-word part. Five dollars an hour in those days for a young mother of one was something to be proud of. Of course, once the movie came out, she saw that her part had been cut down to a four-second, wordless walk-on. But still, it was a brush with greatness.

Yvonne didn't trust Leo Mangiano. He smiled too brightly. When he would come into the café and say *"Buongiorno*, Yvonne," she'd look at him sideways and simply nod a reply.

"His dentures are too white and too straight," she'd tell Willie. "Anybody who would lose that many teeth and buy such white dentures never had a mother who cared for him. He's got too much money! More than a healthy man should have."

Willie would say, "Mom, you've got teeth missing."

"Yes, my precious, but I come from a poor background, and they're only molars that are gone. I have all my front teeth, and that says a lot."

Leo Mangiano knew what Yvonne thought of him. It had become a little game for him, as it can be very boring in this fine ol' state of Georgia. He'd go to the Navy Café sometimes twice a day to eat her cooking and whisper sweet little nothings to her in Italian.

"Ah, hallo, *bella madre di Willie! Como 'sta?*"

Of course, she didn't tell Willie or Leo that his Italian snippets made her heart flutter. On her way to Bible class she would pray, "Get thee behind me, Satan, get thee behind me" whenever her thoughts lingered on him. But the words "behind me" would conjure up an image of Leo bending over behind her, and she would break out in a sweat, squeal "Sweet Jesus!" and make a run for hallowed ground.

Leo was smart. He'd spread it around that he didn't have a lot of money, he was here and there with the odd jobs, and shrimping was the shits. But he always ended the day with a bright denture smile and started it the same way, though in between he took his dentures out and kept them in a glass beside him on the night table.

And so, it was very unusual to find him in a bad mood.

He was about to be in a bad mood.

Leo, aka the Pizza King, was part of a conglomerate with his cousin in Calabria. Amongst many other arrangements, they had a unique system of laundering money—a system which he personally felt was one of his brighter ideas. It had eggs as its center theme, and it was his ingenious idea to use plastic egg cartons to do it with. As a child in Italy, he had always loved his mother's hens and took endless pleasure in organizing the eggs by size, colour and slight imperfections. Not that he wanted to smuggle eggs. Just eggs in the top layers of thousands of plastic egg cartons masquerading as cartons filled with eggs when in reality it was a major load of a variety of illegal drugs.

The cycle, according to his plan, started in Vindenza, Quebec, where a purchase order was given to a company set up by a smaller conglomerate, J & P Plastics, for a large number of plastic egg cartons at a hundred times their value to be bought by his contact in Venezuela. Once in Venezuela, the cartons were used for packing drugs and shipped off to Mexico City where they passed on the drugs and—this is where he took pride in his artistic genius—the dirty money generated by the drug sales in both Venezuela and Mexico City was tightly rolled up and packed along with marijuana into the same plastic cartons. These cartons were then shipped to Savannah, Georgia, and kept in a holding area owned by a company called Pizza King. Leo arranged for the flats to be unpacked, and the dirty money was transferred and stored in the hold of the *Santa Maria*. Then Leo had the cartons melted down, dried into pellets, and sold back to J & P Plastics in Vindenza, Quebec, at another exorbitant price. In the meantime, Leo goes out shrimping and meets a vessel in international waters and transfers the money to be run back to New York, where the cash is cleaned through dry cleaners, restaurants, check-cashing joints and Pizza King outlets. Everyone took a cut along the way.

All arranged beautifully by plain little ol' Leo Mangiano, the shrimper.

But little ol' Leo's system had a crack in it somewhere, and he was at a loss as to how to fix it. Fix it he must, because if he didn't, his cousin … well, his cousin would not be pleased. So he sat on a weather-worn bench on a floating dock near his ship, and he pondered on the weak link that was called J & P Plastics, which was run by two guys called Jack Taylor and Peter Giordani.

Chapter 9

A T FIVE O'CLOCK THE NEXT morning, Andy woke up with a start. For the first time in ages, she had slept soundly. She heard a voice. Someone called her name. At first she thought it was her mother, but the voice wasn't shrill. A softer voice … but the memory of the voice faded away just as quickly as it came upon her. The guest bedroom was very dark and very quiet. Perhaps she had heard Stefano and Maria, but when she cocked her ear to listen, she could hear Stefano's deep, rumbling snore on the other side of the wall in the master bedroom. She listened to Maria's heavy breathing on the bed next to her.

Andy rested her hand on Maria's thin shoulder and allowed her hand to rise and fall with each breath. Funny how Maria still crawled into bed with her the odd night. When Andy and Stefano were still sleeping in the same bed, Maria would climb in between the two of them almost every night. *She's a real mama's baby*, Andy thought to herself.

Quietly, she got out of bed, and gently pulled Maria up. Carefully she straightened Maria's long, gangly limbs. Maria protested sleepily, but Andy hushed her. They shuffled down the hall to Maria's own room and carefully placed the girl in her own bed. Andy swept away a horde of stuffed animals and covered Maria with a Cabbage Patch duvet. She then kissed her daughter on the forehead. Maria protested again with garbled words but immediately fell asleep. Andy stepped out into the hallway, closed the door and tiptoed down the stairs.

She crossed the front hallway into the large front living room—the one they used only on birthdays and holidays. Her bare feet sunk into the deep pile of the pristine white carpet as she peered through the large plate-glass window overlooking the front lawn. Her nose directed her gaze left, right, up and down. Nothing untoward, except for the beginnings of another light snowfall. She shivered and wrapped her nightgown tighter.

Andy turned and walked back through the hallway and into the dark kitchen. In spite of the snow flurries, there was a startlingly bright full moon, and shafts of blue light poured like a beacon through the kitchen windows. Andy silently walked into the patch of moonlight on the tile and looked out. The barnyard was cast in the moon's shade, but the dog pen and the picnic table on the back lawn were as clear as day. The tall pines by the frozen pond slowly swayed in the light gusts, the accumulated snow on and around them sparkling like what she imagined a South Sea ocean would shimmer like under a moon. She sighed.

She stayed gazing up at the sky until a massive cloud blanketed the moon and the stars slowly faded from view.

"Anita," she murmured to herself, her breath fogging the glass. She padded over to the kitchen phone, picked up the receiver and dialled Anita's number. "I don't give a shit what time it is," she mumbled.

The phone rang and rang, but she was determined to let it ring a hundred times if that was what it took. "Answer, damn it," whispered Andy. "Anita, pick up the damn ph—"

"Hello?" Anita croaked. "Jack? Jack, is that you?"

"Jack, Jack," Andy mimicked softly. "No, this isn't Jack. It's Andy. Who else would call you at a crazy hour like this, huh?"

"Andy. Wha … what time is it?" Anita croaked.

"It's about five thirty." Andy leaned into the kitchen to check the time on the stove. "Yeah, quarter after five."

"Morning or night?" asked Anita.

"What kind of drugs are you on?" Andy quipped. "It's freakin' morning!" She lowered her voice. "I bet you haven't slept a wink."

"Well, no. I slept. I took some sleeping pills. I'm fine."

"Yeah, right, and bears don't shit in the forest."

"No really, Andy. I'm fine. Not to worry. Andy, he'll be back."

Andy became apoplectic. "Are you deaf? Read my lips, girl. He ain't coming back!"

Anita struggled against sleep's pull. "Andy. When Jack told me I might not hear from him for a while, I believed him. It's just taking longer than he said, that's all. I know you say a few people saw him with another woman, but—"

"T'yeaaah! People aren't blind, Anita."

"It's just a rumour, Andy. To me, it's still just a rumour. He's in a country where there's little or no reception. He's in a volcano for all I know."

"In Calabria?"

"Well, I don't know! Just deep down inside, I know he's coming back." Anita sighed and mentally crossed her fingers. Just believe, just believe …

Andy also sighed, and heavily. "Girl, you're … Forget it, he's not—"

Anita fell apart and bawled. "Andy, stop it! Hang up now. I don't *need* this!"

"Nothing! Nothing, Anita! You've heard *nothing*! He's disappeared! He's not at work. No one knows where he is," Andy could hear Anita sob. "The police won't help you for shit. Even they know not to waste time." Andy paused and waited, wondering if she'd pushed too hard this time.

After a moment, Anita spoke in a soft and controlled voice. "Andy, something had to have happened to him. This is nuts. I can feel it, Andy." In spite of her bravado, Andy had undone the good that Tricia had done earlier and opened the door to uncertainty long enough for Anita to doubt once again. She could say no more for fear of losing her mind.

Andy knew she had gone too far. "Okay, kiddo. You're coming back here. You shouldn't be alone".

"I can't—"

"Don't do this, girl."

"Andy, I can't. I really can't … I don't have a car anymore."

"What?"

"They repossessed my car."

"Omigod! Who did?!"

"Men. I don't know. Men!"

"So. You think this is just a coincidence?"

"I'll talk to the bank in the morning."

Andy sighed loudly. "Girl … Wait. Just wait a sec, 'Nita!" Andy turned to the stairs and yelled, "Stefano! Stefano, wake up! Get your coat on and get Anita!" Andy came back on the line. "'Nita, you still there?"

"I'm here," Anita whispered. She was giving in. "Andy, it's like in the middle of the night."

"Anita, listen to me, okay? Stefano's gonna pick you up. He's always up this early for those damn animals anyhow. Pack a few things. We're going to that party tomorrow night, remember?"

"I'm just not up to it, Andy. I'm exhausted."

"When you get here, you go straight downstairs to your pullout bed and sleep all day if ya like."

"But what if Jack calls?"

"Oh, for f— … 'Nita, just do it. He freakin' knows where to find you. Wait. Just a sec." Andy put her hand on the receiver and called up the stairs again. "Stefano!"

Stefano, his hairy belly showing from underneath the grey T-shirt sagging slightly over his paisley boxer shorts, lumbered down the stairs yawning. "*Si, capisco*. I get Anita. *No problema*."

"Good," said Andy. She watched as Stefano lumbered into the kitchen and on through the family room to the basement stairs. Downstairs was almost entirely Stefano's world—Stefano's bathroom and shower, his work clothes and boots. "And be careful, Stefano, it's snowin' again," she called after him. Then to Anita. "You still there?"

"Yeah, I'm here."

"Call me when he gets there, okay?"

"Okay."

"I mean it, call me, right? It should take fifteen minutes. Any more, then I need to know. There's something goin' on 'bout that bleached blonde babushka, you remember? I've been hearing stories about some of the guys sneaking out early, presumably for a coffee at Tim Hortons but they're actually goin' to her place, you know what I mean? There's a conspiracy goin' on. Not that I think Stefano would …"

"What?"

"Forget about it. We'll talk, okay?"

"Okay," said Anita meekly.

"So don't forget. Call me," and Andy hung up. Or at least she thought she did.

Anita stood at her kitchen window and watched Stefano's mud-splattered, snow-covered red pickup truck crunch into her driveway. She read the faded letters on the driver's door: "Stefano Giordani & Sons Contractors." It was a curiosity about which Anita never had the courage to ask: Stefano and Andy didn't have any sons. She went to the phone and dutifully called Andy, but she only got a busy signal. *Oh dear*, she thought. She hung up, opened the door for Stefano and gave him a massive hug.

"Stefano, I'm so, so sorry that you had to come."

Stefano held up a bear paw of a hand and shook his head. "No need for sorry," he said softly. He patted his breast, "I know. Da heart-a, she hurt bad, *si?*"

She nodded sadly and said, "*Si*." She wiped away some tears with her sleeve. Stefano bent over to look at her eyes.

"*Questa e una triste situazione*," he said softly. Anita shrugged and shook her head slightly. Stefano straightened up. "Is-a *triste*—sad—this thing." His gentleness was her undoing, and she fell against his padded red and black plaid lumberjack jacket and began to cry. Spasms of grief, days and nights of worry, of immense loneliness, of self-doubt, and a very, very broken heart poured out of her.

Stefano let her cry. At first he wasn't sure if he should put his arms around her or just pat her shoulder, but as he patted, he felt he was shortchanging her out of the comfort she deserved. Just a warm couple of arms to lessen the load a bit. So he wrapped her gently and then squeezed with his strong arms. He could feel her grief so acutely that he found himself tearing up. *Such triste*, he thought. This good, kind, childlike woman was dying, simply dying inside. A tear trickled down along the side of his handsome nose, and because he didn't want to disturb the moment by moving, he let it drip onto her hair. Her beautiful hair was the colour of those sheaths of wheat he used to help bunch together and toss onto wagons as a boy at his *nonno's* farm in Italy. And she smelled like the wild spring flowers that grew on the hills of Marsala just outside Sicily where his *nonno* lived.

The longer he held her, the more that beautiful scent wafted up to his nostrils, and he felt his pulse quicken. *Mama mia!* he thought. He broke out in a sweat and had to gently push her away. He took her overnight bag from off her shoulder and turned and opened the front door. He pointed to the truck. "I-a wait for you-a," he said softly and walked into the icy cold air. "*Caldo, caldo*," he said to the falling snow. "Too hot."

Anita turned off the light in the hallway, stepped outside and closed the door behind her. Stefano's massive galoshes had cut a path for her to follow into the deepening snow, and as she carefully placed her feet into his large footprints, she felt a spasm of guilt once again for putting Andy and Stefano out of their way like this. But oh, this time she was grateful! *I can't sit in that house full of misery*, she thought. *Not right now!*

The eastern edge of the sky showed shreds of a new dawn as she opened the creaking passenger door of the truck and climbed in. Stefano started the truck, and they pulled away from the house. The drive was slow but uneventful. Neither spoke, and Anita felt safe and comfortable enough to close her swollen eyes slightly and partially watch the windshield wipers swish back and forth. The sound comforted her, and soon her eyes closed completely. She fell asleep.

Stefano looked over at her as discreetly as he could. He shook his head slightly. He liked her—very much. Too bad about Jack, he thought. He shook his head again. "*E cosi stupid*," he whispered to himself. "Stupid, stupid man."

"Stefano?"

Stefano jumped with a start and looked over. Anita's blue eyes were wide open.

"Did you say something?" she asked.

"No, no, no thing," he said a bit too loud. He pretended to be very concerned about the amount of falling snow. He shifted his solid body and looked as high as he could through the windshield and shook his head. He motioned to the weather "out there" with his right paw.

Anita smiled and studied his classic Roman profile while she distractedly played with her wedding ring. She stirred and ventured to ask something she had always wondered about. "Stefano. Do you mind if I ... um, why do you have 'Stefano Giordani & Sons' on the side of the truck?"

Stefano's face went crimson, and she immediately regretted opening her mouth. She watched as he purposely killed a few more seconds looking first right, left, and then into the rearview mirror at nonexistent traffic. As she waited, the wipers seemed to boom louder with each slash across the windshield. Finally, Stefano smiled shyly and shrugged. "I always have-a dream is-a sons work with me." His face dropped. "Adriana," he paused, and again shrugged, "well, we only-a have-a Maria an' …" he sighed and pondered on how much he could tell her without regretting it later. "She no sleep-a wid me no more, so no more bambinos … no sons."

Anita's heart skipped a beat. *Oh my God*, she thought, *Oh my God! Too much information!* She stiffly turned to face forward and gaze at nothing. Her mind raced. She could sense the immense emptiness he must feel. Broken dreams … And he would've been so proud of a son. This time, the tears that welled up were not for her alone. It was for the loss of sons he had hoped for.

Stefano's face was drawn as he quietly whispered, "So sorry."

Anita glanced over and saw his brow had darkened.

"No, I'm sorry, Stefano. I'm sorry. It was none of my business and …" She found herself at a loss for words.

"Is okay," Stefano said softly.

Anita gently put her left hand on Stefano's shoulder. He looked over and their eyes locked. Just for a moment.

Suddenly, the truck's right front tire caught a pothole along the edge of the snow-covered road. The truck swerved to the right, and the slippery snow caused it to continue sliding sideways and out of control. Then one of the front tires gripped a dry spot on the pavement and whipped the truck to the left. It finally slid to a stop facing the wrong way. The snowfall was very heavy, and visibility had diminished drastically. Immediately, both Stefano and Anita knew they were courting danger if they didn't straighten out right away.

Stefano quickly put the truck into "drive" again and turned the wheel hard to right in order to do a U-turn. Slowly the tires caught. But the truck lurched and made large grating sounds. Stefano shifted the truck into "park" at what he estimated to be the side of the road and jumped out of the cab to check for damages.

Anita clambered out as well, and they both came around to the front and saw that the right front tire was flat. "*Merda*," Stefano muttered. After looking around quickly, he climbed back into the truck, slowly eased it into a nearby driveway and parked it. He got out of the truck, gathered his tools together from behind the driver's seat, handed Anita a flashlight and then got down on the ground and slid under the truck for the spare.

The close call and flat tire felt surreal. Anita's head swam as she pondered on this new Stefano she had discovered. It was like catching a glimpse of a meteor streaking across the night sky. *Bang!* A fabulous, burning streak splitting the sky above from one end to the other in two seconds. She felt oddly blessed. Stefano, the quiet one, who rarely spoke an entire sentence, turned what she thought she knew about him upside down. Everything felt different somehow. Her own problems felt queerly different.

A chill crawled up her back and along her arms. The light of the flashlight she was holding shook. Stefano pretended not to notice, because deep down inside, he knew with certainty that Anita's shivering was not caused by the simple cold of the early dawn.

Grunting with the spare tire, Stefano desperately regretted telling her. Inwardly he groaned when he glanced over, catching her checking her watch. *Ah si*, he thought, they were both thinking the same thing: Andy. Andy was going to have a fit.

Of late, he had become very tired of Andy's constant fits. It was he who had suggested to Andy that they should help Anita, but her antics seemed to worsen when in front of an audience so gentle and soft-spoken. He wanted to howl, break something, kill something—because Anita's unhappiness and grief were perhaps entirely of his own doing. It was he who had discouraged Jack from breaking out on his own when he started showing signs of greed. Jack thought he could dupe the big guys and it was Stefano who warned him not to even think about it. That it took a big man with luck and brains. Stefano wasn't sure, but Jack may have been dumb enough to take up on that challenge. He looked over at her again and tried to read her eyes. She looked back in innocence. She had no inkling. He felt like a damn cad.

While he pondered on his own thoughts under the truck, something very curious happened to Anita. She wasn't aware of it at first. Her head and heart had conceived a strange little worm, one which started wriggling into the primal depths of her soul. It made her feel smug. And even though they were smack in the middle of a miserable blizzard, it suddenly felt like she was standing drenched in sunshine.

Andy looked at her watch. It had been more than an hour since she had spoken to Anita. She stood by the living room window looking out at the wall of snow as the light of day slowly brightened. Twenty minutes after Stefano left, when there was still no call from Anita, Andy had called her but there was no answer. She began to fret. And as Andy was wont to do, she started to panic. Her panic mounted and overwhelmed her. She called the police, but they told her the obvious: "The weather, ma'am. It's pretty slow going out there. Better just to sit tight."

Every minute that went by only worsened her fears. This waiting drove her crazy. What was worse, it drove her mad.

"*Goddammit!*" she yelled. "They could be *dead* for crying out loud!" She paced in front of the window, clutching at her nightgown, her thin shoulders hunched over. Then she ran to the kitchen and grabbed a pack of cigarettes from behind one of the pots. She lit a match and dragged the smoke in. She never smoked in the house. Stefano wasn't even aware that she smoked. But this time. … "Goddammit!" she yelled again. She paced back and forth, back and forth, like a little locomotive, puffing smoke like a steam engine.

Upstairs, Maria had awakened, and she lay there listening to her mother's complaints. It was oddly early for her mom to be up. Maria climbed out of bed and sleepily walked down the hallway to the top of the stairs. She bent over to look and saw that her mother was fretting in the kitchen. And smoking! Maria frowned and sat down on the top step. She sighed and simply watched and listened.

"I'm not blind, and I'm not stupid!" Andy suddenly argued aloud. "That's what you get, Andy ol' girl, for helping a fucking friend!" She thought of Anita looking at Stefano with those big blue eyes of hers, always feeling sorry for herself.

"You better watch it, kid," she muttered at the window.

And then, finally, she heard the truck turn in and ran to the window in time to see it plough through the snow up the driveway. Angrily, Andy stepped away from the window and turned to go up the stairs. She stopped at the sight of Maria sitting at the top. Andy looked down at the cigarette in her hand, and then she ran up the stairs into the bathroom and flushed it down the toilet. She came out and pointed her finger at Maria.

"You. Not a word. Understand?"

Maria wordlessly got up and went back to bed, closing the door behind her. Andy did the same. Except that she slammed the door as hard as she could so that the entire world could hear how miserable she felt.

Chapter 10

ANITA WAS AWAKENED BY THE sound of chickens clucking and scratching in the snow outside the window above her pullout couch. Brilliant rays of sun cut sharply through the vertical blinds and spliced the opposite wall. It was strangely quiet otherwise. *Perhaps everyone's gone out*, she thought. Or they were still in bed, more likely.

She wriggled a little to loosen up her stiff back. Then she remembered Stefano, the truck, the snow ... then Jack, Nancy, her car. She groaned and wrapped her head in one of the pillows. She was getting used to feeling miserable. She let herself sink into depression and lay there listening to her heartbeat. *Padabum, padabum, padadadadbum.* She wondered if this was how people died of heart attacks—that this was how life killed you.

She couldn't imagine it getting any worse. If it got any worse she'd kill herself, she decided. She thought how Andy didn't want her to be alone with these suicidal thoughts. Bless Andy. Bless her, bless her.

Anita reached for her watch on the arm of the couch. *Holy crap!* she thought. *Almost noon!*

She rolled off the pullout couch, pushed the blinds aside and gasped. It was a winter wonderland out there. Sparkling diamonds covered everything—Stefano's barn, the little paddock, the ploughed garden out back. Pine trees covered in coats of ice swayed under their heavy mantels and rained shards of snow and ice onto the frozen snow-covered pond below. Little multicoloured hens pecked and scratched close to the brick wall by her window where the sun shone the warmest. The sky was a brilliant blue with a solitary white cloud overhead.

A small goat appeared from behind one of the sheds and started nibbling at a fence post. Then one or two of the hens strutted up to the glass pane to study her—first with one eye then the other, jerking their heads this way and that. They crowed gently as if discussing her amongst themselves, holding a ladies' gab about this strange bodiless apparition. Anita smiled and tapped the window. Everything seemed heavenly, and she wondered how one could feel it was the end of the earth and then the earth itself could take that all away and give you a beautiful gift such as that moment.

Anita sighed, stood higher on her tippy-toes and pressed her nose against the glass. The hens seemed perplexed by the sight, and she laughed. Suddenly something heavy smashed against the window and startled her and the other hens. She jumped back and fell on the bed with a squeal.

"What the heck!" She looked up at the window again and saw the strangest rooster. It had a mottled black and white body with the thickest-looking feathers she had ever seen. It looked like a killer dust bunny with a tail about six feet long that jerked back and forth, up and down. It looked like it wanted to kill her. It was evil. *It can't be of this world*, Anita thought. It banged and hammered at the window as if trying to break through. "Jesus," she said. "Demon rooster from hell."

She stuck a foot out to step down off the mattress, but her shifting weight buckled the bed, and it proceeded to swallow her—blankets, pillows and all. It happened so swiftly that Anita found it immensely funny and started giggling. She chortled and laughed so hard that tears ran from her eyes, and then she cried. She punched the pillows, the blankets, the mattress and the arms of the couch, imagining them to be Jack, the repo guys, the bank and, yes, Andy.

Meanwhile, Andy lay in her bed upstairs, listening. Maria had climbed into bed with her again and was still sleeping soundly. Just as well, because Andy didn't want to get up and face Anita. She was still fuming and not too pleased with her so-called friend and husband over that hour-long wait. It did not sit well with her. She thought their excuse of a flat tire was the worst shit she had ever heard in her entire life.

Downstairs, Anita was wiping her eyes and then her nose with the sleeve of her nightie. She felt cleansed and oddly elated. Giggling once again, she slowly crawled and tugged at things until she got out if the couch's death-grip. She threw on a pullover and track pants and then just happened to glance back at the window again. That demon bird was still there, jerking its tail. She could almost hear the *dadah-dadah-dadah-dadah* of *The Twilight Zone* theme.

Anita shivered. She kept her eyes on the window while walking backwards over the cold ceramic tile towards the stairs. She could swear the rooster could read her mind. It disappeared with a loud crow just as quickly as it had appeared once she reached the bottom of the stairs. She shivered and laughed. "Silly," she said to herself and turned and walked up the stairs.

Where is everyone? she wondered as she stopped to listen at the next landing. She not only could still hear the clucking of the chickens, but now Stefano's dogs were barking in accompaniment to the crowing demon bird. She wanted to run up to a kitchen window to look, but she hesitated. She was facing Stefano's gun rack on the landing wall. She reached out and fingered the blonde maple, remembering how she and Jack had given the rack to Stefano. It hung in their house at the time Jack bought it, but because he only had the one rifle, he had taken up Anita's suggestion to give it to Stefano to house his large collection of guns.

Anita remembered how she had picked up Maria, 8 years old at the time, and brought her back to the house because Maria insisted that it sounded like an adventure and she had to be a part of it. Andy was only too happy to get Maria out of her hair, but she would've screamed bloody murder at Anita if she'd known what they ended up having to do. They could only fit the rack halfway into the side of the van. Maria suggested that she could sit at one end to keep it from falling out. Anita thought it was a lark, and they both laughed almost all the way back to Andy's—except when the RCMP, coming the other way, saw them and immediately did a U-ey with lights flashing. When he caught up to them and pulled them over, the officer was ready to give her a ticket, but he waved her away with a smile when he found out she was giving the gun rack to Stefano Giordani.

"I know Stefano and his brother, Peter, well," he said. "They've helped us with a lot of fundraisers. Good people." Then he motioned her to go on and said, "Give my best to Stefano, and have a nice day!"

Stefano loved the rack. He hung it up on the second lower landing going down to his special part of the house. He had a variety of guns, as he had hunted ever since he was a boy in the old country. The fact that it held almost all of his hunting guns pleased him very much. At times, after coming home from work and on the way to his shower, he would stand for a moment and admire his collection.

Of course, Andy hated it when first she heard of it. "Don't encourage him," she had said. "Stefano's got too many goddamn guns as it is! How many guns does a man need, for crying out loud? He only goes hunting once every blue moon!" This was not wholly true. Yes, he hunted only once a year, but he would take two weeks and drive up and over to Cape Breton on the Canadian Atlantic shore. He hunted everything he could get a license for and envied Canadian Aboriginals for having a license to hunt moose. The two chocolate hunting Labs who were now barking in their individual kennels were a result of meeting other Italian–North American hunters up in the woods. He was highly impressed by what he considered to be their dogs' superior intelligence.

Anita smiled at the memory and touched one of the shotguns. She saw that there was no lock on the rack, but she didn't take much notice and continued on her way to the kitchen.

At the window by the kitchen table, she could see the kennels more clearly. The dogs were barking towards the barn door, which was open. She figured that Stefano was probably inside. She looked around, but there was no sign of the devil demon bird anymore … at least, not until she heard it. She craned her neck and saw it perched precariously on the brick windowsill outside the guest bedroom. It threw up its amazingly long tail feathers, stretched out its puffy neck and lifted its ugly blue / purple beak. It gave out a crow that was so menacing and so long that it was still yodeling when the guest bedroom window slammed open and it was knocked off the sill with a backhand.

"Those goddamn shitting machines! I'm going t' *kill* them!" Andy screamed from the window. Anita pulled her head back quickly. She could hear Andy yelling from inside the house and upstairs. "Why do they have to make such a *goddamn racket* right outside the bedroom *window?* So help me *God*, one of these days I'm gonna *wring those chickens' necks!*" Then Anita could hear the window slide shut with a bang.

Andy stomped along the upstairs hallway and marched down the stairs. Anita reached the kitchen door just as Andy burst in, her crinkly red hair sticking up like an unruly scrub brush. Andy was wearing a thin housecoat—an elegant, expensive and certainly not functional Victoria's Secret housecoat—and stood shivering in her bare feet.

She miserably nodded a silent good morning at Anita. "How can anyone sleep around here with those freakin' animals? Where's Stefano?"

Anita shrugged. "I don't know."

"You don't know?" Andy quipped. "Lost sight of him, did ya?"

"Pardon me?" asked Anita.

"Oh, forget it," mumbled Andy, patting her hair down.

"I thought you had all left, it was so quiet," smiled Anita.

"Drive in this goddamn weather? Have you looked outside lately?" Andy pointed out the windows at the bright blue sky.

"Yeah, isn't it beautiful?" asked Anita.

Andy snorted. "Yeah, right! Cold as hell and snow up your ying-yang." Andy stood scowling at her.

"Didn't sleep well?" Anita innocently asked.

The demon bird crowed outside, and Andy snapped her attention to the kitchen window. She pointed a quivering finger outside. "I'm going to kill those stinking pooping pests!" She pushed Anita aside and threw open the window. "Stefano! Where's that shotgun?"

Anita looked out over Andy's thin shoulder to see Stefano charging out of his barn. He looked uncharacteristically angry. In two strides he passed by his sheep pen and then stopped under one of the evergreens to grab a pitchfork. His brilliant aqua eyes flashed like cold steel as he looked up at Andy at the kitchen window. His cheeks were the colour of crimson. He glowered at her.

"Oops," said Andy. This time she knew she had pushed too far. "Roman god hellfire!" she mumbled, slammed the window shut and ran back up the stairs, tripping over Maria sitting halfway up. She reached the guest room and slammed the door so hard the house shook.

Anita, still by the window, looked back out and saw Stefano stomping up to the back door. She could hear the storm door creak open. There was silence for a moment, and then she heard Stefano growl and the screen door slam shut. She watched Stefano walk about halfway back to the barn and then stop to throw his pitchfork with such force that it cut through the snow and into the frozen ground, scattering his hens in a panic. Although angry, he immediately softened and clucked at the birds gently to calm them down. A lamb bleated from the fenced-in paddock, which distracted Stefano even further. He walked back over to the pen and petted the lamb and a goat, letting them snuggle his hand.

Anita was mesmerized. She watched how gentle he was with his animals. Without warning, he looked back at the house scowling, but he caught sight of Anita at the window and their eyes locked. Anita was thrilled and felt herself blush. She waved. Stefano smiled, shrugged with embarrassment and disappeared back into the barn.

"Poor Stefano," she whispered, her breath fogging the glass. She raised a finger and drew a happy face.

She turned to see Maria quietly leaning against the kitchen door frame. The both of them heard Andy yell, "Shit, that was a close one!"

Chapter 11

ANDY THREW TOGETHER STEFANO'S FAVOURITE brunch: sausages, made by Stefano himself; poached tomatoes, grown by Stefano in his little greenhouse; mozzarella, made by Stefano; crunchy Italian buns from Bruno's bakery, nice and crispy from the oven; and a few freshly laid eggs compliments of Stefano's hens, fried up in tons of butter. The coffee was strong, sweet and creamy. It smelled like heaven—and for Stefano, a man of simple tastes, it was. With luck, it might make up for that morning's outburst.

But not entirely.

Anita was setting the kitchen table for five. Stefano had left earlier to pick up Andy's mother and father so that they could stay with Maria for the rest of the day and evening.

"Maria, you behave yourself tonight," Andy said over the sausages. Maria didn't hear, as she was bouncing a basketball against the wall while watching Much Music with the volume cranked up.

"Maria!"

"Yeah!" Maria yelled back as she continued to bounce the ball. "I will!"

"How'd ya sleep?" Andy yelled to Anita, poking at the sausages some more.

"What?" hollered Anita.

Irritably, Andy yelled at Maria, "Maria! Shut that damn TV off!"

The ball kept bouncing, and the TV kept blaring.

"Look at that!" Andy yelled at Anita. "See that? She never listens! I get *no* respect! Someday I'm gonna kill that kid!"

Over the din of the frying, popping, sizzling food and Maria's shenanigans, the front door opened and Stefano apperaed in the hall with Claudia, Andy's mother. They were stomping snow off their boots when Anita poked her head into the hallway. "Hey, Nonna!" she called out. Everybody in the world called Claudia "Nonna."

Claudia threw up her little arms and screeched a happy greeting in return, giving Anita a massive bear hug. Claudia was tiny, her head only as high as Anita's shoulder, but no one could rival her endless energy and love. She also, unfortunately, had a voice that made men cry—a sound like fingernails dragging across the proverbial chalkboard.

"How-a you doing, 'Nita, huh?" she screeched with genuine concern. Anita shrugged and was about to answer when Andy cut in.

"What, Ma? No 'How are you doing, Andy?'" she quipped.

Claudia scurried over to Andy at the stove, arms outstretched. "Si! Shu-a. How is-a my Adriana?" She scrambled over and reached up to give Andy a wet kiss on the cheek, but Andy warded her off with a fork.

"Not now, Ma. I'm busy, can't you see? You'll get splattered by grease!"

The ball was still bouncing off the wall, and the TV still blared.

"Maria!" Andy screamed. "Shut that goddamn TV off or I'll stuff that ball up you-know-where!"

Stefano walked into the kitchen at that moment. Suddenly everyone froze—except Maria, for she was still throwing the ball and sitting in front of the blaring TV. Everyone looked at Stefano and then at Maria.

Stefano's piercing blue eyes were on Andy at the stove, and then he slowly turned to the family room to focus on his daughter. Quietly he called her: "Maria."

Maria stopped bouncing the ball and meekly turned off the TV. She looked over at Stefano with innocent eyes. He shook his head with disappointment, pointed at her menacingly and then winked. Unaware of everyone looking at him, he walked over to sit at the table in his chair. While Stefano took out a cotton kerchief to wipe the melted snow off his face, Andy and Maria locked eyes, and Maria stuck her tongue out.

"Did you see that?" Andy yelled and pointed at Maria with the fork. "She stuck out her tongue at me!"

Stefano shot up his hands and slapped the tabletop. "Adriana!"

Nonna stood with her hand over her mouth watching. She made a little sob. "Adriana!"

"Ma, she treats me like shit!" Andy complained, poking more angrily at the sizzling sausages.

Back in the front hall, Fabrizio, Andy's father, opened the front door and kicked his boots against the door frame before stepping through onto the wet mat. "Ho ho ho," he said, laughing to no one in particular. "Where is-a my little bambina, ha?"

Maria's eyes grew large, and she jumped up and scurried to her grandfather in the hall. "Hi, Nonno!"

She jumped up, and Fabrizio caught her with a grunt. She had grown taller than he, but he took pride in being strong enough to hoist her up. She ended up face to face with him, so she grabbed both sides of his face and kissed him all over. He gently put her down to let her help him take his coat off.

-"*Delicatamente!*" he cautioned. "Bambina, you-a *nonno* is a broken-a man!" He helped her take his coat off and bowed as she took it in her arms. She then playfully curtsied. She took the coat to the closet and hung it on a hanger—at least some semblance of hanging it.

She skipped as she followed Nonno into the kitchen. He raised a stiff arm and wiggled his fingers with a smile at Anita (he had a soft spot for her, though the fact that she was pretty really had more to do with how that soft spot could tingle), and then he nodded at Andy at the stove. He directed his own prominent nose up to the ceiling and inhaled with ecstasy. Stefano's sausages were the best he'd ever known, and he slapped his hands together in anticipation. Maria rushed ahead and pulled out a chair for him. "*Grazie,*" he said.

"You're welcome!" Maria replied, standing at attention at the table. She looked over at her father and noticed that he still had his lumberjack jacket on. She skipped two steps towards him. "Let me take your coat, sir," she said with a smile, eagerly coaxing his arms out of the sleeves.

"*Grazie,*" he said gently with a tiny smile in return.

"*Prego!*"

"Ooooh. Very good-a," screeched Nonna. Fabrizio clapped and nodded, and a smiling Anita cheered. Andy nodded too, but in disgust. When she caught Maria's eye, she tapped the side of her nose to indicate that she was on to her, and then she turned to continue skewering the sausages onto a platter. "Like she's sucking up, she is," she muttered.

Stefano heard her. "Adriana, who-a is the bambina here-a, eh? You or Maria?" he said as Maria climbed onto his lap and lovingly rubbed his stubbly chin. "With-a me she knows. *Ne*, Maria?" and he slapped his hand into the other palm. "*Visto?*" He pointed at his temple. "She alway' listen to-a me." He lovingly cupped his big hand around Maria's face.

"Oh, ya think?" quipped Andy. She pointed her fork towards Stefano. "*You* try staying with her all day every day." Then she pointed the fork at her mother and Anita. "Sit," she ordered them.

"Adriana, how she gonna listen if you alway' shout?" shouted Claudia. She sat herself down beside Stefano and beckoned Maria to come to her. Maria slipped off Stefano's lap and plunked herself down on the other side of her *nonna*. Claudia locked her granddaughter into a tight hug.

"Mariiiiiiiiyaaaa!" she screeched as Maria covered her ears.

Maria let her *nonna* hug her while she also screeched. "Nooonnaaaa!"

"Ma, what's with the screeching and hugs?" Andy asked, walking to the table with the platter of sausages and a basket of crispy hot buns. "It hasn't been that long since you saw her, you know."

"But I miss my *bambina*. I no see her for-a many weeks. She-a grow since, too."

"Try five days," Andy corrected her, reaching over the nearby counter for the balsamic vinegar and olive oil.

"I love Maria, she my on'y *nipotina*," Claudia said, squeezing Maria's nose with her knuckle. "Five day-a too long."

"Whatever," said Andy. "Eat."

So they all began to eat while Andy set the rest of the meal on the table—roasted chicken legs, homemade gnocchi, butter for the buns, a tomato salad and some cheese.

No one spoke for a long time. Anita looked around as she slowly chewed. Silence. She cleared her voice.

"Mmm. Andy, these buns dipped in vinegar and oil are absolutely yummy."

"You had them like that before, Anita," Andy muttered without looking up.

"Yeah, I know," Anita answered meekly. She studied Andy's face. She had already come to the conclusion that she wasn't exactly in Andy's good books, but she had no idea as to why.

Suddenly, Fabrizio made a clatter by dropping his fork and knife on the table as he clutched his chest.

Andy looked over at her father with alarm, holding a fork of sausage in midair. "What's the matter, Papa?"

"Oh, he no feel-a no good dis morning," Claudia said as she took out a crumpled tissue from her sleeve. Her bottom lip quivered. She had always been able to cry at the drop of a hat.

"Oh, for crying out loud, Ma. What's the tears for?"

Claudia motioned to Fabrizio, who still sat with his hand on his chest. "I no want-a him to die."

Andy's eyes widened and she reached out a hand and held his forearm. "Papa, what's up? You okay?"

Fabrizio looked up and silently nodded his head, but everyone kept staring at him with concern. Slowly he sat up straight again, yanked out a kerchief from his trousers pocket, and dabbed at his face and his mouth. He held up a hand and continued eating.

Everyone looked at each other. Andy piped up, "Papa, talk to me!"

Fabrizio waved her concern away. "'S nothing-a," he said.

"This is nothing? Ma? What's up with him?"

"I no know." Claudia dabbed at her eyes.

Andy looked over at her father again. He had started getting some colour back. She got up and stood beside his chair and crossed her arms as she looked down at him. Her dad had an iffy heart, and she was forever concerned.

"Dad, what's wrong?" Andy yelled.

Fabrizio jumped. He looked at her and reached up to his left ear to turn on his hearing aid. He preferred to focus on a good meal and not get distracted while he ate it. "Adriana! No-a yelling."

"Well then, answer the stupid question!"

"*Che?*"

Andy put a hand on his forehead. It was clammy.

"You no look-a good," said Stefano, shaking his head. He was in the middle of testing the sausages to see if they were done to his liking. "He no sleep well maybe," he said, casting a glance at Claudia.

"Oh dear," said Anita. "I hope you're all right, Nonno."

"Oh, he no bad, *ma* his heart," Claudia shrugged her little shoulders, looking crestfallen.

"Oh dear," said Anita. She happened to look at Stefano, who tipped up an imaginary drink to his lips and then winked at her. Anita laughed, and that really peeved Andy.

"Who let *you* laugh?"

Anita was taken aback.

Fabrizio cleared his throat. "No is problem. How you say-a ...?" He pointed from his diaphragm to his throat.

"Reflux? Heartburn?" offered Anita.

Fabrizio smiled and nodded. "*Si.*"

"Enough talk," muttered Andy, giving Anita a look and changing the subject, "Eat. Let's have some respect for the chef, 'cause I've been cooking all friggin' day!"

So, dutifully, everyone settled down to eat again, and for a short time, no one thought of speaking.

Andy rarely ate large meals, so it took her only a few moments before she was satisfied. As per routine, she remained sitting, leaned back in her chair and started picking at her teeth with a toothpick as she looked on.

Anita again broke the silence. "How did you and Nonno meet, Nonna?"

Claudia brightened up. Her favourite subject was herself and all that revolved around her. "Oh, we grow up da same in Sicily."

"You grew up together?"

Andy's least favourite subject was her mother and all that revolved around her. She sighed heavily and rolled her eyes.

"Si ... he my zio's son o' second wife ..." she pointed out.

"He was your first cousin then," said Anita.

Claudia frowned and turned to Stefano. "*Cosa c'e* ... firs-a cousin-a?"

Stefano, mouth full of sausage, said, "*Cugino di primo grado.*"

"Ah, *si, ma* no," Claudia pointed out, "he son o' zio's second wife, not first."

Anita frowned. "That's kinda first cousin as well ..."

Andy guffawed and then giggled. She shook her head as if in disbelief at the general stupidity of the people present, but it was really to take attention away from Anita.

Anita then asked what she really wanted to know: "So, how did Andy and Stefano meet?"

"Aw, shit!," Andy cut in. She banged the table with her left palm. "Ma, you talk too much. Don't you have some TV to watch or somethin?"

"But Anita, she ast me question," Claudia protested, quite upset.

"Well, Anita can 'ast you questions' another time."

Anita shrugged. "Hey, Andy. I was just curious."

"See?" screeched Claudia.

"Listen, I don't know about you, but I got better things to do than to get depressed."

"Adriana," Claudia frowned.

"Ma! Don't call me that!"

"No, I like-a you real-a name! No-a, you have-a nice house, a good-a husband an' ..."

"Yeah, right," Andy muttered.

Stefano abruptly pushed his chair back and stood up. He wiped his mouth with his napkin and nodded curtly at everyone.

Maria piped up, all sweet and innocent, "Daddy, can I watch TV?"

Stefano nodded but put up a warning with his index finger and pointed it at her. Then he drew his index finger across his neck and pointed again. Maria nodded enthusiastically, bounced down to the family room, and turned on the TV. Stefano followed her down, but before he continued down the basement stairs, he drilled a look at her as a warning. Maria pushed on the control and put the volume much lower. She looked back at him for approval. Stefano nodded, winked and went downstairs.

Claudia looked over at Maria. "Maria is so skeeny. She no eat?"

"Ma, what do you think, huh?" Andy suddenly got up and moved some pans around on the kitchen counter. Then she peered at her mother from under the hanging cupboards. "What are you implying? I'm starving her? No, Mom! She's fine! You just saw her eat like a pig."

Claudia reached for the coffee pot in the middle of the table and, while pouring another cup for herself, muttered about the time of day it was and that the poor, growing child was probably hungry for a snack by now. Andy slammed a frying pan on the stove and whipped around, her hands on her hips. "Ma! You don't think I have anything better to do than cook the whole day long?"

"But that wot a momma do, si?" asked Claudia, shrugging her tiny shoulders while she looked to Anita for support. Instead of answering, Anita pushed back her own chair and started to clear the table.

"You put that down, Anita! Ma, take that from her." She waved Anita away. "Go. Do something pleasant. Get ready for the crystal party—or not. I don't give a shit."

Anita stood and watched Andy questioningly. Then she looked down at Claudia, who simply smiled. "Thanks for brunch, Andy," Anita said. "That was delicious."

Andy, pretending to scrub a spot on the counter, said nothing.

⟨⟨⟩

Later, Anita was ready to go any time Andy was. She thought she'd kill some time by throwing on a coat and stepping out into the brilliant sun. Oh, the sun felt good on her face. With her eyes closed, she could almost imagine herself somewhere on a Florida beach with just a bit of a nippy wind whipping her hair about. The joyful song of a red bird somewhere in the upper branches of the pine trees made her open her eyes. She looked around, couldn't see it and then made a beeline straight through the ankle-deep snow to the pen where she had seen the little goat earlier.

She laughed as she reached it. "You're so cute!," she said, and the goat bleated at her like a baby. At the sound of someone chuckling, she turned to see Stefano watching her from the barn door. The sun reflected up off the snow and danced in his startlingly brilliant aqua-coloured eyes. His cheeks were flushed from the cold, and the ends of his lips curved up, forming a shy smile.

"They are-a beautiful, *si. Bellisima*," he said, pleased with Anita's interest. "Come." Stefano walked over and opened the wire gate into the larger of the two pens and motioned for her to follow. She did eagerly. Two lambs came out from the other side of the barn, and then they were joined by another goat. All studied her silently, and one of the lambs walked up to her looking for treats, nudging her, pushing her and searching her pockets. She laughed, totally enchanted.

"Here, you give," Stefano said as he reached over and dipped his hand into a large open burlap sack, retrieved a handful of feed and poured it in her hand. He motioned she should feed them. She stretched out her hand palm up. First one and then all of the animals greedily nibbled at her palm. The feed went quickly. She wiped her hands on her jeans and quickly hopped through the dirtied snow back to the gate. The animals followed her to the fence.

"Oh, that was nice," she said. Stefano nodded, grinning.

Anita happened to look back at the house. There she saw Andy watching from the kitchen window. Stefano noticed, too, and his happy demeanour disappeared. He nodded politely at Anita and went back into the barn.

Anita looked back at the window. This time Andy was gone.

❧

Claudia still sat at what was now a cleared table, cleaning homegrown carrots for dinner, when Anita walked back into the kitchen. "Hi. Andy getting ready?" she asked Claudia while taking off her coat.

Claudia nodded. She held up a cleaned carrot and offered to Anita. "Eat, eat, pleeeeaaase."

"No thanks, Nonna," she said. "I just ate!" She retrieved her purse from under the chair she was sitting on and took out a hairbrush. She didn't really need to brush so much as just have something to fidget with. "So, Nonna," she said, "did you have a good time at your Calabria festival?" Nonna was in charge of her favourite activity at the social club, and she was always keen to talk about it. Claudia grinned and nodded.

"You drove with Mrs. Rossini, right?"

Claudia shrugged a little. "*Si*." She was crestfallen. "Mrs. Rossini-a, she nice. *Ma* she so alone. Antonnio, he die. I feel-a bad. If Fabrizio ever … you know. No wan-a live no more." Claudia's eyes teared up as she continued to peel the carrots.

Anita frowned and imagined Jack dead. Then she was startled suddenly by catching herself wishing he were. "Oh!" she exclaimed.

"*Che?*" asked Claudia.

"Oh, the time," Anita lied. She looked over at the clock on the stove. She saw that they had half an hour before they had to leave for the crystal party. She lowered her voice. "Claudia … how *did* Andy and Stefano meet?"

Claudia's lips formed a slow smile, and her little greyish blue eyes brightened. "Oh, das-a Mother Nature," she whispered, tapping the side of her nose.

"Mother Nature?" Anita was suddenly intrigued.

"*Si*," she said, leaning closer. She whispered. "Fabrizio an' me, we let-a Mother Nature do all da work." And with relish, she started telling the story.

1962

Andy had just turned seventeen, and by this time, Claudia and Fabrizio sadly admitted that within the Italian Canadian community, they knew of no one who would want their Adriana for their son. She had a reputation for being crass, rebellious and profane as well as a troublemaker. Still, people grudgingly admitted that she was very clever and bright. Nonetheless, bad or good, a suitor had to be found, because … well, that's what you had to do when you were Italian in the sixties and had a daughter. And you wouldn't accept anything less than a nice hardworking Italian man—young or old, it did not matter—so long as this man could provide for and love his wife. Well, all right, at least he had to like his wife. However, there was one even more important quality, and that was that he would care for the wife's parents in their later years. Oh, and of course, make many grandchildren, but grandsons in particular.

After endless prayers and anxious wringing of hands, Claudia and Fabrizio finally found the perfect solution: they would write to their hometown in Italy that they were willing to sponsor a fine young man to immigrate to Canada. They would work very hard to find this young man a job, and to top it all off, they offered free room and board until the day that this fine young man could stand on his own two feet. So they put pen to paper, specifying in their letter that this young man must come from either Claudia's family or from Fabrizio's—which, technically, were really the same.

Then they sat Andy down and informed her that they were sponsoring a young relative to come to Canada, that he would be staying with them, and that Andy was to try to be civil. Being the queen of manipulation herself, she immediately saw right through the ruse. "You can do what you want, there's no way I'm spending no goddamn lifetime with some jerk who doesn't speak Canadian!" she informed them. "I ain't falling for no goddamn loser from no shit-faced, backward, godforsaken country!"

But the more Andy rebelled, the harder Claudia prayed, and finally one blessed wintry day, after a hard shift at the clothing factory, she hurried from the bus stop—as she did every night—to see if there were any replies in their mailbox. On this particular heaven-sent day, she found a thin blue airmail envelope from Italy.

"*Favolosa!*" she cried on the doorstep. With her heart almost leaping out of her chest, she scrambled to her back door. She was still praising Holy Mary Mother of God as she burst into the kitchen. Normally, she would grab her apron from its hook on the back of the kitchen door and start supper while Fabrizio, who had retired as a school caretaker by then, finished his daily afternoon nap. But today, she swept on through into the front room to the couch and shook Fabrizio awake.

His eyes snapped open, and he jumped up wide-eyed. "*Mama mia! 'S bomba?*" he screamed in surprise.

"No, Fabrizio. Is no-a war no more. We are-a in Canada, si?"

He peered at her and grabbed his chest. "Claudia, what's a matter for you? You give-a me a heart attack!"

"No, Fabrizio, you no have a heart attack," she beamed. "But your heart-a will-a burst-a into-a song!" She led her husband gently to the kitchen table and sat him down. She held up the blue airmail envelope. Fabrizio beamed, took the envelope and very carefully with a knife sliced it open along its sides. Tenderly he took out the folded thin blue note paper. Claudia stood peering over his shoulder as he unfolded the note and a small photograph fell out onto the tablecloth. They both peered at it. "Fabrizio," she whispered, "this is the perfect husband for our Andy. I know it in-a my-a heart-a."

Fabrizio reached for his reading glasses in his shirt pocket and focussed on the photo more carefully. He saw a slim man in what appeared to be his late twenties, dressed in a dark suit and crisply starched collar. He stood posing rather stiffly in front of a stuccoed wall covered with grapevines which bore heavy and bountiful bunches of beautiful grapes. He was darkly tanned, with thick black hair and piercing light-coloured eyes, and in his arms he was holding a baby lamb. He was smiling with apparently all of his own teeth.

Tears of joy welled up in Fabrizio's eyes. "*Bello, si?*" he asked. Claudia nodded. Fabrizio looked again, and his eyebrows shot up. "I-a remember that-a little boy," he said excitedly. "*Si, si*, I remember he love da land an' help make-a da wine. You think-a Adriana will ...?" He was ever so hopeful.

"*Si, si*," Claudia laughed. "She will like-a!"

Fabrizio peered even closer. "Look-a, Claudia, he has a nose-a like me."

"*Si*, Fabrizio, I see!" An unusually large nose ran in the men of Fabrizio's family, and it was considered highly aristocratic. But unfortunately, Andy had carried on the tradition as well, much to her own chagrin. Hers ballooned to match her father's in her early teens, and that was the beginning of intense criticism and mocking at school. However, after a brief period of tears and heartache, she ended up punching a student in her own nose and quickly gained respect from her fellow classmates. She was the first to smoke, the first to use the Lord's name in vain on the school premises, the first to say "groove, baby, groove!" She became known as the "nose from hell" by the nuns who were quickly at wits' ends as to what to do with her. She was, as the nuns kept telling Fabrizio and Claudia, a rotten apple.

"*Ma* what of our Adriana? She make-a trouble," Fabrizio moaned.

But Claudia said, "No, Fabrizio, this is-a the Mother Nature who will-a work. You-a see. She-a no help but fall in love—he so nice-a!" She laughed, and her heart swelled with the certainty that this handsome young man would win over their difficult daughter. A good Italian boy would magically make their Andy a perfect Italian wife and would give her many bambinos—most especially grandsons, as his virile nose implied. Life was starting to look good finally, for they had lived very difficult lives in Italy—first the depression, then the war and finally having to start all over again in what they found to be a strange, kind and beautiful country.

"Fabrizio," said Claudia. "We don't tell Andy we like-a him. We never, never say a thing-a about-a marriage."

Fabrizio's eyes widened as he recognized his wife's wisdom. "*Si*," agreed Fabrizio, "we no say nothing-a." Fabrizio clasped his wife's hand to his breast, saying, "Oh, *mia* Claudia, we will be so happy!" And Claudia gave Fabrizio a kiss on his rosy bald head.

At that moment, Andy crashed through the back kitchen door, dropped her school bag heavily on the floor and kicked off her boots, spreading slush as far as the chair her father was sitting on. She tore off her snow-covered plastic head scarf and, shaking it, said, "Jesus fuckin' Christ, it's shitty out there!" But neither father nor mother took exception to her swearing this day.

Stunned by their silence, Andy did a double take. She was appalled to see that they were embracing each other—a sight so frightening, so unappetizing, that she was startled and lost her balance. She fell with her tush on top of her wet boots. Claudia and Fabrizio appeared not to notice.

"Oh, puhleeeze!" Andy yelled from the floor. "Don't make me puke!"

Claudia stopped talking the moment she heard Andy coming down the stairs. Andy stalked into the kitchen smartly dressed in a black mohair sweater and black woollen dress pants. Her neck, earlobes and wrists were bedecked with gold. Her red hair was teased and curled, and her nails had been given a coat of red. Blood red. She stopped to look at Anita and her mother. "What in freakin' hell are you two whispering about?"

"Your mother was just giving me advice on love and life," Anita smiled.

"Well, give it up." Andy shook her head. "You're not going to get a freakin' thing worth shit from Ma." Anita looked at Claudia, but Claudia only smiled and shrugged. Anita herself, still hurting from Andy's earlier snipes, looked steadily at her friend, wondering what she could have possibly done to deserve all this anger.

Damn, what's Anita looking at my nose for? wondered Andy irritably. She looked at the clock over the stove. Then she looked at her $400 gold watch. "We gotta go!" She turned to her mother. "Ma. Why don't you do somethin' with Maria tonight? Play a game or somethin'. Maybe shop before you make supper."

Claudia sipped the last of her coffee and smacked her lips. "We-a stay," she said, resuming cleaning the carrots. "I make-a a roast. Maria help-a. 'Ave a good-a time at crystal party. I feed Stefano before you back." She waved Andy away. "You-a go."

"Right," said Andy. "Maria! Get down here!" she yelled up the stairs.

"What?" yelled Maria.

"Get down here!" Andy commanded. She retrieved a dress coat from the hallway closet. Maria skipped down from upstairs. "Grab an apron and go downstairs to the basement kitchen. You'll see a roast sitting in the fridge. Bring it up for your supper."

Maria slumped wearily as she dragged herself through the kitchen and down towards the family room. Andy looked at her awkward, lanky daughter, whose feet and hands—and unfortunately her nose—had grown very large. Maria paused in the family room.

"Now!" yelled Andy. "Like, today maybe."

Maria slowly continued walking through the family room and down the basement stairs, allowing herself to slide down with her shoulders against the wall.

"And don't scratch the walls!"

"Maria!" screeched Claudia. "Bring-a me a pop-a an' for Nonno."

"Can I get a pop too, Ma?" Maria's voice echoed from the basement. "No!"

Claudia frowned. "Oh, she like-a …" Andy shook her head. Claudia shrugged. "*Ma* she so good."

"No, Ma."

Claudia's bottom lip drooped. "Maria," cried Claudia. "You know Momma don' wan' you to drink-a pop," she said as she got up and walked to the top of the basement stairs. Then she whispered down the stairs. "Shh, no tell-a Momma. I give you-a pop."

Andy and Anita could hear her clearly.

"Yaaaay," Maria whispered.

Andy played dumb. She wasn't in the mood. Anita by now had put her coat on and grabbed her purse. She followed Andy through the family room and straight to the garage off the back hallway. On the way into the cold damp garage, there was a large wooden crate to the side with plastic egg cartons full of freshly laid brown and spotted eggs. Virtually all of them were liberally sprinkled with straw and bits of feather.

"Hey, you need eggs, any time," muttered Andy as she passed.

"I love fresh eggs," Anita said as she eyed the plastic cartons in passing. Something about the cartons looked familiar. "Andy, aren't those the same cartons that Jack makes at the factory?"

Andy was pulling leather gloves on as she turned to look down at the crates. "How do I know? I think Stefano's always used them." Andy twitched her nose in disgust and muttered, "Stinking pests, those birds."

Anita's heart gave her a jolt of misery. She wordlessly pulled on her own gloves and moved on, with Jack heavy on her mind.

Andy stopped between her brown ten-year-old Volvo and Stefano's "good" car, a late model—had to be black—Cadillac. "You drive. You know I hate driving." She tossed the keys to Anita, who walked over to the Cadillac first and peeked in through the tinted windows.

"Nice," she said. "Just bought it?"

"Yeah, I know. Every year a new Caddy. We need another car like we need another hole in the head. We use the Caddy about a dozen times a year—at the most! Hey, you wanna see somethin'?" Andy asked, brightening up. "Look here." She stepped to the trunk and opened it.

Anita looked inside. "Empty, right?" Anita nodded. "Okay, under this floor is the spare tire." She exposed the spare tire. "Now, watch this." Andy pulled at a tab under one of the back brake lights and another floor unlatched. Anita leaned in to get a better look. In the shadows underneath the fake bottom was a squared-off receptacle in the shape of a box with foam dividers. Within the foam were two handguns. Anita was speechless, and her pulse raced. She cast Andy a questioning look.

"Yeah, I know. Kind've overkill, ain't it?" she said sarcastically. "No pun intended."

Anita took a closer look at the locking mechanism of the false bottom when Andy briskly closed it on her. "Wow," was all Anita could say.

"Yep!" said Andy sarcastically as she got into the passenger side of the Volvo. "You'd think we lived in the Wild West."

Anita got in the Volvo on the driver's side and started the car, driving it out of the garage and down the driveway. The sun had done a fabulous job of melting the snow. Anita cast a quick glance at the mileage dial. She was amazed to see that it was only just above 70,000 kilometres. "Geez, Andy. You don't drive much, do you?"

"I hate driving with a passion," Andy said tonelessly. "Two miles down that way and over one block is the butcher, baker and the bank. If I go the other way one mile, I'm at Sharon's clothing shop, Sandra's travel agency and almost to my parents' place. The school's next to the church, and you know where that is. Not even a mile behind us. That's all I do—and *only* if I have no choice but to drive. Ma does a lot for me. So I go out maybe—what? Once every two weeks? That's twice a month, and too many times for me, I tell ya."

Anita drove quietly for a moment or two but then realized she didn't know where she was going. "So, where is this crystal party?" she asked. "Whose house is it?"

"At you-know-who's with the pink mink—Roberta! Keep going this way. I'll tell ya when to turn." Andy bent over, turned on the radio and stuck a tape in—'The Best of Claudio Baglioni.' She played it loud. Andy was not in a talkative mood.

This is ridiculous. I don't deserve this, thought Anita. "Listen, Andy, I think I know why you're upset with me. Honest, I called just like …"

"I don't want to hear it," Andy cut her off.

Anita persevered. "Andy, why? I don't deserve this. I called as soon as I saw Stefano drive up."

"Well, that's funny, because I sat and waited over an hour and nobody freakin' called me!"

"Andy, I *called*! It took about fifteen minutes, just like you said, and when I saw Stefano pull up I picked up that phone, and I dialled, and it was busy!"

"Well then, you dialled the wrong fucking number, Anita, because there sure wasn't no fucking calls coming through on my end." Andy's face was concrete, her eyes squinting into rock-hard slits. "You think I'm stupid!? I stood there and I waited. End of story. So, someone's fucking lying!"

Anita reached the end of her patience. "Andy, it was a flat tire."

"No kidding!" sneered Andy. "The ol' flat tire excuse, huh? Come on," she laughed sardonically. "Can't you think of something a little more original?"

Anita glared at Andy. "You know what? I'm getting really tired of you yelling at me. I don't need this. You of all people know that." She sat fuming, barely noticing the traffic as she drove.

"Oh yeah, we're feeling sorry for ourselves, are we? Husband gone? No kids? No car?" Andy sneered. "Looking all teary and blue-eyed at Stefano."

"Shut up!" screamed Anita, the car squealing to a stop. "Just shut up!" Anita had to control the need to physically lash out. She knew she was close to the edge, and her own outburst frightened her.

Andy looked at her askance and then quickly looked around. She had never known Anita to be so aggressive. She sat silently for a few moments and then suddenly and mutely jabbed a finger to the left.' Anita scornfully but dutifully turned left. "There," she said, pointing. "Stop there." Anita saw a group of cars in front of a little bungalow and drove by them to park in the next available spot along the curb. Silently, the two women got out of the car and marched towards the house.

⁂

Stefano, flushed with contentment, poured more of his homemade wine into Peter's and Fabrizio's tumblers. The men were sitting in a cellar below the garage, which was accessed by an open hatchway in the cement floor. They sat on old wooden grape crates under Stefano's hanging bundles of cheese and the carcass of a rabbit he had shot recently. They were surrounded by winemaking paraphernalia, including a deep sink, stacks of empty pint fruit baskets and a row of cleaned demijohns covered in Saran wrap. There was also the odd mousetrap. Behind them were crates of potatoes from Stefano's garden, and an old electric heater glowed brightly at their feet.

The three men puffed at big fat cigars and blew the smoke through the hatchway up into the garage, occasionally watching the smoke waft up into the rafters. Fabrizio suddenly burst out in a fit of coughing, and Stefano leaned over and patted his father-in-law's back hard with a chuckle. Fabrizio caught his breath, and the three of them sat for a moment in silence. Above them in the house, they heard the creaking of floorboards and the distant sound of the odd exchange of chatter between Claudia and Maria.

"Andy's-a friend … she husband still-a gone?" asked Fabrizio, wiping his eyes with his cotton handkerchief and squinting through the smoke.

"Anita? So far as we know," answered Peter, focussing on trimming a piece of smoked sausage. Even though Peter had immigrated to Canada a couple of years later than his much older brother, Stefano, he had quickly acquired North American habits and, for the most part, lost his thick Italian accent. "She hasn't seen hide nor hair, has she, Stefano?"

Stefano shook his head, pointing to his temple. "The man, he is-a stupid."

Fabrizio chuckled and ogled at the younger men. *"E una bella dona."* He kissed his fingertips and grinned. "Me-a? I look after her!" offered Fabrizio with a grin.

Stefano pointed at his father-in-law. "You no do it. You-a too old."

Fabrizio laughed and winked. "Never too old-a!"

"The guy's an ass," said Peter. "Do you think she knows where Jack is?"

Stefano shook his head. "No, I don' think-a she do."

Peter exploded. "What an asshole. A guy makes it big, makes a load of money, spends an even bigger load of money, wants more money, ya know? That guy's just into money, money, money. I mean, we all are, but that guy—he's not smart about it. He's got some bad fuckin' explaining to do, Stefano. You know what he told me once?"

Stefano shook his head and wiped sweat off his brow with his cotton handkerchief.

"He said that life was nothing but a shit sandwich—the more dough you got, the less shit you have to eat."

Stefano chuckled and grinned. "That no bad! Good joke," he said.

Fabrizio also laughed and briefly wondered what a shit sandwich would look like.

Peter continued, "He's got shit for brains. What'd he expect? What'd he take us for?" Peter sucked at his cigar again. "She looks bad, Stefano. Tired. She needs someone to look after her." He grinned and winked at Stefano, but Stefano didn't see the humour in it.

"I look-a," laughed Fabrizio eagerly, motioning with his arm that he would love to catch her alone.

Stefano squinted at his father-in-law and smiled broadly at him, nodding.

"That's not what I mean," Peter mumbled. He rearranged the crease on his pants, wiped off some cigar ashes and took another drag on his cigar. "You think we're gonna get at that asshole through her?" Peter said slyly, looking at his brother. Then he threw a glance at Fabrizio to see if he caught him doing that.

"I tell Adriana she keep an eye on 'Nita," Stefano said, pointing at his brother. "Das all. She don' need no help from you. She-a no know nothing-a." He pointed his thumb at himself. "I do dis, no you!"

Peter leaned in towards Stefano. Briefly looking back over his shoulder up the hatchway and then at Fabrizio, who was focussing on slicing up more sausage, he said softly, "He's gotta show up sometime. We both know he didn't arrive at Luciano's in Italy. I thought maybe if we put a little pressure on Anita, we might be able to beat him out of the bushes."

Stefano slammed his fist on one of the crates and smashed one of the wooden cross pieces, and then he pointed a sausage of a finger at Peter's nose. "You no do anything-a, I say. Nothing! *Niente!*" Stefano scowled at his brother. "Leave 'Nita for-a me to watch-a. Soon-a."

Fabrizio looked at the brothers and realized something was up. He looked down again but sat still. Peter eyed his older brother. He sensed something. "Oh, come ooooon," Peter smirked. "You're not falling for her." Fabrizio looked from Peter to Stefano.

Stefano glared at Peter and put up his index finger. He stabbed into Peter's left shoulder. *"Essere attento,"* he said. "Careful."

"Are you fucking with me, Stefano? Or are you fuckin' with—" He didn't need to finish the sentence.

Stefano bent over and grabbed Peter by the coat collar. He stared into his brother's brown eyes. *"Essere attento,"* he said again.

Peter pulled himself away from Stefano and brushed down his coat collar. Quietly, he stood up. "I think I got a say in this, Stefano. It's for my own best interest. I have a large stake in this." He spit some cigar paper off his tongue. "I've been hearin' things. Rumours. It might be more effective if you start doin' something constructive for a change ... as your brother, I feel I should tell you that they think you're getting soft. I saw her, you know, at the church the other day with Andy. I get the feeling that she might know a thing or two. I can maybe get her to talk or at the least frighten him out of hiding." Peter grabbed the ladder leading out of the cellar. "If I were to put her in some sort of trouble ... We gotta get some of that cash back."

Stefano looked at Peter as he flicked the ashes off his cigar and stuck it back into his mouth.

Fabrizio looked up. "Me's, no mind-a. I wait."

Peter looked from Fabrizio to Stefano. Stefano shook his head and shrugged.

"No mind-a what?" asked Stefano.

"I give-a him. *Si*, five-a. Is all. Stefano, you-a give him same, *si?*"

Stefano shook his head and held up a finger.

"You only lent him one thou?" asked Peter.

Stefano shook his head again and made a rolling motion with his hand.

Peter sat blinking at the floor and then up at his brother. Then his mouth dropped open. "One hundred thou?"

Stefano nodded and flicked more ash around his feet. Peter and Fabrizio both stared at him. Fabrizio straightened up, shrugged again, put a finger to his lips and then pointed upwards. "Shhhh. Claudia." He held up his five fingers and also did the circular motion with his hand.

"Noooo," said Stefano.

"Five hundred thou!?" Peter shouted.

Fabrizio shook his head and put his finger to his lips again. "No, *cinquata!*"

Peter stood up fuming. "Fifty thou. That's it. Not only is he turning on us—Lord knows where he's running to with the dirty cash—but *our* money? We gotta beat the bushes and see where this creep is taking our money. I'm gonna kill that son of a bitch!"

Stefano shot a hand out and grabbed Peter's dress coat. They stared at each other for a brief moment. Stefano sighed heavily. "He's you good-a friend."

Peter plopped back down on his crate. "Not when he steals money meant for the family!"

"Si. To take-a to …" And he motioned to a faraway place.

"Si! First to Italy and then on to Venezuela." Peter dropped his head and jiggled his legs. Fabrizio looked on, not quite knowing what was happening.

"Forget-a 'bout it." Stefano tapped his temple.

"Oh, geez, no." Peter leaned forward and spoke with despair. "Stefano, I'm telling you, they never ever received a call from him in Italy. Hell! They didn't even realize he had left from here! I didn't know that the *famiglia's* money was also being delivered by this creep."

"'N he your partner," Stefano reminded him.

"Not anymore, he ain't!"

"One more-a week," Stefano said simply.

"Okay, but after that we use that wife of his any way we need to. You hear me?"

Stefano pointed the cigar at his brother. "Maybe he will-a still do this-a thing. 'N just-a little cream on-a da top." Stefano motioned to his pocket. "Is normal. Uno week-a."

Peter slumped onto the crate again and fretted, wringing his hands. "I, uh … got another problem. I also gave him stuff that wasn't mine. In fact," Peter looked up and sighed into the rafters, "I lent him a hell of a lot more than both of you." He sadly looked down his nose at Fabrizio.

Fabrizio and Stefano stared at him. "How mo'?" asked Stefano.

Peter dragged his shaking hand over his forehead. "A *lot* lot more, if you catch my drift."

"What is 'drift'?" Fabrizio asked.

Peter didn't hear him. He hung down his head. "Sandra's, and …"

"No!" Stefano shot out. "No' her parents!"

Peter stood up and waved a hand at him. "Of course not, you think I'm that stupid? That'd be like signing my own death certificate. Ha! Listen!" he jumped up off the crate. "Just forget it!"

"You no worry," advised brave Fabrizio. "All da business do-a good! Jack, he's-a gonna come back. You-a see."

"Right. Sure. Like Andy says, and bears don't shit in the forest!"

Fabrizio looked questioningly at Stefano.

"Oh, fuck it," Peter murmured. He turned and climbed the few rungs up the ladder. As his head cleared the floor above, he found himself face to face with Maria—who was sitting quietly, wide-eyed. Peter almost choked.

"Hey! Uh, hi, Maria," he said softly. "You hidin' there all this time?"

Below, Stefano pushed his crate back and jumped up. He climbed up alongside and looked up at Maria. "Maria! Is no polite to listen in."

Claudia's head poked through the garage door leading into the house. "Maria! You leave you daddy alone. You a little girl, you stay wid me!" She stepped forward quickly, grabbed Maria's hand and helped her up on her feet. "Come, Maria, you help-a me."

Nervously she walked back to the doorway with Maria in tow and turned around. "Peter, you wanna eat somethin'?" Claudia could see that both Peter and Stefano were angry, and she was especially bothered by how ashen-faced Stefano was. Fabrizio looked pale too. If there was one thing Claudia could do well, it was know what was up and playing it dumb. "You mus' eat, *si?*"

"No, *grazie*. I have to go home. Sandra wants me to be back early to help with little Stefano and Andrew's birthday party tonight." He turned to look down at Stefano, who had stepped down into the cellar and was looking up through the hatch, watching Maria being towed away.

Stefano wondered how long Maria had been eavesdropping. What did she hear? He relaxed when he realized there was very little she could've heard or even understood.

Claudia quietly chastised the child as they slipped back into the house. "Maria, you no do that. Das for men, no' you. Come! I give you anotha' pop," she coaxed.

Peter followed them into the house.

"Peter," Claudia insisted, "you no wan' fo' sure?" She smiled sweetly.

Peter looked down at Maria for a moment. His niece looked back with large eyes while she reached out to her *nonna*. Peter swallowed. "No, gotta go. Thanks anyway." He turned to go, stopped and turned back. "Are you and Fabrizio not coming tonight?" he asked.

"Ah, no, I stay wid Maria, an' Fabrizio, he tired, he stay too. Is-a too busy for him."

Peter reached the garage as Stefano and Fabrizio came up out of the hatchway. Stefano closed the hatchway door with a slam, grabbed a large piece of oil-stained canvas and pulled it back over the hatchway to hide it. "Anita—she will be there-a too."

"Good, good," Peter said with a vacant look on his face. "Yeah, good. All right." He smiled, first at Fabrizio, then at Stefano. "We'll just have to keep an ear and an eye open for you-know-who, right?" he said nervously.

Stefano nodded silently.

"Great, see you later then ... Fabrizio." Peter hugged him while shaking his hand. "Nice to see you." He started to leave, but Stefano grabbed his arm. "Little Stefano an' Andrew," he said. "How ol' now?"

"You should know, you're their goddamn godfather," Peter chastised him.

"*Dieci*? Ten?"

"*Si*," said Peter. "Can you believe it?" He walked towards the open garage doors but turned back one more time. "Oh, by the way." He took out a thick white envelope from the breast pocket of his camel-hair coat and handed it to Stefano. "The store's up and running and doin' very good. See you tonight."

Stefano silently nodded and watched as his brother disappeared through the garage doors into the waning afternoon light.

Andy was starting to feel awfully hot, and she fidgeted uncomfortably. She was sitting in the middle of an overly large couch in front of a table covered with dirty plates of half-eaten food, half-empty glasses of wine and punch and a myriad of samples of crystal vases, bowls, dishes, decanters and more. The women around her were chatting and laughing loudly while a baby cried in its bassinette in a corner. Andy shivered with mounting paranoia and quickly felt fenced in. She shakily took out a cigarette and a lighter from her bag.

With the cigarette hanging from the corner of her mouth, she called, "Roberta! Hey Robbie!" A woman standing at the entrance to the kitchen stopped talking and turned to look. Andy held up the cigarette at her, questioningly, and asked "D'you mind?" Roberta gave her the thumbs up. "Thank God," Andy muttered. "At least I can smoke without feeling like a goddamn criminal."

Andy lit the cigarette, dragged in deeply and then slowly aimed a long spume of smoke towards the corner away from the baby. Its mother, bending over and shaking a rattle, looked back at Andy and frowned. Andy smiled and waved at her and then got up and went to a window. With so many hot-blooded women heating up the room, someone had already opened one of the windows just a crack—enough to let in a small draft of welcoming cool air. Andy opened it a little more and stayed there for another drag or two.

Bored with that, she threw the cigarette out the window … but the cigarette didn't fall to the snow-covered ground. Instead, it rested on the outside windowsill. "Holy shit," she said, quickly looking around to see if anyone had seen her throw it out. She put her hand through the window and tried to push the still-smoking cigarette off the sill and into the snowy bushes underneath. She only ended up pushing it a little further up the sill.

"Oh fuck," she muttered and looked around for something long and thin. She spied a pen near a few brochures that were left in a sticky spot of spilled wine. She grabbed that and reached out. She pushed the cigarette into the bushes but lost the pen. It fell into the bushes as well. Behind her, Nina, the crystal lady, was talking to another guest and happened to be looking for her pen.

"Now, where's that pen? They never seem to be where you left them, do they?" Nina said, looking around frantically. She, too, was feeling rather steamy and was getting very close to her tolerance level. The mayhem was overwhelming. *Why are Italian crystal parties always so loud and hectic?* she wondered. But she also knew that at the end, she always walked away with a bounty of orders, so she once again decided it was worth it.

Andy looked around and quietly went back to her seat on the couch. She sank down, way down, into the cushions and ended up with her knees high in the air once again. For the umpteenth time, she looked around and in front of her and reached out to fiddle with a few of the crystal objects. "I got this already," she said of one. She picked up another. "Got that." Another. "Yep, got this." She searched through the rest. "Goddamn, isn't there anything new I can buy here? I already bought all this at the last twenty parties," she complained loudly.

The crystal lady heard her and walked over. "Andy," she said, "I do have something new that's just come out. Maybe you haven't seen this yet." She bent down to pick up one of her totes and rummaged through it.

"It's Nina, right?" asked Andy, pointing to the woman's name tag. "Okay, so what you got, Nina?"

On the other side of the room, from a cluster of ladies standing by the kitchen, Anita looked over at Andy. She could tell Andy had had a few drinks and was getting louder and more out of control. Anita was reminded what a loose cannon big loudmouth Andy could be. Presently, she looked away and happened to lock eyes with Josie, another friend of Andy's. They smiled at each other, and Josie got up and walked over. "Hi, Anita," she said quietly. "How are ya hangin' in there?"

Anita's smile disappeared, and she looked at her questioningly, "Oh ... hanging in."

Josie wasn't sure if she should go on. "I'm sorry. I heard that Jack ... We met you before, and I hear you on the radio lots of times."

"Oh, of course." Anita smiled bravely. "He's still not back, but I'm sure there are reasons. There isn't a lot of reception in some parts of Italy. He's been working very hard. I'm sure he'll be very relieved to come home."

Josie frowned and then smiled. She nodded. "Oh, so he didn't run off with some lovely redhead! Oh, I'm so relieved. Everybody's been saying they'd seen him out and about, and I just thought—"

"Well, everyone must be wrong."

Josie nodded silently. To change the subject, she turned to look at the young mother and the baby, who was now cradled in his mother's arms, finally quiet and content. "My God, it seems like yesterday that my boys were that age. They're in their twenties now!"

Anita also watched, and her heart skipped a beat. Would she ever have children? "Jack and I would like children of our own. We're planning to have our own, you know."

Josie looked at her in surprise. "Really? Well, that's wonderful!"

Anita nodded. "We started trying a few months ago. We waited until we were sure Jack's new business was well underway." Her voice trailed away. She suddenly felt a sickly sense of uncertainty. "Can I ask you a question?"

Josie nodded. "Sure."

"There are so many rumours, and I'm curious why anyone would start them. You know, Jack may have meetings with female co-workers, buyers, distributors … so I'm not worried. But I'm curious. Who is it people say he's been with?"

Suddenly Josie felt uncomfortable again. "I don't know her name, but I've personally seen Jack with an accountant from the Catholic School Board offices. Maybe you know her?"

Anita thought for a moment and shook her head. "I don't remember Jack mentioning an accountant, but of course he must deal with them."

"I don't exactly know what her name is. I'll be honest with you; I thought it looked a little weird. I was shopping at this really neat little store up in Tewkesbury, and I looked up and saw your husband. I remembered him from last year at the club. I didn't say anything because he looked right past me. He obviously didn't remember me. Well, I kinda looked around to see if you were there with him, but instead I saw him walking with his, um, arm around this redhead. I thought, 'Gee, Anita dyed her hair,' but then the woman turned around, and I saw it wasn't you." She winced. "I'm so sorry."

Anita's eyes grew large as saucers, and a knot began to form in her stomach. "Tewkesbury?" She was dazed.

"As a matter of fact, I saw her this morning."

"This morning? Where?" asked Anita, wide-eyed. She was loud enough to be heard by Andy, who snapped her head around to look.

Josie moved in closer. "She works at the school-board office behind the old mall. I was handing in a parent's signature form for my daughter's trip to Quebec City when I saw her at the back of the office. A little woman. Big boobs. Red hair. Lots of makeup."

"Is she … you know … beautiful?" Anita meekly asked.

"To be quite honest, Anita?" Josie said. "She can't hold a candle to you, girl."

Anita mustered a slight smile. "Oh, Josie … if that's true, then she must have a heck of a lot of other good stuff that I don't have."

"Somehow I don't think so!" smiled Josie.

Anita was quiet for a moment. "Everyone else is wrong, Josie. Please believe it." She lowered her head and shook it. "I don't know. I just don't know anymore." She looked over to where Andy was sitting and saw that her friend was occupied with the crystal-party lady again. She made a decision. "Well, it's Saturday, but they're open today, you say?" asked Anita, her mind racing ahead.

"They're doing year-end, something like that." Josie looked at her watch. "They might still be open."

Anita thanked Josie and gave her a big hug, but she had to fight back tears. "Thank you," she said warmly. "I have to figure this out or I'll go mad." She then hurried over to Andy. "Excuse me, Andy," she said, "I need to step out just for a moment. Can I use the car?"

Andy coldly looked over at her and shrugged smugly. "We're going to have another 'flat tire' with someone else, are we?"

Anita ignored her comment. Everyone stopped talking and looked at Anita. She blushed. "I'm not going to be long. I'm just going around the corner."

Andy stared at her and then struggled up off the couch.

Anita put up her hand. "It's about Jack."

All the women started whispering together, turning their backs to Anita. Andy nodded silently and waved her away. "You got the keys. Go," she said and then turned back to Nina.

"Thanks, Andy," Anita whispered, and she turned to go.

Andy watched Anita leave and sighed deeply. She turned and focussed again on a small round object that Nina was holding out to her. She reached for the object but it slipped from her fingers and fell, crashing into a thousand little pieces. "Ah fuck!" cried Andy.

A room full of women and one baby gasped. The baby broke out into a healthy wail.

Anita sat in the parked Volvo and peered at the building across the road. She could just make out the odd head and shoulders passing by the office windows. *That woman*, she thought. *That "other woman."* Had Anita become a statistic—one of billions of married woman over the ages whose husbands left them for someone else? She grimaced. It didn't seem real to her. Regardless, she wasn't going to give up without a fight.

Deftly, she undid her seat belt and got out of the car. She crossed the road and stepped into the school-board building.

Inside, she walked up to a receptionist behind a glass window. She knocked on it gently and slid the glass partition open. "Hi," she said smiling to a young woman of about twenty-five or so. The woman looked up at her from her book. "Um, I'm looking for a friend who works here," Anita said. She looked past the receptionist and into the office. By one of the gray partitions, she saw a woman fitting the description that Josie had given her. She pointed towards the woman. "Oh, there she is. It'll just take a moment."

The young woman looked back to where Anita was pointing and turned back. "Rose? Sure. Can I say who's asking for her?"

"Yes, tell her it's a friend from grade school. I'm sure she won't recognize me. I just want to let her know I'm in town," Anita fibbed.

"Sure," said the young woman. She got up and walked over to the cubicle where Rose sat. Rose listened and then got up and walked over to Anita with a small expectant smile on her face. It was evident that she didn't know who Anita was. The young receptionist came back to her desk and said, "You can come in through the door."

"Thank you," said Anita. She stepped through the office door and mutely stood facing Rose.

As if in slow motion, Anita studied the woman from the top of her bottle-red head to the tip of her toes. She was much shorter. Smaller hands, smaller feet. Her hair was clipped short, and she was wearing small gold hoop earrings in her pierced ears. Her dress was a navy blue tunic with gold buttons, and she also wore a gold chain and bracelet. Her face was pleasant enough though heavily made up. Anita noticed that Rose's eyelids were droopy and swollen and somewhat sad.

Rose smiled and asked, "Can I help you?" She had such a tiny voice.

"Yes, I think you can. I'm Anita, Jack's wife, and he's kind of disappeared. I think you may have something to do with it."

"Jack's wife?" Rose gasped and covered her mouth, stifling a tiny sob. She nodded, looked around the office in despair, and frantically waved her little well-manicured hands for Anita to follow her into an empty conference room. As they left the main office, the other employees craned their necks to watch them go.

Inside, there was a large redwood laminated table with eight padded chairs around it. Anita angrily pulled one out and plopped into it. Rose closed the door and remained standing, her bottom lip quivering. She began to wring her perfect little hands around and around. She looked terribly troubled.

If Anita had been in a different mood, she might've felt sorry for the woman. "My Jack's gone, poof!" she said, lifting her chin defiantly. "I don't put a lot of weight into rumours normally, but too many people are telling me that you may be the culprit. I want to know if it's true." She felt her body shaking. "And if you know where he is." She paused and added with a catch in her throat, "He's been away so very long. I'm afraid, and I miss him so very much."

Rose looked shocked and confused. "Are you saying you don't know where he is either?"

Anita was taken aback. "Wait a minute. Maybe I've got this wrong. Are you doing some accounting for him or are you ... you know ... doing what you shouldn't be doing. With him," she asked haltingly.

"What?" exclaimed Rose, her pencil-lined eyebrows shooting up. "No. Why would I do work for him? I love him! And yeah, we are ... doing. We're getting married."

"Er, excuse me?"

"But he told me you knew. That you were separated and everything was friendly-like. He said you wanted a divorce, and that you wanted to go on with your life. He told me you guys were like buds."

"I don't want a divorce! And we're not like buds!" Anita screamed. Rose jumped.

"You liar!" yelled Anita. "He loves *me*. How could you do this to me?"

Rose frowned and flopped into a chair. "You mean you're not ...? You still want him back?"

"Back? I never let him go! I didn't know that I didn't have him to begin with! So ... it's true?"

Rose dropped her head, and after a pause, she nodded. Then she covered her face.

Anita looked at the walls and the ceiling. "Oh, my heart," she said to no one in particular. She gathered herself together. "Where is he now?"

"I ... I don't know. I thought maybe you knew. I thought you came to let me know where he was." She wrung her little hands. "I was hoping he sent you to explain."

"Me? You're kidding, right?"

Rose nodded her head and then shook it, her tiny red curls bouncing on top of her head. "No! Yes!" she cried. She pulled a used tissue from out of her cleavage and wiped her nose with it. "We were supposed to go to Italy together for Christmas. He even showed me the tickets. Then a couple of days before we were to leave, he disappeared. I waited and waited ... I thought I missed something, you know? Like maybe we were supposed to meet at the airport an' I forgot? Like those nightmares you can have? And I was so looking forward to it, too. It's been so very lonely, and over Christmas and New Year's! You know more people commit suicide over the holidays?"

Anita jumped up and grabbed her by the shoulders. "Tell me where he is, or I swear to God I will crucify you!"

Rose cringed. "I swear to you, I don't know!" She pulled away and sat down again. She covered her mouth and started to rock back and forth. "Omigoshomigosh! Maybe he's hurt and lying somewhere in a ditch!" she wailed. "Oh Jack, oh Jack." She stood up and grabbed the phone on the conference table. She started dialling feverishly. "If he's not with you, then he must be in trouble! We've got to call the police!"

Anita slammed her hand on the telephone. "Wait a minute. I've already called. You'll find this hard to believe," she said sarcastically, "but the police say that he's not considered a missing person until more time has lapsed, and that this happens all the time. You know why?"

Rose shook her head, and her curls jumped.

"Because a lot of husbands run off with other women! Ha! Isn't that a hoot?"

Rose didn't get the irony because her mind didn't work in subtleties. In a small voice, she said, "Do you think he ran off with another woman?"

Anita almost slapped her. "Stupid! *I'm* the *wife*, not you!" She poked a finger into Rose's shoulder. "*You* are the other woman!"

"Oh no. I can't be, because he's not run off with me."

Anita was about to laugh. She took a deep breath and wiped her eyes. Her voice lowered as she fiddled with her skirt. "But you're right. I think he's in trouble too."

Rose suddenly looked up at Anita wide-eyed. "I remember just before we were to leave on our romantic—"

"Clam it!"

"—leave for Italy, we were driving back to my place when he suddenly thought we were being followed. He kept lookin' over his shoulder. Oh, do you think someone wanted him dead? It's gotta be somethin' like that, otherwise he wouldn't have left me hanging!"

Anita lifted her hands up as if she wanted to strangle the woman. "He wouldn't leave *you* like this? He's not *with* you, stupid!" The audacity! But Rose took no notice and continued to bawl. Anita stood watching her. This was a bad dream. And now what also made her angry was that she suddenly felt sorry for Rose. "Dammit! You have no right to cry! You … you *twerp!*"

Suddenly, Rose lightened up. "Jack's so romantic, isn't he? We were supposed to see the Coliseum. I was really looking forward to that. Oh! And I wanted to buy a pair or two of those beautiful Italian leather shoes they have there." Suddenly she clammed up and almost died of embarrassment. Meekly she spoke further, "He told me that it was my Christmas present."

Anita flopped back on the chair and sank into it. She seriously believed she had lost a bit of her sanity.

"I believed him," Rose added meekly.

"Rose, talk is cheap."

"Oh no, not with him." She leaned closer to Anita. "I even went to a fortune teller and asked her if he was coming back. You know what she told me? That if I really wanted him to, he'll come back. So, I really want him to," she said, crossing her fingers.

Anita's heart pounded in her chest. "And who really gives a shit!" She suddenly felt nauseous. "I have to go. I'm going to be sick." She turned and ran to the door. All the employees huddled in the doorway suddenly jumped back to let her run through. Then they all turned to stare at poor little Rose crying in the conference room.

Forty minutes later, a drunken Andy and a subdued, red-nosed Anita left the crystal party and walked back to the car. Andy handed a small box to Anita. "Here, got ya somethin'," she said. Anita silently took the little box from her without looking at it. "What is it?" she asked absently.

"Well, it's the same as this," Andy said, holding up an identical box and shaking it. "It was the only goddamn thing I hadn't bought yet. Although I had to pay for three. I smashed one!" she said gleefully. "Oh dear," she said and shook the box again. "Is this one broken too? I swear I will kill the next person who has another goddamn party. Crystal or Tupperware, I don't care." She calmed down a bit. "Anyway, go ahead and open it."

"Now?"

"Now."

Anita stopped walking and let her arms drop by her side. "Andy, I don't want it."

"Oh, you ungrateful cad!"

Anita took the box and opened it. She pulled out a crystal version of an eight-ball. She looked at it mutely.

"What you do," Andy instructed, "is you ask it a question, then you shake it, an answer will pop into this window here."

Anita looked a little closer. It definitely looked like crystal, but it had a black substance within another ball.

"Go on, shake it. It's a hoot!"

Anita looked around the front lawn first and then shook it with her eyes closed.

"No, no. You first ask a question and then shake it. And you don't have to close your eyes."

"But I want to close my eyes."

Andy snorted and grinned. Then she motioned for her to do it.

Anita closed her eyes and silently asked a question, and then she shook the ball.

"Out loud," demanded Andy.

Anita sighed. "Okay." She looked down at the ball. "Will my husband come back?"

"Oh brother," Andy snorted with a roll of her eyes.

Anita shook the ball again and eyed it as a slow swirl of liquid passed the little window. Eventually a word came into view: "Maybe."

Anita lowered the ball and covered her eyes with one hand.

"It's that bad?" muttered Andy. Andy grabbed Anita by the shoulder of her coat and dragged her gently towards the Volvo. She took the keys from Anita, unlocked the car and pushed Anita into the passenger side.

Anita shook her head and sniffed. "No, I'll drive."

"You shut your pretty little trap," said Andy. "You just sit there and be quiet. Here, let me take that friggin' thing away from you." Andy took the ball and threw it along with the bag with the other one in it into the back seat. The ball bounced once and jumped off the back seat onto the immaculate carpeted floor.

Andy turned the car on and crept away from the curb at a snail's pace.

"Thanks, Andy."

"You're absolutely welcome."

Anita looked out and watched the pavement crawl by. "But you have to believe me. We really did have a flat tire."

"So you keep saying." Andy lifted her nose further up in the air, and she squinted at the road.

"I know. When we get home, I could show you the tire in the truck. Would that prove it to you?"

Andy looked over and saw how desperate and sad Anita was. She swivelled her nose back to the road. She nodded once. "I guess. Yeah, it would." She felt like an idiot now. "Listen. I think now that I may not have hung up properly. Maybe you're right. Sorry."

"That's okay, Andy. I can understand not trusting one's husband."

Andy looked at Anita again and laughed. "Yeah, you would." Back to the road. A thought struck Andy. "But if that spare isn't on that goddamn truck, I'm just gonna have to kill you. Fair?"

Anita smiled. "Fair!" Then her face cratered and she started to cry.

Andy patted her lightly on her back. "Shh, shh. That's okay," she whispered. "I'm not angry with you anymore."

Anita stopped sobbing and looked up to stare blankly through the windshield.

Andy looked Anita up and down. "So, where'd you go? What happened?"

"I went to see that woman."

"That woman ...? *That* woman?" She slammed on the brakes. Wheels squealed behind them, and someone honked a horn. "No kidding! You've got some nerve! Good for you! Is she still walkin'?" A car zoomed around them honking. "Eat this!" Andy yelled as she gave them the finger. To Anita, "So, yeah?"

"Yeah," Anita sputtered. She wiped her nose and eyes with a tissue. "But I don't want to believe a single word she said!"

Andy remained unusually quiet for a moment and softly she said, "Believe it, my girlie. Believe it. It's not the first time in history that this has happened."

"You know the stupidest part of it all? He had told her we weren't together anymore and that he loved *her*, and she believed it with all her heart. She was so little, so stupid and so much so that I actually felt sorry for her."

"Pardon me? You feel sorry for her? That's a laugh."

"I'm not laughing."

Andy continued driving, but she was so upset for Anita that she didn't noticed a car slowly pull from the curb a little ways back to follow at a short distance.

Leo Mangiano sat eating Yvonne's hush puppies in his little Navy Café across from his wharf. He liked sitting there in his favourite spot at the end of the counter next to the kitchen window. There were a few of the usuals sitting off in a corner underneath the dartboard. The smells wafting out of the kitchen were healing, inspiring, addictive and pure joy. He loved to relax and enjoy every little morsel of the deep-fried dumplings. They were one of his favourite foods in Georgia, usually along with a good helping of some sort of seafood—always caught fresh that day. These magnificent golden morsels never tasted better anywhere else. They were the best in the state. Hell, they were the best in the entire United States, and they were only to be found in his own humble cafe, steamed or fried by this beautiful ebony kitchen Madonna, Yvonne.

He grinned at his plate, chewing happily. Suddenly his contentment was disrupted by the old faded yellow phone ringing on the wall beside him. He ignored it, casting a weary eye at its smudged handle.

Yvonne heard it as she stood over the deep fryer in the kitchen. After the fifth ring, she wiped her hands on a towel tucked into her apron and answered it on the kitchen extension.

"Navy Café, an' you better be quick!" she quipped. She listened for a moment as she turned to shake the deep-fry basket. "Uh-huh."

Leo could tell by her tone of voice that it was for him. He dropped his fork and started to wipe his mouth as Yvonne turned to the open window. She peeked out at Leo with the evil eye. Leo always got a kick out of it.

"Mr. Mangiano? Is someone for you soundin' like a Mafioso," she drawled disdainfully. Leo pushed back his chair and chuckled as he watched a trickle of sweat course down the side of her beautiful ebony face.

"Yvonne, you could get into trouble talking like that."

She gave him another look from those massive, beautiful eyes and said, "Uh-huh. Like you some big tenpin puffing up his chest. Should I be scared?" she asked.

Leo threw her a kiss as he picked up the wall phone and put it to his hairy ear.

"Leo of *Santa Maria!*" growled Leo. It was Jorge from Venezuela, and Leo instinctively knew the man didn't have good news. "Hold on," he said. He popped a toothpick into his mouth as he leaned to the side to see through the kitchen window. He was always careful to make sure that Yvonne had hung up the phone before he got into a discussion with anyone about anything. She knew he did it, and she stared steadily back at him as she very slowly hung the phone back up. She then patted the phone with those long, amazing fingers he loved so much and went back to her cooking. He chuckled again and sat back down.

"Yeah!"

"Leo, we got a problem here! That asshole of a kid from Vindenza, he pulled a fast one on us."

"Talk to me," said Leo quietly. As he turned his body on his stool to face the wall, Yvonne looked up slowly from under her lashes and could just make out the left side of his body. She'd seen this stance of his before. She didn't like to see him upset. Not that she was frightened of him. Not at all. She just didn't like to see him unhappy, even if she told herself she couldn't care less. She shook the hush puppies into a small wicker basket. As she pushed it through the window, she lingered to listen in.

"Okay, we gave him the money for the first 'order,' if you get my drift," said Jorge down in Venezuela.

"Go on." Leo tensed his jaw and ground his pearly white dentures.

"He must-a hired a couple of these sad-assed mercenaries that hang around looking for trouble. The thing is, we were held up by a couple of guys with machine guns. They drove up in this shit-box of a car and threatened to kill us if we didn't hand over the money. You know how much money we had on us?"

"No."

"We had about five million in US currency. All dirty money, of course, but that shouldn't make it any less heinous."

"What happened?" Leo asked as he sat up straighter. He noticed Yvonne hovering around the window, and their eyes met. He turned his back to her.

"The long and short of it, he made out like he was being held captive by these guys. The one guy shot up in the air, threw this Jack Taylor kid in the car and grabbed the cash from us."

"What were you transporting them in?"

"Just the plain old banker's bags stuffed into larger duffle bags."

"Anyone hurt?"

"Yeah, we think we got one in the leg as they drove away. We caught up to the mercenaries a little while later, and, yeah, we gave them what they deserved, if you know what I mean."

"Good."

"But that Jack guy? He got away, and there was no sign of the money."

Leo's face was grim. He quietly breathed into the phone as he mulled over this unfortunate bit of news. He let out a big sigh. "Okay. Jorge, you go and make sure he doesn't get very far."

"How am I supposed to do that?"

"Use your head, eyes and ears, where you got 'em. Airport, bus terminal, hospital, whorehouses ..."

"Right," Jorge said as he was about to hang up.

"Oh, and Jorge?"

"Yeah?"

"Don't make it too easy on him. You know how to do it. Skin him alive if you have to. And don't let him die before he tells you where that goddamn cash is."

"Right." And Jorge in Venezuela hung up.

Leo slowly turned and hung up the phone. Yvonne stood by the window with her arms crossed under her ample bosom, shaking her head in disgust.

"Did I heaya you right, Leo? You gonna knock someone off?"

"Don't be silly, *bella* Yvonne. It was just a bad rooster making it hard on the hens and so they can't lay eggs, is all." Leo smiled at her and returned to his hush puppies. As he sat down, he felt an odd sensation. His body was shaking slightly, and he wondered if his line of work was finally catching up to him.

The sandy roads normally muffled any traffic coming through to the waterfront, but suddenly there was a massive, ever-increasing roar. Leo put down his fork and cocked his ear. He turned to the kitchen window and motioned to Yvonne to turn off that country music, and she immediately did so. Then, in mid-bite, he heard it more clearly.

The sound was like a train coming down a track, but there were no train tracks in the immediate vicinity, and though there was a military landing strip nearby, he knew it wasn't a jet fighter screaming overhead. It seemed to resonate through the floor and in the walls. As if in slow motion, he turned to gaze at Yvonne. Yvonne looked at him with frightened wide eyes. "Sweet Jesus!" she yelled.

And suddenly, the café around them exploded. It was a tornado that neatly sucked up everything, including the dentures right out of Leo's mouth. The ear-splitting monster pillar of wind carried the carcass of the cafe along with Leo, eventually dumping and smashing it on top of his *Santa Maria*, completely flattening the pilot house. When the storm finally passed after agonizing minutes, he was left sitting on top of his stool staring out where walls once were. He saw instead fallen giant oaks over the cafe's foundations. Fish were flapping everywhere. The fish shack was gone.

He looked over and saw that Yvonne had disappeared with the rest of the kitchen. In a stupor, he gazed down in a haze between his shaking legs and saw the little statue of Santa Maria standing up right in front of him. Leo's heart flipped.

"Santa Maria," he whispered. He grabbed for his handkerchief, but it had been vacuumed out of his pocket with all the other paraphernalia. His fingers and hands trembled as he wiped his forehead with his hand. It came away covered in blood, and he stared at it. He hoped it was his own. For the first time in his entire life, he finally knew what fear was. And loss. *Yvonne.*

Frozen now in a state of shock, he realized he couldn't hear, and everything he saw seemed to crawl almost to a stop. Then a curious light appeared somewhere in his solar plexus. A tiny spot silently wriggled into a smudge. From a smudge it grew and expanded until he sensed a sort of lightness of being, in spite of his grief.

He panicked. Surely he was dying. And the light—it would make him see and remember all that he had done and lived through. He didn't want to see a rerun of his life because it was long and hard and full of evil deeds, things he would never be able to account for. For the first time in his life, the concept of hell seemed real.

Debris floated about him as he sat frozen in his teetering chair. His bottom lip began to quiver. He felt hot repentant tears welling up into his eyes, and a silent moan began to build within his very soul. He sat like a fish gulping for air as the moan built up into his throat and then finally—finally—a cry escaped his tight throat and reverberated back through all his years. Back to when he was a baby. Back to the very first time he ever did something that he intuitively knew was wrong.

Tears streaked and left rivulets on his dusty, grimy face, the blood already clotting. A raindrop plopped onto his bald pate, and he looked up in response. More drops fell. Slowly sound formed in his ears and then *bang*, the sound of mayhem, cries, cars honking and gulls screaming overwhelmed him. He looked down around him again at what was once the *Santa Maria* and in grief, he slipped off his chair and fell onto his knees amidst the rubble of his boat and begged for forgiveness. And then, the sickening realization gripped his whole being. Yvonne. Where was his ebony Venus? And Willie! Overwhelmed with fear, he offered a bargain: Save Yvonne and her son. Bring *them back, he prayed, and I will give up all my evil ways and do what I can to make up for all that I have done wrong since boyhood.*

Shaking, he looked around for Yvonne where once the shoreline was. Now it was a sea of debris as far as he could see. Then he turned to look out over the garbage-strewn harbour. He feared that the love of his heart had been swept away and out into the open sea forever.

"Santa Maria," he cried aloud, "please bring her back!"

Chapter 12

S TEFANO FUMBLED WITH HIS NEW tie. His rough, calloused fingers kept sticking to the fine grey silk. He sighed and dropped his hands. He had shaved, showered and dressed with great care this evening and had even remembered to ask his mother-in-law to polish his good shoes (as Andy didn't "do" shoes). He adjusted his sleeves, checked that his gold cufflinks were in place and undid a button on his tailored suit's jacket.

Content with what he saw in the mirror, he walked out of the cluttered master bedroom into the bathroom and came back with a bottle of aftershave lotion in his hand. He couldn't remember the last time he had used it. He unscrewed the top, and his grand nose and nostrils twitched at the aroma. Then, with an almost tender touch, he took out a fresh, folded cotton handkerchief and sprinkled a few drops on it. He smelled it again, liked the manly scent, and patted his kerchief across his chin and the sides of his broad neck. Satisfied, he left the bottle on a dresser and walked out of the bedroom.

He paused at the top of the stairs and felt a wall of warm, moist air coming up from the kitchen. It put him at ease. He smiled at the cozy wintry feeling, inhaling the mouth-watering aroma of meat roasting and macaroni cooking. The sensations brought him back to Italy, which still beckoned to him as home, but he didn't have the ruby shoes to make it right. But that might change. Their partner, Luciano, might become his red shoes, and the possibility thrilled him. Their cousin back in *Italia* now worked with him and Peter on new developments—small things on the fringes, small enough that bit players like themselves could own a piece of a number of businesses and not step on the big players' toes. Or at least, they wouldn't feel the toes being stepped on.

Stefano was such a gentle person that most people assumed he was completely benign. He just had to stay that way.

He put his hands in his pockets and leaned against the wall to ponder some more. His construction business was doing very well. He'd had to hire three more men, in fact. But the real success was what he and his brother had accomplished in the last two years. They now had a hand in about twenty businesses throughout their own area, and they had planned to do the same at home—in *Italia*.

Stefano frowned and scratched his chin. This unfortunate incident with Jack, however, was upsetting. For some reason, Peter was being a real *bastardo* about it. Stefano didn't like what success had done to his brother; it didn't sit well with him. He sighed. Anita was a woman grieving and helpless who deserved to be left alone to a certain extent, not to be coldly used as bait in order to catch the asshole. He hoped they were able to catch Jack soon so that Anita wouldn't have to be followed any longer. The thought of it made his stomach turn sour.

Maria's laughter from the kitchen brought his thoughts back to the moment. He loved the sound of her little voice and her incessant chatter with Claudia. She was his little sunshine. With a smile, he continued down the stairs. As he went to the front hallway closet to get his dress coat, he could hear Fabrizio's deep rumbling curses at a hockey game on TV. Stefano was worried about his father-in-law's nagging cough and chest pain, but Fabrizio refused to go to a doctor, insisting it was nothing. However, they all couldn't help but notice that it had worsened considerably. Fabrizio was old-school and felt doctors were for women and children and not for "real" men.

Stefano briefly wondered if Fabrizio was afraid: of sickness, of hospitals, of doctors poking at him. That hadn't occurred to him before.

Stefano found his coat on a hanger covered in plastic. He took the coat and tore off the flimsy film. As he threw on his dress coat, he felt a quick vibration of life stir through his body. He was changing; he could feel it. Sure, the old Stefano was still there—an occasional cigar, some wine, good meat, fresh eggs, a nice crusty white bun, lots of olive oil, cheese, fresh air, sunshine and hard work. But a tiny voice kept asking, "Is that all? Is that enough?" He shook his head. The questions hovered over him like a black cloud, but there was nothing to be gained by wishing for the impossible. He would not let that woman be the end of him.

"Maria, get down here this minute and clean this shit up!"

That woman. Stefano's jaw set. With a long sigh, he lumbered into the bright and steamy kitchen. Claudia turned to look at him from where she was stirring the macaroni at the stove. Stefano pulled the tie from around his neck and held it up.

"You wanna me to help?" asked Claudia. He nodded. She dropped the wooden spoon onto the stovetop and scurried to her son-in-law. Claudia had loving hands.

"Maria, *bella*, stir-a da pasta for me please while I-a help-a you daddy."

Maria, who had been about to go down to the family room to clean up for Andy, brightened and immediately skipped back to the kitchen to stir the pot instead. She stood on her tiptoes to look into the boiling pot and proceeded to pop the boiling bubbles with the spoon.

Stefano bent down so that Claudia could reach his neck. "Hmm. You smell-a fine!" she said. Pleased, Stefano smiled and blushed.

"*Si?*" he asked.

Claudia vigorously nodded her head. "Oooooh, *siiii!*"

How could he possibly let down these warm-hearted and kind people? thought Stefano. They were a major part of the good that there was.

While Claudia worked on a Windsor knot, Anita came up from downstairs, dressed and made up, although there seemed to be a large red welt under the makeup. She held two birthday cards and was looking for a pen to sign them with. She saw Stefano and Claudia standing together at the kitchen door. Stefano caught her gaze immediately and blushed crimson, for she looked to be an angel.

He reached for his pocket handkerchief and dabbed at the sweat on his brow. Claudia made the last little touches to his tie and stepped back to look at him. She was very pleased indeed. "There, now you-a look like a *gentiluomo*." He held out his rough hammer hands. She gently touched them and pointed at his heart. "You are a *gentiluomo* here," and she pointed up to his head, "and-a here." She was so proud of her son-in-law, and she beamed up at him, her heart overflowing with love.

Anita watched and smiled. She, too, thought he looked amazing. She tried to ignore her skipping heart but thought of the terrible ordeal Andy had caused when they returned home. It was so bad, so awful, that she broke into a sweat at the mere memory of it. To get back at

Andy, she dared herself to let that little satisfying worm turn again. She wanted to believe she could get back to Andy for all that ugliness.

Stefano caught the sick look on Anita's face and looked away. He returned to the hallway mirror to see what Claudia had done. Of course it was perfect. He touched it gently. Then he looked at his face and hardened. When Andy, giddy and drunk, had driven into the driveway, some sort of ball on the floor had rolled forward and lodged under the brake. She couldn't stop, and the car had continued to drive right into the back of his truck. The truck was old. That really wasn't a problem, but what followed was a nightmare.

Andy had jumped out of the car with her mouth and eyes agape. Anita had to lean over to the ignition and turn it off so that no further damage could be done.

Claudia and Maria had heard the crash from the kitchen and arrived at the car the same time Stefano did. He happened to look over from the barn and see it happen. He was concerned for Andy and Anita and immediately wondered if there was a chance that Maria had been in the driveway and in harm's way. He ran like the wind, but when he saw Claudia and Maria run out of the garage, he felt tremendously relieved. By the time he reached the truck, he wrote it off happily as a harmless accident. There were definite priorities in his life, and his family came first. The truck could always be replaced.

While everyone was looking at the damage, Fabrizio slowly joined them and laughed. Andy looked over at her father and also started laughing. This caused relieved chuckles from everyone else, and the day seemed to be turning out better.

Until Andy happened to look over at the truck's tires.

Earlier, when he had walked with Peter out of the garage, Peter had pointed out the spare tire on the truck. "What happened there?"

Stefano had explained that they had hit that nick in the snow-covered road, he lost control and the pressure blew the tire. "Yeah, that was quite a storm," Peter had said, and Stefano had agreed. It could've been worse. Once Peter drove out of view, Stefano walked back to the truck and started working on fixing his tire.

When Andy saw four very un-flat tires on the truck, her laughter stopped and echoed away across the fields. As if in slow motion, she turned and slapped Anita hard across the face.

After an initial gasp of surprise, Anita burst into tears, holding a hand on her burning cheek and looked over at Stefano beseechingly. This maddened Andy even further, and she was about to slap Stefano when he deftly caught her arm and held it there. He was angry. Very angry. As he watched Anita run into the house, he felt a grave injustice had been done. A massive wave of guilt flowed over him from head to toe.

Claudia and Fabrizio looked at each other and thought they'd better go inside. Maria didn't want to move, as she was amazed and excited by all the drama. Didn't this only happen on TV?

Claudia reached out and gently pulled Maria along with them.

That left Stefano and Andy frozen in position, him dully looking into her eyes and she searching his for a sign of … what? Love? Understanding? Maybe some semblance of actually wanting her? But none of these things resided in those aqua eyes, and her heart hardened. She lifted her nose in defiance.

He had then pulled her across the backyard to the barn, in which she had never set foot ever.

"I'm not going in there!" she screamed as she punched at his large strong forearm. Stefano was very aware of the faces in the kitchen window, but he hoped they knew he wouldn't put a finger on Andy. But his silence had to be broken. She had become too much.

Once inside, he forcefully sat her down on a bale of hay.

"It stinks in here!" she cried. "Let me out of here!"

He now held both her arms and made her look at him. She wouldn't, but he persevered, holding her gaze until she finally, under hooded eyes, ventured to look at him. He held her gaze for a few quiet moments.

Back in the kitchen, Claudia and Fabrizio had exchanged glances. If they had been familiar with Shakespeare's *Taming of the Shrew*, they would've been thinking the same thing. Something had to be done about Andy's uncontrollable anger. Claudia had nodded conspiratorially at Fabrizio. "'S the change of da woman-a time," she said. Fabrizio looked at her and shrugged. He did not understand women and was too embarrassed to talk about it to begin with. He took one more look at the barn and turned away.

Stefano had to explain to Andy the reason for his interest in Anita. He didn't tell all, but just enough—that Jack had a delivery to do for the consortium and had disappeared. The only way they could keep an eye on whether he came back or not was to keep Anita under their wing and wait. Of course, he didn't tell her whose deliveries, where precisely, and how much of anything. He also wasn't honest about his interest in Anita. In fact, he couldn't stop thinking about her. She had touched his heart, and all he could do was hope that it would fade away.

Now Anita stood in the kitchen getting ready for the party, with her one-sided blush and an air of humility. Andy had apologized, as per his suggestion, and Anita had graciously accepted. However, now she truly felt as if she were in the way, and she planned to return to her own house right after the party. She was hoping perhaps to borrow one of their cars.

Stefano raised an eyebrow at Anita when they locked eyes.

"Um, is there a pen handy?" she asked, holding up two birthday cards.

Stefano looked over at Maria, and Anita turned to Maria at the stove.

"Maria? Could you tell me where I can find a pen?" Maria looked back at her and pointed with her little slender arm to the top of the refrigerator. Anita had to squeeze past Claudia and Stefano to get at it. In passing, she looked Stefano over once again. "You look so handsome, Stefano! Maria, what a handsome father you have!" Maria looked back and grinned at her dad, and Stefano smiled at her in response. He straightened up. He turned and thanked Anita with a little grunt and a smile.

Anita then sat at the kitchen table with the pen and signed the birthday cards for little Stefano and Andrew. She reached into her purse and took out four twenty-dollar bills and stuck two in each card.

Andy came into the family room after having used the smaller two-piece washroom down the lower hallway for her makeup. She liked the light in it better than anywhere else in the house, and she could make herself look almost perfect with the right makeup, the right hairstyle. Almost. And in the near dark. She more than made up for what she considered her physical shortcomings by buying the best and most expensive Italian clothes that especially show off her long slender legs. If she looked just so at the mirror, she didn't look half bad. She wore a striking mauve dress that hugged her slim and perfect figure, and she was made up beautifully. And she felt terrific.

Though strange for her, apologizing to Anita had gone fairly well. It made a world of difference to get the scoop from Stefano, and he had made her feel special by speaking to her in confidence of things he had never ever referred to in her presence. Business was never discussed. Now, for the first time in their marriage, she felt raised to another status—perhaps even like a business partner. This was going to be a great evening party after all.

In her stockings, she stepped around the toys still left scattered in front of the TV. *"Maria!"*

"What?" yelled Maria from the stove. "I'm helping!"

"Jesus Christ!" Andy swore as she kicked toys into a single heap. Fabrizio had been sitting in the rocking armchair in the corner watching a hockey game and so had to bend over to look around her.

"Adriana," he said. "Leave da toys. I no-a see." Andy kicked one more toy and shot it under the couch. "Yeah, well, whatever," she mumbled. "Ma, where's my new shoes?" she said as she took the three steps from the family room to the kitchen level in one stride.

Claudia took over the stirring from Maria and then looked back at Andy. "I don' know-a," she said with a shrug.

Anita, sitting at the table with the cards, got up to help look.

"Oh, thanks, Anita. They're still in their shoebox, maybe in the plastic bag."

Anita stood up and bent down to look under the kitchen table. She was surprised to see three boxes—the two boxes from the crystal party and a shoebox. She reached over and picked up the shoebox and was handing it to Andy when one of the shoes fell out.

"Hey, watch my friggin' shoes! They're worth more than a week's wages Stefano pays those schmucks who work for him." Suddenly Andy froze and caught herself. She quickly looked over and caught Stefano's look from the doorway. She turned to Anita again. "Sorry, Anita. Thanks for finding them." She went over and took the box and the shoe from Anita. "Hand me those other boxes?" Andy looked over at Stefano, and his aqua eyes returned the gaze. She then turned back to Anita and said, "Please."

Claudia looked back in surprise, as did Maria from the family room. Fabrizio, of course, didn't hear it, and he wouldn't have believed it even if they had told him.

Anita smiled, retrieved the boxes from the floor and handed them to Andy. "Hey, Ma," Andy said, putting the boxes on the counter. "I got you a little present. 'Nita, show her what I got you guys."

Anita unpacked one of the boxes and took out the little crystal ball. She held it up for Claudia to see.

"Oh, *bella*, Adriana. What it is-a?" her mom asked.

"What does it look like? A crystal ball!" Andy put on her new shoes and stood admiring them from side to side.

"Can I see that, Mom? Please, oh please?" cried Maria. She reached for the ball and grabbed it a bit too enthusiastically from Anita.

"Maria! Watch it. I've already broken one today. I've got enough bad luck without you adding to it!" Andy said.

Anita placed the other little box on the kitchen counter and peeked into it. She noticed a little bottle and an instruction sheet. "Here's some instructions and what looks like a bottle of oil."

Maria leaned halfway onto the counter to see the thing more clearly.

"Pretty, huh?" Anita said to Maria.

"As if Ma needs all this junk," mumbled Andy, "but I thought, what the hell?" Maria traced the etchings on the glass oil dome with her thin finger. "Maria! Don't touch!" Maria stopped touching and instead rested her chin on the counter and stood, like a flamingo leaning on one leg, eyeing the crystal etchings very closely and now very safely. She dared to lean just enough forward that her prominent nose almost touched the ball.

In the meantime, Stefano watched Andy fussing over her shoes. Shoes were shoes. He couldn't understand her obsession with clothes and jewellery. To him, getting a good deal on a good piece of beef was far more rewarding. Strangely, Andy could spend thousands on herself and he wouldn't care. But paying too high a price on basic foods would raise his blood pressure terribly. He looked at his watch.

"Adriana, we go now. You have-a da gifts?"

Andy held up two cards. "A hundred bucks each, like you said."

"Is enough?" he asked.

"Stefano, they're ten freakin' years old, how much money do little kids need?" Andy said impatiently.

"Si, but they-a my godsons," he reminded her harshly. Andy sighed and looked in her bag for more money. She retrieved two fifty-dollar bills and stuck them in the envelopes.

"There, a hundred and fifty cool ones for both. Happy?"

"*Si, signora.* Happy."

Andy did a double take and then smiled at Stefano.

Claudia covered her mouth and stole a glance at Fabrizio sitting in the family room. Then she gleefully clasped her hands and looked up at the heavens.

Chapter 13

S ANDRA AND PETER'S HOUSE SAT at the end of a cul-de-sac and towered over neighbouring houses. It was an eyeful to say the very least—numerous massive windows, three stories, circular cobblestone driveway, frozen pond, Greek statues, box shrub hedges and bright carefully hidden spotlights creating interesting effects of light and shadow on the front brickwork of the house. A half moon of blue slate steps led from the driveway to a massive antique oak door trimmed in bronze and detailed with iron filigree door handles and lock. Above the door was a half moon of brilliant stained glass.

There were about six other cars parked on half of the driveway and spilling over onto the curb. Stefano drove the Cadillac all the way up the other half of the driveway to the front door, where space was especially kept clear for the godfather of the twins. Stefano stepped out of the car and went around to Andy's side to let her out.

Andy wore her black mink coat, which she loved dearly; she wore it at every opportunity. Stefano noted that Andy had an amazing shine to her face, and there was absolutely nothing in her demeanour to mar the sensuality of the total effect. Times like these, when Andy was at her best as a woman, had become unfortunately very rare. But tonight she was absolutely stunning. She swung her shapely legs out of the car and gently took Stefano's hand.

Anita, eyes glued to the house on the approach, slowly got out of the back seat on her own. She grabbed her pocketbook and the birthday cards, and Stefano politely stood back to let her pass. At the door, he rang the bell, and immediately the door was opened by a small boy wearing a two-piece suit, a white shirt and a bow tie.

"Andrew! Look at you!" said Andy. "Who said you can grow up!"

A shy Andrew grinned up at them, his two front teeth missing. "Hi, Thia Andy."

"Zia Andy and …?" Andy asked teasingly.

""'N Thio Stefano," he added.

Stefano chuckled at the boy and held out his massive hand for a manly shake. Andrew swatted Stefano's big open hand instead and ran into the great room directly across from the front door. He grabbed his mother's ample legs while she stood talking to other guests. Sandra, distracted, looked down at her son and then over to the front hall. She broke out in smiles and ambled over.

"Hey! Welcome! And everyone welcome the birthday boys' godfather!" announced Sandra, giving Stefano a hearty hug and a big wet smack on the lips.

Peter, who had been chatting with another gentleman with his back to the hall, turned around to look as well. His eyes seemed to only focus on Anita. He took a sip from a single malt Scotch in his hand before he squeezed his way past a chatting and laughing couple. Other guests looked over at Stefano and Andy and waved or nodded in greeting. A hired pianist was playing Brahms on a baby grand in the far corner of the great room, and its pleasant tones wafted throughout the spacious home. Coloured glassworks and warm candlelight created a magical effect, rounding off the corners and making everyone look beautiful— the female guests especially, some with a myriad of diamonds sparkling from fingers and earlobes and others with cleavages and bosoms covered in gold. Underneath all that richness, most were dressed conservatively but expensively, as good Italian wives do.

Peter walked up to Stefano and slapped him on the back. "Can I get you a drink?" he asked. Stefano nodded. "Scotch?" Stefano nodded again, grinning. "Wine for you, Andy? Or would you like a martini?"

Andy, ready to party, said, "I'll have a Scarlett O'Hara. On ice. Two of 'em."

"On ice it is!" said Peter. He swung around and snapped his fingers at a young man in a white jacket and black tie. "Hey, you, a Scotch for my brother here, and the lady would like a couple of Scarlett O'Haras." He turned back to Andy and asked, "What the hell is a Scarlett O'Hara?" Peter then turned back to the young man. "Do you know how to make a Scarlett O'Hara?"

"Y-yes, sir," the young man stuttered. "On ice, ma'am?" he asked Andy politely.

Andy nodded and took off her fur coat, exposing ample cleavage covered in gold. The young man couldn't help but look and blushed. Quickly he switched his focus to Anita. "Ma'am?"

"Um … You know what? I'll have what Andy's having. A Scarlett what?"

"O'Hara," Andy said. "It's Southern Comfort. Two or three of those babies, and you'll be laughing." The young man nodded with a smile and rushed away to get the drinks.

Anita glanced around and noted the spacious hallways on either side of the front hall, bedecked with beautifully coloured Persian carpet runners and wall niches holding what looked like original sculptures and a variety of artifacts and collectibles. Some of them were stunning, like the brightly coloured antique Venetian glassware lit in its own custom-made display case, or a worn marble bust of a Hellenistic female deity. A large, brilliantly coloured, hand-woven South American tapestry hung on the wall, as did an amazing-looking painting of what appeared to be a man walking with a suitcase. She stepped towards it and read the name. "Alberto Su—"

"Sughi," said Peter. "It's called 'Man with Luggage.' He's an Italian artist and Sandra's favourite. Of course, this one she had to have because of her travel agency—and the best part, this way she gets to claim it as a business expense." Peter tapped the side of his own impressive nose and winked at Anita before looking back at the painting. He pointed at the swirls. "Aren't the swirling oranges amazing?"

"Oh, yes," agreed Anita. She was a born aficionado of both old and contemporary art, long before she had to cover artists and exhibitions for the radio. She turned to look further into the large living room. There were so many candles burning it had to have taken more than one person to light them. At the centre and far end of this expansive space was a large fireplace in which massive logs burned brightly, the light of the flames reflected in large brass fireplace utensils and fixtures. On either side of the fireplace were recesses filled with a variety of antique crosses, and over the massive mantelpiece hung another even larger ancient-looking crucifix in what looked to be age-blackened oak. Briefly she remembered her threat that afternoon (was it only today, she thought?) to crucify poor delusional Rose.

"You like it?" Peter followed her as she moved closer to the great room. She turned to look at him.

"What a beautiful home you and Sandra have, Peter."

"Thank you, yes, we are very happy with our home. Sandra designed it, by the way, and Stefano built it."

She looked over at Stefano, who was still chatting in the front hall with Sandra. "Oh my God, Sandra, Stefano, such beautiful work!"

Both Sandra and Stefano looked over and smiled at her. "Thank you!" said Sandra. Stefano simply nodded.

Peter looked over his shoulder and gave Stefano a nod, but it had nothing to do with the house. He stuck his hands into his pockets and jingled some change. Anita continued looking around.

"My, Sandra must be very talented. She did a wonderful job."

"Yeah. She's quite the artist herself," said Peter proudly. "This house was actually built over the foundation of an older home, you see. You can tell by the surrounding homes that this is not the original."

"I guess so!" laughed Anita.

"Sandra's parents live right next door in the house where Sandra was born. They're getting on in life, and Sandra wanted them to live with us on the other side of town, but they refused to move. So instead, we bought this property, tore the old house down, and—voila!" He spread his arms out to take the house in. He then stepped a little closer, close enough for Anita to smell his breath. She caught a whiff of cloves and Scotch. "We ended up tunnelling a connecting hallway between the two basements so that they and the kids can go back and forth as if it was all one home."

"Oh neat!"

"Well, she's not just a pretty face, you know, our Sandra …" He looked over at his wife, and Anita followed his gaze. Sandra had led Stefano past them into the great room, and one or two of the guests had turned to greet him. Stefano towered over his sister-in-law, but she looked to be pretty close in weight.

Peter tapped on Anita's shoulder to divert her attention back to the conversation. "My bailiwick is landscaping," he continued. "The original house didn't really have any except for a couple of tiny fountains and an old pine tree. To me, what your house looks like from the street is just as important as what it looks like inside, you know? I wanted to make the house look like a millionaire lived in it. I wanted people to look at the house and say, "Those guys there, they don't drink orange juice for breakfast, they drink Dom Perignon, and at three hundred bucks a bottle.'" He laughed loudly for a moment but then quieted down and looked more serious. "It's like a beautiful expensive gift, you know? You don't just throw it in a sack. You wrap it up in lovely wrapping paper and a big fat bow."

He took another sip of his Scotch before he went on. "I had a talk with every landscaping company I could find in Montreal, and as far over as Ottawa and even Toronto. No company was able to come up with any ideas that warranted me giving them my hard-earned cash, see? So you know what I did? I started my own landscaping business!"

"Ha!" laughed Anita, looking around.

Peter followed her gaze and noticed Stefano exchanging glances with Anita. Then Stefano caught Peter's gaze, and Peter raised his glass to him. Peter pointed at his brother as he continued.

"So, with Stefano's help, I designed what I wanted to see not only from the outside as you drive by but also what you see looking out from all the windows." He cupped his hand under one of her elbows and gently led her to one of the windows in the hallway. She looked out and let him explain the various bushes and plants. He then led her to a sitting room that had its own fireplace. He pointed out the marble mantel.

"I shipped over Italian masons with real talent, something these schmucks around here don't have. I mean real craftsmen. You know where I found them?"

Anita stifled a yawn. She widened her eyes and shook her head no.

"In Calabria, where Stefano and I were born!" He tapped his noggin. "And because I built this through newly set-up companies, it's designated as a showroom, and I take the odd potential client in to see what we can do, I got away with writing most of it off! Not only that, I got away with paying these guys next to nothing. They were only too happy to be sponsored to this wonderful, peace-loving country called Canada. It's a win-win situation! That's important, you know," he said. "And now I'm the biggest landscaping company in town."

"No. *we*-a are!" corrected Stefano from behind them.

"Oops. Big brother always correcting me. Okay, 'we' are. And we are doing really well, I must say." Peter grinned a bit too brightly at Stefano.

Anita welcomed the interruption. "The golden touch," Anita said, smiling at Stefano. Stefano blushed a crimson red and looked away, pleased.

Just then, Sandra stepped in the doorway. She had always been a big woman, but over the years she had become hefty. Her hair was dyed blonde, and her nails were always conspicuously manicured. She sported three gold and gem rings on each of her hands. She was a bright and confident woman, an excellent businesswoman, and obviously a proud mother. With a large grin, she reached out to take Anita by the hand. "Anita, we're so happy you could come. It's so nice to see you again!" She noticed that Anita was still carrying her coat, and Peter suddenly noticed as well.

"Oh, here, I'm sorry. Let me take your coat." He took Anita's dress coat, stepped out into the crowded front hall, snapped his fingers and then draped it over the arm of another hired young man who hurried up to them. Anita watched the young man walk down the hallway, the lights cast by the low-slung spots seemingly dancing on and off his head and shoulders, creating a halo of blond hair, shadow, halo, shadow, halo ... She swivelled her head in the opposite direction and noticed an arrangement of more canvases on other walls—this time older ones, all in fancy gold frames and lit by individual display lights.

Sandra caught her attention by motioning for her to follow back into the great room and into a sunken part by the fireplace. She introduced Anita to other guests, some of whom she had already met or seen at the many Italian Canadian dinners and dances—most recently, the New Year's Eve dance. She tried to ignore the women whispering to one another as she passed by. Sandra took her to a second little boy, obviously the twin to the one she had already met. He was wearing an identical suit and bow tie and sat in a large armchair all on his own. He was playing with a portable PacMan game—the newest rage—and sat in the middle of a pile of beautifully wrapped gifts and a basketful of cards. He looked up and spied Stefano. Anita watched as he jumped off the chair with a big grin, brushed past her and tackled his uncle's legs.

As she watched Stefano play with the boy, she thought of his truck with the words "Stefano Giordani & Sons Contractors" along the sides. She continued to watch as he cuddled and wrestled with the boy. Anita couldn't help but think that this was exactly what Stefano should have had: two handsome little copies of himself. The first twin heard the commotion and joined in the fun. Anita saw the joy on Stefano's face as he wrestled with one hanging on his neck and the other clasped to his leg and sitting on his foot. There were chuckles from surrounding guests, and the room was filled with giggles.

Stefano then lifted up both boys almost over his head. They squealed so loudly that Sandra had to come over and tell them to stop. Stefano then put the boys down, kissed both of their heads and tousled their blond hair. He bent down to their level and retrieved two cards from his breast pocket.

"Here," smiled Stefano. "Don-a you spend-a right away, huh?"

Little Stefano shook his head. "We won't," he said, smiling.

But Andrew piped up that he would—and all of it on a He-Man doll. Some of the guests heard and chuckled. At that moment, Anita noticed their aqua eyes. *Just like their zio*, she thought.

"You big-a soon, we go hunting," Stefano said, pretending to hold a shotgun. "*Capisci?*" He nudged little Stefano's shoulder playfully. "*Si?*" He nudged Andrew and laughed. "What you wanna shoot? *Coniglio? Fagiano?*"

Anita turned to Sandra and asked, "What's a *coniglio* and *fag ... fag ...?*"

"Who are you calling a fag?" joked Andy loudly, stepping up closer to them, holding her drink in a precarious fashion. Anita cringed and glanced around in embarrassment. Andy turned to Stefano. "Stefano," she mocked jovially, "watch what you say to the kids, for cryin' out loud." Then she turned back to Anita. "Rabbit. *Coniglio* is rabbit and *fagiano* is pheasant."

"Aren't they a little young to go hunting?" whispered Anita.

Stefano overheard Anita's comment and shook his head. "In-a Canada, *si. Ma*, when I was-a *cieci*—10 year ol'—I already shoot-a much in *Italia*. Is no bad-a. Is-a normal. An' you eat."

Anita nodded and smiled, but she was appalled at the thought of a 10-year-old walking through a forest shooting bunnies.

"I learn-a them, they-a fine," Stefano explained. He looked at Anita and smiled but then frowned, as he could read Anita's thoughts. "Is okay," he said softly.

"Where's your freakin' drink, 'Nita?" Andy asked, looking around, bored with the conversation. She held up her hand and snapped her fingers. Sandra looked around and motioned one of the young men over. He saw Anita's lack of a drink and, wide-eyed, hurried towards the kitchen off the great room. Andy turned to Anita and said, "Sorry. I drank your drink." She wobbled a bit.

Anita mentally tallied up the three drinks Andy must have already had. She watched as Andy bent over and kissed the twins on their heads and tousled their hair before walking away and downing the rest of the drink she was holding. "Where's that cute young man in the white jacket and bow tie?" she yelled.

Just then, more guests arrived and made their way to the two birthday boys to congratulate them, so Stefano and Anita stood back to give them room. Stefano tried to stick his hands into his pants pockets as if he was really relaxed, but he couldn't get them in. Embarrassed, he looked around at the other guests before quietly glancing down at Anita. When she gazed up at him, her pulse quickened, and she quickly looked away. Stefano slowly looked around for Andy and caught sight of her disappearing into the kitchen.

At this point, the pianist took a break, and somewhere speakers blasted out a sunny rendition of Seals and Crofts' "Summer Breeze."

Anita smiled up at Stefano. "Well, forever hopeful, right?"

"*Che?*"

"You know, summer!"

"Ah," he laughed. "*Si.*"

From amongst the guests in the great room, an elderly couple moved towards them, the woman with arms outstretched. What thin hair she still had was a sort of scrub, grey and black and short. She wore black-rimmed glasses, a loose-fitting navy blue dress and comfortable shoes. Her husband, walking with a cane, had two hearing aids in place. He also wore black-rimmed glasses and sported ill-fitting dentures.

"Ah, Stefano! *Zio* Stefano!" the woman sang. They reached Stefano, and she pulled his head down to kiss the top of it. Still with her arms stretched outward, she motioned over to Peter to hurry over.

"*Pietro, Pietro! Capitare! Mettetere frette*, come!"

Peter excused himself from the guests at the front door and jogged over. Sandra's mother grabbed his face, pulled him down and planted a massive kiss on his forehead. She hugged him as hard as she could.

"*Pietro*, she-a good to Leonardo an' me." She held up her hand and slapped it with the other. "She-a make-a *molto denaro*! He a good son-in-law."

Peter smirked. "Of course I have to take very good care of you. It's the least I can do, as you did a wonderful job bringing up my wonderful wife." He turned to Anita and explained, "Sandra's two travel agencies are doing quite well, and now with the funeral home and florist shop, my landscape business and the stonemasons, we do pretty good. Lots of money to spare, really."

"*Si, ma* you-a tell, our *denaro*."

Peter cringed and obviously looked uncomfortable. "Oh, well, I help them a bit with the stock market. You know, I dabble a bit in this and that. Yeah, they're pretty wealthy on paper." He smiled at his in-laws, who were nodding frantically and looked at him with doting eyes and loving smiles. Peter cleared his throat and looked a little awkward before begging leave to welcome other guests.

Anita shook Sandra's parents' hands and smiled at them as she and Stefano moved further into the great room. Stefano looked down an adjoining side hall off the bottom of the great room and called her, motioning for her to follow. Anita followed him down the hall a few steps until he stopped and pointed at a framed watercolour on the wall. He looked back at her and smiled brightly. He nodded to it and said, "Is-a my *familia* home."

"In Italy?" Anita asked, her eyes widening.

He nodded proudly. She stepped closer for a better look. It was a portrait of an old villa set in a beautiful country setting surrounded by gently rolling cultivated fields—a memory of happy days for him, before he had learned how to worry.

"Beautiful," she said, smiling up at him. "Who lives there now?"

"*Mama mia.*"

"Your mother's still alive? Do you see her often?"

Stefano shook his head. "No, *ma mama mia*, she visit here only-a *uno*—"

"Just once?"

"*Si, ma* she no like-a here. Adriana no speak-a *Italiano e mia mama* no-a speak *Inglese*."

"Oh, that's too bad. Why don't you go there to visit her?"

He sighed and frowned. "Adriana no like-a to be alone."

"Oh, sure."

He took a step closer. "'Nita," he mumbled. He seemed to have a problem searching for the right words, but Anita didn't mind and patiently waited, taking the opportunity to study those incredible eyes—all the more brilliant in contrast to the crimson highlights on his cheekbones.

Finally he found the words. "Adriana, she tell-a me you need-a car. You can use-a Cadillac, *si*? *Ma*, also, eh, you come stay. Those-a men take car, maybe-a more problem tomorrow, next-a day ..."

Anita almost choked. *Oh Lord!* she thought, *me in that Cadillac?* That's all she needed, being stopped by police in a car with two guns in the back. She stammered, "Um, Stefano, I d-don't think I should, but thank you so much. Just my luck, I-I'll smash it!" she joked nervously.

Stefano shook his head and smiled. "No, you safe. You use-a Cadillac."

She swallowed hard. "Please, no. Really. I'll check at work and see if they'll lend me the special-events Jeep for a few days until I get the car problem solved."

Stefano continued as if he hadn't heard. "Adriana, she-a ..." he was searching desperately for the right words again, damn this English. "Adriana, she no happy. You make-a Adriana happy. She happy, then I happy."

Just then, Linda Ronstadt started singing, "It's So Easy to Fall in Love."

"You're kidding, right?" Anita blurted out, looking askance. "She's had enough of me, Stefano. In fact, I think I'm about to be a murder statistic if I hang around much longer. I know she insists I stay, but every time I turn around, she yells at me!"

Stefano shrugged. "She yell at-a everybody."

"*Si*," said Anita, smiling. "You're right."

Stefano looked down at his shoes for a moment before aiming those aqua eyes back at her. She was captured by his long black eyelashes. He looked deeply into her eyes, and she felt herself melt. *Oh, Lord*, she prayed. *God, what a man! Oh God*, she thought, embarrassed. She felt such a desperate urge to be held by him, to kiss those lips and those eyes, to ... *What am I thinking!*

He was gently smiling at her, his eyes searching hers. He then hastened to repeat what he had said. "I am-a happy because-a Andy happy." He fumbled. "An' Jack-a ..." He paused.

"*Si*, Jack?" she repeated. Anita's heart flipped at the thought that maybe Stefano had some news, but she was immediately disappointed.

"I help find-a Jack, an' I think he in no-a in trouble. I know here," he said, touching his chest. "He be-a back soon."

"You think he will?" she asked hopefully, but then she lowered her voice almost to a whisper. "I'm afraid, Stefano."

"*Che*? Why?"

"Because right now, I don't know if I love him or hate him."

Stefano was taken aback.

Anita was just about to tell him about Rose when she almost jumped out of her skin at the sound of Andy clearing her throat behind her. *Geez, she has a habit of doing that*, Anita thought.

She turned around to see Andy holding a Scarlett O'Hara in each hand. She quietly took a sip from one and then a sip from the other as they looked on.

Anita cringed in embarrassment, but Stefano remained cool. He simply looked at Andy and said, "I tell 'Nita, she take car an'-a she stay."

Softly seething, Andy said, "That was the plan, wasn't it?"

Stefano said simply, "*Si.*"

Andy twitched her nose and then pointed it up in defiance as she seemed to be weighing what he had said. Then she looked hard at Anita and nodded curtly. She downed both Scarlett O'Haras one after the other, turned and marched straight back to the kitchen, wondering what trouble she could stir up at this goddamn boring party.

Stefano left Anita's side and briskly followed Andy. Once in the kitchen, he grabbed Andy's upper arm and led her away from the hired help. He feigned a smile at the chef, who was singing at the top of his lungs—a selection from "The Barber of Seville"—while touching a flame to something sizzling in a pan. Stefano went straight out the back door with Andy, slamming the door hard behind them.

Under the back door's light, amidst gently falling snowflakes, he pointed a menacing finger at Andy's face. "*Ricordarsi*—remember! You-a," he said quietly, "you-a try-a to be-a nice." His voice and eyes were startlingly cold.

She looked at him silently for a moment, at once frightened and invigorated. Where was all this passion coming from? They'd had such an amazing moment earlier in the day. Should she believe the crap he told her? That they had to help Anita in order to find Jack? No, bullshit, she thought. She knew it had to be bullshit!

"Is this really what's happening, Stefano? Or are you pulling my leg. Huh?"

Stefano simply said, "Trust-a me. Is-a business, Adriana."

"Yeah, right. More like monkey business!" she yelled, tearing her arm away from his tight grasp. She wrapped her arms around herself in defiance.

He wagged his finger at her forehead. "Is-a business wi' Jack!"

Andy stared at him, her face suddenly ashen. "I wanna know more, Stefano. What's so big about this business with Jack?"

He shook his head. "Jus' business." The colour had drained from his face as well.

Andy's face fell as she studied his eyes. "That kind of business? Like in the whole …? Jack in trouble with the …?"

He looked at her steadily. Behind the door, the singing chef filled the silence with his arias while Andy's heart pounded with fear and dread. Jack was in trouble with *them*? That meant he was as good as dead. She'd always turned a blind eye to what the men were up to, and she put it down to an energetic Italian sense of entrepreneurship, which in her mind was great because that's how the money rolled in. All those businesses with one active partner and forty-nine silent ones and a whole bunch of money always shifting around—Lord knows, she shouldn't be surprised that Jack was part of it just because he wasn't Italian. He was an Irish Catholic, for crying out loud. God, she thought, he's probably already dead. Her eyes widened, and she grew ever paler.

Stefano nodded his head slightly and shrugged.

She gasped. "Why didn't you tell me this before?! I thought he ran off with that bimbo! And now this? This is even worse than just keeping Anita safe!"

"Is better you-a know *niente*."

"*Where*, Stefano?"

He remained silent.

"Where *is* he?" Andy yelled.

He put his hand on her mouth and softly silenced her. "I do'n-a know, Adriana. But we will find-a him."

"Don't let them freakin' hurt her, Stefano," she hissed through gritted teeth. His gaze never faltered, and she kept staring right back, although she was fighting tears. "And this shit with her … don't, Stefano." She trailed off and nodded. "This better just be business,

Stefano!" she warned. He nodded silently. She relaxed and smoothed her sleeves. "Okay," she said finally. "Okay, all right." She turned and yanked the door open. Stefano followed. They retraced their steps through the kitchen, but halfway through, Andy—putting on the charm once again—picked up where the chef was in his aria and sang along with him while pretending to conduct him with two wooden spoons. The hired help laughed and sang along, watching Andy with glee.

The dinner that followed was fabulous. The singing chef himself serenaded them proudly all night—a different opera in accompaniment to each exquisite course, describing and explaining each and every dish starting with *polpo* (octopus) and ending six courses later with a selection of *formaggio* and a scrumptious selection of tiramasu and ices. Wine flowed generously all night, and even the children were allowed to drink a small glass during the meal. There were many happy toasts to the hosts, to health, to happiness, to wives and finally, the most wonderful toast to little Stefano and Andrew, who both stood on Peter's chair at the head of the table grinning while the adults held up their glasses and saluted them.

"*Cin cin!*" everyone toasted. "And to the godfather!" Sandra added at the end, and everyone toasted Stefano, who beamed just as brightly as his godsons.

Shortly afterwards, the boys kissed every single guest good night—a kiss on the right cheek, left cheek and then right again—then went off to bed with a nanny in tow. The guests were encouraged to return to the great room for coffee and liqueurs. Some of the men decided to go to a lower floor to play billiards, and soon the crack of billiard balls was heard over Louis Armstrong and Ella Fitzgerald crooning in the background.

In the kitchen, dishes clattered and glasses clinked while guests talked and laughed around the freshly stoked fire. Someone had lowered the lights and replaced burnt-out candles. Anita sat in the middle of one of the couches facing the fire, her cheeks flushed with the glow of the flames and her heart full of optimism. She had mulled over Stefano's words, and although they had at first frightened her, she had now, in her drunken state, forgotten why they did. So she sat half-listening to Andy, who as usual had become quite the life of the party with her witticisms and jokes. Anita could tell her friend was on a roll.

Andy, holding court, sat on a loveseat with her long legs sensually crossed and her hair falling over her brow. In this light and looking straight on, Anita thought, Andy looked brilliant and breathtaking. She watched in a wine-induced haze as Andy knocked off a number of knock-knock jokes. She had bet everyone that she knew more than anyone else at the party, and she was right. She was on her eighteenth, and it was another good groaner.

"Knock knock!" she yelled.

Everyone yelled back, "Who's there?"

Andy shouted, "Tex!"

And the others yelled, "Tex who?"

Andy held up her glass and shouted gaily, "Tex two to tango!"

People groaned and laughed as Andy grabbed Sandra with her free hand and they tried to do a tango together, but not very well. In fact, Sandra almost tripped over one of the guests' legs, her heavy bosom jiggling and heaving as she righted herself. Andy laughed herself silly. She then looked over at Stefano, raised her arm and pointed at him. "Takes two to tango, right, Stefano?"

Stefano was standing with Peter at the other end of the great room, watching her as he sipped a tiny glass of grappa. He wondered where she was going with all this. Peter looked a little glassy-eyed. He leaned into Stefano, who was sober enough to know that of all the people there, he was probably the lucky one who was not going to wake up with a hangover. He turned to face his brother, who was trying very hard to focus on him. Peter grabbed Stefano and dragged him off to the side.

All of a sudden, Anita felt ill. She tried to ignore it at first but finally had to give in. She clambered off the couch and made her way down one of the hallways, hoping to find a washroom. Instead, she almost walked right into Stefano and Peter, who were standing with their backs towards her. They weren't at all aware of her, which gave her a chance to retrace her steps quietly and back around the edge of the wall. She turned to looked into the great room and saw that Andy was still watching her. She tried to look nonchalant leaning against the wall. She could barely hear the two men, but suddenly her ears perked up.

"But it's Luciano I'm most concerned about," Peter slurred. "We have to find the bastard and wrap this shit up fast before Luciano hears it from someone else!"

Stefano grunted a little in response.

"You know, if Jack's still alive, there's still a chance to find that money—but if he screws up, Stefano, all that money's gone! Yours, mine, Fabrizio's, Sandra's, *theirs*—just *gone*! *Poof*, that's the end of you and me, and you know it!"

Peter stopped to take another desperate gulp of his drink but missed his mouth and instead dropped his glass, covered his head and bawled while he slowly slid down the wall into a heap on the floor.

Stefano bent over, grabbed his brother's lapels and pulled him back up. After a moment, Peter managed to stop crying and looked up at Stefano wide-eyed.

"Hey, you think he's gone down to Mangiano in Georgia?"

Anita jumped. She recognized that name! The Pizza King! She took a little step back closer to the hallway.

Peter settled down, and he and Stefano started whispering to each other, looking over their shoulders every once in a while. Stefano slapped his younger brother's shoulder. Peter nodded that he was okay. He brightened up and smiled.

"Oh, I hafta tell you," slurred Peter. "Somethin's botherin' me."

Stefano leaned in to hear and help.

"Have you ever …? I mean, ever? Anita? You know?" Peter made a suggestive motion with his hand.

Anita's heart stopped.

Stefano stepped back and gave him an angry look. Peter saw it and motioned him away.

"'S'okay, jes' wondered, s'all." He looked up at Stefano again. "But you and Andy don't …" He saw Stefano's expression. "See? You don't. I don't know how you do it, man, I mean, I need a broad who can make me go wild! A broad like her," he motioned up the hallway.

"'Nita? Don'!" said Stefano1 angrily.

"Okay, okay, just asking."

Stefano pointed a thick finger at Peter. "You no do a thin'," he hissed.

By now, Anita had forgotten all about her wooziness.

Peter continued to babble. "Maybe she's just not bait enough to catch Jack. Maybe we should use Nancy. She might know more about Jack, actually."

"Nancy?" whispered Anita. And then, without any warning, she suddenly sneezed. She then gasped and hurried back into the great room. Andy looked up in time to see Anita coming in from the hallway. Anita spied her and piped up, "Andy, I think we better go! Fabrizio and Nonna—"

By now, someone had put on an old tape of Elvis Presley's "All Shook Up," and to the beat of the twist, Anita rushed up to Sandra and announced, "Wonderful dinner, great fun. Thank you so very, very much for inviting me!" She started walking backwards and bumped into Stefano's chest. She twirled around and faced him. Stefano nodded to her. "Si, Adriana," he said. "For Fabrizio an' Claudia, we go home now."

"I'll get our coats," offered Anita with a happy little lilt, and she quickly slipped down the hallway—passing Peter, who, with a grin, pointed the way to the study. Anita rushed to the study and burrowed into the pile of coats—which, she couldn't help but notice, were almost all fur coats. She was about the only woman who hadn't worn one that night. Briefly caressing some of the sleeves of the different furs, she wondered why not a single one bore the natty look that fur acquired with wear and tear. She straightened up with her and Andy's coats and turned to go—and came face to face with Peter, looking a little unsteady on his feet. He smiled benignly.

"Hi 'Nita," he said, reaching out for the coats. "Here, let me help." He dropped Andy's mink on the floor and guided Anita's hand into one of the sleeves of her woollen coat. In the background, she could hear Andy laughing and throwing around insults in the great room over the great King of Rock 'n' Roll singing "Hard Headed Woman."

"Did you enjoy yourshelf tonight?" Peter asked softly. Anita nodded silently. "You must come again."

"Thank you."

"I'm sorry about Jack," Peter continued. "It must be very difficult for you, being alone and without a man—hic—around."

Anita nodded silently again.

"Have you heard from him at all?"

Anita shook her head wide-eyed.

"Do you know where he ish?"

Anita looked up at him and tried to read his mind. His eyes were bleary, almost sad. She shook her head no again. He gently started leading her out of the study.

"You know, Jack is a very shtupid man because you are a very beautiful lady, and no beautiful lady should be left alone." She stopped him and pointed back at Andy's black mink, still on the floor. "Oopsh," he said and bent over to pick it up. He looked back at Anita. "You had a white mink, didn't you?" he asked, frowning.

"Yes, Jack bought me a beautiful shadow mink with silver fox."

"Yes! I remember!" he said excitedly. "You see, I sold it to him."

"Oh?"

"I got him a good deal on it, too—wink-wink, nudge-nudge kind of thing," he joked as they continued down the hall. Peter caressed the back of Anita's neck until they reached the great room. It made a shiver go up her spine, and not a nice one.

Andy was loudly teasing Sandra when they got there. "What goes *vroom, screech, vroom, screech, vroom, screech*?" Sandra shook her head while everyone else grinned and waited for the punch line. "A blonde going through a flashing red light! Hahaha!" Andy guffawed along with everyone else. Sandra went to slap her in jest.

Stefano, in the meantime, stepped over, took the black mink from Peter and deftly manoeuvred Andy into the coat, dressing her as if she was a child who couldn't stand still.

"Andy, you tell 'Nita I sold Jack that boootiful mink of hers. It wash my idea to get a shadow mink with f ..." Peter fumbled. "With f ..." He frowned, a bit surprised that he couldn't remember.

Andy piped up. "Yeah, but I bet he didn't tell her how much he paid for it!" she quipped. She held up her hand and rubbed her fingers together. "Like falling off a fucking *truck* 'good deal!'"

Most of the guests stopped chatting and looked over.

"Adriana!" Stefano yelled. Andy fell silent and looked back at Stefano while swaying on her feet. Anita looked from one to the other and back again. Stefano put an arm around Andy's shoulders and gently led her to the front door.

Peter slid up to Stefano. "Brother, I wanna talk some more about dat ..."

Stefano nodded and grunted as he stepped past Peter to give Sandra a big hug. "*Si si*," he said to Peter impatiently. To Sandra he said, "*Grazie, bella.*"

Anita gave Sandra a big hug while Andy went ahead and opened the door before turning around again. "Another dumb blonde joke!" she started, but Stefano grabbed her and pushed her out gently before she could finish her sentence. Andy's red hair bounced as she stomped down the slate steps. She reached the car and leaned against it. "I gotta tell dumb blonde jokes 'cause we have two dumb blondes here!" she said cheerily.

Stefano ignored her and instead looked at Sandra and shrugged. "Sorry, she too much-a drink." Then he motioned to Anita to follow, which she did wordlessly. Stefano nodded a final good evening to Peter and Sandra, stepped out into the cold night and shut the heavy front door behind him.

Chapter 14

ANDY SAT ON THE GUEST bed in the dark, still tipsy but miserable, listening to the freezing rain that had started while they made their way home. Stefano had yelled at her and hit the steering wheel in real anger when she had stupidly muttered "Miss Goody-Goody fucking two shoes" at Anita. Stefano didn't like that one bit. She sighed deeply thinking she couldn't help it—she simply could not help it. There was something that bugged the hell out of her about this business with Anita and Jack, and she just wanted to throw someone, anyone, out of a moving train.

She looked over at the night table and shakily reached out for a framed photograph. She looked down her nose at it and studied the photo closely in the light of the back porch light coming in through the window. *Where did all the years go?* she asked herself. She touched the faces in the photo. It was their wedding, so many lifetimes ago. Two young people, barely smiling, standing stiffly and partially facing each other. She could hardly recognize herself, and Stefano—he was so innocent and so strong. Her mind wandered back to the beginning ... *Where was the beginning?* she asked herself. She let her mind go back so many years.

1962

Andy raced down to the long set of concrete steps on Elm Street the day her distant "relative" was to arrive from Italy. Weather permitting, she and her friends always met after school to sit on the top steps sharing cigarettes and laughs before going home. Today was no exception. She had been thinking about her parents' latest obsession of this relative of theirs, and she had to admit, she hadn't heard anything from them about "good Italian husbands" or her "marrying" or wanting "bouncing Italian bambinos." If anything, she wanted to thank the guy for being such a great distraction. He could stay as long as he liked for all she cared.

So Andy was actually in a pretty good mood for a change. She arrived to find her best friend, Sandra, already sitting on the top step, one up from schoolmates Sharon and Louisa. Andy dropped her books on the ground and took out a pack of cigarettes and a fancy gold lighter. She lit a cigarette and plopped down beside Sandra.

"So, today is the day, right?" Louisa asked Andy.

Andy looked down at her like she had horns growing out of her head. "Sorry?"

"You know," said Louisa, "The big day!" Andy simply looked at her blankly. She scraped a line into the grit and sand on the step with her heel.

"Aren't ya curious?" asked Sandra, grabbing the lit cigarette and taking a drag. Sandra was big and bosomy. Her parents owned the local travel agency, and the two girls had known each other since kindergarten.

Andy snatched back the smouldering cigarette and puffed at it as if it was a roach between two fingers. "Curious about what?" she asked, blowing a thin stream of smoke above her head.

"You know—the *guy.*"

"What guy?"

"Oh, come on Andy!" demanded Sharon. "You know perfectly well who she means! This guy's supposed to be a relative or somethin'?"

Andy shrugged nonchalantly.

"Jesus, Andy, I still think it's a set-up!" teased Sandra.

"Ohmygaaaaahd!" teased Louisa. "They're marrying you off! Just to get rid of you!"

"Oh for fuck's sake. Just shut up, okay?" Andy yelled, covering her ears.

"Andy's getting married, Andy's getting married,"
sang Sharon, and then Louisa joined in. Two younger
boys from school squeezed past them down the steps
and picked up the song, "Andy's getting married, Andy's
getting married. Na na na-na na!"

Andy picked up a stone and threw it after the boys
as they scurried down two steps at a time, their school
ties and shirt tails flapping behind them.

"Omigod!" said Louisa, grabbing Andy's shoulders,
"If you get married, you can do anything you want! You
don't have to do 'this'!" she said as she took a fistful of
her uniform's pleated skirt. "You know what? If it was
me, I'd just say, stuff it. I don't need to go to school no
more. I'd do anythin' I want. I'd be the woman of the
house, have babies …"

"Then *you* marry the guy!" said Andy.

"Don't be silly, I don't need no guy. I already got
one!" Louisa held up her hand and showed a thin gold
band with a tiny red garnet. "See?"

"Please, take it away, it's blinding me," mocked
Andy. She took another drag on the cigarette, squinting
her eyes against the smoke. She flicked the ashes off
before she gave it back to Sandra. "Hey," she said, "I
got a joke!" The girls leaned in towards her. Andy's
jokes were always risqué, and her friends absolutely ate
them up. "Okay, listen," she said. "A nun and a priest are
crossing a desert and halfway across, the camel they're
riding dies. They wait to see if anyone comes by to
rescue them an' no one does. After a while, they start
praying, but still nothing happens. Finally the priest
says to the nun, 'You know, Sister, I'm about to die, an'
I've always wanted to see a woman naked. Would you
mind taking off your clothes so I can look at you?'"

The girls giggled and snickered. Andy continued,
"So the nun takes off her clothes and then she says,
'Father, now that I think about it, I've never seen a
man naked. Would you mind taking off your clothes?'
So the priest takes off his clothes. Suddenly the nun

says, 'Father! Father! What's that little thing hanging between your legs?' And he says, 'That, my child, is a gift from God. If I put it in you, it creates new life.' An' then *she* says, 'Well, forget about *me*! Stick it in the *camel*!'"

The girls hooted and hollered with glee. Suddenly, the odd heavy drop of rain fell—here in the bush, there on the step and then steadily on their heads. Andy was the first to pick up her books. She pushed through between Louisa and Sharon and skipped down the steps. "Wait up!" cried Sandra, but Andy just waved with one hand over her shoulder and sang, "When the moon's in the sky, like a big pizza pie, that's amore ..."

"Hey, ho! The princess is home!" yelled Andy as she banged through the back door and tripped over a large old suitcase on the floor. "Hey, he's here! That only took, like, three months!" she yelled to no one in particular. "What'd he do? Swim?"

She peeked around the corner and looked into the kitchen. Claudia and Fabrizio were sitting at the table with a ruggedly handsome man. To Andy, he looked ancient. At least late twenties, she thought. She could tell that the three had been drinking, as there was a jug of Fabrizio's homemade wine on the table. They were in the process of dipping bread into saucers of olive oil and vinegar when she startled them. At the sudden sight of Andy, the man jumped to his feet and accidentally knocked Fabrizio's glass over, spilling red wine all over the red-and-white-chequered tablecloth.

"Andy, please, why you no come in gentle for one time? Look what you do here to poor Stefano!" screeched Claudia.

But Andy as usual ignored her. In front of Claudia lay a bunch of glorious flowers, and Fabrizio was holding a beribboned clay bottle of grappa. She saw a second bunch of flowers over on the kitchen counter.

Pointing towards Stefano with her chin, she asked, "This him?"

Before her mother could answer, Stefano moved from behind the table and stretched out his massive arms, pulling Andy towards him to do the traditional Italian greeting of several kisses—right cheek, left cheek and right again. Andy hated being touched (never mind kissed), but something quite unexpected happened— something overwhelmingly comforting. Stefano's nose kept getting in the way. Not hers. His. *What a schnozz!* she thought.

Then she *really* looked at him. That nose, that same big goofy nose that looked so amazingly ugly on her, was surprisingly handsome on him. And he was kinda nice, she thought—in a Tony Bennett sort of way.

He babbled to her in Italian, smiling brightly, his gorgeous aqua eyes shining on her like spotlights. She felt like a rabbit mesmerized by the headlights on a car. Suddenly she felt a bit bashful, which in itself was a very strange thing for her to feel.

"Yeah, yeah, whatever," Andy muttered. She looked over at the flowers on the counter. "Those mine?"

"Ah, *si, si, flore!*" he nodded. He leaned over and grabbed the flowers. He bowed slightly as he held them out to her. Andy took them gently and poked her own schnozz into the blossoms. "Gee, what do ya know," said Andy, "my first bunch of flowers—and from a pizza man no less."

Stefano frowned at her, not understanding her jest. "Pisssa …?"

"It's okay, just forget it," quipped Andy.

Stefano smiled and turned to Fabrizio and Claudia. "*Tua figlia e bella,*" he said shyly.

Fabrizio opened his mouth to agree but hesitated. Claudia chirped up instead, "*Si, si, molto bella,*" she said proudly. "Very beautiful, my daughter!"

"Oh, give me a freakin' break!" Andy said. "I'm gonna puke, Ma!"

"Puke?" he asked.

She looked at him again. His smile, his eyes beseeching her, trying so hard to make her like him. *Holy crap, this guy likes me!* she thought. And for the first time in her entire life, Andy cared.

She really, really cared if this man liked her or not. And he did "like" her. She felt a very tiny point of light grow deep within her soul. The sun was shining. It was shining from this man's face, she could swear! Feeling strangely weepy, she made herself stand straighter. For once, she wanted her young breasts to fill her cardigan. She wanted to have smouldering eyes, soft lips, panting breath and all that other crap. She carefully tucked a wayward strand of hair behind her ear. "Er, Ma? Um. How is he related to us again?"

Stefano, not understanding, looked questioningly at Fabrizio and Claudia for translation. Fabrizio was stupefied and suddenly wondered how this gentle voice could possibly be his daughter's, but then he finally found his own voice and falteringly translated her question. Stefano brightened and held up a finger. With a massive smile, he pulled out a photograph from his pocket and pointed at it, holding it out for her to see. He babbled in Italian but too fast for Andy to understand. She looked to her father, who said, "Adriana, that-a man you see-a der? He is-a my stepbrother, an' he's da father of Stefano. So, to me, he is-a my nephew—so he is-a you cousin."

"A step-cousin?" Andy's heart beat faster.

"*Si*, a step-a cousin," Fabrizio nodded.

Holy double crap! she thought and froze.

"Adriana," said her mother softly. "Say-a something." Andy kept staring. "Say-a thank you, maybe, for da flowers?"

Andy nodded slowly. But Stefano suddenly held up a finger. "Ah, *ma una presente per tu*, Adriana!" He bent down and pulled out a small, beautifully wrapped box from a carry-on next to him on the floor.

Andy woke up a bit and shook her head. "Adriana? Since when does everyone call me fucking Adriana?" she mumbled as she unwrapped the gift.

Fabrizio choked suddenly and coughed. Claudia panicked and whispered, "Omigod, Andy. Don't-a say such bad words."

"Why?" asked Andy, looking up briefly. "He doesn't understand English." Which was true. Stefano kept on smiling and waited patiently for someone to translate for him again. So Claudia smiled graciously and in Italian outright lied, "She say-a you shouldn't have, but-a please, she say to call me-a—she—'Andy.'"

This absolutely gracious and handsome man said, "Oh, *si*," and then repeated, "Andy." He shook his head, "No Adriana!" he said, smiling.

"*Si*, no," added Andy. "No Adriana. Andy!"

"*Si! Si! Bella Andy!*" He bowed his stately head of blue-black curls (like fucking Superman, thought Andy).

Andy pulled out the gift: a pair of exquisitely soft, light grey, Italian calfskin gloves.

"Aaaahhhh," aaah'd Claudia.

"Aaaahhh," aaah'd Fabrizio.

Andy fingered the rich, luxurious leather. *Yeah, fucking aaaahh*, aaah'd Andy to herself. "Jesus Christ, these must cost a mint!" she blurted. Her parents both inhaled sharply and held their breath, but they were relieved when, after a moment, she quietly said, "*Grazie. Con tutto il cuore.*" *With all my heart.* In spite of never giving a damn about love, her looks, her manners or what anyone else ever thought of her, she suddenly was petrified that she might not be beautiful or charming enough for him.

She was also discovering that she had a taste for the very fine and pricey.

Later that night in bed, a very tired but happy Claudia whispered to Fabrizio, "See-a, Fabrizio? The Mother Nature, she is-a working, no?"

Fabrizio, half asleep, grunted softly, "*Si*, Claudia, you right." And for the first time in all of his daughter's seventeen years in his care, he fell immediately into a blessed and most comfortable sleep—as if a massive burden had finally been lifted off his shoulders.

But then, of course, that is exactly what happened that first magnificent day of Stefano's introduction into their family.

The baton was passed.

Chapter 15

ANITA DROVE STEFANO'S CADILLAC HOME, in spite of how eery it felt to her. When she got to her driveway, she reached up to the visor to press the garage door opener, but of course it wasn't there. *You idiot*, she thought to herself. *It's in the repossessed car.*

She sighed, because she didn't have a house key either. She stopped the car, hit the steering wheel with her forehead, and said, "Duh." It was on the key chain with the car keys that she'd simply handed over.

Miserably, she sat back and watched the wipers and the freezing rain as she pondered her predicament. Depressed as hell, she decided to brave the rain and test every single door and window of the house she could. It took about half an hour, but she finally spied an unlocked basement window with a loose screen.

It was a small window set in a very deep window well. She knew it would be tight, but she stubbornly persevered. She took off her high heels and coat and let herself drop about three feet into the icy gravel well—the top edge of which was almost as high as her underarms when she stood up again.

She heard a hiss, a squeak and a squeal at her feet, and then something black and furry rubbed her leg. She screamed as a skunk climbed up her body and over her face before scooting in the direction of the neighbouring trees.

"Holy *shit!*" she yelled. She flew back out of the window well and scurried away in the opposite direction of the skunk. Her heart pounded in her chest as she shivered with shock and cold, frozen on the spot in her stocking feet. Slowly she became aware of the most disgusting and pungent aroma she had ever, ever experienced in her entire life. She could almost taste it, and she wanted to barf! "Oh no!"

she wailed as she haltingly walked all the way around the house back to the Cadillac for some shelter and solace. But as she was about to get in out of the freezing rain, she froze.

Andy would kill her if she ruined the leather interior of a new car, and in pristine condition. She had no choice. It would've been too, too cruel.

Tearfully, she walked to the other side of the house yet again. She stopped and stared at the same basement window. Looking around for something long and pointy, she found a rake by the garden faucet out back. Gingerly, she poked the rake back into the well, but there was no sign of more furry things. She held her breath and dropped back into the putrid well. She managed to slide the glass window open with her wet palms. It was tough going, but eventually she forced herself through the tiny opening feet first and face up, getting only momentarily stuck halfway through.

She took another breath and groaned trying to find a footing somewhere beneath her in the dark. She had to shimmy and roll, cracking her back and scraping her thighs and behind. Finally she fell and landed on the basement floor on her side, her dress hiked right up to her neck and her nylons ripped to shreds. The broken screen fell in with her and landed on the floor beside her, frightening her. She screamed before she realized what it was.

"Omigod, I'm in!" she yelled.

Leaving the window open to air out that terrible smell—of course, to no avail—she ran through the dark basement and up the stairs, cracking her baby toe against the corner of the wall. She grunted with the pain and hopped up the stairs wet, stinking, hurt and traumatized.

When she reached the top basement step, she plunked down on her wet behind to grasp her toe. "Oh, my God ouch, oh my God ouch!" she chanted through clenched teeth. She knew she had broken her little toe. She smelled her arms and sniffed at her plastered hair. The *smell*!

The basement door faced into the front hallway, and at the base of the front door of the house she saw a pile of mail scattered over the ceramic tile floor. She reached over and with her fingertips carefully spread them towards her to see if there was something—anything—from Jack. Nothing but bills. Then she saw a post office notice for registered mail.

"Omigosh," she said to herself as she held the card to her heart and prayed that it was from her dear, adorable, shit-face Jack. Of course it had to wait till Monday. She studied the card wishing there was a clue as to what it was about and where it came from.

Full of renewed energy, she pulled at the doorknob to pull herself up, but her hand slipped free and she plunked right back down on her stinking, soggy behind, hitting the door jamb with the back of her head.

"Okay! I give up!" She threw up her hands. "Go ahead. *Kill* me!"

Her voice echoed once, and then there was only silence—save for the sound of the icy rain outside. She crawled to the main stairs, leaving wet streaks on the tiles, and wearily crawled up the cream-coloured deep-pile-carpet stairs. She stopped in mid-crawl when she remembered the car was still parked outside the closed garage and that her coat and shoes were still out in the rain.

"Fuck it." She stood up as best she could at the top of the stairs and hopped to the master bathroom, feeling as if she had peed her pants.

Her dress and underwear were soaking in the bathroom sink, though she suspected she would end up throwing them away. She sighed as she slid deeper into the tub until her nose stopped just above the bubbles. With the toes on her good foot, she turned on the hot-water tap and let it run until she felt the heat crawling up her thighs. She turned it off and let her one leg float. *Fat makes it float*, she thought stupidly.

She stood up carefully, bubbles falling off her in clumps, and grabbed a towel off the wall. Gingerly, she stepped out and vigorously dried herself before wrapping her hair in another towel. Putting on a bathrobe, she walked into the bedroom and plonked down on her bed. She stared at her sorry self in the mirror. She thought of her coat and things lying out there in that icy rain. Now totally ruined, of course. At least she hadn't been wearing her fur coat.

Her fur coat. What was it Andy had said? "Off the back of a truck."

She remembered how Jack had surprised her with that beautiful coat on their anniversary the year before. It was so completely out of character, and it was wonderful! He was normally a miser, and though she was frugal herself, the gift made her feel warm, loved and beautiful. Jack told her that it cost over ten thousand dollars but that she was worth every single penny. She had cried. She was so happy.

It was the same with her beautiful diamond ring. He had sat her down one day before they were married and announced that they were going to go to Hawaii. She thought it was a wonderful idea, but was it practical? she remembered asking. It demanded a longer trip than just the seven days she was able to take off from work. It turned out he had already spoken to her boss, who had agreed to let her go for the two weeks. Jack had told him he was going to elope with her, and they couldn't do it in anything less than that. So he gave the two weeks' vacation as a wedding gift.

She remembered thinking she obviously didn't hear him right. *Elope.* No, Jack said, she heard right, and then he took her hand and slid on the ring. It was massive. She wasn't an expert on diamonds. but he was, he had said, and he'd chosen the best-cut diamond he could find in Vindenza.

She looked down at the ring on her finger. This beautiful ring. Surely something so expensive was not flippantly given. Then she thought about how little Rose's hands were, and she remembered there were no rings on those little fingers.

The coat, the ring, all the plans they had for the future—she'd dared to believe she was worth it all.

She thought back to the day he had come home announcing he'd insured the coat for a whopping $15,000 and added it to the house policy along with the ring for another $10,000. She had pointed out to him that as far as the coat was concerned, it was more than what he had paid. But he had gotten a good deal on it, he said, and $15,000 was what it was worth.

More than once she had looked at the coat, as well as the ring, as insurance against bad times. But Jack was still supposed to be with her—in sickness and in health, for richer, for poorer. Something still did not sit right.

She must be pretty stupid.

With a rising sense of urgency, she hobbled into the walk-in closet to look at that fur coat. She grabbed the heavy coat off its hefty hanger and dragged it back out into the bedroom. She tore off her bathrobe and pulled the coat over her naked body. She touched the embroidered "Anita" on the inside lining before she wrapped it around herself. She looked at herself in the mirror for the millionth time since Jack gave it to her. So beautiful!

Andy had said, "Off the back of a truck."

What did she mean? Suddenly, Anita got a kick in the gut. She remembered all those fur coats that night at Peter and Sandra's place. And the cloakroom at the Italian Canadian Club at New Year's was also packed with fur coats to the brim.

Oh Lord, she thought, Andy had meant that it was stolen goods! Taken from the back of a truck!

She hobbled in a daze up to the dresser and grabbed the wedding photo. She peered at it, trying to remember all the details of their wedding ceremony on the island of Maui. There was this underlying feeling of sadness. What was it?

Then she remembered. They were standing facing each other under a banana tree. The justice of the peace did the ceremony without a witness present, as his wife, who was to be the witness, didn't want to get up so early in the morning. She had signed the papers before he left the house.

During the ceremony, Jack had startled her and the justice of the peace by changing part of the vows. He had said, "till love do us part." She had told herself it was just a slip of the tongue. Now she realized it was his lack of sincerity.

Till he loved her no longer.

Screaming in anger, she hurled the picture against the wall, where the glass smashed into a million pieces. Then she tore the coat away from her. It all meant nothing to her any longer. The coat and the ring, the plans and the promises—they were now nothing but hateful lies and deceit. She didn't want anything to do with them any longer, and she wouldn't have cared if it was the fur coat lying in the mush and stinking like a skunk.

She bundled up the coat, opened a window and threw it out into the rain.

She deserved better than to be treated like that by that lout.

After a moment's pause, she thought better of it. She hobbled and slid back down the stairs and out the front door. Naked save for a towel around her hair, she ran through the rain to where her poor fur coat lay in a wet heap. Caressing it as if it were a pet, she brought it back in and lovingly hung it on the back of a kitchen chair.

Andy knew, and it looked like every woman at that party knew, that her coat fell of the back of a truck. Or did they all know? Were some of them as naive as she was? The thought of the nasty way Andy had told her made that sour little worm that had been conceived so silently while standing beside Stefano's truck take on new life, and it burrowed deeper into what was once a very gentle soul. Ever so slowly, it split and then split again. It continued to multiply …

Chapter 16

ANDY TOOK A DRAG ON a cigarette and then held it as far out the kitchen window as she could. She waved away little errant bits of smoke that strayed back into the kitchen. She heard stomping and crashing at the back door, so she flicked the cigarette out into the wet grass below. "Let the chickenshits eat that," she mumbled to herself. She quickly closed the window and continued to wash a pot in the sink.

This time it was Maria, who had just finished helping her father feed the sheep and chickens. She discarded coat and boots en route to the family room and then plunked down on the floor cross-legged, turned on the TV, and without looking up said, "Mom, you shouldn't smoke. I'm telling Dad."

"Don't you have something better to do than to hang around here botherin' me?" Andy yelled, one hand on her hip and the other still in the soapy water. "Go help your father!"

"I just did. I'm finished!" yelled Maria without taking her eyes off the screen.

"You can't have, 'cause you weren't out that long." Andy stood glumly watching the back of her daughter's head. She still had remnants of the hangover that killed all hangovers, and she felt lousy. The only reason she got out of bed when she did was because Stefano would've given her hell. She'd been cooking because Claudia and Fabrizio were to come for supper. If she could only last till bedtime. But until then ... She peeked out the window. "Where is your dad?"

Maria twisted back to face Andy in the kitchen. "He's in the cavern," she said, leaning on one arm. "Mom, can I have a—."

"No, you can't have a pop."

"Uh, Moooom!" whined Maria. "Nonna lets me!"

"Well, Nonna ain't here, is she!"

The phone rang.

"I'll get it!" yelled Maria, jumping up and into the kitchen. She grabbed the phone on the wall at the desk beside the fridge and said, "Hello?" She stood there, small but gangly and happily expectant. "Oh, hi Zia!"

"Which zia?" asked Andy, walking over with her hand held out.

"Yes … Yes … No …"

"*Which zia?*"

"You wanna speak to Mom?" Maria held up the phone. "It's Zia Sharon." Andy snatched the phone away from Maria, who bounded and crashed down the few steps back to the TV.

"I just saw you freakin' last night, what the hell do you want now? … Uh-huh … Yeah. You're kidding, right? … Maria? … I'll think about it!"

Maria looked up from the TV. "Think about what?" asked Maria.

"Are you freakin' nuts?" her mother said into the phone.

"What, Mom?" Maria jumped up and ran back to Andy, tugging at her fine tan mohair sweater. Andy slapped her hand away. "*What, Mom?*" Maria repeated.

"Like I said, I'll think about it!" Andy hung up without a goodbye.

"Moooom, what?" Maria pleaded.

"Sharon needs people for her fashion show, an' she needs a kid. You feel like struttin' your stuff on a runway?" asked Andy, dialling the phone.

"Uh-uh!" Maria grunted, shaking her head. "No way, Jose!" Maria was no longer interested, skipped back into the family room to sit cross-legged in front of the TV once again.

Andy stood listening to the phone ringing on the other end. Finally Anita picked up the phone. "Hello?"

"'Nita?" Andy said. "Forgot to tell you, you're in a fashion show, kid."

Anita, who Andy had just woken up, whispered groggily, "What time is it?"

"Time to get up, lazy!" Andy relished catching people unprepared—especially Anita these days.

On the other end, Anita squinted and tried to read the clock radio on the dresser. Instead, she saw the wedding picture with its broken frame and no glass and remembered the awful night before. She put her head back on the pillow and groaned.

"Those Scarlett O'Haras can do that to you. They last, don't they?" laughed Andy.

"Oh, no, it's not that I'm hung over." Anita said, struggling to sit up. She winced as her broken toe rubbed against the blankets. She sniffed the air and then sniffed her arm. She groaned again.

"Liar, liar, pants on fire," Andy said.

"Do you know how to get rid of skunk smell?" asked Anita.

"*Skunk* smell! What'd you do?" Andy switched the phone to the other ear.

Maria looked over from the family room. "What did she do?"

Andy pointed at her and made a motion of cutting a throat. Maria went back to watching the TV. *Sesame Street* was on, and she watched as Bert and Ernie sang a duet of "Row Your Boat." Even though Maria was getting old enough to appreciate groups such as Culture Club, she still liked her all-time faves—*Sesame Street* and *The Muppet Show*. She sang along with Bert and Ernie in a tone not previously known to man.

"I frightened a skunk—was it only last night?" Anita said, covering her eyes.

"On the road?" Andy asked.

"No, I stepped on it."

Andy cogitated for a moment. "Excuse me?" said Andy, completely at a loss for words.

"Andy, don't tell me you're at a loss for words." Catching Andy off guard felt somewhat satisfying, and with that satisfaction her sour little worms squiggled and writhed, and she blurted, "'Cat got your tongue? For someone who never shuts up, *that's* a first!" Anita slapped a hand on her own mouth. *Omigod!* she thought. *Where did that come from?*

Andy straightened up. On the one hand, being at a loss for words was indeed ever so rare. She dropped her voice. "Where'd this … this attitude come from?"

Anita rolled her eyes and groaned.

Andy hung up on her, slamming the earpiece into its cradle. In fact, she slammed it so hard that the phone cracked in two and fell onto the floor. Andy picked up the thing, tried to push it back together, gave up and slammed the cracked piece into the wall unit even harder. This time, two pieces fell to the floor and she kicked them, the pieces sliding and slithering along the ceramic floor and smashing against the opposite wall. Maria swivelled to look at her mother. Andy pointed a finger at Maria and then at her mouth and zipped it up. Maria, unfazed, turned back to Bert and Ernie.

Andy wiped her forehead and grabbed the neck of her sweater to waft cooler air at her throat. Hot flashes. Another cursed thing. She walked back to her corner in the kitchen, dug deep into a cupboard behind small bottles of spices and pulled out her pack of cigarettes. She took one out while she looked right and left out the window to see if Stefano was in sight. Satisfied, she opened the kitchen window, lit her cigarette and was turning to blow out the smoke when the demon rooster from hell scrambled past the open window and catapulted shit onto her and everything around her.

◈

Anita sat stiffly on the bed still staring at the earpiece. How could she be so rude to Andy? Andy had been so kind and so generous. Why the hell did she push the envelope that way? In a panic, she dialled to call Andy and apologize. But then she thought about it some more and slowly hung the phone back up. Didn't Andy deserve to be razzed every once in a while? Hadn't she been a real bitch lately? *Yeah*, Anita thought. *You want attitude, girl? Huh? Andy wrote the book on attitude! Well, she's not going to get away with this crap anymore. Let her taste a bit of her own medicine for a change!*

This strange new wave of self-confidence bubbled up from a deep, dark well of empowerment that had seemingly sat dormant her entire life. She looked around the room. Something profound had happened. She saw colours she'd never noticed before. She looked at the furniture, the walls, as if it were another house, another time …

She jumped out of bed to get dressed. Forget Andy! She had far more important things to occupy her mind with—like finding Jack and breaking into the factory.

◈

Andy stood facing the stove and felt a tear trickle down her shit-strewn cheek. Maria stood a distance from her, wide-eyed and stunned. Andy looked at her hands, the stove, the counter, the sink. The tears kept coming. Astonished, Andy groaned. She couldn't remember the last time she'd cried. In fact, she didn't think she'd ever cried in her entire life. Humiliated by a dumb bird, she now finally sensed she had met her match.

"A friggin' bird," she sneered—which wasn't good, because the stuff launched onto her face stuck to her teeth. She wildly spit it out.

"Mom, are you crying?" asked a pale Maria. Forget about the bird shit—it was her mother crying that startled her.

"Me, crying? What freakin' for?" Andy looked around helplessly. She sidled towards the open window and screamed, "Stefano!"

Inside the barn, Stefano looked up from a box of stored potatoes on which he was checking the eyes. He thought he heard something. He dropped a potato and quickly stepped outside and looked towards the house. He saw a great swath of splattered bird shit across one of the kitchen windows, which happened to be open. He could see at a glance what had happened.

He grinned to himself as he hurried across the wet ground and sloshed his way in his massive rubber boots. As he ran, he couldn't help but visualize the bird shit over the cupboards, the counter, the sink, the floor. He understood quite well that this was something that would drive Andy over the edge. He couldn't help, however, but see the damn humour in it. He pulled open the back door, threw off his galoshes and sprang upstairs. At the bottom of the kitchen steps he stopped and stared.

Andy stood as still as a statue. As a matter of fact, part of her did look like a statue. He pulled off his Portuguese fisherman's cap and scratched his head, but he did it to hide behind his cap as he grinned. Unfortunately, Andy caught sight of it before he could hide it in time.

"It's not fucking *funny!*"

Maria covered her ears quickly.

"Adriana, no-a say that-a."

Andy looked askance. He hadn't called her that since the day they met for the first time.

Stefano looked around for towels, rags, anything. Maria jumped up and ran out of the kitchen to the hallway and grabbed a small woven rug. She brought it back, but Andy pointed at it and screamed, "No!"

There was a brief pause before Andy took a step forward and then another, all the while trying not to drip any bird poop on the floor. Stefano stepped aside to let her pass and watched as she started down the basement stairs. He and Maria looked at each other and giggled.

Both figured Andy was going down to wash up in the larger basement laundry sink and were perplexed when Andy knocked something over on the landing halfway down. They went down into the family room in time to see Andy stumble back up with a shotgun in one hand and shells in the other.

Stefano reached over and gently took the shells before putting an arm around her, guiding her down the stairs to his own shower stall. Maria began to follow them, but Stefano simply shook his head, and she stopped. She watched her parents go down and around the corner out of sight. They had touched each other! "Weird," she mumbled.

She shrugged and skipped back to her *Sesame Street* friends. She plopped down on the floor as the phone rang. She whirled around and looked at the broken handpiece of the phone still lying on the floor by the fridge. She jumped and went over. She stared at the mounted base of the phone on the wall and then down at the broken handset.

Stefano yelled up from the basement. "Maria!"

Maria bent down and picked up the handset. It was loosely held together with a few wires, so she carefully held it to her ear and mouth and jiggled the wall unit. "Hello, Giordani residence."

It was Claudia, and Maria could clearly hear shouting and shrieking over the broken phone. "Quick-a, Maria! Get you Mommy! You *nonno* is-a *ammalarto!*" she sobbed. "He is-a sick-a! He-a die! Hello? Hello? You *nonno!*"

Maria exhaled as if someone hit her in the solar plexus. "Daddy!"

Chapter 17

"GO AHEAD! POOP ALL OVER me!" Anita muttered to the blue heavens as she drove the stinky Cadillac to J & P Plastics. She felt stronger now, like an Amazonian—powerful, beautiful, brave. She glared at the road in front of her, imagining herself as the heroine of a romance novel. She was once a piece of flotsam on the ocean of life—a victim of the heart. Now, with the beautiful tapestry which was her love for her husband unravelling before her very eyes— with her dearest cruelly torn away, her car repossessed, a skunk running over her face—she would fight to the end and find her beloved in the nick of time! He, on the brink of death, saved by his devoted wife and lover! He, brainwashed by a bimbo, hopefully soon to wake from a deep drug-induced stupor after being held captive!

She banged the steering wheel with her palm. "Lovers!" she yelled. "No longer! I shall reclaim him!"

"Rose is a cover-up," she told herself. "Yes!" Her eyes widened as she dared to believe this figment of her imagination. "A cover-up by evildoers to draw his love away from me."

The freezing rain from the night before had stopped, and the day had dawned a bitterly cold though sunny one. One of the wheels skidded over a black slippery spot, and she took her foot off the gas and coasted. There were no other cars about, and the loneliness of the windswept land around her now aggravated her inner beast. She felt her courage starting to ebb away. She quickly turned on the radio.

"So, Adriana," she whispered. "What bad taste do you have in music, hmm?" She punched in every preprogrammed radio station. News, news, rock, rock—no classical music, not even Anita's own radio station! "Some friend you are," she muttered. She turned it back off.

She looked at the mileage meter and smiled. She knew the car was basically Stefano's, but she could tell that it was never driven beyond their neighbourhood either. "Talk about new!" she said to herself. It had only 23,000 kilometres. Well, she knew she was going to rack up another few hundred. Probably more mileage in one day than Andy's Volvo had done in four years. Andy would have a fit. "Good! I don't give a shit!" she yelled at the dashboard.

She reached the outskirts of a neighbouring town and continued on past farmland still spotted with mounds of snow and ice along ploughed ruts. Beyond that, she reached an eyesore: a new industrial park made up of similar drab brick units built on spec for sale or rent to small businesses and factories. Since it was Sunday, there were absolutely no cars anywhere to be seen, and she felt free as a bird. She drove two more blocks and turned right. Jack's factory sat at the end of a cul-de sac. (*My life is full of cul-de-sacs*, she thought.)

She slowed the car down but didn't stop. Instead, she looped around to the next block and parked on the road behind the factory. She put the car in park and waited for dusk.

An hour later, she sat facing a beautiful purple and orange sunset. When she closed her eyes, the rose-coloured light penetrated her eyelids. Once the sky darkened, she felt an urgency to make her move. She looked around and, satisfied, stepped out of the car. As she did so, a nauseating aroma wafted out of the car with her. She grimaced as she put the keys into a zippered pocket in her ski jacket and reached back into the car to grab a small crowbar.

She strolled unabashedly along the road until she came to a leafless hedge, which she quickly ducked behind. She hustled down the side of the office building behind Jack's and then ran through the back adjoining parking lots. She skipped through large pieces of rusted metal she could barely make out lying in disorderly piles among scattered weeds. She slid along the deepening shadows until she reached the long narrow window of Jack's office. She knew that there were alarms at the front door and at the back loading doors but none on the windows. She also counted on the fact that her husband never remembered to lock windows. What she had to do was get a good hold of the window and shift it back and forth until it opened wide enough for her to slip through. It went far more easily than she had expected. Within five minutes, she was in his office, with only one scratch on her inner thigh. *So much for a security system*, she thought.

She walked straight through Jack's office to the front lobby and then onto the factory floor. It was a hideously ugly place, full of massive machinery usually deafeningly loud and now sitting idle. This was where the women poured plastic pellets into hot moulds and where they assembled the parts. They made and packed egg cartons, housings for calculators and a variety of garden tools and spray heads. She cast her eye up and down the aisles to see what jobs were being worked on. Then she saw massive blocks of laden pallets of finished product waiting for shipping. Not like the old days, when they couldn't make product fast enough and it rushed out as soon as it was packed. Not a good sign.

She walked back to Jack's office. There were piles of unopened mail on his desk—both personal and business. She rifled through the papers and found his daybook. There were no notes or appointments for the previous six weeks, save for the one he'd missed with the bank. But prior to that, there certainly were a number of interesting items.

One entry said, "Rose's Birthday, order flowers." Some more dreaded proof. After staring at the words, she picked up a pen and drew a little heart underneath the words. If Jack should ever come back to normal and take up his daybook for a normal day of business, he would recognize that someone other than himself had drawn it. Would he think of her drawing it and be overwhelmed with guilt?

She doubted it, but she hoped he might.

With a sigh, she continued searching for more clues. There were notes about flight times and flight numbers to Italy. She was getting a scrap of paper to copy them down when she noticed discarded bills and notes in the garbage pail. She rifled through them as well, keeping them and figuring they would never be missed.

She continued through the daybook and found doctor and dentist appointments, meetings with customers, meetings with staff members, meetings with Nancy—all before Christmas. Notes on tax days and holidays. She was intrigued to see that he had "Peter" written on the Friday before his scheduled trip. There were what looked like international phone numbers and other initials that didn't mean a thing to her.

She pulled Jack's desk chair closer and flopped into it. This was all hard to take. Flowers, birthdays, another woman's name, and not one entry that had anything to do with her. *Where the hell am I in all of this?* she wondered. Where did little reminders of Anita end and Rose begin?

She slumped into a momentary depression. Dear asshole Jack. He had always been unpredictable, and so busy at times that she saw him only at stray moments. There were one- to two-week business trips all over the world, and he constantly complained that he was tired. She slapped her forehead and shook her head. "Duh!"

For a moment, she leaned back and pondered on various forms of retribution. Arson? Nah! Poison? Nah! Anita drummed her fingers on the desk. She looked up at the clock on Jack's wall. It was almost five fifteen in the evening, and it was already dark. She ran to the window, shut the blinds tightly and turned on the lights. Then she took the daybook to the front office and turned on the photocopier. While she waited for it to warm up, she leaned on Nancy's desk and looked it over. The work area was as neat and tidy as it always was. She had a lot of respect for Nancy and cared very much for her. What would Jack have done without her? She was one of those rare individuals—kind, honest, hard-working if at times crisp—but she was a valued employee. The best.

The photocopier light went green, so Anita put the daybook upside down on the screen and pressed the button. As the page printed, something odd caught her attention. She took a closer look at the wastepaper basket underneath Nancy's desk. There was a slip of paper with her and Jack's name written on the top. She bent over and pulled out the paper and gazed at it. "What the ...?" she said. It was a faxed bank statement dated the end of November. Someone had circled all the large withdrawals on the account. This was a joint account under her and Jack's name, but she didn't recognize it. How did Jack do that? And where'd all this money come from? It certainly couldn't be theirs. Jack's?

Intense anger shot through her. She quickly went back to Jack's office and went through the piles of mail on his desk in a frenzy. Her heart pounded hard against her chest as she opened envelopes and sorted, putting aside material for copying.

Most of their personal mail went straight to Jack's office. Though they both put their wages into one joint account to cover the bills, it was Jack who wrote the cheques, as it was easier for him to do it while in the office during the week.

She sat back in dread. Most of the letters were final notices—final-final notices, for the leases on both cars, the power company, the phone company, the oil company and, yes, even the mortgage on the house. Jack hadn't made a single payment on anything for four months. She sat back stunned.

She dipped back into the pile, looking for their joint account statements. She found one and quickly ripped it open. She scanned the statement. Her wages were deposited into the account every two weeks, but the balance was far less than it should be. Someone had been withdrawing money from the account as late as … she checked the top of the statement for the date. The statement covered a period two weeks past the day Jack had left. That could only mean one thing.

"Holy shit!" she yelled. "Oh my God, oh my God!" she cried as she jumped up and paced back and forth. She felt as if she had awakened on the edge of a precipice. She swallowed hard. "Jack! You're alive!" she yelled. "Where are you?" she screamed.

She walked out of the office and into the front lobby. Lord, she didn't know what to do. Tears welled up and trickled down her cheeks, but she couldn't tell if they were tears of joy or of frustration. She walked to Nancy's desk to grab a tissue from a box that always sat on the corner of the desk. She snatched two sheets from the box, toppling it over onto the floor by accident. She bent over to pick it up and froze.

On the underside of the box was taped a photo of Nancy and Jack smiling, cheek to cheek, in front of the Coliseum in Rome. The photo had been taken by Jack himself, holding out the camera in front of them. Nancy's auburn hair was blowing in the wind and partially covering Jack's face. Red hair. Just like Rose's.

Anita slumped to the floor with the box in her hand. This was too much. She let her head drop back against the wall, and she closed her eyes. She could've sworn that she was losing her sanity. She let out a deep breath, and then she let her mind dwell on Jack's and Nancy's photo. Did it really prove anything? Nancy might have had to be in Italy with Jack strictly for business. Maybe he didn't want to tell his wife because she may have thought it was something more than business.

A voice said, "Then why didn't Nancy tell you she went?"

Well, she told herself, for the same reason perhaps.

Did she really believe that?

She spent a long time that night sitting against the wall staring at that damn photo.

⟢

They got to the house in less than five minutes—and a full five minutes before the ambulance arrived. Fabrizio was on the living room carpet gasping for air like a dying flounder. Claudia had already placed a pillow under his head and was sobbing loudly as she hovered over him. Stefano immediately listened to Fabrizio's chest and heard the struggles of a set of terribly congested lungs. He called Fabrizio by name, but Fabrizio only slightly moved his right hand in response. Stefano looked up at the silent and petrified Andy and realized she still hadn't cleaned up from her ordeal with his rooster.

"Maria."

Maria had been watching intently with frightened eyes.

"Maria!" he said again. She jumped and looked at her father. "Help-a you mama." He motioned to wash her mother's face and turn on taps for a bath. Maria reached for Andy's hand and gently tugged.

"Adriana," said Stefano. Andy looked at him blankly. He motioned for her to go away with Maria down to the bathroom. She turned and mutely let Maria lead her down the hallway.

He then in Italian gently directed Claudia to put a small bag together with Fabrizio's medications, some underwear and his false teeth, figuring it was better to have Claudia focus on something productive than continue to wail and moan and stand in the way of the paramedics. After they had arrived and checked him over, they loaded Fabrizio onto a gurney and into the ambulance, Claudia wanted to go with them, but the young paramedics took one look at the distraught Claudia and shook their heads. Instead, Stefano suggested that Andy, finally washed and wearing some of her mother's clothes, go along with her father, and that he follow with Claudia and Maria in the truck.

At St. Joseph's Hospital, the paramedics immediately took Fabrizio to the ICU, and there was nothing for the rest to do but wait. Almost an hour later, Andy was getting agitated. They still hadn't seen a doctor.

"Can't anyone tell us what's happening!?" Andy cried while pacing up and down the sitting area. She looked extremely tired and pale, and she kept her arms crossed tightly across her chest. She was wearing the clothes that Maria had found in Nonna's closet for her to wear—clothes that Andy would normally not be caught dead in, but as it was, she was completely oblivious to the fact that the hem of the pants was above her ankles and the top was too short for her.

Stefano, holding a sleeping Maria, looked up at his wife. Then he glanced over at Claudia beside him and saw that she was still clutching a rosary and had her eyes shut.

"Adriana," he said softly and shook his head. Andy shook her head, too, and flakes of dried bird poop floated down from her hair. Stefano watched them float down onto the floor and chuckled in spite of himself. Andy looked down and then checked her shoulders and arms for more. She brushed off what she could but failed to see the humour in it.

Suddenly, the frosted door at the far end of the hallway hissed open and a nurse came out dressed in a smock with cats of all kinds printed on it. Maria stirred awake. As the nurse came closer, everyone's eyes were glued to those little cartoon multicoloured cats playfully socking large balls of wool. For some reason, Stefano numbly wondered why he never kept cats around the barn to keep the mice at bay. Maria thought of how her mother never let her have one.

Claudia had heard the door hiss open and was halfway up the hallway by the time the nurse reached her. She stopped and looked at Claudia and then over to the rest of them.

"Are you Mr. Fabrizio di Giovanni's family?" the nurse asked. Stefano nodded silently as Maria sat up. Andy took a few steps towards her.

"Yes, we are," Andy answered loudly. "He's my father and this is my mother, Claudia di Giovanni. How is he?"

"The doctor will be coming out soon to talk to you. Right now, as you know, Mr. di Giovanni feels some discomfort, although we've given him a mild sedative and that certainly made him feel better."

"Discomfort?" asked Andy.

"Yes."

"What does that mean exactly?" demanded Andy.

The nurse remained calm and subdued. *She's done this before,* thought Stefano.

"He's in stable condition. As you probably noticed, unfortunately, we're a little short-staffed today."

"Can we see him?" interrupted Andy.

The nurse shook her head. "No, I'm afraid not. It's best to let him rest." A beeper on her belt beeped and she looked down at it. "Oh dear. I must go. There's a beverage machine down in the cafeteria if you need anything, but I'm sure the doctor will be with you shortly."

"This doesn't help us one freakin' bit!" Andy snapped.

"Adriana," Stefano said softly.

"What!?"

Stefano shook his head.

"Don't shake your head at me, Stefano. This is my father and I need to know—" Andy's voice cracked, and she had to stop for fear of losing control. She slapped her hand over her mouth to try to shut up. Maria stood up and pulled at Andy's hand to calm her down.

"Maria, don't!" yelled Andy, pushing her daughter away. Maria broke down and cried, hurt and overwhelmed by what was happening.

Stefano took one gigantic step forward and grabbed Andy by the shoulders. She tried to push him away in anger but couldn't. So she snapped, "No, Stefano! They could at least tell us if he's fucking going to die or not!"

Claudia also broke down and wailed again at the thought. Stefano suddenly felt overwhelmed himself and apologized to the nurse. He could feel his heart race, but he was careful to keep his hands on Andy's shoulders while she unhappily stared at the nurse.

"He's not dying, if that's what you're afraid of," the nurse said quietly. "But he's very, very sick." The nurse looked at the four with sympathy. "It's best to wait for the doctor to explain everything to you. I'm sorry that there's nothing more we can do until the doctor takes a look at him. But I can tell you he's asleep and a lot more comfortable. He's going to be fine."

Andy shook free from Stefano's grasp and walked into a corner to brood. The nurse silently watched her go and turned to Stefano. "I'm sorry, but we had a few people waiting for over two hours before you arrived, and we're short-staffed."

Stefano nodded and watched her walk back through the frosted door.

Anita worked diligently into the early hours of Monday morning. She photocopied statements, banking information and correspondence with the company's latest customers, along with Nancy's notes from her own daybook and travel itineraries of recent business trips. She photocopied anything and everything that she could use to her advantage, either in finding her husband or divorcing him. She shook her head, but she realized it was truly possible that Jack himself might want to pursue a divorce under these circumstances. She was consumed with love in finding her man, but at the same time she was ready to be filled with anger and remorse. Either way, her focus now kept her mind from going crazy. She felt it was productive work, and it made her feel strangely closer to Jack.

An hour later, at six in the morning, she put all the new copies into a large folder and tidied up the office. She made a point of remembering to put the box of tissues back in its corner on Nancy's desk.

Now for the finale, thought Anita. She licked her finger and proceeded to write in the dust of the plate glass window, "Nancy and/or Rose stole my husband, Jack, who is an asshole." She then returned to Jack's office, took his daybook out and wrote in that week's schedule, "Jack is one big asshole." She looked at what she wrote and felt bad. Then she added, "P.S. I love you with all my heart!" even though in the back of her mind, she realized that was asinine.

She went to the washroom off the office and slapped cold water on her face, brushed her hair and straightened out her clothes. She turned off the lights, pulled the blinds on Jack's window to the side and then cranked open the window. Straddling the windowsill, she looked around Jack's office one more time to make sure that everything appeared exactly as it had before she broke in, save for the mail having been opened. Even then, it would take someone to want to open the letters to discover that someone had beaten them to it.

She climbed out through the window and gently swung it back into a closed position. Dawn was starting to shoo the darkness away, and one solitary bird crowed in the quiet cold air. She made sure that the coast was clear before she ran through the back parking lots and back to the car. She was greeted by that retched skunk smell as she opened the door, and it knocked the breath out of her. She started the car and checked the time on the dash. She had just enough time to go home, change and get to work at the station. She couldn't afford to test her boss's patience any further. But more importantly, she couldn't afford to miss any more days' income.

She drove out of the cul-de-sac and back to the entrance of the industrial park. She stopped at the stop sign and looked right and left, and then her heart jumped. She saw an approaching car. *Damn, it's an early bird*, Anita thought. The closer it got, the more it looked familiar, until finally she recognized the car. Nancy's!

The car slowed down, and as it turned the corner, their eyes locked. At least, Anita swore they did. After all, she was in a strange car with darkened windows. But then Nancy turned in and looked away from her as if nothing had happened. Anita took in a deep breath. She continued going around the corner and sped home.

෬

Nancy craned her neck and followed the lights of the Cadillac as far as she could see. It was unusual to see other cars this time of the morning, more unusual to see a new-model Cadillac. It didn't sit right with her.

She parked at the front of the factory and quickly located her keys. She unlocked the front door and tapped in her security code, turning off the alarm. Then she stood frozen on the spot as she slowly looked around. Nothing seemed disturbed. But there was an odd smell. She sniffed the air. Skunk. It had to have come from outside.

She hung up her coat and prepared for another workweek. Typically, Peter would've made his daily calls later that morning for more product numbers, and she would've been making up some purchasing orders. Her resolve that things would eventually get back to normal started to crack. To her, routine was everything, so in spite of the fact that there was very little to do, after making a pot of coffee, she turned on the computer and sat down.

Suddenly, as she swivelled into place, something looked awfully wrong. Someone had changed things over the weekend. With Jack not coming in and a skeletal staff for the floor, she was basically the only one in that office throughout the week, so no one else should have come in. There were no shifts over the weekend, no overtime clocked like there used to be. Could it be a sign that Jack had been back and was still in hiding?

Although none of them knew where Jack was—and there were some who even wondered if he was alive—they still kept their eyes open for any sign of him returning. They felt sure he couldn't hide forever. She had even hired "eyes" to watch out for him in Italy, Georgia, and Venezuela. Nancy didn't think that Anita was a big enough reason for him to return, but the combination of her, this Rose she had just learned about and any secret stashes he may have had would have to call him back eventually.

Maria had fallen asleep with her head on the lap of Claudia, who sat slumped over the child while still clutching the rosary. Andy thumbed through a magazine she had already gone through a number of times. She finally gave up, tossed the magazine onto a corner table and recrossed her legs. She was exhausted.

She looked around and saw Stefano standing at the window looking out at the traffic and the rising sun. In his lumberjack jacket and big rubber boots, he looked massive. Andy looked at his reflection in front of him on the windowpane and studied his face in the rising light. She really looked at him. In the past few days, she seemed to have become more aware of him—her husband, someone she had spent the last two decades with but never took the time to get to know. Has she only seen him as someone who provided for her and Maria?

The sun slowly streamed in and shone on Stefano's face, and she was startled at how brilliant his aqua eyes were—almost as if they had a light of their own. They flashed dramatically, two beautiful lights in the colour of the heavens. She studied his profile and was suddenly filled with remorse and a sadness so deep she was afraid she would drown in it. She let her eyes drop to her hands and felt ashamed.

Suddenly, the door at the end of the hallway hissed open and a tiny Oriental man in a lab coat and with a clipboard in hand scurried straight towards them. Claudia pressed the rosary to her chest and looked beseechingly at the doctor.

"Ah, Mrs. di Giovanni?"

Claudia stood up and Maria rolled off her lap, waking her up. "*Sì!*" cried Claudia.

"We would rike to keep him here for a day or two." He turned to Stefano. "We make sho he's comfo'table. You go home and get some lest. Touch base wi' us. We may end up moving him to anotha fwoh, but we know moah about hi' stay of heahf as time goh by."

Stefano, Claudia and Andy stared at him as he kept a steady gaze on them in return. He looked down at his clipboard and up at them. Then he peered down closely at the clipboard and up at Claudia before he brought the clipboard right to his nose. He pushed his glasses up to his forehead and squinted. Looking again at Claudia, he said, "Ah, Mrs. di Giovanni?"

Pause

"Mrs.—"

"Yeah! We are Mrs. di Giovanni! Keep talking!" yelled Andy. The doctor jumped with a start at her outburst, but when he realized he wasn't being attacked, he looked at the clipboard one more time.

"We have, er, Mr. di Giovanni in staboh condition. Aftah some X-lays and othah tests, we have come to the concwusion that he has PAH disea—"

Andy jumped in, "'PAH disea.' What is that?"

"Ah, it stands foh Puhmonary A'telial Hypahtension. It is a disea' that affect the brood vessehs in the rungs and specificahry the vesseh that reave the haht cahying the oxygenat' brood to the rung. Mr. di Giovanni, his vesseh have become thickah, stiffah, and the tubes that go through them have deterioyated, thinneh, so that theh is a lesistance of the frow of brood. This couh cause the haht to fail. In thi' case, it didn't, but he is very ill. The inceased workroad of the haht then makes him vely short of bleath. He's bee' on oxygen since awiving heah, and it may be that he will need to lemain on oxygen foh the time being. Well, at reast until we see how he pwoglesses."

Claudia, struck numb by this dialogue, looked up at Stefano. Stefano look at Andy, and Andy looked down at Maria. Maria looked from Andy to the doctor. "He's my *nonno*. Is he still alive?"

The doctor looked confused. "Arrive? Oh, arrive! *Sì!* I mean yes."

"Can we take him home now?"

"No, Maria," said Andy. "He's too sick right now—at least that's what I think he said."

Crimson-faced Stefano bowed his head and said, "*Si*, thank-a you."

"Doctor, here's my *nonno's* bag," said Maria as she leaned down and dragged the bag through her legs from under the chair. She held it up to the doctor.

The doctor raised his hand and shook his head. "He won't need that light now, but if you have his medication, we will keep it on han'. But keep the lest of it wi' you foh now. He may want it rater. So, foh now, we' just have to way."

"*Si*," said Stefano again, and with that the doctor turned and walked back to the frosted door and disappeared.

"I didn't understand a freakin' thing he said," mumbled Andy as she followed Stefano. "What's wrong with learning how to speak English?"

Stefano glanced back at her.

"I mean, wouldn't it help to know the language when you're cutting people open?"

Stefano did not dignify her statement with a reply. "We go-a home," he said simply, and they followed him out the hospital and into the crisp sunny morning while Maria patiently and maturely explained to them what the good doctor had said.

Chapter 18

AT THE RADIO STATION, ANITA'S eyes still stung from her unfortunate incident with the skunk, and it certainly didn't help that she hadn't slept in twenty-four hours. She had to stop reading every once in a while to rub them for some modicum of relief. She was at her desk struggling through press releases, circling the interesting ones and crossing out the dregs. She paused and nervously tapped her pen on the top of the desk. She took a deep breath and then sighed loudly. Finally she put her head down and, in spite of the loud music piped in from the sound studio, fell sound asleep.

At the best of times, Mondays were the busiest day of the week for her. Weekends typically generated more accidents, shoplifters, domestic mishaps, lost pets and increased news content carried over from Saturday. The station's policy dictated that Sundays were for good positive news items only. However, even on Mondays, it was mostly soft stuff because of the tri-town lack of bad stuff happening. There just wasn't any crime. Besides, this wasn't CNN. In fact, it was one of thousands of insignificant local radio stations that survived almost entirely on ad revenue generated by car-lot owners and Italian jewellers and butchers.

The headquarters of easy-listening CHJX-AM sat atop the local drugstore and consisted of a small foyer, three little offices and a sound studio—all very nondescript. The station had started out as closed-circuit campus radio back in the early sixties and had just celebrated its twentieth anniversary as an AM station. It operated at thirty-three watts, and at times reception was pretty patchy. However, they were waiting for the official go-ahead to make a switch for an increase in power, and they wanted to hit the deck running for a major position on the airwaves by adding innovative projects such as a mobile capability and a high-profile special-events program. Ergo, a station promotional Jeep and lots of reporting on local activities and mall openings.

The station's small staff plus three or four high school and college volunteers had been fundraising for a new transmitter and antenna so that the station could convert to high power. The money needed to make the switch seemed nearly impossible to attain, but fundraising—especially during annual Italian Canadian Club festivals and graduation events—had paid off. They were actually almost ready to upgrade and were waiting on pins and needles. So Anita knew that now was definitely not the time to slack off and do a lousy job of reporting. Advertisers were lily-livered to begin with, and it didn't take much to frighten them off. The staff had to work hard to maintain their support.

They were happy to have garnered a bit of influence through the Italian Canadian community and their many affiliated businesses, but that brought with it an increase in responsibility and a higher demand for quality of content. No one could afford to have a bad day on the job and inadvertently put out faulty ads or say the wrong thing on subjects that were important to the listening community. Back when no one really listened, there was a large margin of comfort, but those days were over. Now there was constant scrutiny from all sides.

Roger Drummond, the DJ on air, saw from his perch in the recording studio that Anita had dozed off, and he knew that she was programmed to be on air, live, within the half hour. Playfully he tapped, and then knocked, on the plate-glass window that separated the sound studio from her office, but she couldn't hear him. The grey sky outside lifted and the sun cut through sharply from a side window, streaming into the office and onto her face. Roger saw her shift her head a bit. He went off air for a moment and called to Anita through the intercom. She jumped almost to the ceiling and glanced around.

"Over here!" he said and tapped on the glass partition. She looked over with swollen eyes. He sat back suddenly. "Whoa! What happened to you!? Bad night?" the intercom blared.

She shrugged then said, "You can say that, I guess."

Roger looked sad, for he knew all about her missing husband and the rumours.

"I'm okay," she assured him.

He smiled and motioned to his watch. "Half hour. Will you be ready?"

She glanced at the clock on the wall and then down at the press releases. She nodded sleepily. Roger held up his index finger and wiggled it as he mouthed, "Naughty, naughty." He joked because he didn't want to let on that he knew about her problems and so embarrass her. He turned off the intercom and jumped on the mike just in time at the end of a song to introduce another. It was the eleventh commandment not to allow dead air. Every second had a monetary value.

Roger read from a sheet of paper, "And now we have a request from Mrs. Santori for her lovely granddaughter, Tina Tuscani. She is turning four today—happy birthday, Tina!—and this song is for you: 'Go to Beddy-Bye, Little Fried Chicken Legs.' Oh! I mean, 'Little Chicken Legs.'" Anita giggled as Roger, rolling his eyes, sat back in his chair and started hitting his forehead with a book in mocked mania and in beat with the music, *"Fate la nanna coscine di pollo."*

An awful smell rose in the heat of the sun. Anita sniffed and gagged at the *l'eau de skunk*. There simply was no getting used to the pungent odour.

Just then, she heard the *ping* sound as the elevator doors slid open, and she turned in time to see her boss, Mike Whitney, step off. Wearing a long heavy coat and a plaid scarf, he looked boyish and young for his age. He carried a soft leather briefcase in one hand and jiggled a large bunch of keys in his other. Anita waved at him and crooked her finger silently for him to come over. He shook his head and motioned to her that she should come over instead and continued on into his office off the hallway.

She stood up and ambled to Mike's door. The door was ajar, and she knocked on the door frame. Mike popped his head from around the back of the door where he was hanging up his coat.

"Hi," she smiled.

"Hi," he said. "Beautiful day!"

Anita nodded. "Sure is!"

Mike looked back at her. "Hanging in there?"

She nodded.

Mike stopped to sniff, and she groaned silently. "Holy crap!" he said. "What's that smell?" He held up his arm and smelled under it. Then his nose led him along the wafting current of the pungent smell up to her. He stopped and stared at her.

She smiled apologetically and nodded.

"Skunk?" he whispered.

She waggled her head in embarrassment and nodded again.

"Grooooss!" he yelled.

Anita motioned from bottom to top. "Climbed right up my body and over my head," she said, cringing.

Mike mutely stared for a few moments. Then he suddenly burst into jovial guffaws so loud that he had to clap a hand over his mouth because of the "on air" light on the wall. He snortled a little quieter this time. "Sorry," he said. "I'm not going to ask!"

"Yeah, well, long stor—"

"Yep, I know, long story. It has to be," he cut in.

She nodded again. "Um, something else," she said. He raised his eyebrows expectantly. "I, uh, no longer have a car. I was wondering if I could borrow the Jeep until I sort this thing out."

"The skunk took off in your car?"

"It's been repossessed," she said, embarrassed.

"The skunk?" asked Mike, nonplussed.

"No, those who repossess cars," said Anita.

Mike opened his mouth and then shut it.

"I didn't know they could just come over and take these things away!"

Mike said, "Oh," then frowned. "Money problems?"

"Yes," she said and shrugged. "And, no! I mean, it's not me, see. It's Jack."

"Jack? See, he's alive, right?"

"Yes," she said smiling, and then she frowned. "But he's been cleaning out our joint account these last few weeks. I wasn't aware of it till last night. Nothing's been paid, you see— the mortgage, the lease on the cars, house insurance, silly stuff like that." Anita's face cratered, and she burst into loud tears. She waved Mike away, even though Mike wasn't moving in anyway. He would've preferred to die first than to come any closer to a crying female. Especially one who smelled like skunk.

Instead, Mike sank into his desk chair and took a deep breath— which, of course, was a mistake. He gagged and coughed and coughed.

Then he took out a tissue from his pocket and wiped his face. He chortled again and had to wipe the tears away. Finally, he straightened his face again, picked up a roster on his desk to look at it and then tossed it back on the desk.

"Tell you what," he said. "This might work out for us. If you cover Joe for the special events as he's, quote-unquote, 'sick,' you can use the Jeep. How about that? Does that work for you?" he asked.

"I guess it buys me some time." She let her voice trail. She fiddled with the roster Mike had just thrown on the desk. "I, uh, also need to make as much money as I can, of course." She licked her lips. "Is there any overtime I could put in with any ultra-special events?"

Mike looked at her. "Anita, it's only you and Joe to begin with. Except for the repeats, the two of you are it. And you're doing 'it' already with news and special events. There's nothing else that's overtime."

Anita held up her hand, looking to the ceiling. "So are you saying, then, that if I'm covering Joe, I'm also doing more hours on his behalf? I mean, I'm on a biweekly wage and not paid by the hour, per se, but ..."

"No. But he just finished covering for you all this time, and you can moonlight on your own if you want—voice-overs, on-location promotions outside of the radio station. It's against the station's policy, but I think this is an exception. Will that help?" clipped Mike. He watched Anita smile and relax. "But only on one condition, and it's a tough one," he added.

Anita frowned. "What's that?"

"That you do something about that smell. I've discovered that these offices are too small for the both of us."

Suddenly, over the intercom, Roger said, "Anita, sixty seconds to the news."

Anita jumped and motioned to Mike. "I gotta go! And thanks, Mike. I'll remember this." For the first time that day, she felt just a little less desperate.

Back at her desk, she decided to drop by Andy's after work to see if she wouldn't mind driving her back to pick up the Jeep. But at the thought of seeing Andy, her stomach lurched. She covered her face with her hands and groaned. How in the world was she going to explain the stink in the car? She shook her head, sat up straighter and watched as Roger did the countdown with his fingers: three, two, one.

"Good morning! This is the ten a.m. news. First, international. The Georgia coast was hit hard by tornadoes, with damages totalling in the millions and many feared dead ..."

They had returned home from the hospital a bedraggled lot, drained and weary. Andy told Maria to go to bed and then called the school to excuse her from class. When she got a hold of the school secretary, she was told that they knew already and weren't expecting Maria for a couple of days. Great. Having lived there all her life, the speed with which news got around didn't surprised her, but her dad wasn't even out of emergency yet!

She hung up and yawned, rubbing her neck. Claudia was slumped at the kitchen table, still sniffling into a wet handkerchief. "Ma, you go to bed too. Get some sleep now while you can. Dad'll be okay." Andy looked at the clock on the stove. "You've got a few hours before we go back for visiting hours, okay?"

Claudia looked at her, and it occurred to Andy that this stricken look on her mother's face was something she had never seen before. Ma was frightened to death. She pulled at Claudia's chair and tried to nudge her mother off. "Go on, Ma. I'm going to bed too."

"*Si*," sniffed Claudia. She let Andy help her up. "*Ma* I no sleep," she argued. Andy almost dragged her mother to the hallway and up the stairs.

"Go," she said as she pushed her mother into the master bedroom. "I'll come back up with a blue pill, okay? That should help."

"I no sleep-a," insisted Claudia.

"Ma!" yelled Andy. "If you don't get some sleep, I'll have *two* sicko parents, okay?"

She made her mother lie down on the bed and pulled an extra comforter over. She walked into the en suite, rattled some medicine bottles and came back with a glass of water and two small blue pills. "Here, Ma, drink. Take these." She stood with her arms crossed as she made sure her mother took the two pills. She retrieved the glass and put it on the nightstand. "Sweet dreams, Ma." She closed the curtains and turned to walk out of the bedroom.

As she went through the doorway, she noticed an old photograph Stefano must've stuck under the corner of the light switch. She froze and gazed at it for a moment. It was her and Stefano standing together, he behind her with his arms gently cradling her swollen belly. It disturbed her to no end. Memories.

Andy returned to the kitchen, and her eyes automatically glanced at the time on the stove again. Normally she would reach for an apron and make preparations for that day's dinner. "Not on your life," she muttered. Today would be cafeteria food, like it or not. "Yippee aye yay, it's colon cancer chow!" Then suddenly, her own eyes were heavy with fatigue, and she let her body slump. Wearily, she climbed the stairs, pulled herself up with the handrail and tiptoed into Maria's room. Gently, she climbed in beside her daughter. She placed one arm over Maria's shoulder, and with the other hand she brushed a bit of hair off her forehead. Maria stirred but did not wake up. *What a good kid*, Andy thought, remembering how Maria had tried to console her so lovingly during the night.

Andy closed her eyes and tried to relax, but her body shook with each pounding beat of her heart. She found she couldn't breathe. She felt an overwhelming panic freeze inside of her and astutely recognized that she was dangerously close to a nervous meltdown. She wanted to scream and run away. She didn't, of course. Not now, she thought. Not yet.

Too much going on, she thought to herself. Memories, emotions, unhappiness, insecurities, even babysitting Anita while she suffered from the thoughtless actions of her husband.

Husbands! She thought back to what Stefano had shared with her about the businesses needing to find Jack. What businesses was Stefano actually referring to? Was it just being friends and, in the case of Peter, partners that made them owe Anita so much care and concern? Women were a special lot in Italian families, especially widows, who were respected and looked after in their community. Did Stefano mean they owed her the same support? Was he implying that Jack was dead?

Andy didn't know, because none of their acquaintances had ever been separated or divorced, just widowed. So there was nothing really within their tiny community that dictated what to do with divorced women. A very unique situation in this modern era.

And that terrible photo tucked under the light switch. Oh, why did these things have to come back and haunt her? Terrible, terrible, awful things that could never be undone. "I don't know how to make it right," she whispered to the back of Maria's head.

She rolled over, sat up and covered her face. She stayed like that for a very long time. *No tears, Andy, no tears.*

She got up and returned to the kitchen. She needed a smoke. Over in the corner by the stove, she reached for the cigarettes in the back of the cupboard. She lit a cigarette and slid the window open very gingerly. "Fucking bird," she muttered as she looked right and left. No birds. She didn't have to worry about being caught by Stefano, either, because he had briefly left to check up on one of the construction sites and was to be home in time to take them back to the hospital.

She dragged and then exhaled out the window. In a way, she was relieved Anita had the Cadillac and the Volvo was being repaired, because it freed her from having to drive, and she had no compunction about making Stefano drive all over hell's half acre for them. Suddenly she heard one of the hens cluck loudly below the window. She immediately slammed the window shut and smashed the cigarette in half.

"Dirty shitty filth!" she yelled as she pulled the smashed cigarette out of her mouth and threw it into the sink.

Stefano's birds. Her thoughts went back to Stefano and that photograph. She admitted to herself that she feared him in many ways—mostly because she knew she was the cause of his unhappiness. But she had no choice. No choice but to keep a massive black hole between the two of them. And something else she knew but tried to ignore was that the massive black hole was eating them alive. "Like living with a fucking monster and pretending it's not there," she muttered.

Her father's collapse truly shook her. It made her realize that her father and mother were getting on. *And once they go, who's next?*

She sighed and leaned back against the stove. That photo cruelly brought back horrible memories of two heartbreaking miscarriages and an even more tragic stillbirth. And of Stefano losing a chunk of his heart each time until there was nothing left. Maria was their first surviving child, and Andy had determined to make sure that pregnancy was her last.

"Let's leave it at that," she had told herself for years. Maria was a miracle. Wasn't that good enough? What was worse, it was all their fault! Their own stupidity! Where innocence was no excuse and a pound of flesh could not make it better. A million Hail Marys did squat and a billion Lord's Prayers could do nothing to lessen hell's burning fire waiting to consume her soul. She felt the heat of that fire now again and was afraid it would eat away her gut, her heart, her mind. She loosened the top buttons of her mother's sweater because she suddenly couldn't breathe, and she closed her eyes and tried to inhale and exhale slowly, inhale, exhale.

A tear burst free and ran down her cheek, but with a violent slap on her cheek she obliterated it. The pain felt good.

She straightened up again, fished the soggy cigarette out of the sink, opened the window and tossed it out. The chickens rushed to the cigarette on the wet ground and gobbled it up, destroying the evidence.

As usual.

Anita steered the Cadillac up the Giordanis' driveway. By now, the sun was hidden behind late afternoon clouds, and the temperature had dropped accordingly. She drove right up to the closed garage doors and stepped out. There was a bit of a breeze through the pine branches, and she could hear the delightful clucking of hens and the sudden machine-gun rattling of a woodpecker.

Stefano's truck wasn't in its usual spot. Thinking that someone might be home, she went around to the back door and knocked. No answer. She jiggled the doorknob but it was locked. That was unusual. No one ever locked it unless they were all gone, which was in itself rather unusual. She walked over to a garage window and peered in. Empty.

Not knowing what to do, she stood listening to the breeze a bit more until she shuddered from the cold. She walked back to the Cadillac to sit in it for a bit just in case someone would be coming home soon. But as she opened the driver's side door, the truck suddenly pulled into the driveway. She saw Stefano raise a hand, and she responded and waved back. He parked and stepped out.

"I brought back the Cadillac. I can use the station's Jeep for a while, but I need a ride back." Anita looked up into the truck, expecting Andy and Maria to step out, but the cab was empty.

She looked at Stefano questioningly. "Um, where's Andy?" she asked as she held out the Cadillac keys.

Stefano leaned into the truck and pushed on the remote for the garage door. The door jumped into life, and Stefano motioned her to follow him into the relative warmth of the garage.

"Andy, she is-a in hospital. Fabrizio is-a sick."

Anita's eyebrows shot up. "He's sick? What happened?" she asked with sincere concern as she followed Stefano through the garage.

He motioned to his chest and tapped it. "He-a no breathe. They took-a him to the hospital."

Anita gasped. "Oh no! Is he going to be all right?"

Stefano nodded. "Si, *ma* he is-a very sick." He led her to the hallway door where he kicked off his boots. "Adriana, Maria, they go visit."

Anita also kicked off her boots and followed Stefano through the family room. "I'm so sorry to hear that. Can I do anything?" she asked.

He turned and looked down at her from the kitchen. He shook his head and said, "No."

"Now what?" asked Anita.

"They keep-a him," he said. "For a little bit-a."

Anita went up the few steps to the kitchen level and sat down in one of the kitchen chairs. Stefano opened the fridge and took out the milk. He held it up questioningly. Anita shook her head and said, "No, thank you." She watched as he drank from the bottle and almost emptied it. He wiped his mouth with the sleeve of his lumberjack jacket and put the bottle back into the fridge. He closed the fridge door and stopped. His handsome nose twitched, and he reopened the fridge. He tucked his head in as far as he could and sniffed the corners.

"Oh," said Anita. "That would be me."

Stefano smelled his arm and then opened the little freezer. He shut everything and walked to the garbage container under the sink. He leaned down and sniffed. He was hidden by the counter.

"Stefano," she said, "it's me. I'm the smell."

Stefano popped back up from behind the counter and stared at her.

"It's me. Something, er, happened the other night." Stefano frowned. She held up her hand and said, "It's all right! I didn't hurt the car! Well, at least, not really." Stefano walked over and sat down opposite her at the table. He waited expectantly. Anita saw his nostrils still twitching. "Um, there was this skunk." She squirmed in embarrassment.

Stefano's eyes grew large in surprise. Then he broke out in laughter so loud that it echoed through the house. "*Puzzola!* A skunk-a?

"Ah, er, yes, a skunk-a."

Stefano grinned, and his eyes sparkled. "How happen?" he asked gleefully.

"Well, it was really stupid, Stefano. I was locked out of the house."

He chuckled.

"And so I tried to find a window to climb through, and I found a basement window unlocked. I had to get into this ... this ..."

"A hole-a," Stefano offered.

"*Si*," she said. "A hole-a. Well, a 'well,' really."

"*Che?*"

"A window well, and it was dark, and when I stepped into it, all of a sudden ...!" She raised her hands in mock surprise.

Stefano laughed so hard he couldn't breathe, and tears were running down his ruddy cheeks. He wiped them away with his handkerchief. He shook his head, and he shook his body. It had been decades since he had been able to laugh so hard, so freely.

"'Nita. Ho ho, ha ha, 'Nita!" He raised an index finger. "I have-a secret for clean-a."

"Oh yeah?" she asked. He nodded and again motioned for her to follow, this time back through the family room and down the basement stairs. He walked into one of their cold cellars. This particular one was filled generously with canned goods: roasted green peppers, applesauce, tomato sauce, pesto, pears, cherries, pickles, jellies, pig's feet, head cheese ... enough to feed an army for a year. He reached for two large glass jars of tomato paste and handed them to Anita, who silently studied them under the swinging bare bulb hanging from the rafter.

"Is this for my ... hair?" she asked, confused.

Stefano shook his head yes and no. "You-a take a bath an-a you-a do you-a hair. *Si?*"

Anita was taken aback and made a face. He chuckled again, his eyes sparkling with glee. He pointed to the cellar door and hurried her out and to the other end of the basement where he had his own shower and sauna. He grabbed a fresh towel and handed it to her.

"You put on you-a self an' sit-a in here," he said, opening the sauna and turning it on. "Then-a, when you-a finish, you-a go here!" He pulled back the shower curtain of the shower stall. "You-a wash."

Anita looked back at the jars, "And that will work?"

Stefano chuckled and nodded. He pointed to himself. "I-a look at-a the car, *si*?"

Anita frowned and grimaced in apology. She nodded helplessly. "*Si*, it smells in there, too, Stefano. I'm sorry. It was so cold I had to sit in the car to warm up before I tried the window again."

"No problem-a," he smiled. He nodded one more time and backed out of the little bathroom. He closed the door gently, and she could hear him going back upstairs and out of the house.

She looked at the jars one more time and shrugged. Very tentatively, she started to undress.

Peter sat drumming his fingers on Jack's desk. "Apart from opening the mail and photocopying a bunch of stuff, what else did he do?"

Nancy stood in Jack's office doorway. "As far as I know, nothing! I checked the safe. Nothing's gone from there, and that's the part I don't understand. If he was going to take anything, it'd be the black book and the cash. I'm sure he must be desperate by now."

"Maybe he photocopied that too?" Peter said, making a bad joke. Nancy didn't answer, and she looked very sad. In the back on the factory floor, the mould machines were pounding and creaking, pounding and creaking. Peter took a deep breath and stood up. "How can you be so sure that it was Jack?"

Nancy shrugged. Peter stepped past her and closed the office door. He took Nancy by the shoulders and turned her around to face him. "Listen," he said, "I know you think you're responsible." Nancy looked up at him. She had intensely dark brown eyes, and they seemed to pierce his gaze. "You did your best to make sure he finished what we set him up to do." She looked down and averted her eyes. He held her chin with his thumb and index finger and lifted her face up to his. "So," he said. "What makes you think he'd show his face here again?"

"Because of something he said the night before I left him in Italy."

"Oh, and what was that?" asked Peter softly.

"Something about not liking to share his business. That he never intended you, Stefano, or the rest to call the shots. That if he hadn't needed to borrow from you guys in the first place, he'd still be full owner of this place. He was depressed. He wanted to feel good about himself again," she explained.

"Jack? Depressed?" Peter grinned in amusement. Then he looked questioningly at her. "You didn't fall for him, did you, Nancy? I thought your heart was mine alone? You were to make sure he made the delivery to Luciano, Nancy. Not marry him." Nancy stood silently, still averting her eyes. She remained quiet. "You ungrateful bitch," he whispered. He grabbed her behind with both hands and pinned her close to himself. "So now what?"

Nancy wiggled and pushed him away. "All I know is that other than you and I, Jack's the only one who knew the new security code." She fumbled for words. "I'll ... I'll call Anita and see if she's learned or heard anything. Maybe he's contacted her. She's a real dunce, but she's still his wife, still in that house."

Peter nodded slowly, letting his eyes graze over Nancy's face. Then he gazed at the piles of mail on the desk again. He reached out and fingered the daybook.

"Unless ..." she said, letting her voice trail.

Peter looked at her sideways. "Unless?"

Nancy exhaled. "No. Nothing."

"You sure?"

"Yeah ... well ..."

"What?" Peter demanded.

"There was a smell," she said and paused.

"Smell?"

"Yeah, a weird smell. Like manure. Can't you smell it?"

Peter sniffed with his version of the famous di Giovanni and Giordani nose. He caught a scent and stood up. He followed the scent as best he could—out into the front lobby and back into the office. He shook his head. "Nothing," he said.

"Come over here." She motioned him to come by the window. Peter stepped towards Nancy and sniffed some more. "Yeah, you're right! Skunk," Peter said finally.

Nancy's eyebrows shot up. "Skunk? That's right! Skunk!"

"Yeah, but a skunk doesn't break into a place and use a photocopier." Peter rubbed his chin and looked outside. There were woods about, and skunks lurked and sprayed.

"What if?" Nancy paused, because the thought frightened the dickens out of her. "What if it was Luciano's guys? Maybe Jack didn't make the drop, and they're hunting him down."

"Well, I hope it's him they're looking for instead of blaming us for sending him." Peter thought about that one for a bit. He had been trying very hard *not* to think about it. But for Nancy's sake, he kept a calm facade. "No," he said. "They wouldn't do that. They know we're like this with them." He held up two fingers stuck together.

"Well, someone still got in!" A thought occurred to Nancy, and her face paled. She marched across the office to the window. She cranked the window open and then looked back at Peter, who simply stared at the open window.

Peter shook his head. "So? There's still the alarm."

Nancy cringed. "No. The windows aren't part of the security system. Only the front doors and the loading doors out back."

Peter hiccupped as his heart skipped two beats in a row. *Then it had to be Luciano*, he thought. They stood quietly staring at each other until the phone on Nancy's desk rang and she had to leave and answer it. Peter was left alone in a cold sweat to wonder at the awful repercussions if Luciano found him first. For a fleeting moment, he seriously thought of running away. If they had gotten into the safe ...

Stefano hurried. He had to put feed out for the sheep and the goat, and then feed the hunting dogs in their pen before he was off again to pick everyone up at the hospital. He was dipping a makeshift scoop made out of the bottom of a Javex bottle into a burlap bag of feed when he heard the barn door creak open. He squinted through the glare of the single light bulb just above his head. He made out Anita, and he chuckled and nodded, smiling. "Feel-a better?" he asked. His breath billowed out and hung in the heavy cold air of the barn. Anita smiled and sniffed at her arm.

"I think so," she answered, smiling. She held out her arm for him to smell. He sniffed at her sleeve and nodded, returning her smile. Then she sniffed the air around her and took a deep breath. "I love the fresh smell in here. Like freshly cut grass. Like spring." She looked around the barn. "Stefano, can I help?"

Stefano stood with the scoop in his hand while he looked around. He pointed in the direction of the henhouse. "*Si,* you can-a take da eggs-a."

"Oh, what fun!" She stepped towards the coop and stopped to look at the hens in their nests. "Do I have to get my hands under those chicken bums to get their eggs? Won't they bite me?" she asked, wide-eyed.

Stefano laughed and shook his head. "No, no. She-a no bite. Come-a." He waved for her to come closer and showed her how to do it. He placed his hand under one of the hens; the hen complained loudly but didn't fly away. He pulled out a straw-covered egg and held it up to the light daintily, with his pinkie finger sticking up. He motioned for Anita to do the same. She walked up to the next nest and gingerly placed a hand under the brooding hen. The hen clucked loudly, and Anita jumped back in surprise. By accident, she stepped onto a rake, and the handle hit her in the back of the head.

"Ow!" she yelled, holding her head. She lost her balance and started to fall, leaning on a bale of hay. The bale slipped from its pile and fell to the ground. Anita fell with it and went headfirst into the hay.

Stefano looked askance and couldn't believe what had just happened. He laughed so hard that he couldn't catch his breath. Anita howled with ridiculous laughter as well, rolling on the bale of hay and trying to get a hold of something to help her up. She gave up and held up her hand to Stefano. Stefano reached out to help her up, but instead he tripped over the same rake and fell on top of her. Anita howled at the absurdity of the moment, but she couldn't breathe very well because of Stefano's weight on top of her. She started to pant and tried hard to get air into her lungs. Startled, Stefano pushed up and leaned on his hands. His brilliant eyes searched Anita's to see if he had hurt her. He struggled to get off, but each time he reached for something, all he grabbed was slippery hay.

Anita stopped laughing and looked at Stefano. She became aware of Stefano's big strong arm muscles flexing under her touch, even through his lumberjack jacket. With her right hand, she felt those muscles as she trailed it up his right arm. Her heart pounded, and she felt an intense physical longing. She could hear her blood pulsating in her eardrums like a percussion band. She trembled uncontrollably. Oh, she wanted him so much!

Her eyes dropped to his lips and then back to those eyes. She raised her left hand and cradled Stefano's flushed cheek. He lowered his head a touch and hesitated, but she pulled his face all the way down to hers. He pulled away but she whispered, "Please … please …"

He let her lips gently brush his. He didn't know what else to do. Then she pushed him away a bit to look in his eyes again. The intense sexual appetite that Stefano aroused in her was the most amazing feeling she had ever known in her life. Hungrily she kissed his face, his cheeks, his eyes and then his mouth.

Stefano's heart burst, and his mind reeled. He had neglected that part of his life for so long that he'd thought it was dead. Suddenly he kissed back hungrily. Their mouths locked together. Stefano, who was in his prime with so much love to give, knew that there was absolutely nothing left in this world that could hold him back.

Stefano grabbed at Anita's pants button and fly while he kept kissing and kissing. She in turn pushed his jacket over his strong shoulders and unbuttoned the front of his shirt. Her hands explored wherever she found flesh. His broad, hot and muscular chest came bare, and she let her left hand explore through his chest hair to his shoulders, to his chest again, his stomach, his upper arms …

Somehow, Stefano was able to slip off her jeans without letting go of her lips. She, too, frantically grabbed his jeans and undid the top button. Then, as if to tease herself—to reassure herself that this was real, that this wonderful specimen of a man really did desire her when another didn't—she let her left hand cup his groin and felt his living, pulsing, wonderful … She moaned at the feel and hastened to take his pants off. He leaned back and deftly took off his jacket and shirt as one, and then lowered his jeans. Anita grabbed him fully, his hot velvety skin over steel, and the beauty of it made her moan again.

He pulled her shirt back off her shoulders and lifted her bra. His searching, warm lips found her breasts. He moaned. A woman's breasts. How he had forgotten what they were like. He murmured in Italian that needed no translation. She felt so wanted, so needed, that just by his caresses and sucking her breasts, she could feel close to that wonderful precipice. His mouth found her other breast and this time, amazingly, she came. But it only served to make her want more. She leaned up and threw off her shirt and bra, knocking the naked bulb hanging from the ceiling with her shirt and causing it to swing in long arcs. The light and shadow played on their faces, their closed eyes, their shoulders.

Stefano leaned up on his arms to look at her and to stretch his muscles like a cat. Gently, Anita let her fingertips trail along the curves and hills of the muscles in his back. Tears welled up in her eyes. This was so good ... so good.

Stefano nursed further down her body to her belly button. He pulled his head away a bit to look at that beautiful body. Then, with a swiftness that made her dizzy, his mouth desperately sucked at the small mound just below her belly button and then furrowed further down. He grabbed her thighs and lifted her, furrowing deeper into her body.

Anita arched her back. She opened her eyes wide as her body exploded and her eyes blindly trailed from hay, to the rafters, to hens, to a swinging bulb. She had died and gone to heaven. Then Stefano grabbed her by the buttocks and pulled her closer. He grunted as he got up on his knees and pulled Anita's body up and over on top of himself. For fear of hurting her, he stopped just short of his goal and slowly rotated her body ever so slightly as he lowered her down and down and deeply down on himself. They clung to each other as one, not able to let go and not able to be still. The magical moment of coupling—the most primitive of all sensations, with no fears, no inhibitions, nothing to distract them—seemed to last an entire lifetime.

She came again, and this time she grabbed his strong elbows and forced herself further over him. She rotated her hips persistently and took glee in breaking down his resistance until finally, with a shout and a moan, Stefano came, his locks of blue-black hair hanging over those dancing eyes, that beautiful face, that strong and sensitive mouth. Anita watched his almost mystical trance, the twitching of his eyelids with those long thick black eyelashes, the sweat glistening on his skin, the inner tremor that she herself could feel down in the depths of her solar plexus. *Oh heaven*, she thought, and "Oh heaven," she moaned.

He cratered and fell on her. She cradled him close and kissed his sweaty brow. Her fingers interlaced his thick black hair, and she murmured love and sweet things to him. He slowly caught his breath, and she felt tears run down from the outer corner of her eyes to trace tiny rivulets across her temples and into the hairline of her scalp. She was happy.

Back at the house, the phone rang and rang.

Andy was calling from the hospital to see why Stefano was taking so long in coming back to pick them up. Visiting hours were over, and Andy hated having to stay any longer than she needed to. It smelled in the hospital—of blood, and urine, and feces. A hospital can only be a sad place. Even babies seemed to cry with grief. For her, it was a painful reminder of children lost.

She was, of course, blissfully unaware that at that moment, Stefano and Anita were gently dressing each other, nibbling here and kissing there and still oblivious to that other world outside the barn.

Eventually they made their way to Stefano's truck. Anita clung to his hand as she kept her eyes glued to him. Stefano started the truck, and they sat silently save for their breathing. He put the truck in reverse and slowly backed out. Anita dreamily pointed in the direction of the radio station. In ten minutes, they finally turned into a multi-storey open-air garage and stopped beside the station's special-events Jeep. Tenderly, Stefano led her to the Jeep, where he leaned over her and kissed her one last time. Then he regretfully had to let her go and get back into the truck. He started the truck, smiled gently and nodded.

Anita put her hand on her pounding chest and gave him a very grateful and tender smile. She watched as he drove away. A moment later, she was still standing by the Jeep, having lost sight of the truck but not the feel of the man.

She was a most happy and fulfilled woman for the first time in her life, and as she climbed into the Jeep and started it, the radio blared out

Aretha Franklin singing, "What a Difference a Day Makes." Twenty-four little hours …

The worm, it had won.

And she hadn't even remembered to tell Stefano that she knew Jack was still alive and well … somewhere.

Leo had searched everywhere. There were a number of people from the little community of Shellman's Bluff missing, and so there was already a sense of general alarm. Medics came in from everywhere, some having to clear the roads themselves in order to get to where the real damage had been done.

Leo, terribly sad and in a daze, made his way back through the debris towards the tilting wharf where his ruined ship lay. There was so much garbage and bits of clothing, radios, televisions and furniture on the marsh that it appeared solid enough for anyone to walk across, never mind Jesus.

He asked here and there, "Have you seen Yvonne? Do you know where Yvonne went to?" but no one could help him.

He had a very good cry over the possibility of losing of Yvonne. He sat on a rock clasping his statue of Santa Maria and prayed for the umpteenth time. He had learned to appreciate how precious life was now. Though he had never been far from knowing death, it was always the death of other people, and usually people he didn't like, and they were dying at his hand. It had never occurred to him that perhaps life was not as cheap as he had been brought up to believe.

Losing Yvonne made him a new person. He became born again, except through what he believed was the grace of the Son's holy mother. So he continued to fervently pray to Santa Maria, his pact clear and uppermost in his mind. He begged her to please save innocent and God-fearing Yvonne, she who was pure in heart and had the soul of a beautiful child and the face of an angel. He again promised that he would never hurt or kill another person, and he prayed that he would be forgiven for those he had killed, forgiven for not having seen that he had taken away a son from a loving mother, or a father of some innocent child, or a husband of a woman who worshipped and loved him and was therefore alone and helpless.

Ghosts of faces churned through his soul, and he asked to be forgiven for every single life he had taken or caused to be taken. He knew he didn't deserve to be forgiven, but he believed in the teachings of his church in Italy. "Please forgive me for all the bad things I have ever, ever done," he concluded. "Please bring back Yvonne."

At that moment, as if a door had been opened, he knew what his next step was to be. That sensation of an almost tangible inner and strangely silent force of guidance was something he would never forget for the rest of his life.

Chapter 19

ANDY STOMPED AROUND THE HOUSE perturbed. They had finally given up on Stefano and called Peter to pick them up at the hospital to take them home. She was terribly upset. Stefano knew they were waiting to be picked up, so where the hell was he?

Also, the Cadillac was back. That meant Anita had been there ... alone with Stefano. How rare it was for Stefano to be home alone. It made her feel sick, and she felt the first trickles of alarm.

Finally she heard the truck pull in. She didn't even wait for him to get into the house. She stomped out through the garage onto the cold driveway. In her stocking feet, she lunged at the truck and yanked the driver's side door open. Stefano, surprised, sat back and stared at her.

"Do you fucking know how long we waited for you?" she yelled. "What the hell happened, Stefano? Where were you?"

She stepped back as Stefano got out of the car. He slammed the door shut, shooting her an icy glare. He pointed to Peter's black BMW. "You come-a home wi' Peter?" he asked.

"Yeah, after we waited for an hour."

He wordlessly passed her, went into the garage and pointed at the Cadillac. "She-a use-a Jeep from the work-a," he said, making a slight motion with his head. "I drop her off-a."

Andy folded her arms and glared at his back. "Oh yeah? Where to? To goddamn Timbuktu?"

Stefano stepped towards her, red-faced. He pointed a finger at her face. "Adriana," he warned. "I no feel-a like yelling."

Andy stepped back and lowered her eyes. She straightened up her shoulders and pointed down the hallway. "Peter's inside. He wants to talk to you," she muttered.

Stefano nodded curtly and shuffled in his heavy boots through the garage to the hallway door. With deliberate movements, he let one boot slide off one foot, and leaning on the doorjamb, he let the other boot slide off, letting it fall on top of the first. He tucked his gloves into his jacket pocket and took off his jacket. As if in slow motion, he hung it up, tucked his shirt further down into the back and sides of his pants, and then pushed a lock of his jet-black hair back into place. As he passed through the hallway into the family room, he was very much aware of Andy's eyes drilling into the back of his head. He didn't care.

Peter sat at the kitchen table jiggling his left leg and fingering a mug of coffee. Stefano walked up from the family room and nodded at him.

"Where have you been?" asked Peter, picking up a biscotti from a dish and tapping the crumbs off.

"I bring-a Anita to another car. She no car." He motioned with his big hands a steering wheel.

Peter nodded silently, took another sip of his coffee and continued to drum his fingers on the table. He looked pointedly at his brother. He was just about to say something when Claudia came into the kitchen, having roused herself from the plastic-covered couch in the living room where she had been resting. She looked beseechingly at Stefano. "Stefano, coffee?"

Silently, Stefano nodded. "Fabrizio?" he asked, looking at Peter and then at Claudia.

Claudia moaned and held her head. Fresh tears sprang from her swollen eyes. "Still very sick-a," she whispered. Her bottom lip and little chin trembled, and her face crumbled in grief as she began to sob. Stefano's heart ached at the sight of her pain, and he stepped towards her, hovering protectively over her for a moment before taking her in his arms. He tenderly patted her back, tucking her head against his chest. He rocked her gently while her muffled cries poured into his underarm. He was startled at the love he felt for his poor mother-in-law, and he had to fight back his own tears suddenly.

Andy quietly stepped into the kitchen. She stopped and stood with her arms crossed, staring at her mother and Stefano. She tilted her head back and pointed her nose to the ceiling. Intuitively, she knew Stefano had changed. And, goddammit, it had to have happened during a two-hour window over which she had absolutely no control.

"Something smells fishy around here."

Peter glanced sideways at his sister-in-law and saw her sour look. He did a double take.

Claudia looked up from under Stefano's underarm. Sniffling, she said, "Is-a no fish. Is-a skunk." At the sight of Andy, she broke down again. "Oh, Adriana, you no have a papa soon-a," and she burrowed under Stefano's underarm again.

"No, it ain't no skunk I'm smelling. Just a big fucking fish!" Andy yelled angrily.

Peter slammed his fist down on the table, which made his coffee jump and spill. "Christ, Andy. What now, huh? Leave the freakin' guy alone!"

Andy's nose slowly rotated towards Peter. "Who made you king shit around here?"

Suddenly, Stefano let go of Claudia and threw up his hands. "Andy!" He stared her down and then motioned to a chair. Andy angrily plopped down next to Peter, who averted his eyes and rotated his body away from her. He silently took another sip of his coffee.

"Andy," Stefano hissed. "You Mama is-a right. Smell-a is skunk!"

Peter looked up. "What about a skunk?"

Andy ignored Peter and threw up her hands. "I'm not talking about no skunk!"

Peter slammed his mug down on the table and trembled as he desperately tried to control his temper. "Andy, with all due respect, you're my sister-in-law. Wife to my brother, zia to my sons. But I am getting so sick and tired of your—"

Andy pointed a finger at him. "You know what you can do? Stick it where the sun don't shine!"

Peter shot up but stopped as Stefano leapt forward and clamped a hand on his shoulder. He gently pushed Peter back down onto the chair. Then he pointed to the front hall and looked pointedly at Andy. Andy slammed the table hard with her right palm and stomped out of the kitchen, yelling, "This is my fucking house!" But she went anyway, up the stairs and into the guest room, where she slammed the door so hard the dishes rattled in the cupboards back in the kitchen.

Stefano gently led Claudia to the table and sat her down. Then he himself leaned against the back of the fourth chair and directed his attention to Peter, who glared back and said, "You know you spoil that rotten wife of yours."

Stefano shook his head. "She-a *my*-a rotten wife." He took a deep breath and exhaled slowly. "So," he said. "Fabrizio?"

"Yeah. Fabrizio." Peter studied the bottom of his coffee cup. "I saw the doctor, but I didn't have a chance to see Fabrizio. Visiting hours were finished, but the guy said that Fabrizio's hanging in there. Right now he's on twenty-four-hour oxygen."

Claudia slowly crossed herself and rolled her eyes to heaven. Peter watched her do it, and then he downed the last drops of his coffee. He cleared his throat loudly. "Stefano? You got a minute?"

Stefano pushed off from the chair and nodded mutely, motioning for Peter to follow him to the *caverna* under the garage floor.

Claudia sadly watched the men disappear from the family room. Her swollen eyes looked over to the armchair where Fabrizio always sat in front of the TV. She saw the gilt-framed photo of her and Fabrizio on top of the cabinet and got up and walked to it. She held it as she sank back into the armchair. She broke down in tears again and rocked as she hugged the photo to her breast.

At the end of the hallway, Peter and Stefano stepped into the garage and removed the tarp from the *caverna* hatchway. As Stefano yanked the hatchway open, Peter caught a whiff of the terrible smell. "Must be skunk season," he said to Stefano. "You can smell it everywhere."

Stefano climbed down the little ladder. "No, is Anita. She-a step on-a skunk," he said offhandedly.

Peter froze and frowned down at his brother. "Anita?" he asked quietly. Stefano looked up at him and then suddenly flashed him a brilliant smile. "Si, skunk-a run like-a so," and he motioned a sweep from his toes to up over his head. He belly-laughed at the thought.

"She was here?" Peter asked.

"*Si*, bring-a Cadillac."

"When did this skunk thing happen?"

Stefano grinned and shrugged as he reached over to a cloth-covered jug and poured a couple of glasses of red wine. "Hmm, *Domenica*. Sunday-a."

Relieved, Peter brightened up and laughed as he climbed down the ladder into the *caverna*. "Thank God! Anita! Ha! Boy, do I have a story for you!"

"I tell ya, operator, he does have a number. He is in Venezuela. ... Look, we just went through a tornado here, and I've lost everything. I have no number for him, but it is a life and death situation here. Yes, collect call." Leo fretted, his eyes swivelling this way and that at the upheaval around him. "I swear on my mother's grave that ... Yes, Jorge Pessek."

Leo leaned back and took a deep breath. Keeping his temper under control was going to be a real challenge. This "becoming a nice guy" shit was going to take all his energy. He made the sign of the cross and silently promised again to turn over this new leaf. He promised and promised. On the other end of the line, finally, the phone was ringing. And ringing.

Finally, *"Ola, Pessek residencia?"*

The operator said, "This is a collect call from Leo Mangiano for Mr. Jorge Pessek."

There was a long pause and some chatter in the background. Then the phone was hung up.

"Sir, it seems to me they do not want to talk to you or that the person you are calling isn't there."

"Don't you understand what I'm tryin' to say to you?" Leo looked around at what now looked like a bombed-out parking lot. He was standing in a phone booth somewhere in Brunswick, Georgia, because all the lines were down in Darien, Eulonia and Shellman's Bluff. "It's a matter of life and death! Santa Maria destroyed my boat! No, no, you don't understand. Santa Maria!" he mumbled. "People all around me, gone, out somewhere in the ocean. *Phhhffft!* Dead! Just like that!"

"I'm sorry, sir. Maybe you should contact the police." With that, the operator hung up on him.

"No!" Leo slammed the phone back into its cradle and leaned against the grimy glass of the phone booth with his aching shoulder. He had helped lift a section of a roof with other people to free someone who was crying from underneath. There they found an elderly man, a young woman and a child of 2 years old. They were safe but pretty banged up, as most people walking around in a daze were. He rubbed his face with one hand. His five o'clock shadow had thickened to a twelve o'clock beard.

"This Jack guy's gonna get killed," he muttered to himself. He stood still and closed his eyes. He felt his heart beat a little slower, and he relaxed. He visualized having to go after Jorge and get to that young man, Jack, before Jorge did. He shook his head. But he saw it again and then realized he had no choice. He groaned and opened his eyes.

He happened to look up at a badly damaged car slowly rattling into the congested intersection. It occurred to him that the passenger must've really been hurt, because he was heavily bandaged from head to shoulders. Then he did a double take—one of those double takes you remember for the rest of your life. He saw it was Willie at the wheel, and it slowly dawned on him that the guy sitting in the passenger seat beside him was a woman, and it was Yvonne.

Leo's eyes widened, and he slapped both hands on the glass of the booth and yelled at them to stop. He grabbed the door and yanked, but it wouldn't open. He banged at the glass with his fists again and screamed, "Yvonne! Willie!"

Willie was focussing on the debris piled high in the middle of the intersection and tried to snake around it. He, too, did a double take when he saw a crazed man banging on the inside of a phone booth. He then squinted and focussed on Leo's face. "Ma, look!" he cried, pointing in Leo's direction. Yvonne looked over and saw Leo. She slapped a hand on her cracked but still beautiful lips and stifled a cry.

Leo Mangiano threw a kiss to heaven and thanked Santa Maria.

He knew fully that his bargain with Santa Maria had amazingly been accepted. And once again, through that wonderful silent inner voice, he knew exactly what to do next.

Chapter 20

ANITA SAT CROSS-LEGGED ON THE bedroom floor holding up her engagement ring to the light. She had several pieces of jewellery in a little pile beside her. She gathered them and put them into a Ziploc bag and zipped it shut. *This should bring in some money,* she thought. Her beautiful engagement ring (bought in Paris), her bracelet with each link embedded with a blue sapphire for a total of twenty-five sapphires (bought in New Orleans), a gold tennis chain necklace (bought in Spain), gold bangles (bought in Portugal), gold and diamond earrings (bought in Mexico)—all went into the bag. She sighed. Tomorrow she was going to a jeweller to get her jewellery appraised, and then she was going to sell the whole lot.

"Good riddance to you, Jack!" she shouted at the bag. She had stopped having her paycheck automatically deposited to the joint account and had it rerouted to a new account of her own. "How do you like them apples?" she asked Jack in the wedding picture. It was her first real step towards establishing a new life without him, and she felt great about it. She next had to deal with the threatened foreclosure on the house. "Oh well," she said to herself in a drawling Southern accent, "Tomorrow is anothah day!"

She stood up and skipped down the stairs. *Stefano, oh my God, Stefano,* she thought. *You, my dear, have given me an entirely new lease on life.* She started to hum a bit. Her heart felt light and cheerful in spite of the circumstances, and in her perhaps naive and innocent way, she decided that all things happen for a good reason. *Good riddance, my dear Jack,* she thought.

She went to the kitchen to start dinner: steamed rice with oyster sauce, tofu chunks, and miso soup. "Yum," she said to herself. As she opened the pantry cupboard, she happened to glance at a large bottle of olive oil that Andy had given her.

Andy ...

The human brain has a peculiar ability to justify almost anything under the sun, no matter how big the lie. In Anita's case, her brain simply took what she and Stefano had done as a blessing solely for her own comfort, and therefore it was okay. After all, she began to reason so easily, Andy was a terrible wife and mother, and she perhaps didn't deserve the respect she would otherwise have earned from Stefano.

And because as humans we are a peculiar breed, she decided she'd compensate for what she had done by becoming a far better friend to Andy than she ever would have been. As Sir Walter Scott once said, "Oh, what a tangled web we weave when first we practice to deceive." Especially when we deceive ourselves.

Anita decided she would do anything and everything to help poor Andy. After all, it was time to return all that Andy had done for her. With a light heart, she picked up the phone and dialled.

"Hello?" answered Maria.

"Hey, Maria. It's me, Anita!"

"Hi, Zia Anitaaaa!"

"What's new, babe?"

"Oh, nothing," Maria said, bored. "We got a new phone 'cause Mom broke the old one, and oh, Nonno almost died."

"Oh dear, I know—"

"'An' I saw him, and guess what? He looks like a zombie, like in that movie."

"Oh dear. You don't mean *Night of the Living Dead*, do you?"

"Yeah. Also, Mom had a fight with Peter, and she's crying. Oh, an' you know what else? Spring break starts tomorrow!"

"No kidding? Tell you what! I have the radio Jeep this week. How about you come with me and help me do some reporting tomorrow? Maybe give your Mom a break while she takes care of Nonno."

"Really? All right!" Maria yelled.

Anita could hear Andy stomping into the kitchen in the background. "All right what? Who's on the phone?"

"'Nita's gonna let me report the news!"

"Like heck she is," yelled Andy.

Maria whined, "Aw, Moooom!"

Andy grabbed the phone from Maria. "Give that to me," she demanded. "What?" she yelled into the phone.

"Andy? I'm so sorry about your dad. Stefano told me he was in the hospital."

"Oh he did, did he?"

"How is he? Is he going to be okay?"

"Who, Stefano or my dad?"

"No, your dad, stupid," quipped Anita.

"He's just gonna need twenty-four-hour 'round-the-clock care for a bit an' oxygen. That's all. Piece of cake! Can you imagine? Now I got four people to take care of. Somebody give me a gun!"

"I'll help you, Andy," offered Anita. "It'll be fine."

"Oh, ya think?"

"I'll take Maria out for a while, will that help?"

"You gotta drive around a lot?"

"Well, yeah, Andy. I have to promote or report on things, and it takes me all over the place. Have you never listened to our station?" Anita knew the answer but couldn't help jabbing her with it.

"Well, I'll think about it."

In the background, Maria was still whining. "Ah, Mom!"

"Anyway," Andy continued, "we're having to pick up some damn oxygen tanks and—as the good doctor says—'get acquainted' with the stuff. You know what? I couldn't understand a single word he said. What's wrong with these people who moved here? They don't even learn how to speak English properly."

"Andy, most people at the club can't speak English. This is not meant to be a criticism, you understand, but Stefano, your mom and dad ..."

"They're not goddamn doctors with lives in their hands. Think, for crying out loud, before you say anything."

"Oh, Andy, you're right. Sorry to get you so upset."

"Girl, you don't know what *upset* can be. Anyway, all this garbage is going to be a real pain. That's what you get for being an only kid!"

"Well, at least you have a lot of support from Stefano."

"'Nita, you just lay off of Stefano this and Stefano that, okay?"

"Yeah, but I was just saying ..."

"You leave Stefano out of this."

"Okay. Sorry again. Um, how's your mom doing?"

"She thinks that any moment she'll become a widow."

"Poor Claudia."

"Not 'poor Claudia.' Poor *me*."

"Okay, poor you."

"Yeah, poor me. So, what precisely are you doin' with my daughter?" Andy demanded.

"'Thought she'd get a kick out of helping me tomorrow. I'm zipping around in the station's Jeep and doing live promotions. It'd be a good experience for her. You know, radio and all."

"I don't care if it is a good experience or not. It's good for me, okay? Take her, please! That's one less thing for me to worry about—but only if you go easy on the speeding around. How long?"

"A few hours? I'll pick her up around ten in the morning?"

"Make it nine, and you get to keep her all day."

"Er, yeah, okay then, nine it is. Maybe after work I'll just drop her off at the hospital. You're going to be there around five thirty? I'd like to stay a bit for a little visit with Fabrizio. Is he up to it? Will you be there?"

"What do you expect? It's my new vocation. And no, better not tire him out, but thanks anyway. We'll say hi to him for you. See ya tomorrow at nine." Andy hung up on Anita as usual and was pleased that Anita would be taking Maria off her hands. *Geez, what was wrong with me? Why the jealousy?* she thought. She shook her head and marked it up to that time of life. "Wonderful," she said out loud.

Feeling elated in spite of her dad, Andy decided she would buy herself a new dress before visiting him. That always made her feel great, and she knew that Sharon had all the winter stuff on clearance, since all the summer stuff was already in. "Goody," she said.

Then suddenly, the thought of a new dress made her remember Sharon's fashion show. She picked up the phone and called Anita back.

"Whaaat?!" mimicked Anita.

"Very freakin' funny! Forgot to tell ya—Sharon's fashion show."

"What fashion show?" Anita asked.

"This is a favour I'm calling in, 'Nita, okay?"

"Another one?"

"Very sassy! You know Sharon?"

"Of course I know Sharon."

"One of her ladies reneged out of helping her with her fashion show." Andy started tapping her toe against the bottom of the fridge.

Looking down, she decided her slippers were frumpy. Hey, new slippers too.

"Helping in what way? Makeup? Dressing?"

"No. She twisted elbows for that already. She needs models, you idiot. And I don't want no guff from you either, 'Nita!"

"Why don't you model?"

"With this schnozz? I don't think so. It's too good for that rabble. Anyway, who do you think is helping with dressing?"

"*Toi?*"

"*Moi.*" Andy lowered her voice. "Besides, if you do it, then Maria will want to do it. Sharon desperately needs kids."

"I don't wanna do it!" yelled Maria from her colouring books at the kitchen table.

"What are you? A mind reader?"

"Why don't you model as mother and daughter?" Anita was getting used to this.

Andy ignored her comment. "Ma's in it too, by the way. They're doin' this cultural crap, and Ma and her friends are wearing the traditional costumes of their provinces back home. Ma does Calabria, and they have Benevento, Asti, Avellino, Latina, Rome of course, Ravenna … It's Carnevale, the biggest fundraiser for the club of the year other than the Italia Unita Annual Festival."

"All right, whatever you say. I should cover that for the station anyway."

"Yes!" Andy cheered.

"When is it?"

"Three weeks Saturday."

Maria yelled from the table. "Yes *what*? Mom, *yes what*?

"Anita said you can go on the radio all this week if you model Sharon's clothes with her."

Maria sat and stared at her mother for two seconds, and then she jumped and screamed, "Yeeeees!"

Anita yelled into the phone, "No! Just tomorrow! Andy!" But Andy had hung up on her once again.

Chapter 21

A NITA BARRELLED UP ANDY'S DRIVEWAY in the radio station's fun but gaudy Jeep with its radio blaring. The Jeep was bright and small, with the station's call letters, CHJX-AM, splashed across both sides in lime green and purple. She had about an hour before her once-every-half-hour promotional spots started for the day.

She parked where Stefano always parked his truck, turned off the radio and stepped out of the Jeep. She could smell the fresh, brisk air of an early spring and paused to listen to the chirpings of birds clustered around the numerous bird feeders that dotted the property. A festive feeling wafted over her and made her feel so, well, wonderful! It was a mystery to her how life could be so miserable yet still feel so good. The word *mania* came to mind.

She jumped when Maria suddenly popped out of the open garage and grabbed her by the sleeves. She was ready to go, in her pink coat and mauve boots and a rainbow-coloured knitted hat. Maria's thick, dark hair bounced up and down as she hopped and skipped in a circle around Anita.

"I see you're not eager and keen!" joked Anita.

"I'll be on the air, I'll be on the air ..." sang Maria.

Anita held up a finger. "Maybe—if you're good and you only say what I tell you to say, okay?"

Maria nodded eagerly. She continued skipping and singing as she followed Anita back through the garage and into the house.

"Andy?" Anita called, knocking on the walls as she made her way to the kitchen. "Yoo-hoo!"

"What!" yelled Andy from the stove.

"Oh, you're there," said Anita as she made her way to the kitchen.

"Where'd you think I'd be? Florida?"

Maria grabbed and hung onto Anita's arm. "Mooom?"

"Now what? I thought you were gone." Andy leaned against the counter and made a face at Maria. "Let go of Anita's coat."

"Anita's a nice person, right Mom?"

Anita looked down at Maria and blinked twice.

Andy looked at Anita with a sparkle in her eye. "Ya think?"

Maria stomped her foot. "Yes!"

"Yeah, so?"

"So she could be a saint, right?"

Andy made a face at her. "Mariaaaa. Don't waste our time."

"At school we were taught that Mary, Mother of God, was very, very good and that we have to *strive* to be like her."

Andy hunched even further over the counter. "Strive? Is that the shit they teach you these days?"

Maria nodded.

"What a waste of time and money," she said as she flicked a crumb off the counter.

"So," Maria continued. "Why aren't you a mother like Mary?"

"Excuse me?" Andy yelled.

"Well, you're the one who sends me to that school, and you always tell me to listen to the teacher!" said Maria.

"Yeah, an' it was a big mistake! I shoulda sent you to Alaska."

Maria ignored her. "The sisters teach us to be gentle and kind. To be loving like Mary, Mother of God." Maria fidgeted with a button on her coat.

"Don't you ever stand still?"

"And Mary Mother of God never yelled at Joseph, right?" Maria asked, now fidgeting with a lock of her own hair.

"They told you that?"

Maria nodded.

"Well, they *lied!*" announced Andy. "Even Mary had to ride on Joseph's ass sometimes!" she laughed.

Maria snapped to attention and stared at her mother as she digested that bit of information.

Anita guffawed, which caused a coughing fit. Andy held out a packed brown paper-bag lunch and waved them away.

"Here, snacks and a lunch—for both of you! And stop coughing all over my kitchen."

"Gee, thanks, 'Mom.' You didn't have to do that," Anita said between coughs.

"I know. I'm freakin' Mary, Mother of God. Didn't you know? Go! An' try not to come back."

"See you at the hospital then," Anita managed to say as she led Maria out of the house.

Maria ran and jumped into the Jeep and buckled herself in. Then she flipped through clipboards, papers, press releases and schedules and poked at the car phone and the radio.

"I'm gonna be on radio, I'm gonna be on radio!" she sang. She held up the bag of jewellery Anita had put together earlier and asked, "What's this? Treasure?"

Anita snatched it out of her hand and tucked it into the pocket of her jacket. "Yes, and it's mine. All mine!" Anita started the Jeep and backed out.

"I found buried treeaasure, I found buried treeaasure." A couple of blocks away, Maria was still singing when Anita stopped in front of a jewellery store.

"You stay here, Maria, okay? I'll be right back."

Maria watched as Anita got out and disappeared into the store. As she waited, Maria pressed her nose and mouth against the passenger-side window and then leaned back to admire the smudges. She wiped them away with her sleeve and then pressed her mouth against the glass to make rude farting sounds. Then she played with the clock on the dash and accidentally set it back twenty minutes. This was going to be a fabulous day!

Claudia had been waiting fretfully at the kitchen table for over an hour. She looked at the clock over the stove for the tenth time and called out, "Adriana, is-a *ore due*! Two-a o'clock!"

From deep down in the basement kitchen in the bowels of the basement, Andy's voice was barely heard. "I know it's frigging two o'clock!"

Claudia shook her head. "Alwa' dese words." She clutched her purse a little tighter. She was getting overheated in her coat, hat and gloves. "Adriana!" she bleeted in her shrill voice. "Such language," she again mumbled to herself.

From far away, she heard, "Afternoon visiting doesn't freakin' start until two thirty, and we're five minutes away!"

Claudia looked again at the clock and then at her watch. "*Ore due. She-a late. Ore due.*" She shook her head and then looked down at her feet. "I go put my *scarpa* on-a now!" she announced.

"Wear your boots!"

"No, not-a da boots, shoes—*scarpa*," Claudia yelled as she got up and made her way through the family room and out into the hall where her shoes were neatly tucked away with the rest of the family's. She bent down to pick hers up and tried to put one on while standing on one leg. It was arduous work for her. She had too many layers of clothing on, and bending over was so uncomfortable she couldn't breathe. She straightened up for a moment to catch her breath. Then she put her purse down and tried again. She almost got the one shoe on when she lost her balance. She hopped a step or two before she toppled over and landed on her hip in the pile of shoes. There was a big *crack*, and the fall knocked the breath out of her. She tried to call Andy but nothing but a squeak came out. When she finally found air, she let out an ear-shattering scream.

Andy crashed and banged her way up the basement stairs wide-eyed, still clutching some laundry. Claudia lay splayed out on the pile of shoes.

"*Ma!*" Andy stumbled over the shoes and bent over her mother. She automatically reached out to help her up, but Claudia screamed again. "Ma, stop, my ears! Hold still!" Andy checked Claudia's head, shins, hands and arms. "What happened? Where are you hurt?" She touched her mother's hip, and Claudia screamed so hard that she fainted.

"Holy shit!" Andy yelled. She ran off to call 911 for the second time in three days.

Andy sat rocking and swaying beside her suffering mother, who was lying on a stretcher in a speeding ambulance. Claudia was now fretting about Fabrizio.

"Oh, ooooh! Adriana, you no tell you daddy that I-a fall-a. He no need-a know. Aaahh, ooooh!"

"Oh, yeah, right, Ma. We'll keep it a secret all right!" Andy had to yell over the noise of the sirens for her mother to hear.

"*Si,* no tell you daddy." Claudia winced and moaned again as she grasped whatever she could find around her. The siren and speed of the vehicle was frightening her to distraction.

"Sure, Dad will never guess," Andy yelled. "Even though you may be in a cast from head to toe, who'll notice? Just throw your coat over the cast and no one will be the wiser, huh, Mom?"

"Ooooohhh," Claudia cried.

Andy threw up her hands and then pointed at her mother as she spoke to the paramedic. "See what I have to live with? Have you ever heard such garbage?" The paramedic opened her mouth to speak but didn't know what to say, so she closed it again and said nothing.

"No tell you daddy," murmured Claudia.

Andy covered her face with her hands. "All right already!"

Back in the Jeep, Maria was chatting up a storm—but for the most part, Anita only half listened as she thought about the value of the jewellery she had left for appraisal. Then something Maria said caught her attention.

"… and I heard Zio Peter say that Zio Jack ate doo-doo sandwiches," Maria said, giggling.

"I'm sorry? What did you say?"

"Doo-doo sandwiches! Zio Jack said that life was a sh …. Can I say 'shit'? He said life was a shit sandwich." Maria giggled again. "That's what Zio Peter said anyway! And you know what? Is Daddy soft, Anita? Zio Peter said Daddy was. You know why he said that?"

"Well, no, but your daddy has a soft heart. Maybe that's what he meant."

Maria put her feet up on the dash of the Jeep and slipped deeper into the seat. "Or maybe because Daddy won't push you to talk. They said that all Zio Jack thinks about is money, money, money. I think of money too, but Mom won't give me any."

Anita interrupted. "When did you hear all this?"

Maria sat up straighter and opened the glove compartment for the tenth time. She took out the manual and some maps. "I heard it when Nonno and Daddy were in the *caverna*. It was um ..." She shook her head, "Let me think." She tapped a finger against her chin. Then she brightened up.

"Oh, yes, I remember! On little Stefano and Andrew's birthday day."

Anita, stunned, didn't know how to digest what Maria had just told her, but she had to put it aside for later, as they had arrived at their first radio spot for the day. Anita pulled into a parking lot at a new discount warehouse mall that was in the final throes of construction. She had to gather information on its grand opening scheduled for three weekends later and was to build up an awareness of upcoming events during the next three weeks with five thirty-second live spots a day. She was also scheduled to do a live promotion all day that Saturday and half the day Sunday, helping with handing out door prizes. However, for now, the only people she saw were construction workers who looked like they were doing final touches on the front entrance.

"Okay, Maria. This is our first stop." She undid her seat belt and took the clipboard from Maria, who had been fingering and playing with the different tear sheets that were clipped on it.

"Can I come?" asked Maria.

"No, not quite yet," Anita said as she looked around for her pen. "What'd you do with my pen?" Maria held up the pen, and Anita tried to snap it away. Maria smiled as she held it closer to herself. Anita put on a strained smile. "It's very important that I keep that pen by me, okay?"

"I'll need it when I write my own reports. You just tell me what to write!"

"Um, no. This isn't how it's gonna work. Now give it to me, Maria."

Maria pouted and stuck the pen behind her ear. "I saw Dick Tracy put a pen behind his ear like this. Do I look like a reporter?" She took the pen away from her ear and stuck it in her mouth and dragged at it like a cigarette.

Anita sighed and held out her hand. "Now, Maria. Give me that pen." Maria took it out of her mouth, pretended to blow out smoke and then finally handed the pen back to Anita.

Anita wiped the pen on her sleeve and looked at Maria with a wary eye. "Okay, you wait here. I'll be right back."

"But you said …"

"I know, I know. I have to get all the facts about this place before we can do anything. Otherwise we have nothing to say, right? I won't be long." Anita stepped out of the Jeep and pushed the automatic lock on all doors before poking her head back into the car to face Maria. "Don't … touch … anything, okay?"

Maria panicked and shook her hands in the air. "Wait a minute! Wait a minute!"

"What?"

"Will you be long?"

Shaking her head, Anita turned, slammed the door shut and hurried to the mall's main doors. "Holy moley!" she muttered. Maria was definitely her mother's daughter.

Inside, she hurried passed a small group of workmen clearing away debris. They did the usual whistling and catcalls as she passed them and ignored it all until someone shouted, "Hey, Anita! You lady widda fock fur!" This of course brought out more crass catcalls. Anita stopped and looked. There they were, Stefano and Peter's cousins, Mario and Guido.

Anita hung her head and shook it.

She waved them away and continued walking, following signs pointing the way to the main office. She crossed a large, sun-drenched, exquisite marble court topped by a magnificent domed skylight with a mature, tall maple tree standing in the middle, its branches almost reaching the top of the glass dome. Around the base of the tree was a cement moat or circular pool about four feet deep, and along both sides of this "moat" was a wide, three-foot-tall marble containment wall. All along the length of the trough were water spouts about four feet apart. The cascading water created a sound similar to that of a large waterfall. Lights flickered throughout the trough, causing dancing light to reflect on the walls and floor around the central court. Off on the opposite side from where Anita was coming stretched a narrow hallway that led to the main mall offices.

Anita opened the glass office door and stepped inside. Carpets had just been laid, and office furniture sat partially unwrapped. The air smelled of glue and fresh paint, and there were technicians here and there wiring computers and phones. She was pleased to see that someone was listening to her radio station on a ghetto blaster. She checked her watch for the time and figured she had about fifteen minutes to get the info and write it up and then do the spot fifteen minutes after that. She knew she was cutting it close, but she'd done this before without any problem. Just ask the questions and write up a three-minute announcement.

She looked around and saw a man standing in the doorway of an inner office. Calling out to him, she said, "Excuse me. Sir?"

The man turned around. It took a moment for the two of them to recognize each other in such an unexpected setting.

"Anita! Small world!" The man seemed surprised to see her.

"Peter. Ha! What are you doing here?"

"I could ask the same." He pointed to her jacket with the radio station's call letters. "Though I see you're probably here professionally. What happened to the special-events guy?"

"He's on extended sick leave," she said, looking around.

"Covering our grand opening for us then?"

"Us?" asked Anita, confused.

"Yeah, well, I'm one of the owners!" Peter said, holding up a finger.

"No kidding?"

"Yeah. No kidding." Anita looked puzzled and still stood open-mouthed. "I can see that you don't believe me."

"No, it's not that. It's just, you know, maybe Jack could've mentioned it. And it's not like I haven't seen you often enough. You never mentioned it." She looked around. "It's kind of a big deal."

"Okay. We kind've kept it a secret. You know, didn't want to jinx it. Okay, so. I am one of the major investors in this mall, Stefano is the contractor but is doing it as another partner, so he's also investing in the mall."

Peter walked to an inner one-way glass window and swept his hand across what they were looking at. "Once we're finished and up and running—which will be very soon, as you know, in about three weeks—I will personally have three out of the twenty new stores, including a pizza kiosk in the food court, a more formal pizzeria and pasta house next to the front entrance and a florist. Not bad, huh?"

"Wow," she said slowly. "That takes a lot of capital."

"Er, yeah, I guess."

He impatiently motioned for her to follow him into the inner office and pointed at a chair, still in plastic wrap. Anita remained standing. Peter sat down and swivelled in his new chair. "So, everything's goin' like gangbusters."

"I see that," said Anita. "A lot of big bucks, though," she repeated.

Peter stood up, jiggled change in his pocket and curtly nodded once. He looked anxious, Anita thought. She suddenly felt awkward and looked down at her clipboard. A lot was racing through her mind. Then she remembered why she was there in the first place.

"Uh, well, I need to talk to someone for some info—you know, the who, what, why, where and how."

"Yes, of course! Take a seat," he offered again, and this time she sat down. He continued to smile as he sat and leaned back. She put her clipboard on the desk and poised her pen.

"Okay, let's start with confirming the name of the mall."

A knock at the door behind her interrupted their conversation. Anita turned and looked straight into Nancy's face.

"Nancy?" said Anita.

Nancy's eyes darted at Peter and then back at Anita. She smiled quite awkwardly.

"Oh, hi! Fancy meeting you here!"

At CHJX-AM, Roger sat back listening quietly to one of the year's greatest hits, Billy Joel's "The River of Dreams." He suddenly straightened up and looked at the wall clock. He picked up the phone and dialled the station's promo Jeep.

Maria heard the car phone ringing and found it under Anita's jacket. Like a pro, she answered it. "Hello?"

"Are you about ready for the first spot?" Roger asked, concentrating on his monitor and the log lineup.

"Oh *yes!*" said Maria.

"Whoa," he laughed. "You're sounding eager and keen. Happy to be back to work, are we?"

"Yep!"

Roger looked at his watch and then at the digital readout on the console. "Okay, ten seconds, so stand by. Don't go away."

"Oh, I won't!"

Roger put the phone down and waited a few more seconds for Billy Joel to wrap up.

In the Jeep, Maria turned on the radio and jiggled in rhythm to the remainder of Billy Joel's song.

Back at the station, Roger slowly turned down the volume on the music. "And that was Billy Joel and his 'River of Dreams'—crossiiiinnnng 'the river so deep.' Now, it's time for our nifty reporter, Anita Taylor, who is on the ground as we speak, digging up fabulously fun activities for today and for this weekend coming up. Anita, where's you at, chil'?"

In the Jeep, Maria bit her lip as she quickly thought about what to say. "Oh! I know!" she said, her voice echoing over the car radio. "Yeah, hi, this is Kermit the Frog."

She paused for a moment, thinking. At the station, Roger frowned into his mike.

Maria went on, "And, I'm reporting to you from the studio of our famous alphabet songwriter, Mr. Alphabet." She paused again, and then continued.

"But first, a message from our sponsor." She dropped her voice. "Do you feel sluggish? Big, fat and perhaps stinky? Buy today's new brand of baking soda. You will be glad you tried it. Now for our song of the day. 'A, B, C, D ...'"

Roger shot out of his chair, looked through the plate glass separating the studio from the press room and then jumped on his intercom. "Mike, are you there?"

In the mall offices, Anita cocked her head at Nancy, who in turn looked back puzzled. In the background, she could hear ear-wrenching singing on the radio.

"Ha, sounds like Maria," Anita said.

"Pardon?" Nancy asked, looking confused.

"Oh, nothing."

Nancy struggled for something to say. "Er, hear from Jack yet?" She looked at Anita in what she was hoping to be sincerity and concern.

"No, not yet. But I'm still hoping for the best!" she said before she was cut short by people giggling. A young woman came up to the office door.

"Wanna hear somethin' cute?" She pointed to the radio. "A kid is singing the A, B, Cs on the radio. Some gimmick to get our attention, I bet." Peter, Nancy and Anita stopped to hear the tiny, scratchy voice that sounded oh so terribly familiar.

"Cute," Anita mumbled. "Sounds just like Maria."

Nancy and Peter looked at each other, confused. "Maria?" asked Peter.

***

Mike leaned into the speakerphone. "Yeah, Roger. What's up?" he asked as he continued to look through paperwork.

"Turn the speaker on, Mike," said Roger over the intercom.

Mike reached up and flipped a switch on a wall speaker and heard Maria singing, "L, M, N, O, P."

At first he simply listened, but slowly his face went white. He leaned closer to the intercom. "This is a joke, right? Very funny, Roger."

"Uh, no, it's not a joke, I'm afraid."

"W, X, Y an' Z."

Mike frowned and bent even closer to the intercom. "But it's not even Anita's voice! It's got to be a joke."

Roger nodded his head violently and then smacked his forehead with his palm.

Mike continued to listen.

"Won't you sing along with me. Very good! And now, for some Culture Club!" Maria started singing, "Do you really want to hurt me? Do you really want to make me cry? Precious kisses …"

***

At the mall, Nancy looked at Peter, who shrugged at her and looked back at Anita. But then something struck Peter, and he sat up straight.

"Holy shit! *Is* that Maria singing? Can there possibly be someone else cursed with that ... voice."

Suddenly there was an ear-splitting scream.

Everyone looked at Anita, who in turn wondered why they were staring at her, until she realized it was she who had screamed.

⚜

In a hallway at St. Joseph's Hospital, a strange little girl's voice echoed from the radio at the nurses' station. Andy, standing nearby, leaned wearily against the door of her father's ward room as she watched her father sleep fitfully. Her mother was still in ICU on the bottom floor, under observation. She had been given a mild sedative and was fine enough for Andy to feel she could nip upstairs to check on her dad.

As she stood there in remorse and worry, she was startled at how frail her father looked.

"Words that burn me, lovers never ask you why, in my heart the fires burning ..." continued the shrieking voice from the radio.

"Turn that screeching off!" yelled a nurse.

"No," another said. "Leave it on. It's cute! What radio station is that?"

"Same one," said the first. "CHJX-AM."

"Huh," said the other as she worked at her charts.

⚜

Back in the Jeep, Maria finished her song and was wrapping it up. "And that's it for now. Stay tuned for our next special announcement. This is Hot Lips Maria saying, 'I'll be back'"

Roger was stunned. He was still staring at the console, and there was a full three seconds of deadly silence before he jumped back to life with a shock. "Er, thank you, er, Hot ... uh, Maria!"

He fumbled through his playlist and queued up a song, any song, as he mumbled, "Jesus wept."

Maria hung up and simply beamed with pleasure at her own cleverness. As if searching for applause, she looked around the large parking lot with pride. Suddenly, she stopped and did a double take. Maria's eyes widened, and she excitedly unlocked the passenger door and jumped out, her elbow accidentally sliding over the automatic lock on the door and locking it behind her. Maria yelled at someone, "Hey! Guess what!" and she ran away from the car.

She did not hear the car phone ring before she slammed the door shut.

Anita shot out of the front mall entrance and raced to the Jeep. She grabbed the passenger door and yanked, but it was locked. All the doors were. And Maria wasn't there. She pressed her face against the windshield and groaned when she saw the keys hanging in the ignition. The car phone was ringing. She tried the other doors again, but in vain. She angrily slammed her hands on the roof of the car. "Shit! Shit! Shit!" She looked around frantically. Save for construction equipment at a trailer and the back end of a truck just driving out of sight, there was absolutely no sign of Maria.

"Maria! Mariiiiiaaa! Oh no!"

Peter, Nancy, Guido and Mario crashed through the front doors of the mall. Anita looked over, yelling, "She's not here! And I can't get in. I don't know what happened to her!" Peter caught up to her and grabbed her by her forearms as his cousins looked into the Jeep and walked around it.

"What happened?" asked Peter.

Anita was distraught. Tears were running down her mascara-smudged cheeks, and she was trembling with fear.

"Omigod! My job! Andy's going to kill me! Maria!"

"You had Maria!?" Peter asked. "Where is she!?"

"I don't know. But I saw the back end of a truck before it disappeared around the corner! We have to find her! Andy's going to kill me!"

Peter looked around and tried to think of what to do.

"You say you saw the back end of a truck go out of here?"

Anita nodded and stared around with fear. Nancy looked around helplessly.

Peter turned to his cousins. "Mario and Guido, go look for Maria throughout the mall. Nancy, go check all the washrooms."

Anita called after Guido and Mario. "Wait! Can you break into this car? Quick!"

The cousins looked at each other and nodded. Peter turned to Anita.

"They'll need to get some tools. Guido, you look for Maria. Mario, you get some tools, *in fretta*! Quickly!" Then he turned to Anita. "I'm going to get my car. It's out back. And I'll drive around the neighbourhood. The guys'll get you back in the car. As soon as they do, you also drive around. See if you can find the truck you saw. What colour was it?"

"It was big, red and dirty, that's all I saw, but I couldn't see who was in it!"

Anita looked at her watch and groaned. She was due for another report on air in less than an hour. And she knew pretty well who was trying to reach her on the car phone. She watched Peter run back to the mall, and then she looked around again. Nothing! She gazed at the convertible top of the Jeep and seriously considered just tearing through the rooftop. The wind had picked up, and it was getting bitterly cold.

"Maria! Maria!" She couldn't remember if Maria had any gloves with her.

She looked over just as Mario scampered over with a wire and immediately set to work on the driver's side. While Anita was still frantically looking around, she saw Peter's black BMW squeal from the back of the mall and race out the next exit. In the meantime, Mario had the wire between the window and the body of the door and was fiddling around with it. The phone was still ringing. Finally, with a click, the door unlocked. Anita threw the door open and grabbed the phone just as it stopped ringing. She then plopped into the driver's seat and turned on the ignition. Hoping Nancy would find Maria in a washroom, Anita raced away.

She was going to find that truck. Just in case.

Chapter 22

ANDY STARED OUT THE WINDOW as she sat by her father's bed. The day had become overcast, and the first few drops of sleet and rain slapped against the window. She went over and sat down in one of those uncomfortable chairs that reminded her of Catholic school. She couldn't help but remember the day she first met Stefano in her parents' kitchen after school.

Exactly one year later, they were married.

1963

Claudia and Fabrizio threw Andy the biggest wedding the club had seen since it first opened the doors back in 1954. After all, they only had one daughter, and nothing but the very best was good enough for their Andy and their future son-in-law. The vows were said at Our Holy Mary Mother of God Catholic Church on Father Constanza Street not far from Andy's school.

Claudia designed the bridesmaids' dresses as well as Andy's wedding gown. Everyone said Claudia had an eye for design, and they couldn't wait to see what she had up her sleeve. Unfortunately, because the dresses were so big, only two or three bridesmaids could fit into one limo at a time, so instead of just two limos, they had to rent six.

But nothing was too much for Andy's wedding.

For the bridesmaids, Claudia chose tight bodices with layers of crinoline under the skirts, which were made from gossamer peach taffeta with a layer of peach netting over all. She chose peaches-and-cream sequins and tiny pearls, all hand-sewn and embroidered, which sparkled from every seam and edging. Light flickered like light through crystals on walls and ceilings with every move they made. Claudia had chosen silver silk stockings with delicate silver patent leather pumps—handmade, of course, in Italy. Each bridesmaid wore white gloves and carried a bouquet of peach-coloured rosebuds and a delicate spray of white baby's breath. Lucinda, Claudia's hairdresser, had sprinkled sparkles over their well-teased backcombed black beehives, thus single-handedly creating a new fad in hairstyling that had yet to fade away by the eighties.

For the men, Claudia chose baby blue tuxedoes with dark blue satin cummerbunds and dark blue satin edging along the lapels and down the outside seam of the legs. Beneath their jackets, they wore light blue ruffled shirts buttoned up not with buttons but with tiny gold and onyx baubles. Claudia was thrilled with how the blue matched Stefano's brilliant aqua-blue eyes framed by long black eyelashes.

The matron of honour was Sofia, Claudia's good friend and co-worker at the shirt factory. She wore exactly the same dress and hairstyle as the bridesmaids but considerably larger, as she weighed three hundred pounds and counting. Claudia had chosen the bridal party with a particular agenda in mind. No one was to be better looking than Andy.

No photos were to be taken of Andy's profile, as head-on there was no hint of a beak. Andy didn't want photos taken at all, but she finally compromised, after weeks of debate with Claudia and Fabrizio, by hiring a sickly looking waif with an unusually long red beard and a brown ponytail. Andy instructed him, "No boob shots, no ass shots and no nose shots, ya hear me? Straight on shots only." But Claudia hired an Italian photographer anyway who took profile shots regardless.

"Ma," Andy had yelled from where they posed together for a group shot outside in the chilly park next to the club, "If you use any of this WASP's shots, I'll kill you!"

Though her face was problematic for photographers, there was no such problem with Andy's figure. To accentuate her perfect curves and legs, she wore white with an abundance of peach pearls sewn into the dress and covering the entire bodice, which sported a mandarin collar with sleeves that stretched elegantly and ended in a point above her well-manicured fingers. From the collar, a teardrop opening showed just a tiny bit of cleavage. As the pearls descended, they eventually lessened in number until there were only hints of them along the hem. Andy was to wear a fifteen-foot train that would be carried and checked by the bridesmaids.

Andy was also given a teased, backcombed beehive hairstyle, but it didn't last. As soon as she left Sofia's shop, she took out all the hairpins and brushed out the sparkles and sticky hairspray. She called all that crass and pretentious.

In the church, peach-coloured flower arrangements hung at the end of every pew and in every corner of the church. In front of the altar were massive sprays of white roses, sweet pea and white carnations tied together with ivy.

For added effect, Claudia arranged for the 4-year-old granddaughter of another co-worker and friend to carry a silver-sprayed basket with white rose petals to spread around before the bride. She, too, wore peach taffeta and netting and had sparkles and white rosebuds in her hair. Claudia had also chosen a young ring bearer, the grandson of another good friend, who was dressed as a miniature version of the groom. He carried a wine-coloured velvet cushion trimmed in silver braid and tassels upon which were his-and-her wedding bands.

Once at the altar, the ring bearer stuck out his tongue at the flower girl who commenced to bawl ...

and then dump the basket before throwing it at him. The boy's mother grabbed him from the side and dragged him out of the church screaming.

Back at the house, Claudia and Fabrizio had cried when Andy stepped into their small cozy living room looking like a queen. She was surrounded by dancing light and looked like a princess out of a fairy tale. Their friends and colleagues were going to be so amazed by how beautiful Andy really was. But it didn't magically change Andy at all. In the limo on the way to the church, Claudia had to gently lean over to Andy and suggest that perhaps chewing gum wasn't appropriate. Andy took the gum out and stuck it in the small ashtray on the door. "Don' forget to smile-a," Claudia had reminded her. Andy had rolled her eyes in response.

At the church, the sun's rays poured through the stained glass windows and drenched family and friends in a cacophony of colour. Telemann blared as Andy and Fabrizio waited at the back of the church while Claudia, before being escorted down the aisle to the first pew, leaned over and whispered to Fabrizio, "We are-a being blessed, Fabrizio."

Fabrizio looked at Claudia and then at Andy. He was startled to see a blue and fire-red aura around their daughter's head. Fabrizio's bottom lip quivered as he fought back tears he hadn't shed since childhood. He gladly took the beautiful aura as a sign from God, and his heart swelled with joy.

As Fabrizio finally escorted Andy down the aisle, her long sparkling train trailed behind them, inching its way along the plush red carpet with every halting step they took. Andy's eyes clamped onto Stefano at the altar, where he stood patiently waiting at the head of the line of ushers. Her heart flipped at the sight of him, and all she remembered of the service afterwards were his brilliant aqua eyes showering her with adoration and how he looked at her as he lifted up her veil to kiss her. "Adonis" came to mind. Once again, she wondered at how such a beautiful man could even exist. And he wanted her!

They stood at the receiving line outside the church doors and greeted all the guests. Andy thought it would go on forever. The photo session by both photographers (hers left early and was later found soused under a table at the banquet hall) was agony. She detested having her photo taken endlessly and only smiled while looking at Stefano. As a result, almost all of the photos showed her profile.

Finally, at the reception, hundreds of guests crowded into the large hall of the Italian Canadian Club. The meal was even more extravagant than the wedding itself. Four hundred people were invited, and four hundred and thirteen showed up. Although Claudia and Fabrizio had been making their own wine all year in preparation, they still had to buy a large variety of other wines and champagne to ensure that good will continued to flow generously throughout the evening. The meal was magnificent—prepared, naturally, by Italian widows who volunteered to cook in their homes and in the club's kitchens.

The feast began with an antipasto of olives, stuffed mushrooms, cheeses, salami, mortadella, calamari and prosciutto. A dinner of pasta followed, and then chicken, veal, soup and vegetables all served by hired wait staff dressed in crisp white jackets and black bow ties. Twists of fried dough with powdered sugar and Italian wedding candy were generously spread on every table across fine white pressed linen tablecloths. The guests were given little net bags of mints and anisette-covered pecans along with white and silver-edged matchbooks with Andy and Stefano's names and the date of the wedding embossed on the front.

An accordion player played traditional Italian songs throughout the two-hour meal but had to stop constantly at the clinking of spoons on crystal glasses. Calls for *"bacio! bacio!"* were never-ending (mostly started by Claudia), and each time, Stefano and Andy would push their chairs back to stand face to face and, to whistles and cheers of *"evviva gli sposi!"* carefully gave each other a kiss without stumbling over each other's noses. At one point, Andy lost her patience and complained to Stefano under her breath, "More of this and I'll mash my pasta into someone's friggin' face!" Naturally, Stefano only generally understood and surmised she was tiring of standing up and sitting down. He gently patted her hand, and Andy looked over to see Stefano smiling lovingly at her. The next time they were bidden to kiss, she had relaxed, and she savoured being held by him. As his breath gently warmed up her mouth, she felt physically overwhelmed and started to clasp him tightly, only to suddenly jump back and shout "Holy crap!" The music and laughter stopped, and everyone looked over at Andy.

Unbeknownst to all, Stefano had hidden a piece of iron in his pants pocket. It was an old Italian custom for a groom to ward off the evil eye and to help keep away the envy and jealousy that might destroy his happiness. Andy jumped further back when Stefano dipped his hand into his pocket and took out the piece of iron. He held it up with a bashful grin, and all the older men laughed and chuckled knowingly. Even Andy couldn't help but laugh.

All the old and not-so-old men joked about Stefano's big nose, *wink, wink, nudge, nudge*, and perhaps it's double the pleasure with a wife with a nose like that, *wink, wink, nudge, nudge*, and gee, looking at her from the front, she actually didn't look half so bad. And look at those *mammellas!*

During the cheese course, Stefano and Andy formed a cookie dance line to lead the guests around and across the dance floor over to the buffet of desserts and Italian cookies. Everyone in the train grabbed a cookie as they danced past. There were cannoli, cakes, pastries, nuts, and fresh and dried fruits. Sweet liqueurs were served at the table, as well as espresso, cappuccino and dessert wines. An eight-piece band played big-band music interlaced with waltzes and traditional Italian tunes. Andy's bridesmaids were hoping to do the new twist and swim dances, but no such luck. Her parents had chosen the music carefully, making sure that it suited the over-45 crowd—which happened to be most of the guests.

Claudia and Fabrizio wiped their tears and blew their noses as they watched the bride and groom dance in the centre of the dance floor. When, during the dance, Andy tore off her high heels and threw them at the head table, they almost died of embarrassment—until they realized everyone else thought it was hilarious. Then they, too, laughed with glee.

Andy and Stefano were given a red glass vase to smash to the floor. The number of broken pieces represented the anticipated number of years a couple would be happily married. The guests craned their necks to note all the pieces as Stefano bent down to count them. A slight hush fell on the crowd. Unbelievably, the vase had broken into five large pieces. Impossible! But there it was, clear as day. Claudia's heart sank momentarily. Oh, but these customs were silly after all. Everyone shook off the momentary lapse in happiness.

Everyone, that is, but Andy. She couldn't shake it off. She, of all people, knew that the custom was silly and meant nothing. But her mind couldn't help but remember their earlier discussion of a honeymoon. She had wanted to go to colourful, sun-drenched Miami and linger on warm sandy beaches wearing one of the new fashions—the bikini—or maybe fly to exciting Las Vegas to listen to Frank Sinatra and Dean Martin. But Stefano had insisted on taking her to meet the rest of his relatives in Calabria. She was appalled. And though real arguing was as yet almost impossible because of the language problem, she and Stefano had come to words, all translated by poor Fabrizio and Claudia.

Stefano had made it clear, and Fabrizio and Claudia had meekly agreed, that the man in a true Italian marriage made the decisions. So, Calabria it was. "No, Calabria it ain't!" Andy had screamed, and the topic was never raised again without heated words.

It would get worse. Stefano's aging widowed mother was flown over for the wedding and was to stay for two months. Unfortunately, ten days was more than enough time for her to acquire a strong distaste for her new daughter-in-law, and she hurried on home, claiming that if Stefano wanted to see his mother, he should come to Calabria on his own. This truly hurt Stefano.

All that, however, was yet to happen on their wedding day. Stefano's heartbreak was light years away, and he basked in the warm glow of his intense happiness at the wedding.

In a hungry search for something to make up for the dismal honeymoon disappointment, Andy spent hours upon hours daydreaming about the gifts they would receive and how much cash they would raise. Throughout the wedding feast, she snuck looks at the mounting pile of beautifully wrapped gifts and the large decorated basket overflowing with envelopes of money. She wasn't the only one craning her neck. Guests, too, wanted to see if they had been outdone by another in the size of their gift or the thickness of their envelope.

In the end, Stefano and Andy were deluged with espresso machines; silver-plate fruit bowls; baskets of Parmigiano, smoked Provolone and peppery-tasting Rustico; delicate hand-painted wine glasses from Venice; gold and silver serving bowls and platters from Rome; Tuscan tapestries; a rather large marble musical statue of Michelangelo's *Pieta* from Calabria; a washer and a newfangled dryer; a marble-topped coffee table; five blenders; two spaghetti-making machines; one biscotti gun and maker; five sets of delicate tablecloths and napkins for twelve settings; green satin bedsheets and matching pillowcases; a large replica of da Vinci's *Last Supper* done in alabaster; wine decanters; a corker; and a large wine press and a smaller fruit press. They "made" enough money for Stefano to build their home on the fifty acres of land he had already saved for and bought.

Andy had wanted to use some of the cash for things she wanted, but Stefano said no and stuck to it. In the end, Andy only liked the wine glasses, and she swore she didn't plan to be stuck in a kitchen blending stupid cake mixes or slaving in front of a washer and dryer. Not on your life, mister.

To pay for the wedding, Fabrizio and Claudia had to remortgage their debt-free home to the hilt, and even though it took until Maria's tenth birthday in 1980 to pay off the debt in full, they still felt it was worth every penny. They would do so again if they had to. But they did occasionally wish the investment had yielded more grandchildren. Unfortunately, Claudia brought that up on every single birthday and at Christmas time.

And the memory of the sad and tragic loss of a fine young president in Dallas, Texas, naturally upstaged their anniversary every time.

ANDY SHOOK HER HEAD HARD to rid herself of memories—silly memories, sad memories, unfortunate memories, memories of grief and loss. She straightened up, wiped her tears away and looked at her sleeping father one more time before turning away to walk over to the nurse's station.

"You wanna give it another try, Andy? Tell Stefano about Claudia?"

The nurses all knew her by her first name as she did them; they had all grown up together. Curiously, only the doctors were from out of town, and they were unfortunately not adequately armed against the likes of Andy Giordani. The nurses explained that patient and long exposure over time was all the good doctors needed to be able to take her finally with just a grain of the proverbial salt.

Andy reached out wordlessly as the nurse handed her the phone. "Thanks," she said as she dialled Stefano at work. She was still in a fog of memories, but as the phone kept ringing at the other end, it burned off under the heat of her mounting and customary impatience. The phone just kept on ringing.

As Andy stood there, a few of the nurses were discussing what they had just heard on the radio.

"Well, I think it's cute," said one. "It might be a gimmick, as you say, but it worked. I, for one, never took notice of which station this was until now."

"Yeah, CHJX-AM! This is the first I even noticed, and we've had this station on for years—every single day I've worked here."

Another said, "That little girl sure was cute. What an awful voice she had, but how can you not love it?"

Andy wasn't listening. It was just white noise in the background. "Goddamn it, Stefano. Answer the damn phone," she demanded quietly. She slammed the phone down loudly for the third time that day, and it made two nurses jump and grab at their chests for the third time. One of them glanced over at her with a look that could kill.

"You'd think that Stefano would have an answering machine by now! I hate answering machines but it's a business, for crying out loud!" Andy complained to the nurse by the phone.

The nurse, whose name was Jeanine, nodded her head lamely and shrugged. "Even the smartest of people still cannot fathom having to live with today's technology, Andy. Some still think it's terribly impolite to force an answering machine on people. I can't handle it myself. I guess I'm just showing my age."

"Showing your age?" snapped Andy. "If my memory serves me right, you were two grades behind me. If you're showing your age, then what am I supposed to be showing? Petrified rock?" She laughed bitterly. "Besides which, you can't run a business these days without either having a living being answer that damn phone or breakin' down and gettin' one of those freakin' things. People should get with the times. It's the eighties, for crying out loud," Andy murmured as she straightened out her dress. "Shit," she added for good measure.

As she walked away, the phone rang. The nurse answered it and then looked up.

"Andy, it's for you!"

Andy hurried back. "Stefano?" she asked. The nurse shrugged as Andy took it.

"What!?"

"Andy? It's Anita."

Andy frowned. "Okay. What's the matter? What happened?" The nurse looked up, concerned, but Andy shook her head and walked over to a chair to plop into. "Tell me. What?" she yelled into the phone.

"Now don't get upset. Have you by any chance heard from Maria?"

Andy shot off the chair. "*What happened to Maria?*"

"Andy, she's fine, honest. Um, we're just not sure where she is at the moment, that's all. I mean, she can't go very far," Anita explained quickly. "I mean, she was in the Jeep—"

"Where's the Jeep?"

"I'm in the Jeep. But she was on her own while I—"

"She *was?*" yelled Andy. She grabbed her bangs and yanked them.

"She did my first on-air report, Andy, and—"

"*She did an on-air report?*"

Jeanine looked up and then at her fellow worker. "That must've been Andy's little girl!" she said.

The other cocked her head. "You think? We should ask Andy."

The third nodded as she bent over a clipboard. "Little Maria," she murmured. Her eyes rose to meet Jeanine's. Jeanine straightened up.

"Oh, yes," she whispered. "That child was our first and only ..."

The others turned to look at her.

"Well, you know. She was a very, very special child."

"Oh?" said the other as they huddled closer together to whisper.

Anita hurried on. "Peter's out looking for her as we speak. I'm on the road at the moment and—"

Suddenly Anita stopped talking. /"And?! And what?" cried Andy.

"Wait a minute. I think I found her!" And Anita hung up.

"*Wha—?*" And Andy had an apoplectic fit.

Anita hung up the phone and made a U-turn. She spotted the back of the same truck she had seen briefly earlier and bumped over the curb into the parking lot of a Tim Hortons. She jumped out of the Jeep and first looked into the truck before running towards the front door of the doughnut shop. Through the window, she saw two familiar faces.

"*Anitaaaaa!*" called Maria. She started jumping and squirming in her chair and held up a half-eaten doughnut. "Did you hear me? I done good!"

She calmed down somewhat. Anita stopped and took a deep breath. Everyone there tried not to look at her. She calmed down somewhat, made her way towards them and sat down. Stefano followed her every move and blinked at her.

"You-a no know she-a with me?"

"No, I did not," she said stiffly.

Stefano looked at her pale face and then menacingly at Maria. Maria wilted and fidgeted under his gaze.

"You-a tell me-a Anita know," said Stefano.

Maria shyly shrugged her thin shoulders and then traced her finger through spilled icing sugar on the sticky top of the table. Stefano shook his head and pointed a finger at her, and then motioned slicing his throat. Maria starting swinging her legs while slowly chewing on her doughnut.

"Andy's all upset. Maybe you could call her, Stefano, and explain?"

Stefano squinted his eyes at Maria and nodded silently.

Suddenly, Anita thought to look at her watch. "Holy shit! I missed it *again!*" She slapped her forehead and hurried out.

Chapter 23

LATE THAT AFTERNOON, ANITA STOOD at the elevator door waiting to go up to her office. Music from the radio station was piped into the lobby, and to the tune of Olivia Newton-John's hit "Physical," the elevator doors scraped open and she stepped in. Her stomach ached; she knew she was in deep trouble.

She sighed deeply as she stepped out at the second floor and took a deep breath before opening the glass doors and stepping into the small lobby of the radio station. Quietly she scooted over to the press release office and got busy sorting out the releases that had come in that day while she was out. As she bent over the releases with pen in hand, Mike walked in and cleared his throat loudly.

Anita dropped the pen and slowly turned around. She raised her eyes to Mike's face and groaned inwardly. Mike did not look happy.

"'Nita, what happened today?"

"Mike, I'm so sorry. It got out of hand."

"You're not kidding. I repeat, what happened?"

"It's all my fault."

"I surmised that but hoped it wasn't."

"I made a silly promise to take my friend's daughter with me while my friend visited her father in hospital."

"This is Andy we're talking about?"

Anita nodded. "Yes," she said quietly. "She's delightful but a bit of a handful."

"Maria," he offered.

"Yes. I wanted to give a hand, that's all."

Mike took a deep breath, and he frowned and cocked his head. "How is it that Maria got on air this morning?"

"I was at that new mall digging up the details for my first report. I ran into Peter Giordani ..."

"Andy's brother-in-law."

"Er, yes, and while I was talking with him about the details of the upcoming grand opening for the mall, he asked me if I had heard from Jack, and—"

"You were distracted," Mike offered.

"Yes."

"And you left her in the promo Jeep."

"Yes."

"I see."

"Oh, Mike, I'm so so sorry. Please, I promise, I'll make up for this stupid mistake."

Mike pulled up at the knees of his trousers, sat down in an empty chair and leaned back. "And you missed the second spot entirely."

"Yes." Anita was close to tears and dreaded losing her job. It's the last thing she needed. She looked up and studied his expression, frightened to see how angry he must be.

Mike got up and sat on the corner of Anita's desk. "You do realize, don't you, that how we do business these days could make or break us and our plans?"

Anita silently nodded as she looked down at her scuffed shoes.

"You also know that I like to work with employees and help them work through their problems any which way I can."

Anita nodded again. "Mike, you've always been great."

Mike's face scrunched together. "So then ...?"

"Mike, really and truly, I'm so sorry."

"You know what? I'm not in the mood for excuses." Mike looked up and saw Roger regarding them from his perch and quickly stepped over and closed the blinds, blocking Roger's view. He turned once again to Anita. "You're pretty close, Anita. This last little while you've been distracted, you end up borrowing the Jeep because your own car's not working, you take along a little girl—absolutely against policy—this girl does your spot and does a *Sesame Street* show and tell and scratches through Culture Club, and then you miss another spot entirely!"

"It was repossessed."

"What was repossessed?"

"My car."

Mike was taken aback. "Repossessed?"

"I told you the other day. That's why I had to—"

"My God, Anita. I thought you were kidding! What kind of trouble are you in?"

"Jack's been taking money out of our account."

"So at least you know he's alive."

"Yes!" she cried and covered her mouth.

Mike looked serious. "Anita, do you need money?"

Anita looked down again. "I'm okay, Mike. I just can't afford to lose my job."

Mike adjusted his clip-on tie. "You know I'm not being unfair when I say that you can't have any more of these, er, incidents. I'm going to give you a warning, but this is the one and only. Okay?"

Anita nodded. Her nose started running, and she wiped it with her sleeves. Mike turned to go but then turned back around to face her.

"So, if he's somewhere cleaning out your account, where does it say he's been doing this?"

"First Panama, then Mexico," she said.

"In the States? Not Italy?"

Anita shrugged. She was also just as confused, but at least she had a clue as to why he was there: the Pizza King.

"Why don't you take a few days off and work at finding your husband?"

"Mike, please let me work for a few days before I try that. I could use the money, and I truly feel more grounded with something I can focus on. Please."

Mike nodded, tapped her on the head and said, "No more Culture Club divas." And he left the room.

A half hour later, she was still sitting there.

Jack came back ...

... after she had crawled home from one of the most dreadful days she had experienced since his disappearance. But there he was, scaring the living daylights out of her while she stood by the sink washing a few dishes.

He knocked on the window with a quick and desperate *rat tat tat*, causing Anita to drop a glass into the sink, shattering it into a million tiny pieces.

"*Omigodomigodomigod!*" She rushed through the kitchen and out the patio doors screaming. When they reached each other outside, she jumped on him and Jack caught her, holding her straddled around his hips. She kissed and pecked all over his face as Jack struggled back into the kitchen, leaving a trail of slippery slush and mud on the ceramic tiles.

He let her slide off and drop to the floor, still clinging to his legs as he went around turning off all the lights. He slammed the patio doors shut and locked them. Then, in the dark, he lifted her up and they stood face to face, inhaling each other's breath.

"Are you really here?" she whispered at the dark image of his face. He looked ruddy, thinner and worn—and wonderful.

"I'm really here." He kissed her. "Was there any doubt?"

"Never! Never in a million years!!" she lied.

"That's my girl." He smiled.

Anita cocked her head and gazed at him curiously. "Jack, what happened? Why ..."

Jack put a finger on her lips to shush her. "Shhhh. I'm just happy to be here. I missed you so much."

"Oh, I missed you!! I missed you terribly. I thought you were dead or—"

"Shhhh."

Anita burst into tears. She blubbered about the rumours, about Peter's aggressive search for him, about Rose ...

"Listen. Who's this 'Rose'?" he interrupted. "Who's telling you all these lies?"

Anita straightened out his frayed collar as she pondered on the words to use. "Jack, people are saying you had another woman on the side and that you were supposed to go to Italy with her." She swallowed. "I spoke to her."

"Bullshit!" shot Jack. Anita jumped, her eyes batting a few times quickly. He softened his tone and smiled. "I mean, darling, really, I have no idea why people would say that. Or why this woman would. You know I went to Venezuela. You know I had business to do there."

She looked at him quizzically. "Venezuela?"

"Yes, Venezuela. Remember? I told you."

She frowned and looked at him quizzically. "Not Italy?"

"That was a cover, remember? Don't you remember? I told you before I left."

Anita shook her head and blinked. "No, honestly, I don't remember hearing that."

"Do you also remember me telling you that it might take a little longer to get back?"

Anita felt nauseous. "No, but I figured something happened to hold you up." She looked around the dark room. "Actually, that makes more sense. Of course, you could have problems getting back to me, couldn't you? Unless you stayed in the larger cities. But you didn't stay in the larger cities, did you?" She traced his jaw and realized now that he was sporting an unkempt beard speckled with grey. In the dark, she saw that his eyes were more hooded, and there were more creases around them. He looked gaunt and weary. "Then why are you hiding, love? What turned a business trip into … this!" She threw up her hands.

Jack didn't answer at first. He took both of her hands and kissed her palms before putting them on her knees. They were now sitting on the floor in front of the couch side by side, cross-legged.

"Let's just say that I've run into a bit of, er, a roadblock. No, strike that. Many roadblocks."

Anita bent back to take another look at him. "What roadblocks?"

He rubbed his beard with his right hand as he frowned. Then he looked at his nails. Anita noticed they were very dirty—very unlike Jack.

"I can't tell you, Anita. It's better that way, believe me."

Anita crawled onto and straddled his lap. She whimpered slightly as she snuggled her face under his chin. He softly caressed her back in silence. "I'm stunned, 'Nita. Someone's been nasty, and I'm having to hide from them. That's it, short and simple."

"Hide from whom, Jack?"

Jack wouldn't answer.

"But you went all that way to get that contract for plastic egg cartons, didn't you? Or was that for the guy in Italy?"

"Well, heh heh, I did get that contract, yes. And no." He shook his head. "'Nita, I can't tell you the whole story, I told you. Not just yet. The less you know, the better."

Jack suddenly stood up. Anita slipped off his lap once again and landed on her tush. She watched as he walked over to the window, taking care to stand to the side. He looked at the dark bushes at the end of the backyard. Then he looked left and right. Cautiously, he walked to the window over the kitchen sink and looked around.

"Jack. How did you get here?" asked Anita.

"It's a muddle. I had to bribe, lie … I hitchhiked."

"From Venezuela?"

He shook his head and then held up his arms towards her. Anita gratefully walked into them again. He lifted her chin up and kissed her. Desperately, Anita wrapped her arms around Jack's neck and passionately kissed back. Then she let her hands fondle, squeeze, pet. She ran her fingers through his longish hair. Slowly she walked backwards, still kissing, leading him to the stairs. Anita let him go and led him by the hand up to the bedroom. There, Anita frantically undressed him, then herself. She playfully pushed Jack onto the bed and straddled him, kissing him all over his face. *Is this a dream?* she wondered. *Oh what a dream!*

Their lovemaking was different from before. Jack always used to like the lights on. He was more visual and liked to watch her make him "feel good." But tonight, in the dark, it felt more subdued. Though her heart was glad and her body ached for him, she just, well, couldn't. To her, it felt like he wasn't really all there. *How could he be? He's just gone through a hell of a lot of trauma*, she reminded herself.

Whatever. No matter what condition he was in, Anita had her Jack back, and she wasn't never gonna let him go again!

Very early in the morning, they were back in the kitchen before the sun rose, and Jack finally began to talk.

"I see these guys—these German chicken farmers—about what was supposed to be my biggest contract yet. I mean, they wanted 30,000 plastic stackable egg cartons, holding forty eggs apiece, due delivery one month from signing, and they were willing to pay many times over what we would normally charge in Canada. And that was only the beginning. Not only a continuous standing order for cartons, but also they were to provide seed money for engineering and production for other plastic products—you know, replacing with plastic things that are normally made of metal—credit card machines, garden products, plumbing products. I mean, 'Nita, it could mean millions." He sighed. "After signing the contract, they gave me—get this—a bag of U.S. bills. I told them a bank draft would've been more businesslike. What was I supposed to do with large amounts of cash? Smuggle it out? They said I was absolutely right!"

Jack took a sip of the very hot black coffee Anita had made for him. He put the cup down and waggled a finger at her. "Funny. The most ridiculous thing I've ever heard is a thick German accent used to speaking Spanish but trying to speak in English. I didn't understand half of what they said. Anyhow, they decided to give me a lift back to Simon Bolivar Airport and stop at their bank on the way for this bank draft. But, oh no, they weren't going to let me go so soon." Jack scratched the back of his ear. "You see, one of them—his name is Jorge Pessek ... or rather, *was* Jorge Pessek."

Anita straightened up in her chair. "What do you mean *was?*"

Jack held up his hand to stop her and shook his head. "Just a minute. There's more. This head honcho invited the bunch of us back to his plantation, you see. I mean, it's in a jungle! We drove south from Los Pijiguigados into nowhere!"

"Piji ... what?"

"Pijiguigados. Or is it Pijiguidos? Never mind. Anyhow, I don't know how many thousands of acres this guy owns." Jack suddenly looked morose. "Owned." He rubbed his eyes.

Anita's pulse quickened as she waited patiently for him to continue. He leaned back and stretched his legs out under the kitchen table.

"So this guy says to stay the night and then we'd all go the next morning, get the deed done, so to speak. Then this Italian guy who happened to be staying there. What's his name?" Jack was still very weary, Anita could tell. She watched as he rubbed his eyes once again.

"Uh, oh yes! Leo Mangiano, the—"

"The Pizza King," said Anita.

"Yeah!" He frowned, cocked his head and looked down his nose at her.

"I overheard someone mention him."

"Where? Who?"

"Two people, really. The first time I heard it was from Peter. Or rather, I overheard it while at Peter and Sandra's place. Peter was kind of drunk."

"Who's the second?"

"Nancy."

"Well, this guy's bad news."

Anita watched his face closely. Jack slicked right past the mention of Nancy. But he'd done the same thing with the mention of Peter. Was she reading too much into this?

"Real bad news. He's the godfather of bad news."

"What about him?"

"Well, he kept asking me questions in this ... hyper way of his. Where did I live, what was it like in Canada, was it a great place to do business, what was my wife like, where do we live, did we know so and so, and on and on. This guy kept chomping on a cigar, and he always had a Scotch and water in his hands with, you know, his hair slicked back. He gave me the creeps. Anyhow, the next day, he comes along for the ride too! So we're driving through the jungle to get to the coast, and suddenly, about mid-morning, we almost run into these crazy soldier guys dressed in camouflage sitting in camouflaged trucks and Jeeps. They completely block this garbage of a narrow road—if you can call it that. Then soldiers on foot came out of the jungle and stood behind us, so we were trapped. I mean, they pointed these rifles at us! And, 'Nita, I was so shit-scared that I pissed my pants! I really did! I yelled at them that I was Canadian, that I was there on business, that I had a plastic moulding factory in Canada. We're supposed to be known as kind and polite people! I don't know why, I guess I thought if they knew I was Canadian they'd leave me alone. They ignored me. They had us all empty our pockets of everything."

"You mean everything?"

Jack blinked and backtracked. "Well, yeah. It was like a holdup. Well anyway," he waved something away in the air, "all the time, everyone was yelling at once, and you know what, 'Nita? They all spoke Italian! Not Spanish." He shook his head. "At least, I think they did."

Anita shook a bothersome thought from her brain to focus. "Oh, Jack. You've been around Italians all your life. You gotta know the difference between Spanish and Italian."

"No, Anita. Almost all our friends are from southern Italy. If it was Italian, it sure was a different dialect."

"No, you're right." Anita fidgeted on her chair. "They speak Spanish in South America, though."

"I know," Jack scowled. "Don't be so stupid."

Anita was taken aback but sat back and let him go on with the story.

"And this guy who led them pointed his gun at the first guy he sees and shoots the poor guy in the head!"

Anita gasped.

"*Shit!* Just like that!" Jack snapped his fingers. His voice broke like a schoolboy in puberty. "Then another guy pulls out a pistol and waves it at us, telling us to stand in line. Then he pulls the trigger. *Shit!* Then *everyone* pulled out a goddamn gun! It was World War 3! I didn't even stop to think! I bolted and ran like my life depended on it—which it did, I tell you. I was standing at the end of the line and closest to the jungle, and while everyone was shooting at each other, I took off!" He bit the back of his knuckles at the memory of it all.

Anita felt faint. "Omigod!" she whispered.

"Yeah, I know. So I stayed in the jungle, see, God, I don't know how long exactly, but I didn't give a shit about bugs or swamps or whatever! I wasn't going to come out of there until I knew I was in the clear, and I didn't care how long that could be, if I had to stay there till I was a hundred years old."

'My God, Jack! You could've died!"

"You know the stupid thing? I was most afraid of something Jorge told me over dinner once, about these kids in the jungle with long arms and dewdrop-shaped heads. Apparently they like to kill with these massive spikes by gouging out the intestines and eyes from animals, even people. The locals call them vampires."

"Lovely," said Anita, choking.

"I'd hear these screams sometimes, and they sure didn't sound like animals to me!"

Anita screwed her eyes shut. "Um, where was the money?"

"What?"

"The cash. All that money you said you had to smuggle—?"

"Oh. Well, I still had this bag of cash with me, you see ..."

"Where?"

"Well, *on* me."

"But wh—"

"You want to hear the story or don't you?"

Anita stiffened. "Of course," she said quietly.

"Okay then," he said in exasperation as he threw his hands up and let them drop. "You see, everything else, you know, my luggage and stuff, was back with the car. Even my passport!" He sighed and continued. "Anyhow, a couple of days later I figured enough time had gone by. I kept walking till I got to a road again, and I heard what sounded like a bus coming. Like the crazy guy I was, I ran into the middle of that damn trail and waved the thing down! The driver thought I was highjacking the bus, so I threw some cash at him and yelled at him to take me anywhere except Simone Bolivar Airport. The guy didn't even flinch. He nodded his head and pointed me to go to the back. So I made my way through these chickens and goats and baskets, people of all ages and sizes, kids bawlin'—and they didn't even seem to notice me. Like they were used to seeing crazy people jumping out of a jungle. Which I guess they were. At the back, someone let me have a corner of a bench, and I fell asleep."

"Did you finally get to an airport?"

"No. I stayed hidden on that bus for as long as I could. Here and there we stopped and I stayed at—I don't know—they're not what you'd call motels, or even houses, but I stayed and ate at these places where no one spoke English or had a phone. No power. No running water. Eventually I took another bus to El Tigre, and then all the way to Barcelona, where I figured I could catch a plane. It was in Barcelona that I thought I was a goner again. I tried to buy a ticket outa there, but the authorities wouldn't let me go! They took my photo, my watch and my bag of money! They accused me of drug-running and bribery!"

"Then what happened?"

Jack looked at her dully.

"I mean, how did you finally get out, Jack?"

"I told one of them that they were going to be in trouble holding back a Canadian citizen. That the money was mine free and clear, and that I was going to make an international scene if they didn't work with me and so," he motioned to the air, "they let me go."

"And the money?"

"They kept it." He looked grim.

"In other words, you bribed them?"

Jack smirked. "No, they bribed *me!*"

"Oooomigosh!" Anita said carefully. "All of it?"

Jack snorted. "Yeah! Just like in the movies! So this guy brings back my bag and what was left in it. I told them I needed cash to get home with, but they didn't care. Told me I was lucky they didn't arrest me for drug-running."

"But you weren't doing that!"

"Well, no. So one of these guys I guess felt sorry for me, 'cause he took me to the airport and told one of the mail runners that I was supposed to hitch with him. So I ended up at least as far as Mexico City."

Anita looked over at the windows, noticed a slight lightening in the sky and jumped up. "I gotta get ready for work! Could you come upstairs and keep talking while I get ready?"

Jack followed her up the stairs and stood leaning against the bathroom door frame shouting out the rest of the story over the noise of the shower. "I hitchhiked up to the American border and then someone smuggled me over." He looked back over his shoulder and disappeared into the bedroom. There he touched the bed sheets and knickknacks and then fingered through her jewellery box. He picked it up and looked into it more closely. He picked an earring up and studied it.

"How did you manage from there?" Anita yelled over the shower.

He tossed the earring back into the box and moved back to the doorway, lighter in step. "Well, ever since then, I washed dishes, swept floors, I even begged on the street in New York for crying out loud!"

Anita stepped out of the shower finally and grabbed a towel from a brass ring beside the shower door. Jack looked at her and lunged. He grabbed her to tickle her. She was relieved he was in a better spirits.

"Ooh, baby, d'you hafta go, huh?" he whined.

"No. Yes, I mean. Let me go!" she laughed. "I need to work!"

Reluctantly, Jack let her go. She smiled back at him as she towel-dried her hair.

"So how did you withdraw money from the account if you didn't have your wallet?" Anita asked. She turned to the mirror and was going to pick up her toothbrush when she paused to look at him.

He stood with his mouth open and looked stunned.

Anita looked at his reflection in the mirror. "You did take money out of the account, right?" She put up a hand, "But that's okay. Obviously you needed it, but I thought you said you lost everything, even your wallet."

Suddenly, Jack looked at the clock in the bedroom. "Oh, geez. I better let you get ready. I'm going to grab another coffee downstairs."

"Yeah, okay," she said, a little puzzled.

Jack rushed away, and she could hear him run down the carpeted steps.

A little later, Anita came into the kitchen dressed and made up, though she was going to let her still-damp hair air-dry on the way to work. Jack was at the stove, making himself a couple of fried eggs and toast. As he sat down to eat, she asked, "How did you get here from New York?"

"Well, you see," he said, gulping down his food, "I didn't care how I got back—boat or bus or donkey train ... oh, you want some of this?" he asked with his mouth full.

She shook her head and waved at him to continue.

"I didn't give a shit. By the time I reached Buffalo, I looked pretty beat up. Without a passport, they held me back, asked all sorts of questions. But they checked into my citizenship and finally had to let me through, see. Then I hitchhiked from Niagara Falls to here. Christ, I'd forgotten how cold it could get here!"

Anita frowned. "Jack. Why didn't you just call me? I would've flown down to Venezuela to get you!"

Jack had that stunned look again. "Well, er, couldn't do that, see," he said, wiping his mouth with a napkin. "I think I was set up, and I didn't want you involved. Wouldn't want one little hair on your head to get hurt."

"But Jack, who would want to hurt me? And why would you be set up? And by whom?"

Jack looked at her pointedly and whispered, "Peter."

Anita was stunned. "Peter? Peter, your partner, Peter?"

Jack nodded. "And Stefano."

She couldn't believe it! "Andy's Stefano?"

Jack threw up his hands to stop Anita's interrogation. "Listen," he cried, pointing his finger at her, "can you keep this a secret? Can you act like you haven't seen me?"

Anita was silent for a moment. She frowned. "But I ..."

"Listen. I've already said too much."

"But, Jack. Why would Pete—"

"Just take my word for it. I was supposed to die."

Anita felt numb. She was dumbstruck. With a gasp, she looked over at the clock. "Omigoshomigosh! I have to go!"

She jumped towards Jack and gave him a big wet kiss. "See ya tonight!" She stopped at the garage door and turned. 'Oh, wait! I still have Christmas presents for you." She jumped in excitement.

"'Nita, you're late!" he chuckled.

She grabbed him by his T-shirt. "No, at least one, only one!"

She rushed off and ran upstairs. Jack brushed his hair back from his face. He could hear her fumbling up in their bedroom and then her jogging down the stairs. She ran up to him with a small box wrapped in Christmas paper. "Go ahead," she smiled. "At least open this one!"

Jack tore off the paper and opened the box. In it, nestled amidst fine tissue, was a handmade gold-coloured necktie.

"Oh, look! A necktie!" he mocked.

Anita fingered the beautiful silk. "It's handmade from Italy. Don't you find the colour gorgeous?"

"Actually, yes. It's quite the looker." He turned a smile at Anita. "I'll wear it for you tonight … and nothing else."

Anita giggled and kissed him on the lips again. "Does that mean you're not going anywhere soon?"

He stretched and stepped closer. "Yup, I'm lying low. Just don't tell anyone, okay? I need to get my head around this before I know what I want to do. See you tonight."

"Want anything picked up?"

"Yeah, pick up a steak or two. The fridge is empty. What do you live on, straw?"

Anita felt immense guilt as she visualized the straw tumbling over her body while with Stefano in the barn. She shook it off. "Okay, I'll pick up some groceries. See you tonight." She turned. "Will you answer the phone if I call?"

He shook his head. "No, it could be anybody. It's safer that I don't."

"Even if I let the phone ring three times and then hang up and call again?"

He was starting to feel a little irritable. "Don't want to take the chance." He tried to smile again and blew a kiss at her.

She blew one back and then disappeared into the garage. He stepped forward and gently shut the door.

As she drove out of the driveway, she was upset and perplexed. There were too many unanswered questions. Like, where was his car? And why, oh why, didn't he simply call? And why didn't he tell the authorities about the outright murders he witnessed in Venezuela? Oh, he could be so distant and secretive, she thought. Then she berated herself for already criticizing her long-lost, and finally found, husband. She pushed all the negative thoughts to the back of her mind, if only to clear her head enough for work. *Tonight, I'll have him tell me more*, she thought. "And he's back!" she yelled at the windshield as she sped away.

Jack watched her go. He noticed that she was smart enough to have borrowed a car from work. It hadn't occurred to him that she was that capable. And she obviously knew how to take care of herself. She'd looked pretty good to him when she opened that door last night.

He rubbed his hand against his beard and reminded himself to never try to grow one again. At least it helped him look the part, he had to admit as he admired his reflection in the window. He had a lot of stuff to do that day and needed to make sure he was back by the time Anita came home.

Anita rushed home. It was already getting dark. She jumped out of the Jeep and ran into the house. "Jack! Jack! Honey, I'm hoooome!" she called out.

She turned on the lights as she ran through the house. There was no answer. "Honey?" She looked throughout the house, the bedroom, the rec room, the kitchen, the bathroom, the living room. No Jack.

Anita stood in the kitchen wondering where in the world he could have gone. *Oh no*, she said to herself. She was afraid she would lose him again. "Jack?" she called out feebly.

She walked around and looked out the windows at the deepening darkness. She saw the change house beside the pool. She went out through the patio doors and ran to it—and screamed as she opened the door.

Someone clamped a hand over her mouth and pulled her in. The door slammed shut behind her. Jack moved her over to the wall and slid down to the floor with her. He put a finger to his lips.

"Shhh!"

Anita looked at him in the dark. "What's wrong?" she whispered. "Why are you hiding in the cabana?"

"Someone was trying to get into the house earlier, so I ran out here to hide."

"Who are you afraid of, Jack?"

"There are people," he said, waving a hand in the air.

"What people?"

"What do you think I just lived through this last month?!"

Anita frowned and then stood up.

"Where are you going?" Jack really sounded frightened. It made her want to take care of him.

"You wait here and I'll check around, okay?" Before he could answer, she had left. She ran into the house and looked everywhere. Nothing was out of place … well, actually, nothing was in its place, but that was a happy sight, because it meant Jack was home! It was apparent to her, though, that no one had tried to break in. She knew personally that it was impossible.

Suddenly, something crossed her mind. She rushed to the back door, grabbed a flashlight and ran outside. She hurried around to the other side of the house and stopped at the window well. Slowly she stepped towards the well. She leaned over to look in, and a few leaves suddenly moved. She jumped back with a squeal.

Silly! she said to herself. Again, she leaned over and shone the flashlight into the well. There, moving around in the leaves, was a skunk. As it moved, some of the loose twigs tapped the window. She clapped a hand over her mouth and stifled a laugh.

She ran over to the change house and threw the door open. "You silly twerp!" she yelled. "It was just a skunk in one of the window wells!"

"A skunk?" Jack looked perplexed in the beam of the flashlight.

"Yeah, a skunk. And can I ever tell you a skunk story or what! Come on, scaredy-cat!" She held out her hand, pulled Jack up off the floor and led him back to the house.

Jack wiped his forehead and went to sit on the couch. Anita ran over and jumped up to sit on his lap. "What would you want for dinner?" she asked suggestively.

"Come on, 'Nita. I'm not in the mood," Jack snapped. "I'm starving. What'd you bring home for supper?" He pushed her off him, and she fell on her tush once again.

"Oh, of course! Hang on." She struggled to her feet. "I left groceries in the car! I'll be right back!" She kissed his forehead and ran outside.

She opened the door, took out three bags of groceries and slammed the door shut. She hummed her way back into the house. As she took out the groceries, Jack walked up to her from behind. Anita smiled, expecting to feel a couple of strong arms grab her from behind. Instead, Jack's hands came into view as he held up a package of T-bone steak.

"My favourite!"

Outside, someone in the bushes at the back of the yard watched Jack and Anita talking by the sink. The person dragged on a cigarette and threw the stub to the ground. It landed on a pile of cigarette stubs.

An hour later, Jack pushed back from the table. He had shovelled in a T-bone steak, baked potato with sour cream, Caesar salad, potato chips, strawberry jello and a bottle of Grant's blended scotch. He burped, wiped his mouth and smacked his lips. "That was A-1, 'Nita!"

Anita smiled and stood up. She took the two plates and dumped them into the sink with the pile of dishes that Jack had used during the day.

"'Nita," said Jack.

Anita turned around. "Yeah?"

"We have to get to the office," he mumbled.

"What?"

"We need to get to the office and get something out of my desk. I figure that maybe Peter wants me dead." He burped again and excused himself. He wavered a bit.

"My God! Why would he do that?!"

"I can't tell you now." Jack walked up to Anita and turned on the tap. He splashed his face and then stared blankly down the drain.

"Jack?"

"The factory. I want you to go there." He kept staring down the drain.

"I've been there." She turned and looked at him.

He threw her a look. "My office?"

Anita nodded. "I looked for clues as to where you could've gone to." She didn't tell him she was looking for confirmation that he was cheating on her. And Rose? It wasn't worth even thinking of Rose now. Besides, how could she have ever believed that? "I looked for our mail—they repossessed the car, and I expect the power will be turned off any day."

"Is that why you're driving the station's Jeep?"

"You noticed," she said.

Jack stood looking at her. "How'd you get in there without the password for the alarm?"

"I knew that the window wasn't connected to the alarm system. It was closed, but I knew you wouldn't think to lock it. I had to shift the window back and forth, but eventually I was able to get through."

"The window, eh?" Jack quietly pondered on that. He kissed her shoulder and patted her bum.

"You have to go back there, Anita. But the place is probably being watched now. If I go and get caught, I don't know what will happen to me. But you, Anita …"

"Me? What if they catch me?" asked Anita, looking into his eyes questioningly.

"You can say what you want. That you were looking for statements because of your crumbling finances. Or simply that you were desperate to find out what happened to me. It would be a great cover because it's true in a way, right? Besides, I doubt Peter would hurt you. Why should he? And you can tell him that you wanted to find proof of my alleged infidelities."

Her heart flipped. "Alleged infidelities, Jack?"

"Yeah, you know," he said, not looking at her. "Those stupid rumours about me and a red-haired bimbo."

Anita nodded slowly. "Okay." Suddenly, she felt uneasy. Something didn't feel right, but she shook it off.

"I need to prove my innocence in a matter of some business enterprises Peter and I have in common," Jack explained. "You see, I didn't agree with a lot of what Peter's been doing." He looked away again and paused.

Did she want to know what these "enterprises" were? If they had anything to do with Peter, she knew instinctively that it had to be dirty business. She shook her head and focussed on the matter at hand. "When, then, darling?" Anita whispered.

"Tonight."

Anita nodded mutely.

He put a finger on her lips. "We need money, 'Nita. If what you say is true about our finances, then we have nothing. They're going to put the pressure on me, Anita. Like a rat pushed into a corner. We can't let him know that you and I know. It's important."

"Know what, Jack? I don't know what you're talking about."

Jack looked down at his bare feet and ignored her last statement. "You still have your fur coat?" he asked quietly.

Anita's heart skipped a beat. "Yes," she said. "Why?"

Jack looked up. "'Nita, I need for you to let me take that coat and your jewellery. I need to sell them. Anything else can be traced."

Anita placed a hand on Jack's chest and looked up at him. "I don't have my jewellery with me, Jack. I've already taken it to a jeweller to be appraised. I already knew I would probably have to sell them."

"Did you get a receipt for them?" he asked.

Anita went to her purse on the counter and took out a slip of paper. She handed it to Jack. "This is where they are now. I was only getting an idea as to value, that's all."

Jack put the slip of paper on the counter and left it there. "Anita, I promise you, darling, when this is all behind us, I'll get it all back for you. Even more than you would ever have dreamed of, okay?"

"That's not important, darling. It's you that's important."

"Then can you do that? Are you okay with that?"

Anita pulled Jack closer. "I'd do anything for you, Jack. You know that."

He gently held her chin. "You know, kid, I love you."

With her bottom lip quivering, she said, "And I'm so glad you didn't do what they said you did. I'd die if it was all true."

Jack gave her a tender kiss on her lips. "It's all lies, love. I never did any of what they're saying I did, no Rose-whoever, no Italy—forget about it. Okay?" Anita nodded and wiped away a tear. "Good goin', kid. Now, tonight you go back to the office." He found a pen and took her hand, palm-side up, and wrote a number. "Here. This is the combination number for the alarm. Go to one of my drawers in my desk—my right-hand bottom drawer. You'll find a latch if you close the drawer halfway. Then put your hand as far as you can along the right side of it. You should find what feels like a flat toggle switch. Push that in, and you should hear the false bottom click open. Inside that false bottom you will find a keyring with two keys on it. Take those keys and bring them back to me, okay baby? It's very, *very* important. It represents a new future for us."

Anita nodded, wide-eyed. A new future?

"You don't have a key for the front doors, do you?" he asked.

"No, but I hope not to have to go that way."

Jack went to his study and banged a couple of desk drawers around. He came back with a key in his hand. "Here, just in case. Take this, though there's a good chance you'll be able to get through that window still. There's no reason for them to check it now if they hadn't before you last visited."

Anita took the key and put it in the pocket of her blue jeans.

"While I think of this, Anita, you have a heart-to-heart with your boss at the station. We need that job for now. And tell them to hand over your paycheque from now on—no more direct deposits."

"But I've just opened a new account, and it's being deposited automatically starting two weeks from now."

He shook his head. "No, Anita, that won't work. I want that money in my hand at the end of the two weeks."

Anita took a step backward. What he said made her stop and stare at him.

"What?" He watched her. His face softened. "Darling, we need to work together on this."

"But I still don't understand what the problem is between you and Peter, and even Stefano. I have a right to know."

He bent over her and kissed her lips. "Just do this for me. I'll explain later."

So Anita retrieved her fur coat and gave it to Jack.

"I'm sorry, love. But don't worry. It will be replaced. One even more beautiful than this one."

When she finally left to go back to the factory, he held her tenderly and said, "You're the greatest, 'Nita. And don't worry. Everything's going to be fine."

"What if something goes wrong and the alarm won't work, Jack? What if someone locks that window?"

"You got a phone in that Jeep?"

Anita silently nodded.

"You give me a call. Let it ring three times, then hang up and call again. Just like you suggested this morning. I'll answer it only then."

Anita nodded and gave Jack a quick kiss before leaving with the flashlight.

⁂

Driving to the factory, her mind wasn't at peace, though her heart still sang with joy at Jack's return. There were a couple of things, however, that Jack had said that didn't sit right. Of course, it was silly to even dwell on them. She felt pretty naked without her wedding ring, and that in itself was enough reason for her to feel queasy. She sighed loudly. Why would she even want to doubt Jack? But damn it all, her mind had a will of its own. It mulled over this and over that, thoughts that weighed heavy on her heart. Each time she managed to shake it off. She reminded herself that Jack was not guilty of anything. *He is the victim*, she told herself.

But Jack had mentioned Italy. She didn't even mention Italy. And she remembered he had asked who Rose was. And now he seemed to know her? And the colour of her hair? He couldn't have been home long enough to hear any of the rumours. Was it possible he was lying?! Ever so slightly, a cold shiver crept up her spine. She was almost dead sure that she hadn't mentioned any of these details. Anita sighed. She was upset with herself. It was as if a demon inside of her wanted to blame Jack for everything. "Stop it!" she yelled.

She shook her head and forced a broad smile. *Focus on the good*, she reminded herself. So she thanked the good Lord that her Jack was finally back. *Hang in there*, she thought, *the best is yet to come*. "Everything's going to be all right," she told the dashboard.

What she didn't know was that a black Cadillac Eldorado Biarritz with a license plate that read *ZIO* was following her. And if she had known and seen who was inside, she would've recognized the nasty duo of Guido and Mario.

Chapter 24

T HE SIDE DOOR LEADING TO the garage slammed open, and Andy awkwardly directed Claudia through the hallway with her walker. Claudia wore an elasticized girdle around her hips to help keep pressure on the broken hip.

"We're almost there, Ma," Andy said. "Ma, keep moving!"

"I go! I go!" squealed Claudia. They kept shuffling along the hallway and finally entered the family room. Andy directed Claudia to Fabrizio's favourite armchair. "No, no! Is-a Fabrizio's!" Claudia complained and pulled away with the walker.

"Ma! Sit! Sit or I'm going to break your neck!"

Claudia whimpered.

"Shit. I'll go get the friggin' wheelchair. Don't move!"

Claudia nodded and nodded in between little prayers to "Mama Maria mia." She moaned and groaned, but once Andy disappeared into the garage, she settled down. She mopped her sweating brow with a dainty handkerchief already thoroughly wrung from the morning's stressful activities. Andy clunked the door open again with a folded-up wheelchair, stumbling over shoes on the way. Claudia started moaning and praying again.

"You wanna sit in the wheelchair, Ma? Is that better?"

Claudia moaned and nodded, then shook her head.

"What's that supposed to mean? You want to sit or have the wheelchair? *Tell* me!"

"*Si*, no-a," Claudia whispered. "I-a sit."

Andy sighed and left the wheelchair folded and to the side. "All right. Hold on then." Andy helped Claudia slowly sink into a chair.

"Owowow!" Claudia cried as she sat down.

Andy straightened up. "Ma, I'm gonna make some lunch. You want the TV on?"

Claudia pondered on it a bit.

"Now, Ma, now," pressed Andy. "It's not a thousand-dollar question. You want it on?"

Claudia nodded. Andy held up the control and turned on the TV. Then she handed the control to Claudia. "Here, Ma. Watch what you want." Claudia took the control and let it drop on her lap. Andy froze in front of her and held up her hands. "What?" Claudia didn't say anything and just moaned, shaking her head. "What, Ma?"

"I no see-a TV when Fabrizio is-a—t'you-a know-a." Claudia started crying.

Andy took the remote control and held it out to the TV in the corner. She turned it off again and in disgust dropped the control on Claudia's lap. She walked up into the kitchen and took some buns out of the freezer. From underneath, on one of the lower racks in the fridge, she took out a Tupperware of cold cuts and carried everything over to the counter by the microwave, where she stuck the buns in to defrost. As she waited, she leaned back into the corner of the counter and surveyed all that she could see from her point of view. She could hear ice pellets hitting the kitchen windows. Through the spotless kitchen, she watched the back of Claudia's head in the family room. It occurred to her that now was a good time to sneak a cigarette, but while she reached into the corner cupboard for her hidden pack, the phone rang.

"Now what," she mumbled to herself. She went over and picked up the broken phone, which was still dangling in two pieces. "Yeah!"

"Andy. It's Sharon. How are you?"

"What'ya think?" Andy quipped.

"I hear you've got two sick puppies."

"You're tellin' me! These last few days have been hell, let me tell you!" Andy laughed in spite of her frustrations. "So what you want?" she asked quickly.

"I need to do fittings with you guys, so how's about coming in day after tomorrow? Are you available?"

"Say again?" Andy looked at Claudia in the family room. She had by now turned on the TV to *Jeopardy* and the volume was far too high.

Andy covered her mouthpiece and yelled, *"Ma! Can't hear for shit! Turn that friggin' thing down!"* She went back to Sharon. "Say again?"

"Fittings," repeated Sharon. "It's too bad for Claudia. How do you think she'll be in two and a half weeks for the big show? I've already got her costume for the province of Calabria ready."

Andy covered the mouthpiece again. *"Ma! The TV, down!"*

Claudia yelled back just as loudly, *"Si!"*

"Down!"

"Si!" And Claudia finally turned down the volume.

"You don't want to be in this province thing for the fashion show now, do you?" Andy shouted at her. "Ya can't do it."

Claudia swivelled her head and winced in pain as she did so. But she was panicking. *"Si si!* No-a tell Sharon no! I do!"

Andy rolled her eyes and tsk'ed loudly. She threw up one hand and let it drop in disgust. "You can't do it!"

"Si, si. If-a someone push, *si!*

Andy sighed heavily. "Sharon, tell me. How in fu—" Andy paused and looked over at Claudia again, who was staring at her wide-eyed and wildly. "Ma, really!" Claudia's bottom lip quivered. "Oh for—" she whispered into the phone. "For fuck's sake, Sharon. There's no way she can do it. You'll have to find someone else to do Calabria. Try Louisa Antonuzzo. She's from there—"

"No! Louisa-a no do it!" bleated Claudia. "This-a my home, my Calabria!"

For the umpteenth time, Andy covered the mouthpiece. "Ma! Louisa Antonuzzo *also* comes from Calabria!"

"Not-a like-a me-a!," argued Claudia.

Andy put the phone back to her ear. "Sharon, you there?"

"Yeah, Andy, I'm still here."

"Will you kill me please. Save me from this hell." Andy put her hand to her forehead and shook her head. Now she really, really needed that cigarette. "Why don't we skip this for now. When did you want to do Maria's fitting?"

"Make it day after tomorrow, after school. How's about four o'clock?" Sharon suggested. "And tell Anita."

"Who? Anita? I don't know no Anita. You tell her yourself."

At the other end of the phone, Sharon sighed. "She's not your friend anymore?"

"Sharon, I don't even recognize that name!"

"What the heck could she have said to you for you to be like that?" asked Sharon patiently. She'd known Andy all her life and had seen it all before.

"Say? Nothing! Ask me what did she do?"

"Okay, what did she do?"

"I tell you, Sharon, I almost lost my daughter. That woman took Maria for the day and the moment Maria was in her hands, poof, Maria was gone! I almost shit bricks! *Never mind* that my mother had just broken her hip that day and *never mind* that my father lay dying in his hospital bed while Maria could've *also* been lying dead in some Chinese underground opium den or sold to white slavery!" Her voice echoed in the kitchen, and even she was surprised to hear the glasses clink in the cupboards. In a smaller voice, Andy said, "Okay. I'll call Anita. Day after tomorrow. Around four."

"Great," said Sharon. "See you then!" And she hung up.

"Yeah, see ya then," Andy repeated. She slowly hung up the phone as best she could and then took it off the wall mount again to dial. She thought better of it and hung it up again. *First things first. I'm gonna have my smoke*, she told herself.

⌘

Anita arrived at the factory after what seemed like an eternity, but only forty minutes had gone by. An icy rain had started falling after she left the house, so there was very little traffic. There were lights on in some of the neighbouring factories, but there seemed to be only one or two lights on in Jack's. Good—there was no graveyard shift. She continued slowly and stopped at the stop sign to look up and down the road one more time for any sign of cars. There was one, but it was well hidden, and she never saw it. She did a U-turn into the intersection and drove back to the building for one more look. Confident that everything looked quiet, she drove away and back into the street behind the building, parking exactly where she had parked the last time.

She put her gloves on and grabbed the flashlight, and then she stepped out of the Jeep and locked it. Quietly she crept towards the back fence and climbed over it quickly. Then she stood in the dark for a bit to listen. All she heard was the soft pelting of the misty rain onto the dead weeds around her.

She ran over to Jack's office window again, but this time someone had locked it. "Crap!" she whispered to herself. She pressed her face to the glass and saw that the only light on was the hallway light just outside of Jack's open office door. She ran around the building and tried every other window. No luck. It looked like she had no choice but to use the keys to the front door. She groaned at the thought of having to stand under that bright front-door light, but she had no choice.

She ran to the front corner of the building and looked around carefully. Then she ran like the wind to the door and stuck the key into the lock. It wouldn't turn. She took it out again and tried again. Nothing. She bent down to see if there was any debris in the lock. The key went in all right, but it just wouldn't loosen the toggle in the lock. "Crap again," she whispered to herself.

With her heart pounding, she ran around to the back and sprinted back to the Jeep. She quickly climbed in and grabbed the car phone. As she waited for the phone to ring three times, she looked around the deserted factories. She frowned when she thought she saw a moving point of light in an exceptionally dark corner of a lot but decided it had to have been her imagination. She hung up and dialled again. Jack wordlessly picked up the phone.

"Jack?"

"Yeah. Where are you now?" he asked.

"I'm here at the factory, but someone's locked your window and the others are locked as well, plus the key won't turn the lock."

Jack was quiet for a moment.

"Jack?"

"Yeah, wait, I'm thinking." There was a long pause before Jack came back on. "Okay, were you able to get the key into the lock?"

"Yeah, I did. It just wouldn't turn."

"Okay, go back to the front door …"

"Yeah?"

"… and blow softly into the lock. It's freezing rain, and sometimes that lock freezes up. Other than that, I couldn't imagine what else to do. But try blowing," he chuckled.

She didn't answer. She thought she saw that point of light again. She shook her head.

"'Nita, are you there?"

"Sorry, I thought I saw something, but it's not there."

"Good. Try that trick."

"Okay!" She jumped out of the Jeep and hurriedly made her way to the front door, standing once again under that damn front light. She looked around and then bent over and put her lips on the lock. She gently blew into it, warming up the lock. She straightened out and put the key into the lock and jiggled it. Nothing happened. She bent over once more and blew. She stuck the key in, jiggled it and finally heard the lock click open.

She pocketed the key and looked around as she pulled the door open. As expected, she set off the pre-alarm beep, and she quickly stepped over to the alarm keypad. She silently hoped that no one had changed the alarm code. She quickly pulled her glove off and was perturbed to see that sweat and the wet weather had run the numbers on her palm. She squinted at her palm and then quickly punched in some keys. The alarm kept beeping. "Shit," she swore, because she was well aware that she was standing in a bright doorway facing the main road and could be seen clearly by anyone passing by the industrial mall. "Shit, shit!" she yelled. With a trembling hand, she pushed in a slightly altered alarm code. She was immensely relieved when the alarm stopped. She took a deep breath and then moved on. "Holy mackerel!" she said as she pulled open the interior glass doors. The quicker she got into the offices and out of sight, the better.

She ran past Nancy's desk and into Jack's office. She plunked herself into Jack's chair and swivelled into place. She used her flashlight to check around the desk and opened the bottom right drawer. She pulled it out completely and dumped the contents out. She rapped it with her knuckles, and the bottom sounded hollow. She shook it and something rattled in it. "Bingo," she said quietly.

Clumsily, she put the drawer back in and then opened it halfway. She put her right hand in and felt the sides. She made a muffled squeal as she felt the toggle switch. She pushed it, and the bottom fell open slightly. Slowly she opened the drawer all the way again and the whole bottom opened. And something fell out of the bottom. The keys!

Her heart pounded as she quickly threw papers back into the drawer and slammed it back into place. She ran out of the office and crouched behind the receptionist's desk in the shadows to make sure there were no headlights or sign of people outside on the road. Satisfied that all was clear, Anita stepped away from the desk … and then she remembered that awful photo she had seen on Nancy's desk. Her heart did a flip. My God, she had forgotten about that photo! How could she have forgotten?

She stepped over to Nancy's desk and was tempted to look at it again. *But why bother?* she asked herself. Jack was home, and all of these questions were no longer important. He was back, wasn't he? Wasn't that enough proof that it was all one big sad joke? All just a big misunderstanding and rumours built up to ridiculous heights. But she was curious just the same. She reached out shakily, lifted up the frame and turned it over.

For some reason, she was startled to see that it was still there. There it was, as if from another life. She looked at it closely. Was it really at the Coliseum? Could it be a poster they were standing in front of? And then it dawned on her. Nancy's red hair. And Rose's red hair. Two red-headed women.

She fell against the wall and slid down on her haunches, deep in thought. There were too many questions. Suddenly, she felt anxious, trapped in a box. She was afraid she was losing her mind. She started questioning *everything* he had said. Jack couldn't be that mean. He loved her. But did he lie about Rose, about Italy, about Calabria, maybe even about Venezuela?

Impossible. But she stayed where she was, trying to catch her breath, control her pounding heart and maintain some level of sanity.

It wasn't until the small hours of the next day that she slowly struggled to get up and leave through the front door. She locked it behind her, looked around and ran around back to the Jeep. She saw on the Jeep's clock that it was getting on to six o'clock, and she was afraid she'd bump into Nancy again at the stop sign. She started the Jeep and quickly drove away.

She may have beaten Nancy this time, but in the black Cadillac slightly hidden by bushes, Mario elbowed a sleeping Guido and woke him up. *"Che?"* Mario pointed at the speeding Jeep. They sat up and turned on the motor. As they pulled away, another set of eyes watched them move. The guy took a final drag on his cigarette and threw the butt down onto a little pile of butts.

But Mario, Guido and the unknown stranger were still not the only sets of eyes watching her. Unbeknownst to Anita, almost every move she'd made had been caught on the new video surveillance system that Peter had recently put in.

When she got home a little later, she found a tired Jack sitting cross-legged on the bed. She held up the keys and rattled them, but she did not show him the photo of Jack and Nancy in Italy. That she kept in the pocket of her jeans.

He didn't even ask what took her so long.

Chapter 25

ANDY DROVE THE CAR AWKWARDLY up the driveway. Maria was screaming, and Andy was screaming back.

"Moooom, you promised I can!"

"You are *not* going with Anita again!"

"I'm gonna call her!"

"No, you're not!"

"Yes, I *am!*"

"Goddamnit, Maria, get out of the car and open the garage!"

Maria threw the passenger door open and stomped to the garage door. She held a finger over the button but stood scowling at Andy.

"Push the button," Andy yelled in the car.

Maria didn't budge.

Pushed to the edge, Andy rolled down the window and screamed, "Maria, you push that button or I'll make your head into a button. *Open the goddamn garage!*"

And suddenly, the demon rooster from hell flew by the car and shit through the window, covering the dash, the steering wheel, the stick shift, and, oh yes, Andy.

Maria was so shocked by the demon rooster's dastardly deed that she pushed the button, if only just to get the hell away from a *really angry* Andy.

Andy screamed, jumped out of the car and followed a fleeing Maria through the garage. Maria ran into the kitchen and looked back to see Andy go straight to the basement stairs, stop at the second landing, take down a shotgun, pocket some shells and stomp back out through the garage and outside.

The Giordani neighbours were curious as to where the shotgun blasts could possibly be coming from.

Twenty minutes later, the shooting stopped.

The garage door flew open, and Maria, who had sat trembling in the hallway chewing her nails, almost hit the ceiling when Andy stomped back in with the rifle over her shoulder and an unrecognizable bloody lump that had once been the demon rooster from hell hanging limply in her hand.

The phone on the wall had been ringing nonstop since the first blast echoed throughout the fields. As Andy stomped up the steps to the kitchen, she grabbed the phone and let it uncoil as she stomped to the sink and slam-dunked the demon carcass.

"Yeah! Uh huh. Me? No way. Why? You thought I finally came to my senses and killed Stefano? What then? You think?" She hung up. The phone rang again. "*What!*"

"Andy? It's Peter."

"What do you want?" she said, leaning into the corner cupboard for her cigarettes. "No, he's not here yet. Yeah, I'll tell him. See ya. Oh, Peter? If you see Stefano before I do? Tell him we're having chicken for dinner tonight. Heavily peppered! Yeah." She hung up.

She struck a match, lit her cigarette and threw the smoking match down on the carcass in the kitchen sink.

⚮

Back at Peter's office at Vindenza Village Mall, Peter, Nancy, Guido and Mario had given up waiting for Stefano and sat watching the surveillance video of Anita going through the offices. Much to Nancy's chagrin, the men kept wanting to see the part where Anita was blowing at the lock. A lot of *wink, wink, nudge, nudge*, and smirks and guffaws. She grabbed the remote and fast-forwarded a little to where Anita entered Jack's office. They suddenly strained forward in their seats to watch closely as Anita bent down towards the right side of Jack's desk.

"There." Peter pointed his finger at the screen. "Look. She's taking out that drawer. She dumped everything out of it. Can you tell exactly what she's doing with that thing?" Everyone squinted at the screen.

"Here, I'll play it again in slow motion." Peter pushed the video recorder into rewind and played it again.

Nancy shook her head. "I can't tell. Wait! Stop right there!" She walked up at the monitor and pointed at the fuzzy image of Anita's hands. "Look there. She's got her hands in the desk itself. It looks like ..." She paused as she focussed a bit more.

Guido got out of his chair and stepped up to the monitor as well. "She-a take little thing."

Peter stepped up to take a closer look. All three cocked their heads at one point and then straightened them out again in unison. Suddenly, Mario jumped up. "Keys-a!"

He snapped his fingers. "Nancy, you were going back to the office, weren't you?"

"Yes. I'll take a look at that drawer," said Nancy.

"Yeah, do that. Guido, you go with her. Are there any staff working today?"

Nancy shook her head. "Laundering this stuff is so much easier than running a business of thirty employees. There's just a skeleton staff on the floor for this week. You know, make it look good. The employees don't like the cutback in hours, but tough beans. I'm a little worried about Sam, though."

Peter loosened up his Italian silk tie and leaned forward in his chair. "Why? Is he starting to get onto us? Be honest with me, Nancy. I know you like the guy."

Nancy pushed away a tendril of wavy red hair and nodded. "Yeah, he's a nice guy. You know, one of those honest, down-to-earth guys. He's really sincerely worried about Jack and the diminishing workload we've been getting in and out through those shipping doors."

Peter sat back. "Yeah, we have to get more of those orders going from Venezuela. I might have to go down. So how do we get a hold of this Jorge guy?"

Everyone shrugged and shook their heads.

"That was Jack's part of the workload," Nancy said, frowning. "We only have an approximate address and a phone number that doesn't work. For the life of me, I don't know how Jack communicated with the guy. That's why we have to find him, and fast!"

Peter looked at Nancy sideways. He leaned back in his new office chair ... a bit too far, because he suddenly fell backwards. Mario and

Guido turned around in time to see Jack's legs sticking up in the air. The two of them scrambled to Peter and awkwardly helped him up, putting the chair back on its rollers. Peter glared at the chair and straightened out his suit jacket and tie. He swiped his hair back into place.

"We'll have to figure this out, but it's going to be tough without Jack's numbers, paperwork and now the *goddamn money!*" He gripped his perfect hair and pulled it. "*Aarrgh!*" He whimpered into his hands for a moment. "And this guy in Venezuela, this Jorge guy …"

"Ah, *si*. Jurg," said Mario.

Peter frowned. "You mean Jorge."

"No, Jurg. He is'a German."

"German? I thought he was Venezuelan?"

"*Si, ma* she-a padre is-a German 'n she-a *madre* is-a *Italiana*," explained Mario.

Peter frowned. "Well, I still think Jack did him in. All he cared for was the money, obviously. Everyone's money."

"No, everyone else's money," corrected Nancy. She redirected a strand of red hair behind her delicate ear. She frowned. "Wouldn't we have heard if there was anyone killed in Venezuela? Don't they cover news like that on TV, radio, in Venezuela?" Nancy looked around and shrugged. "Well, wouldn't we have?"

"Those are wild jungles out there, Nancy. And there's tons of mercenaries and killers. Lots of things happen and no one hears about it. It happens all the time. Old news. And who knows? Animals will have finished him off anyways."

Nancy shot him a dirty look. "How can you talk like that?!"

"*Che* animal?" asked Guido.

"*Elifante? Cocodrilo?*" suggested Mario.

"Guys, don't be stupid. There are no such things as elephants and crocodiles in Venezuela!" Peter said impatiently.

"No, Peter. You're wrong. There are crocodiles in Venezuela, and they can grow up to ten feet in length," Nancy pointed out with chin held high in the air.

"No, those are alligators," said Peter.

Guido raised a finger and opened his mouth to speak, but Peter cut him off.

"All right! Alligators, crocodiles, what's the difference!?" he yelled.

"There's a very big difference," yelled Nancy stubbornly.

Peter threw up his hands. "All right already! Whatever!" He leaned against his desk and fidgeted with a pen. "And what about those orders? We have to get those going again, otherwise we don't have a carrier for the cash and egg crates, and they're going to start asking questions in Italy, and I'll be a dead man if they find out before we fix this fix we're in." He shrugged and then grabbed his torso. "Oh, my guts," moaned Peter.

"Is-a *ulcera*. You no drink-a coffee," said Guido, pointing at the paper cup of cold coffee that Peter was about to bring to his mouth.

Peter put the cup down and stared into it for a moment. Then he picked it up and dropped it into the new wastepaper basket. Unfortunately, it was a new wire mesh basket, and coffee splattered over the pant leg of his Italian silk suit.

He threw up his hands. "Ah, shit! *Cazzo!*" He frantically looked around for some Kleenex. Nancy took one out from in between her cleavage and held it out to him. He snatched it away and dabbed at his pant leg.

"You speak-a *Italiano!*" Guido yelled happily. He and Mario exchanged looks of delight, Mario's eyes moistening with emotion.

"All right already!" Peter yelled. He saw the emotion on his cousins' faces and settled down a bit. He continued to dab. "There's a lot of money at stake here," he mumbled.

All three—Nancy, Mario and Guido—said, "We know-a."

Nancy suddenly stood up and headed for the door. "I'm going to check out Jack's desk and whatever other clues I can find."

Peter waved at her back and watched her behind. "Hey, kiddo," he said. "I want ya to make sure that Stefano doesn't get wind of any of this. Does he still think this is all bona fide?"

Nancy turned with her hand on the knob of the office door. "As far as I know. He's still concerned, but more for Anita's sake, really. I think he's lost his stomach for it. On the other hand, Stefano not only is a child of deep waters, he's also not dumb. He knows very well what's at stake. But he's sure angry with you!"

Peter waved the thought away. "I can handle Stef. Not to worry. I also know that he's gotten a little too concerned for Anita's sake. He's now a liability."

"*Che?*" asked Mario.

Peter ignored him. "I have a feeling that our little Anita might know too much. Once she does, she's also on a hit list, you mark my words. After me." He gulped and shook for a moment and then motioned to the cousins. "Get back out there and keep tabs on Anita. I think we're getting close to somethin' here. At least we know where Jack is right now."

Mario got up and stretched while Guido checked his shoulder holster and harness, his leg holster and harness, and then his other shoulder holster and harness before sauntering out with Mario in tow. Nancy opened the door for them and cast a strange and vulnerable look at Peter before leaving and closing the door behind her.

Peter watched her behind shift under her grey knit dress. Then Peter frowned. He knew where Nancy's heart was, and intuitively he figured she could become quite the wrathful woman.

But then, he could ride on that to his own benefit. He sat back in his new chair and interlaced his fingers together behind his neck. He tipped a little further and then suddenly fell backwards with a crash. It took him five minutes to extricate himself from the tight hold a lodged chair could have between a corner and a desk.

"Where were ya?" Andy was leaning into her corner by the sink.

Stefano had just come up from his shower in the basement. He looked at Andy and his eyebrows shot up. He looked over by the silent TV and his arms went up. "Is-a TV broken?"

Maria was sitting quietly on the carpet in front of the TV. She simply stared up at him with wide and frightened eyes. He looked back at Andy and cocked his head. He waved her question away. "At-a work."

"Oh? Peter was looking for you."

He shrugged. "So?"

"So, where were ya?"

Stefano looked around him confused. "I was-a wi' Trini. He hav-a new lamb. I look." He jiggled his head. "*Ma*, he wan' too much ..." He held up his hand and rubbed his thumb against the other fingers. "Too much-a," he stated once again. Something caught his eye. He focussed on the object, stepped toward it and picked it up. A feather. A long blue feather. He looked quizzically at Andy.

She motioned to outside. "That damn bird sheds everywhere he goes!"

Stefano mutely nodded and pulled out his chair. He poured the wine. He slowly looked over at Maria. He put the carafe of wine down. He frowned and patted his lap.

Maria stood up and tiptoed towards her father, then gently allowed him to lift her up on his lap.

"Wha's-a matter for you-a, *he*?" He put his large hand on her tiny forehead. "You-a no feel-a good?"

Maria nervously stuck a finger in her mouth and swivelled those eyes at Andy. Andy sighed and stood up straighter, reached for a large pot and brought it to the table. She plunked the pot on a hot pad, grabbed a dish and slobbered chicken stew all over it and partially off it. She dumped the dish in front of Stefano. Hot broth slopped out of the dish, onto the table and onto his lap.

"*Che?*" he asked angrily as he pushed his chair back in surprise.

Andy looked around and said, "Nothing. Why?"

Stefano picked up a fork and stuck it into a piece of chicken. Andy went over to get potatoes and broccoli and came back to ladle some of that onto his plate.

Crack!

Andy stopped in mid-ladle. Maria swivelled her eyes at Stefano's mouth.

Stefano sat frozen while his tongue searched around and came up with a … shotgun pellet. He took it out gingerly and held it up. He stared at it while his tongue searched and found the broken tooth.

He silently looked over at Andy, still holding the pellet, still holding Maria on his lap. Slowly Maria slid off Stefano's lap and slipped away upstairs to her bedroom, where she gently closed the door and very carefully moved a dresser to block it. She then slid under the bed, tugged at Ernie from a basket of toys and held him tight.

Andy was still holding the vegetables in mid-ladle and stood staring down at the pot of chicken.

"Is-a from …?" Stefano pushed back his chair, walked down the steps and headed down the basement stairs. Andy heard him moving things around. By the time he appeared back in the kitchen with the shotgun, Andy was sitting down and had started eating the chicken.

"You know what, Stefano? I don't think I've ever tasted such lovely chicken. So tender! Hmm hmmm!" She ate the bird with relish. "Oh, I forgot! I want you to go see what your very expensive sweet and sour bird did to your precious Cadillac." She speared another piece of chicken and grinned as she popped it into her mouth.

Chapter 26

ANITA HAD A GREAT DAY at the office.

She drove to work whistling along with the radio, and brightened up even more when she heard the weather report for the day. It was to be unseasonably warm, and she looked forward to driving around town with all sorts of tidbits to offer her listeners. The day before, she had said live on air, "Beep your car horns when you see me in the CHJX-AM Jeep." And no sooner was she off the air than a few cars honked their horns as she drove through an intersection. That gave her a real thrill. "They listen! They listen!" she said aloud as she waved at them with a big grin.

Going up in the elevator from the parking garage, she was really looking forward to the press releases that would be waiting for her on her desk. She loved doing both the news and the promos, and she couldn't remember the last time she had felt so very happy. Better than that, in spite of all the money problems she and Jack had, she was quite content. She meant it when she had said to him, "So long as we have each other, darling."

With a delightful *ding*, the elevator doors opened, and standing waiting for her was her boss, Mike.

"Good morning! I'm sorry I'm late." She looked at her watch and then remembered she had dropped it off with the rest of her jewellery. "I'm not late, am I?"

"Hey, it's up to you. So long as you're on the air in time with some great news for our listeners, I don't really care." Anita nodded happily. Mike followed her to the press room. "Um, by the way, I owe you an apology, it seems."

Anita turned back to look at him.

"I received a load of calls yesterday and last night …"

Anita's face dropped and she frowned. "Uh oh," she said.

"No, actually, quite the opposite," he said, still quite surprised.

Anita cocked her head. "Really?"

Mike scratched behind his ear. "Er, yeah. People seemed to love that kid, uh, what's …?"

"Maria."

"Yes, Maria. People think we did that on purpose. Nothing but positive comments coming over the phone line. Maybe we should think of doing more of that. It's especially effective during spring break. Kind of like a theme, isn't it?"

Anita smiled. "I guess." She looked down at her shoes. Funny how things turned around. Twenty-four little hours. "I'm really happy. Thanks for letting me know, Mike."

"You're welcome." He pointed a finger at her and shot it like a pistol. "Keep up the good work," he said. "Oh, and by the way, you're smelling a hell of a lot better these days!"

Anita had a fabulous day.

After work, Anita thought she'd drop by the jeweller's for the appraisal and her jewellery before going on home to see her honeybun.

When he caught sight of her parking in front of his store, the jeweller turned the open sign to closed and tried to make a run for it.

Too late. She had reached the door before he successfully disappeared, and he had to acknowledge her rapping at the door. He smiled shakily, minced to the door and unlocked it. She entered, chimes ringing, and bounced straight to the counter ahead of him.

"Hi!" she smiled brightly. "I'm here to—"

The jeweller normally scoffed at people who believed in psychics and fortune tellers, but at that precise moment, he saw a vision so clearly that it startled him. It had a lot to do with death; like the wing of a butterfly, whatever he said and did to her at that precise moment would either cause or prevent World War lll thirty-three years hence. He had to tell her the truth. *It's too bad*, he thought. *She seems to be such a fine lady.*

"Hi, how are you?" he said as he stalled for time. "Of course I remember you!"

"Oh, I'm fine, I'm here—"

"Yes, of course I remember you."

"Great!" she smiled. "I'm glad you do! Are you finished with the appraisal?"

"Yes, I am, and yes, I have, and no, your jewellery isn't here." He did the deed. He nodded to himself, knowing he had prevented a terrible war. Too bad no one would ever know how courageously he had prevented such a catastrophic and historical event.

Anita looked a little perplexed, partly because of what he said and partly because of how he said it.

"Ebrahim, my employee, was here at the time. A gentleman came by with the claim ticket apparently."

"Oh, my husband. Yeah, that's okay. Did he pay you for the appraisal?"

A slight little man with large horn-rimmed glasses, the jeweller didn't look very strong, but he was able to lift a large roster up onto the counter. Anita noticed the sweat running off his forehead.

"Let's see here," he said as he traced all the lines with a finger.

While he was searching, his employee, Ebrahim, came in from behind the back curtain. He nodded at Anita and then bent down to get some ring boxes.

"Ebrahim."

"Yes, Mr. Fraser?" He popped back up.

"This lovely lady is the wife of that gentleman who came by to pick up a small velvet bag of jewellery and the appraisal I had made for them."

"Ah," said Ebrahim. At that instant, he knew he'd made a grave mistake somewhere. Suddenly, he had a primal urge to run home and have some nice hot rice pancakes. It felt like he was on a precipice of sorts and that everything he did at this very moment had potentially catastrophic effects on the world around him. Like that butterfly wing thing. He looked at her wide-eyed as he listened to his boss.

"And did Mr. Taylor pay for the appraisal?" Mr. Fraser said, smiling tightly.

Ebrahim's head jiggled in embarrassment. "Yes, sir, he did, but—"

"But what?" asked Anita.

Ebrahim held up a small brown digit of a finger. "He did not take the ring." He jiggled his head and clasped his hands together to keep them from shaking. Anita looked at two small men with very big tight smiles, both heads slightly on a tilt, both looking quite afraid. She looked around the store to see if there was a crouching criminal somewhere training a gun on them. Had she walked in halfway through a stickup?

"Ah … my engagement ring?"

"Your engagement ring!" echoed Mr. Fraser.

"Why wouldn't he want to bring back my ring?"

Mr. Fraser held up a finger of his own and bent down behind the counter. In an instant, he popped back up with her engagement ring in a tiny zip-lock bag. Anita stepped towards the counter and admired her beautifully set diamonds. She smiled at the sight of it, as she always did. And then she looked up at Mr. Fraser, who she saw was not smiling.

Neither was Ebrahim.

"Why didn't my husband pick this up at the same time?" she asked quietly.

Mr. Fraser cleared his throat, and Ebrahim looked over in fright. He was about to go to the back again when Mr. Fraser's hand shot out and grabbed him by his shirt to keep him in place. He felt that Ebrahim's presence was very necessary, even if just as a scapegoat.

"Er, why don't you tell Mrs. Taylor what happened?"

Ebrahim shook his head.

"Tell her please," he almost hissed.

Ebrahim licked his lips. "Your husband, madame, was not the one who picked up the jewellery." He stopped to clear his throat.

Anita felt a little ill.

"A red-haired lady, very beautiful—" Mr. Fraser kicked him. He jumped. "Not as beautiful as you, madame," Ebrahim smiled. "Well, this lady came in, had the appraisal ticket," he emphasized carefully, "paid for the appraisal, and then afterwards she went back to a little red sports car. There was a man sitting in the passenger's side of the car. I believe it was Mr. Taylor. They talked for a little while, madam, and then he sent her back in. That's when she left …" He held up the little bag. "This ring, this delightful little ring."

"Little ring …"

"Yes, madame." He swallowed hard and couldn't look at her face. "And then they just …"

"Just what?" she whispered.

Ebrahim waved both hands in the air. "They sped off, madame."

"This is a joke, right? Yeah, it's gotta be," she muttered. She slipped her engagement ring back onto her finger. Mr. Fraser and Ebrahim stood looking at it while she admired it first this way, then that. The bit about the red hair made her brain crash, and she was completely unaware of what she was doing by rote.

"And why did they leave this ring here?" she asked shakily.

"Because, Mrs. Taylor, it's zirconium."

"Zirconium? Is that a type of diamond?"

Here he precisely listed its character as from a dictionary: "It is a strong, malleable, ductile, lustrous silver-gray metal and its chemical and physical properties are similar to those of titanium."

"Chemical? Titanium? What does that mean exactly?"

"It means that it is worthless, madame," Ebrahim blurted. Mr. Fraser's mouth opened as he looked from her to Ebrahim and, without meaning to, out the windows for any sign of danger. "It is not worth more than two or three hundred dollars." He straightened up. "Canadian dollars, madame."

Anita stepped backwards and fell. Ebrahim screamed like a girl, and Mr. Fraser jumped over the counter. Both pulled her back up on her feet. They brushed her down. She turned and slowly walked out of the store.

"Oh, dear," said Mr. Fraser.

"*Oh bhaanchod shit!*" said Ebrahim in urdu.

They had both saved the future of Western civilization.

Anita had a fabulously rotten day.

⚬

Somehow, she made it home. She wasn't fully aware of how she got there, but she did—and, thank goodness she at least arrived home in one piece. Which was more than she could say for her shattered heart.

Jack wasn't home. Jack's clothes weren't home. His shaving paraphernalia, their camera and all his shoes weren't home either. Neither were the microwave and the coffee maker.

Chapter 27

TWO DAYS LATER, ANDY WATCHED as Maria stood stiff as a statue, letting Sharon's dressmaker creep around on her knees to pin up the hem of a frilly pink dress. Maria was watching her mother wide-eyed. Andy had already yelled at her when Maria pouted and refused to put the dress on. It wasn't her "style," she had complained, but Andy threatened to "style" her into a corkscrew if she didn't smarten up.

Sharon floated in from the back of the store. She had an ingenious and uncanny flair for the business of women's clothing and accessories. She knew her clientele well—most of them were her oldest friends. She knew that a) they all had money; b) they wanted to buy the best in clothing, jewellery and accessories no matter the cost; c) they all wanted to buy Italian—Italian leather, Italian silks, Italian brocades, Italian hats, Italian gloves, Italian pumps, Italian perfume, you name it Italian, they wanted it and they bought it; and d) they all wanted to outdo each other—especially Andy. In short, Sharon's store offered all that a healthy, wealthy Italian woman would love.

Even the decor and ambience were carefully orchestrated. Subdued lighting, a martini or a strong espresso while browsing through the latest fashions, personal fittings and free tailoring, an almond cake perhaps while you waited at the cash ... Everywhere one looked, there were large gold-gilded framed mirrors and white marble statues of naked women and satyrs. Expensive fake and real flower arrangements were everywhere—the real ones accompanied by a little card promoting Peter's florist shops. Garlands of the stuff hung along the tops of the cupboards and in front of shelves and around the inside edges of displays under glass. Inside her shop it was warm, rosy and exciting; frigid Canada was left outside those front doors. Here, you could believe you were in Europe: on the Riviera, in Rome, anywhere but "out there."

Andy had never been to Europe or anywhere outside of Quebec, so she thought of Sharon's store as being the closest she would ever be to "getting away from it all." At times, she watched jealously as her friends and acquaintances tried on lounge suits for their trips to Miami or absolutely incredible bathing suits and silky throws for their trips to Hawaii. *Forget 'em*, Andy jealously thought. *They can go to hell. I wouldn't be caught dead in a bathing suit anyhow*, she'd sniff, even though she knew damn well she had the best bod in town.

She salivated over the gold lamé two-piece swimsuit that hung off one of the fitting-room doors, but she tried desperately not to look at it, as to buy it was pure futility. In spite of its exquisite beauty and elegance and her bod, she still worried that her nose would upstage it all. This, more than anything, pissed her off. So instead, she made herself feel better by scoffing at anyone trying on a bathing suit.

"Who do you think you are, a two-hundred-pound Marilyn Monroe?"

"You're hopin' your husband don't look too closely?"

"Won't do, look at how your tush jiggles as you walk."

She whispered these things and practised a form of ventriloquism. She'd go over and pat them on their bums and revel in how they jiggled. "See? Who are you kiddin'?"

Sharon tried not to hear, though several times she had come this close to telling Andy off and threatening to bar her from the shop. But then, everyone knew Andy quite well and never took her comments seriously—or so Sharon consoled herself into thinking.

"Everything all right here?" she asked, smiling her best smile. She stood and looked from Maria to Andy and then to Maria's reflection in the full-length three-part mirror. She deftly ignored Maria's frown and pout. She turned to Andy. "What do you think, Andy? Doesn't she look like a princess?"

Andy smirked. "She's no more princess than Prince is a prince," she said, referring to the hot new extravagantly coiffed rock star. She cackled at her own joke. "What do you think, Maria?"

Maria opened her mouth, but Andy cut her off. "Forget it. I know what you think! You're doin' this fashion show in whatever stupid outfit

Sharon wants you in, you get my drift?" Andy turned to Sharon, "No offence meant, Sharon."

Sharon looked down her own nose and smiled tightly. "No offence taken, Andy. Of course not." She turned back and studied Maria's image in the mirror while walking slowly around her, looking her up and down, adjusting a button here and a knot there. She then put her hands on both sides of Maria's head and fluffed up the girl's hair a bit. Maria rolled her eyes. "You know," started Sharon, "I would cover the cost of doing Maria's hair if you'd let me. Make her look less like a boy. Why don't we send her to Alessi's House of Style?"

"Let's not," quipped Andy.

Sharon turned to face her. "And why not? She needs a little bounce, Andy. Just here and here." Sharon fluffed the hair again on both sides. Maria started shaking vigorously as she willed her mother to read her eyes. *No*, she willed her. *Noooooo.*

"What?" Andy asked Maria, knowing full well what.

Maria cast a quick glance at Sharon and then to her shoes.

"What *what*?" asked Sharon, her bright, innocent eyes open wide. Sharon had completely moulded herself into what she and the girls always imagined a Parisian dress designer would look like—at least what one must have looked like in the sixties, while they were still in their teens. It was a vision they had conjured up while sitting together smoking cigarettes, whether at their favourite spot at the top of the concrete steps or in the girls' washroom at school. Basic black or navy blue with slim hips (or as slim as they could get them), perfect posture, volumes of hair piled on top, one well-manicured hand always clasping the other, a smile with bright white teeth and perfectly lined lip look— as much like Chanel as any buxom Italian girl could possibly look. Lovely, luscious, lively, languid, ladylike Sharon.

"What *what*, what? You sound like a friggin' helicopter!" Andy turned to Maria. "Get it? Whatwhatwhatwhat."

Maria stamped her foot. "I *know*!"

There were customers in the store, and they all turned to stare at Maria. Sharon cleared her throat. Then she looked at her diamond-encrusted watch. "Oh dear, Anita's not here yet. I wonder what's keeping her?" Sharon walked to the front of the shop and looked out on the street. It was rush hour and already dark outside. She was fretting that Anita might be late or have forgotten the fitting entirely. She was the last to come, and Sharon didn't want to be too late going home to make supper for her husband, Claudio. Lately he had spent more time out at night than usual. She knew his work took him out and about at all hours of the day, but still, she had this sickening feeling it wasn't all business.

Sharon turned to walk back to the fitting when suddenly the door opened and the tiny little doorbells chimed melodically. Sharon turned to see Anita scrambling in. She wore a bulky purple ski jacket with the radio station's call letters, CHJX-AM, printed across the left breast and on the back. On her head was a snow-covered purple toque, also with the call letters on the front. She wore black denims that rumpled and bunched at the top of an ugly pair of black, scuffed boots. Sharon looked at her with a slightly quivering rise at the corners of her upper lip. She couldn't help it. It was an automatic reaction whenever she saw a major faux pas in fashion. She quickly recovered and smiled, lifting her ample arms in a welcoming embrace.

"Ah, finally, and just in time. Anita!"

"*Anitaaaaaa!*" called Maria, jumping on the spot in front of the large mirror and making the seamstress prick her finger. The woman sighed as she sat back and sucked at a bead of blood. She shook her head impatiently and then continued with her sewing. She couldn't wait to go home. She wasn't paid enough to do this shit.

Andy looked up and sniffed. "So you decided to show up, huh? You look like shit." Then she dug her nose into a woman's magazine.

Anita waved happily at Maria and looked her up and down. "Wow, you look great!"

Andy sniffed loudly. Maria lifted her skinny little arms towards Anita. Anita stepped closer and carefully bent over the seamstress to give Maria a hug.

Anita turned to Andy. "Hi, Andy, how's your dad?"

"Ask me how my ma's doing too."

"I'm sorry?" asked Anita, frowning.

"Nonna's broken her hip!" said Maria excitedly.

Anita covered her mouth in surprise. "Oh no! How?"

"She fell on my shoes," Maria offered.

"Yeah, they're as big as canoes," sniffed Andy, nose still buried.

"Is she in pain?" Anita asked, genuinely concerned.

"She'll live," answered Andy.

"So now you have both …?"

"You got it!" Andy snapped back.

"Oh dear," muttered Anita.

Sharon changed the subject deftly. "You are just in time. Come and see!" She led Anita to the back where, with flair, she stepped to one of the display racks and pulled out a bundle of clothes all zippered up in their own individual see-through garment bags. "These, my dear, are what you are modelling for us!" She motioned to an available dressing room and followed Anita to it. She flicked the powder-blue brocade curtains to the side and hung up the heavy bundle on one of the gold filigree hooks on the brocade-covered wall.

"If you need any help, Anita, just call. Then we'll take a look at whether we should be taking anything in. Would you like some coffee? Tea, perhaps? A biscotti?" Anita silently shook her head and morosely stepped into the cubicle. She was about to close the curtains when she turned to see Sharon standing with her hand held out. Anita raised her eyebrows questioningly. Sharon's fingers twitched. "Let me take your, er, coat and hat. Leave the boots off to the side. I'm going to find you some footwear for each outfit. What size are you?"

Anita looked down at her boots and began to push one off with the other foot. "Size nine and a half," she said.

"Ah, just like Andy!" Sharon said, turning to Andy with a big smile. "You both have big feet."

Andy frowned and threw her a dirty look, but Sharon ignored it and rushed off to help another customer waiting for assistance at the cash counter at the front of the store.

Andy swivelled her nose and threw Anita a dirty look as well. She was happy that Anita caught it just as she closed the curtains to the change room.

You bad, girl, Andy thought to herself. She crossed her legs and tapped a rhythm on the side of the faux Louis XIV armchair she was sitting in. With a huff, she suddenly got up and hovered over the seamstress. "How much longer?" she asked.

The seamstress sat back on her haunches and looked up at Andy forlornly and with pinched mouth. There were pearl-headed pins stuck between her chapped lips as she tried to reply.

Andy got impatient. "What? A minute? Thirty seconds?"

The seamstress, needle and thread in hand, shook her head this way and that. She held up a pinky.

"A minute?"

The seamstress shrugged and then nodded.

"Well, hurry up. We have to get home. I have a man to feed."

You and the Easter Bunny, thought the seamstress.

"Can we invite Anita home for supper, Mom?" cried Maria.

Andy shook her head, glared at her daughter menacingly and mouthed, "Shut up."

"Aaaaah, Mom! We haven't seen her for ages!" complained Maria.

Andy held up a manicured finger in warning and then menacingly stabbed it through the air at her daughter. Maria kept pouting but remained quiet, stamping a foot instead. The seamstress bleated and held up her hand to see another drop of blood on one of her fingers. She shook her head in exasperation and then looked up at Maria, furious. Maria didn't notice. And Andy didn't care.

Anita stood listening in the fitting nook. She hadn't been feeling very well, and she'd had a very difficult week waiting for Jack to come back. But that in itself was another ball of wax trouble-wise, because the more time that lapsed since his most recent disappearance, the more holes she could see in Jack's explanation of things. He had also been far from amorous. She felt cold and unwanted and it only added to the same suspicions she now started entertaining anew. So Andy's attitude almost took the biscuit.

Anita had little heart to spare for Andy. She hadn't slept a wink the last few days. Questions, questions, questions. She had driven herself sick with questions. Why did Jack lie to her about Italy? Why had he taken her ring and coat and then taken all that jewellery. Had he just simply not bothered to show up, or was he lying somewhere in a ditch dead as a doorpost?

To cap it all off, she'd had to go alone to the bank that morning about Jack's mortgage. The bank was going to foreclose on the mortgage regardless.

"Just because we're three or four months behind!?" Anita had asked incredulously.

"Try a year," the banker had said.

Anita's mouth had dropped.

"But," the man pointed out gently, "we begin with a letter of intent. We have to follow a strict procedure. You must remember, you can always bring back payments up to date at any time. But we consider this a serious matter, Anita. The next step is up to you—or rather, your husband, Jack. But money talks, no matter where it comes from."

Ever since then, she had felt continuously sick to her stomach. She figured she had ulcers and realized that she hadn't eaten a thing all day. She turned to look at herself in the mirror and saw a very pale, sickly looking thirty-something woman wearing very ugly clothes.

Out by the mirror, the seamstress finally moved away from Maria's hem and struggled to get up with a groan and a loud crack in her back. "*Finito*," she said, and she stood back to admire her work. She motioned for Maria to turn. "Good, good," she said, and with that, she gratefully picked up her sewing materials and slunk into the back, where she was desperate to get her coat on and leave before Sharon asked any more of her.

While she stood behind the back curtains, she quickly ran a finger along her lips. She had kept pins clenched tightly between her lips for so many years that sometimes she forgot they were there. Once she fell ill with something entirely unrelated, but her X-rays showed two suspicious dashes in her esophagus. Apparently, she had swallowed two pins at some point. The doctor, though he had never seen such a thing, advised her not to do anything—no surgery, nothing—as they would work themselves through and out her body on their own time.

He was right! One day she had an odd itch near her belly button, and when she scratched the spot, she was able to dislodge a straight pin! One down, one to go. Ergo, her habit of checking her lips.

Out in the fitting area, Maria and Andy looked at each other for a moment. Andy cocked her head towards the fitting rooms. Maria jumped down off the low pedestal and skipped slowly to her fitting room. "Now, not tomorrow!" warned Andy.

Not wanting to meet Anita face to face, Andy hurried down to the front of the shop and waited for Maria at the cash counter. She busied herself by browsing through the many beautiful things on display: fabulous sunglasses for those going south for the winter (*they can drown while they're at it*, Andy thought jealously); breathtakingly beautiful earring and necklace sets with matching rings; designer jewellery buttons to replace boring buttons on outfits; colourful purses and billfolds; delightful makeup bags and satin pull-string bags in which to store the sheer and expensive nylons Sharon sold; shoulder pads that were the latest fad, all neatly packaged; little trinkets in gold, silver and pewter, encrusted with tiny diamonds … there was enough booty for a whole week of browsing.

Suddenly, though, Andy didn't feel interested in any of it. Anita looked shitty, and in spite of everything, Andy was concerned. For a moment, she even forgot what it was that she was angry about. However, not being a forgiving sort at the best of times, she decided she wasn't going to be nice tonight; she'd let Anita suffer a little longer. She didn't like how Stefano fretted about the fact that Anita was alone. He had gotten in the habit of listening to her on the radio, both at the construction site and at home, and Andy hated that with a passion.

Andy couldn't take the waiting anymore. She wanted to bolt. She cleared her throat loudly, but that only made Sharon turn to look. Quietly, Sharon excused herself from her customer.

"Ready, Andy?" she smiled. "Perhaps I should help Maria undress?" It was obviously a hint for Andy to do it. Sharon was afraid that Maria might rip something while undressing. This was a valid concern.

"I doubt it," said Andy. "She's been undressing herself for ten years, and I think she can manage quite well."

Sharon frowned. "Yes, but taking off play clothes and taking off five-hundred-dollar dresses are two very different things, Andy. Wait, I'll go back and help her." She turned to go.

"Fill your boots, but make it quick!"

Sharon froze in mid step. She did a double take and then rolled her eyes. She was struggling through menopause, and Andy was easily the most frequent trigger for her hot flashes. She had heard about menopausal woman murdering people.

Andy, completely oblivious to Sharon's violent thoughts, turned to look outside and fretted. She hated driving, but she hated driving through snow and dark of night even worse. "Shit," she muttered to herself. If she had been on good terms with Anita—or rather, if Anita had been on good terms with Andy—she would've asked her for help driving them home. Instead, she shook her head. "You dumb-ass," she said to herself.

Sharon finally returned with Maria in tow, back in her school clothes. Sharon didn't look too happy, and Andy didn't need to ask. Sharon was carrying the frilly dress over her arm, and it had a tear in the new hem.

"Great! Let's go, Maria. Okay, Sharon. See you at the club. I guess you want us early to get ready for the show?"

Sharon raised her eyebrows. "Oh, no, Andy! Didn't I tell you? First of all, we need a rehearsal—"

"Oh, shit," said Andy.

"—and second, the fashion show's part of the grand opening for the new Vindenza Village Mall!"

The fundraiser had always been held at the Italian Canadian Club, so this was a real change from routine. Andy didn't like change. She cocked her head at Sharon and looked through half-closed eyes.

"At that new mall?"

"Yes. I'm opening a second store at the mall, and Peter thought it would be great to invite all the club members to the mall instead. There's going to be food and drink, music, and balloons. And there's this absolutely gorgeous marble central sitting area with fountains and lights, with a large tree growing under a cupola of glass. Oh, just exquisite!"

Maria jumped with glee. *"Balloons!"*

Sharon smiled tightly at Maria. "Yes, lots of balloons."

Andy stood back. "Peter," she drawled. "My brother-in-law Peter?" She hated not being in the know. "What has he got to do with this friggin' mall?"

Sharon looked askance. "Well, he built it, Andy. Or at least he's heading a consortium of sorts that have invested in the mall along with him and Stefano."

"Stefano. *My* Stefano?"

"You didn't know? Your Stefano was the contractor, and I was under the impression from Peter that he was also an investor. Er, I mean, well, I should say, *you* and Stefano."

Andy stood looking down her nose at Sharon for exactly five long seconds. Suddenly she motioned to Maria. "Come," she commanded, and she hustled Maria out the front door. The girl was still dragging her coat with one arm in a sleeve. *"Mooooom, I'm not dressed yet!"* she cried.

But the door slowly swung shut behind them, and Maria's whining mercifully diminished with the wind and traffic noise outside.

Sharon sighed and stood for a moment to gather her wits together. She heard a noise behind her and turned to see Anita stepping out of the fitting room in one of the three outfits she was to wear for the fashion show. It was a blue denim-like braided-cotton two-piece with a long tunic as a top over matching denim-blue tights. Sharon walked over and smiled, nodding and motioning for Anita to step in front of the large mirror. Quietly, Sharon tucked a fold here and straightened a fold there. She looked at Anita in the mirror and was surprised to see tears in the woman's eyes. She reached behind one of the statues and pulled out a box of fancy tissues. Anita pulled a few out wordlessly and dabbed them at her eyes.

"You shouldn't let Andy get you down like that," said Sharon. "You know she's a loose cannon. She can be so cruel sometimes."

"Sometimes?" Anita said grimly. Of course, she couldn't blame *everything* on Andy. But she didn't feel like enlightening Sharon about all that was tearing her apart. So she nodded and didn't say another thing. She knew if she were to open her mouth, she'd be unable to control herself, and she seriously feared losing her sanity. How could she explain to Sharon—a relative stranger—that she was losing her home, had lost her car, was on the brink of losing her job, had no money, had lost her jewellery and fur coat, and worst of all, had lost all of it to Jack and lost him once again. No, scratch that, she thought. Worst, worst of all, was that Jack had lied to her. And lord knows what all he had lied about. So she'd also lost her marriage. Anita wanted to go to sleep and never wake up.

As if feeling her pain, Sharon gently patted Anita on the shoulder. "Wait here. I'm closing the shop now. We can talk over a cup of coffee, if you like. I'll be right back." Sharon walked the length of her exquisite ladies' fashion store, locked the front doors and turned the "Open" sign over to "Closed."

Behind Anita, the seamstress walked through the back drapes with her coat and hat on. "*Buonanote*," she said, smiling. As she passed the cash counter, she spied the frilly pink dress hanging over the edge. She grabbed the hem and shook her head in anger. "*Mama mia!*" She looked at Sharon and sighed. Sharon made a small jerky motion with her shoulders and shook her head. She unlocked the door for the woman.

Before stepping out, the seamstress grabbed the dress, threw it over her shoulder and walked out onto the slush-covered sidewalk cursing under her breath.

Sharon slowly closed and locked the doors again. She put a hand on her ample breast as she watched the traffic go by. Sometimes it just wasn't worth getting some people to volunteer. But Andy was indeed her best customer, and Sharon desperately needed children in the show. *Oh, the things we do in desperation*, she thought to herself.

Part of what made Sharon such an excellent saleswoman and entrepreneur was her big heart and sincere concern for her clients' well-being and satisfaction. It was this same concern that drew Sharon to Anita that night. "You okay?"

"Yes. No." Anita looked at Sharon with welling eyes and shrugged. "I'll be okay. Really."

"Your husband?" asked Sharon.

Anita nodded, but she quickly held up her hand to keep Sharon from saying another word about it. She then changed the subject.

"Did I hear you say that the show's at the new mall and not at the club?"

Sharon bent over and started picking up the scarves that Andy had scattered over the carpet and furniture. "I take it you didn't know either?"

"Well, I knew of the grand opening. In fact, I'm covering it for the station. But the fashion show was supposed to be that night at the club, right?"

"Yes, it was originally scheduled for that night, but just the other day the committee agreed to combine the two. It meant that much more exposure for the mall, and it saved a good buck for the club. That much more cash in their pockets. Everyone thought it was a fabulous idea. Is it a problem?" Sharon had moved on to the shoe display and checked for a perfect pair of casual shoes to go with Anita's outfit.

"Yeah, a bit of a one. I'm working during the entire day interviewing and promoting the mall on air. I'd like to do your show, Sharon, but work comes first. There's no way I can do both of them at the same time."

"Gee, Anita, you just have to do it. I'm really counting on you to carry this part of the show. Not only do you make my clothes look great, but you're also a bit of a star."

"A star?"

"Well, of course! You're a local celebrity, Anita. You're on air, you zip around town in the station's Jeep, telling people what to do, what to see, where to see it! I'm sure you're a major part of why that station has so much of an advertising base. Didn't you know that?"

Anita looked down at her outfit and gently smoothed the front of it. Oh, she felt so sick. "No, not really. It kind of feels like the complete opposite." She sighed. "I'm sorry, Sharon. I don't know. I'll ask my boss. Maybe I can reschedule the live-on-air spots and do the fashion show in between. Would you mind if I walk around in whatever outfit I'm wearing if I don't have time to change for the following live-on-air spot?"

"Are you kidding? I'd love for you to do that. If you do that, I would be more than happy for you to keep whichever of the three outfits you are modelling for yourself." Sharon clasped her hands against her bosom and beamed.

She walked over to the front counter, picked up her somewhat gaudy white and gold antique phone, and dialled with a pen. She stood quietly as she waited. "Well, hello, Darlene? How are you? Yes. Oh good! Yes, actually, I was hoping Mike was there. Thank you!"

Anita was in the middle of putting on the shoes when she was surprised to hear Mike's name. She frowned. Mike, her boss, Mike? She stopped to listen.

"Yes, hi, Michael, how are you? Well, I'm here standing beside one of my favourite people. Who? Anita! Yes, isn't she wonderful? Michael, Anita tells me she has a conflict and I was hoping you could sort it out for me. Anita was to model for me at the club's annual fundraiser, but because it's now part of the grand opening of the new Vindenza Village Mall, she can't do it because she's also on-air all that day. Yes. Okay! Great! I knew you would. Thank you, Michael. [pause] Well, I was thinking she could do spots afterwards while wearing my outfits. She could just do them right from the runway even? [pause] Wonderful! Thank you, Michael. See you at the fundraiser! Oh, and by the way. I'd like to sign up for another three months of seven spots a day in the usual thirty-second spots … Oh, good. I'm ever so glad. Goodbye!"

Sharon hung up with a singing heart and sauntered back to Anita. "Everything's arranged! You're still in the show. He said that you were quite capable of combining the two things during the day and that if anything, I well deserved the extra exposure with you doing the show and walking around in my outfits."

Anita was nonplussed. "He told you all that?"

"Well, no, but he meant to," said Sharon as she took another close look at Anita now that a pair of matching shoes had been added to the ensemble.

"Well, okay then," said Anita. "I guess I'm still doing the show."

Sharon stood with her head cocked to the side and stared at Anita with a glazed look. "Maybe we'll do four outfits! Can you handle that?"

Anita shrugged and nodded. "Sure," she said.

Sharon smiled and walked over to a round red plush-velvet couch in the middle of the fitting area. "Come, Anita. Sit down and relax. Oh, those shoes look great! I'll make a note of that! I'll get us some coffee first. Or would you rather have a glass of wine?"

Anita didn't really want to extend the fitting any longer, but she didn't know how to bow out of the offer politely.

"Wait," Sharon interjected, "I'll give my husband a call and tell him supper's going to be a little late. You're not in a hurry to go home, are you?"

Anita walked over to the couch, sat down and pretended not to cry while she took off the shoes and placed them back in their box. Tears trickled down her nose and cheeks. "No," she blubbered. "I have no one to hurry home to."

"Can you tell me about it?"

"Oh, I don't know, Sharon. It's nice of you to care, but there's nothing anyone can do about it."

"Oh yes there is. I know." She held up a hand to stop Anita from arguing.

Andy slammed her way into the hallway. She shook off her boots, stomped into the family room and stopped. The wheelchair sat in the middle of the carpet. However, Claudia wasn't in the armchair, and her walker was also gone.

"Oh shit, now what?" she muttered. *"Ma?"* she called. She stood and listened. *"Ma!"* Maria stumbled in and slammed the hallway door shut behind her. Andy turned on her. "Maria! Stop slamming doors!"

Maria gave her mother a sideways glance and hopped in front of the TV. She turned it on and stood for a moment to see what was on. She saw it was *Sesame Street*, so she hopped a step back and flopped down into a lotus position.

"Jesus, Maria, you're too friggin' old for that!" Andy walked to the front hallway and yelled up the stairs. *"Ma!"* She hurried back into the kitchen and dropped her coat on the floor as she headed for the basement stairs. *"Ma!"* she yelled downstairs. Suddenly she ran back up and raced for the phone. "Jesus, Mary and friggin' Joseph! This is freaking me out!" She dialled quickly. "Yeah, hi. St. Joseph's? I'm Andy ... Yeah, hi, Julia!"

Maria quietly looked at her mother before turning back to the screen. Then she got up from her spot on the carpet, skipped to the kitchen and sat down at the table to listen.

"Holy Toledo! For fu—"

Maria licked her fingers and drew smudgy circles on the kitchen table. Then she rubbed them off with her sleeve and drew a stick figure. She started humming with the music on *Sesame Street*.

"No kidding!" Andy yelled sarcastically. "Who does she think she is!? Giving me a heart attack like that! All right!" She slammed the phone back on its hook.

Maria leaned onto the table with her elbow and looked back at her mother. "Is Nonna okay?" she asked.

Andy looked over at the stove clock and then hauled open the freezer door. She wordlessly took out a package of frozen Italian buns.

"Mom? Is Nonna okay?"

Andy looked over and saw the concern on Maria's face. "Yeah, your *nonna's* okay, but she's not goin' to be when I see her!" Andy turned on the oven to preheat. Two things she was pissed off about: first, her mother being unable stand still for one moment even with a broken hip—she probably bugged the hell out of Peter to take her to the hospital—and second, Stefano with his finger in Peter's shady business deals.

"But how's Nonna coming back if she can't walk?" continued Maria. "Did she take a taxi? Mom, did she go to see Nonno? Mooom?"

"Maria, quit bugging me!" Andy yelled.

"But I wanna know!" Maria whined.

"Maria! Get the fu— ... get the hell upstairs and stay out of my hair!"

Maria bolted up and knocked back her chair noisily. She ran upstairs, banged the walls with her little fists and slammed her bedroom door hard. The windows beside Andy at the sink rattled. Andy turned to look at them. It was pitch black outside, and all she could see was her blurred reflection. She turned her head slightly to the right and left and studied the image of her nose. That nose. Her mother, her father, Stefano ... She looked down into the stainless steel double sink and whispered to herself, "I don't know if I want to be here." A point of heat began to form behind her aching eyes, but she refused to let herself break.

There was a familiar loud bang outside by the back door. Stefano was home. She knew he would go straight downstairs, have his shower and dress. She looked at her watch. She had about ten minutes before he would appear in her kitchen. *Her* kitchen. Her one and only domain. "Andy-land," she said aloud.

Maria. What kind of a life did that kid have? No friends, nothing to stimulate her. But that was Andy. It was Andy who didn't want kids running amok in the house. Also, Maria had inherited Andy's disdain for Stefano's pets and gardens, but she had begged to have a pony and in spite of having more than enough money and the room, Andy wouldn't let her. It occurred to Andy suddenly that perhaps she was being unfair. Then she thought of the article she had read in one of those curled-up old magazines at the hospital that Disney had opened another theme park: Epcot Center. Florida. Florida. "Andy's always wanted to go to Florida," she mumbled.

Andy was still standing at the sink when Stefano finally walked up from the basement and into the family room. He walked straight to the TV and turned it off before he turned to walk up the few steps into the kitchen. "How you-a think wid dat-a noise?" he said as he pulled out his chair at the table and sat down.

Andy took a partly filled carafe of red wine from the corner of the counter and grabbed a short glass on her way to the table. She put the glass down in front of Stefano and poured in the contents of the carafe.

"Welcome to Andy-land," she muttered, and she plopped the empty carafe in the middle of the table. Stefano glanced upwards and then mutely took the empty carafe and got up to refill it down in the basement. As he turned to go, Andy piped up, "So you got money in Peter's new businesses, I hear."

Stefano stopped and turned around. "*Si*," he said as if she should've known. He looked at her and shrugged. "*Che?*"

Andy mimicked him. She shrugged and said, "*Che? Che?*"

A dark cloud descended on Stefano's brow, and he slowly walked back to the table, put the carafe down and waited.

Andy fidgeted. She turned and put the frozen buns into the hot oven and then walked to the fridge and took out a bag of frozen spaghetti sauce. She turned her back on Stefano at the stove and shrugged again. "I dunno. Like I have no say in all of this?" She turned to face him, and her heart started pounding. "I didn't even know! You didn't think to tell me? I had to hear it from a clothing store owner, for crying out loud!"

"She no-a jus' owner. Sharon is-a *tua amica!*" Stefano shook his head, picked up the carafe again and turned to go. "I get-a *vino*."

"Why?" Andy retorted. "Is *vino* so much more important than I am?"

Stefano froze for a moment. When he turned, his face was beet red and his aqua eyes were shining like two aquamarine diamonds. He pointed here and there as he spoke. "You have-a bad life-a?" He pointed at her clothes. "You no-a have-a all da *vestiti?*"

"Yeah, Stefano. I have lots of clothes and more clothes! That means I should be happy?"

Stefano frowned and stepped heavily around the side of the table. "You no-a do much. You no-a work," he started counting on his fingers, "you no-a do da garden-a, you no-a do da animals," he said, pointing in the direction of the barn. "You no-a do grass-a, no-a *vino*, no-a *formaggio*, no-a *salciccia!* You kill-a my bird!" He poked a thick forefinger into his breastplate. "Wot-a you do-a all day, eh?"

"You know what I do all day, Stefano!? I cook. I cook and I cook, then I clean, then I cook! Yeah, I shop. I shop till my heart explodes, Stefano. You think that's enough!?" Andy yelled.

Stefano fumed and smashed his hand into the middle of the kitchen table. It sounded with a huge *crack* and trembled on the floor. "You-a think-a dis is enough for-a *me?*" he bellowed. "Dat una bambina is-a enough?" He pounded on his chest. "'N-a I have-a no *sons!*" (His voice cracked, which shocked the hell out of Andy. She was to remember that crack in his voice for the rest of her life.) He grabbed one of the kitchen chairs and threw it across the tiled floor towards Andy. She watched it slide and stop against her feet.

Andy had wondered when the issue of sons would come out in the open. In selfish defence, she'd never worried about Stefano's unhappiness. It had become a constant over the years and something that Andy simply ignored. It was easier that way.

She finally looked up to find Maria standing at the kitchen door. The girl had crept down during the shouting, and she now stood leaning against the door frame, crying with silent, body-shaking sobs. Stefano stood looking at her, and in quiet desperation, he moved towards her with arms open wide in reassurance. Maria didn't wait. She turned and ran back to her room, screaming, *"I hate you! Both of you!"* Again she slammed her bedroom door hard enough to rattle those stupid windows over the stupid sink again.

Stefano had tears in his eyes, and with a broad fist he rubbed them away from each eye. He silently reached down and fidgeted with the empty carafe. Suddenly he picked it up and smashed it against the kitchen wall, and then he turned and stomped out into the hallway towards the garage. At first, Andy thought he was heading for his *caverna*, but then she heard the truck engine roar, and she watched the reflection of the truck lights quickly back up out of the driveway. She ran from the stove out into the living room to watch through the front window as he skidded on the frozen wet road and roared away.

Andy covered her eyes and stood in the dark for a few moments until her head cleared. Then she turned and slowly climbed the stairs to the bedrooms.

She tried Maria's doorknob. The door opened slightly, but it was prevented from opening any further by a heavy object. Maria had pushed her dresser against the door, and she was hiding under her bed, crying.

"Maria?" Andy whispered. She knocked on the door. "Maria? Let me in."

"No! Get away!"

Andy leaned her head against the door. She rattled the doorknob. "Come on, Maria. Let me in."

"No!"

Andy took a deep breath. She slapped against the door.

"Go away!"

Andy pushed harder against the door, easily moving the dresser out of the way. Andy looked around. "Maria?"

"*What?*"

Andy kneeled down and looked under the bed. She saw Maria's swollen eyes and tear-stained face and her heart broke. Though they argued relentlessly, Maria never cried. Andy couldn't stand the sight of her child this way. She lowered herself on her belly and crawled partly under the bed. Maria moved a fraction away from her.

"Why are you crying?" asked Andy gently. Maria turned her face away from her. Instinctively, Andy knew that whatever she did now would leave a lasting impression on Maria and affect their mother-daughter relationship forever. With a shaky hand, she reached out and gently stroked Maria's little shoulder. Maria didn't move and continued to sniff, maybe even a little louder.

Slowly, Andy reached out her other hand and gently pulled Maria closer to herself. Then she slowly crawled backwards, pulling Maria along. She finally cleared her from under the bed and held the child on her lap, kneeling on the floor and leaning against the bed. "Shhh," she said. "Shhh."

Maria rested her head on her mother's shoulder. It felt strange to be this close, other than during a night's sleep—to be touching somehow. She closed her eyes and sank a little further into her mother's lap. Andy rocked her back and forth. "It's okay, little kiddo-mine. Daddy's not mad with you. Just with me."

Maria frowned and lifted her head slowly. She wiped her eyes with the sleeve of her baby-blue sweater. "Did Daddy want me to be a boy?" Maria's eyes were as big as saucers, and Andy almost couldn't bear the sight. It would've been so much easier to make a crass remark, to brush this aside with a swipe of her hand, but she knew in her heart that refusing to deal with the emotional pain and vulnerability would be deadly to Maria. Instead, she held Maria's face and looked straight into her eyes.

"No Maria. Weather you are a little girl or boy, you are our special little angel. Who loves you more than anything? We do!" She straightened out Maria's bangs and pushed them away from her eyes. Then fervently she locked eyes with Maria again. "Look at me, Maria. You know with all your heart that you're Daddy's little girl! You know you can—and you do—" Andy joked with a smile, "get away with everything! Of course, not with me you don't," she smiled and chuckled. Maria looked up at Andy's smile. She nodded and smiled slightly.

"I know," she said.

Andy grabbed her and held her tight. Oh so tight! She held her precious daughter and gently continued to rock back and forth, back and forth. Eventually, Maria's body relaxed, and the girl fell asleep. Andy struggled to her feet and half dragged the sleeping child up with her and she lay Maria gently down on the bed. Andy straightened up and turned the lights out but left the door open to allow the hallway light to spread softly into the room. She slipped down to the kitchen and turned the oven off, leaving the buns to rest for the next day. Softly and quietly, she returned to the bedroom and lay down beside Maria, allowing her mind to wander back to when sons were indeed "an issue."

1964–1969

She'd had two miscarriages and one stillbirth by February of 1969. The first time she lost a baby was within five months of their wedding. Stefano had started building their own house immediately, wanting to have it ready for the baby. In the meantime, Claudia and Fabrizio insisted the newlyweds stay with them.

Life was intolerable for Andy. The last thing she'd expected was to have to continue living with her parents. And she was seriously frightened at the thought that Stefano was expecting her to be just like her mother. Every day, Claudia catered to Stefano and Fabrizio, shrieking, "Eat, eat!"

"Andy, see?" Claudia would say, usually while dishing out more macaroni for Stefano. "You need to learn how to make the macaroni like Stefano likes it-a."

Andy felt sick. She'd been feeling sick as a dog since the day she conceived. And if this was what you felt like pregnant, she hoped it was the only snotty-nosed kid she would ever have. And Stefano and her parents wanted a slew of sons and grandsons? Yeah, right! Forget it.

One night, Fabrizio pointed his fork at his daughter. He grunted and wheezed and pointed at her stomach. Then he flexed what little muscle he had left in his arms.

"What, Pa? You're telling me I should eat more so that I can be sicker than I am now?"

He shook his head and pointed his fork to the ceiling. "Ma ... ma ... Santa Maria," he muttered.

Claudia looked at Andy and shook her head as well. "Andy," she said, also pointing her fork but at Andy. "You-a lucky. Other poor *madres*, they can' have no bambinos."

"So is that so bad?" she had asked, watching Stefano shovelling the food into his mouth. Suddenly she slapped a hand to her mouth, and she rushed out of the kitchen into the cramped little bathroom right next door.

She slammed the door shut. God, even in the bathroom she could smell garlic and tomato and onions. She slammed the toilet seat up and bent over and heaved. The problem was, there was never anything to heave. She didn't know which was worse: throwing up something and that's really gross, or heaving up nothing, but the pain of heaving was so overwhelming. Once she heaved so intensely she broke a blood vessel in her eye, and she'd been walking around with it ever since.

She leaned back on her haunches as she continued to cling to the nice cold white porcelain. She pressed her forehead to the front rim of the bowl. Then there was a knock on the door.

"Andy! You-a need more food. You eat-a. You throw up because you no eat!" Claudia screeched. Then she heard her father and Stefano jabbering in Italian.

What in hell happened? she wondered. *Since when does the whole world unite against me? It's the kid. That's all they worry about.*

"Annnnndddyyy!"

"Ma, *shut up!*"

She could hear her mother mumbling her way back to the kitchen table. She let herself flop onto her behind with her back against the toilet.

Her mother came back to the door. "Annnnndddyyy! Maybe someone-a need the bathroom!"

She could hear Stefano tell Claudia that it was no problem. No one needed the bathroom. Not yet, anyhow.

Suddenly, Andy was racked with pain. She bent over double and thought she must be dying. "Aaaah," she winced. She tried to get up. "Ma! Ma!" She waited for her mother, but now her mother wasn't coming. "*Ma, I'm dying here!*" She heard her mother stop talking. As a matter of fact, there wasn't any talking at all. As if the world outside that locked door had disappeared like in *Twilight Zone*. "God help me," she whispered.

Then Stefano kicked in the door and picked her up and placed her on their bed in her old bedroom. They had switched the single bed for a double, but it cramped almost every other stick of furniture that was in there.

Andy groaned and clasped her midriff. Stefano turned white in the face. "Santa Maria," he whispered, watching her helplessly.

They had called an ambulance, and by the time they arrived at emergency, the paramedics had confirmed what she had eventually guessed was happening to her. She'd miscarried.

Claudia grieved. Fabrizio was quiet, as women's issues were a mystery to him, but he did manage to say to Stefano that he would just have to keep trying, *wink wink, nudge nudge*. If Andy had heard him, she would've been fatherless and her mother a widow almost immediately.

Stefano was in shock. It had never occurred to him that they could lose a little baby. They were both healthy. But then he started looking for blame. Andy still smoked the odd cigarette. She didn't eat right. She was only concerned about her weight—for some reason, she kept thinking they were going to go to Miami one of these days. He had said no, he didn't want to be near any of those Mafioso goings-on down there. He was still terrible naïve.

The doctor explained that miscarriages occurred in nearly 20 per cent of pregnancies, and when it happened, it was very common within twelve weeks of conception. It could've been caused by stress, by hormones. The doctor had shrugged his shoulders and said, "Go try again. You fall off the horse? So get right back on it!"

Andy didn't appreciate being compared to a horse, but she got the message. Stefano had asked how long he had to wait before he made another baby. The doctor had winked and said, "Give it a week. She'll be ready."

By the time she got pregnant again, the foundation for the house had been poured. And because Stefano was so grateful that she would allow him another child so soon, he insisted she tell him what she wanted out of the house he was building.

He had given her the drawings and gently held her hand as he led her over the clumps of mud and cement to take a look at the footprint of their new home. She had sniffed at it as he pointed at this, and that, and there is going to be the kitchen ...

She sniffed again. She shook her head and said, "No."

"No?" Stefano had asked.

She shook her head again. "I'm not moving into a house where the kitchen is the biggest room, Stefano. What is this, a restaurant?"

Stefano had been surprised to even notice that the kitchen was the biggest room. "But where-a bambinos?"

"I don't know about you, Stefano, but we're not going to give birth to a football team."

He understood "football." He laughed and nodded, "*Si, si!*"

And Andy said, "No, no!" She grabbed his drawings from him and looked at the layout. She looked around the muck and construction equipment to get her bearings. She pointed off to the far side about a hundred feet out. She stumbled in her high heels (she was a "woman" now) and walked out where she wanted the master bedroom and the ensuite. She picked up some rocks and placed them at the corners of the new bedroom. She picked up some more and showed Stefano a big living room at the front of the house. She also pointed out that they would need at least four bedrooms if not more, and of course a very deep basement. That could be where the original kitchen was supposed to go, but lower by a floor. She walked out another kitchen. She also insisted that he have his own shower, toilet and garage, because she wasn't going to be picking up after him all day and night.

Stefano scratched his head. He looked at the rocks and at his new bride. She was carrying a possible son, and he had already come to realize that the sooner the house was finished, the sooner she would calm down. He loved Claudia and Fabrizio, but he could see that they didn't get a moment's peace.

He had nodded and said, "*Si!*"

Andy had looked back at him. "*Si?* For sure?"

And he grinned and said, "*Si*, for-a sure-a!"

Andy was so happy she forgot she was hiding gum in her mouth and started snapping away at it. Stefano shook his head, disappointed.

"Oops!" she said and happily threw away the gum. It ended up at the precise location marking her future clandestine smoking corner in the kitchen. It was also where she was going to be cooking and cooking and cooking. But this she didn't know. There are small mercies throughout our lives, and this was merciful for Andy, because if she had known all the cooking she was going to have to do over and over in that spot, she would've run away with the circus.

A month later, she had another miscarriage.

She cried. She worried and she fretted. And Stefano cried.

This time the doctor offered other explanations. Sometimes, he said, genetic defects could cause a fetus to miscarry. It could also have been due to a faulty egg or sperm.

Andy was quiet. She wasn't really ready to give up. Now that she saw in her mind how beautiful the house was going to be, she was determined to fill that wonderful picture with her and Stefano's children. It had to happen. It was part of the plan.

Claudia wasn't much help. She said that the problem always rested on the woman's shoulders. She didn't eat right, sleep right, should stay away from smoking and drinking, high heels, should eat for two, and on and on.

Now Andy started feeling uncomfortable whenever Stefano reached for her during the night. She had loved his touch, and the surprise that the whole act of lovemaking was almost as wonderful as she had heard and read about. But now. But now.

It took a little longer to conceive this time. It was as if her body was waiting to sleep in their own home on their new bed with the duvet and satin sheets. She already knew which seamstress was going to make their curtains and drapes. She wanted all new furniture—specifically that new stainless steel look with heavy red leather and white plush carpets. She already decided she was never going to hang up wash. *She* was going to have a dryer and—

"No," said Stefano. "We save-a money." And that was that.

Now she definitely didn't feel cozy with her husband! Now she understood precisely the old joke of, "Not tonight, dear, I have a headache!"

She started having headaches. She even went to the doctor about these headaches. Until one day, the doctor sat her down and said, "Andy, you've never been one for headaches. Except for your two miscarriages, you've been healthy as a horse. Tests show nothing. Can this have something to do with fear of another miscarriage perhaps?" He was a kindly man.

She thought hard about that one. "Nope," she said with certainty. "I don't know where they come from. Allergies, maybe?"

And her doctor sighed and decided to play along with her game, prescribing what was essentially aspirin. She would take them last thing at night as she sat perched on the side of the bed while Stefano was hoping that *this* was the night. *Si*, this was going to be the night.

No, it wasn't going to be the night.

Finally, it got so that she was afraid Stefano was going to complain to her father. She would've died of embarrassment. Walking on hot coals was a decidedly more attractive alternative. But if they could just wait a little longer; the house was almost airtight, and it would be just a month before the kitchen was finished.

"Oh, Stefano," she said one night, "I just know that once we're in our own house, it'll be peachy."

Now, Stefano was still getting the hang of this English, but he knew that "peach" was a fruit and therefore it had to be good. And that was enough encouragement for Stefano to actually hire a few other immigrants to help him build the house and finish it two weeks ahead of schedule.

Two weeks and three days later they moved in. Stefano allowed her to buy a whole bedroom suite, from a tallboy to a chest of drawers with three matching mirrors that could be angled so that you could see all three sides. (She did it once and never again; after that, she pushed the mirrors flat against the wall and kept them that way for almost twenty-five years.) The set included a queen-size bed with two nightstands, along with matching duvet, pillow shams and even curtains.

They moved in before the summer kitchen was finished. Her argument was that if they had their children right away, they would never finish the house, as she'd come up with some great ideas for the front of the house. "Archways," she said. "Lots of archways made out of the same brick as the rest of the house." If he really loved her, he would wait until they had that beautiful patio completed as well, after the house. So Stefano made the archways himself. They were beautiful. And the patio.

"Now-a?" he asked.

"Um, yes! Okay!" But Andy got herself a diaphragm without telling Stefano and managed to buy herself some time. Stefano wondered if they would ever conceive a bambino again. When the house was finally finished, and the patio, *and* he allowed her to have a dryer, and a washer, and then a dishwasher, she decided she had waited long enough. She relented and three months later, she was pregnant once again.

By now, she had come to believe that she was the culprit and that it was, indeed, ultimately her fault. She started going to church. She went to confession and confessed to things she hadn't thought of for years. She stopped smoking, and she ate more. She gained a bit of weight, and her nausea was not as bad. Just in case, Stefano insisted she lie down as often as she could. He accepted Claudia's offer to cook but not to stay. He kissed Andy tenderly when leaving for work, and at night he hurried home anxious to see if her stomach had grown, and if there were any signs of kicking. And yes, she had started to feel that delightful little velvet touch, like the touch of an angel's wing on the inside of her womb. Life.

It was magical, and she and Stefano were truly, finally, actually happy.

At twenty weeks, her water broke, and she gave birth to a tiny creature that mercifully died minutes after birth—mercifully, because it was cruelly deformed.

Andy had been sedated, as was the custom at the time, and when she awoke, they carefully discouraged her from looking at the child. Andy fell into sleep once again and woke up to Claudia crying beside her hospital bed. Stefano wasn't there, but Fabrizio was. She almost didn't recognize him. He looked gaunt, weary and forlorn. He also looked a thousand miles away.

The doctor came by to have a little talk with her. He said that sometimes, Mother Nature appeared to be very cruel.

"Cruel! Don't ya think this goes *beyond* goddamn fucking cruel!?" she had cried.

"Andy, yes, you have had your share of sorrows, but God hasn't turned away completely. What you have lost was a twin."

At that moment, Stefano crept into the room. He stepped over and pulled another chair over to the bed. He sat down and leaned against his knee with his elbow. He was carrying a bouquet of flowers, which he placed at the foot of the bed. Then sounds dwindled away, and everything was in slow motion. He slowly looked at Andy and she looked back. The doctor's words slowly hit home. She still carried a child.

She'd had a most traumatic loss, but she promised herself, Stefano, and God, that whatever happened, this child was the most important thing in their lives, now and forever.

Andy remained on her back—most of it on their newish queen-size bed—until the day the baby was due. Then they put her in a wheelchair, carried the wheelchair up into an ambulance and rolled her into the hospital. Maria was born at five in the afternoon on the fifth day of the fifth month by Caesarean section.

And everyone saw very clearly that Maria was indeed a special and unique child. In fact, she was atypical. And perfectly beautiful.

Chapter 28

"I DON'T UNDERSTAND," ANITA SAID. "THERE has to be something you can do." She was upstairs in the bedroom, pacing back and forth with the phone held tightly to her ear. "I'm afraid something might have happened to him this time around."

The police lieutenant on the other end of the line tried to be patient. "I understand your concern, but your husband is a healthy man who you admit had been away just recently on extended business trips. And as far as taking your jewellery, ma'am, I'm afraid we can't do anything about that. You willingly gave him the authorization to pick it up when you gave him that claim ticket. At the very least, it's a matter between a husband and a wife. There's no reason why at this point this should be a police matter."

Anita put a shaky hand to her moist forehead. It was Sharon who had insisted she call the police right away. They might not be able to help, but at least it would make Anita feel as if she was doing something constructive. What Sharon did not tell Anita was about the men who had disappeared over the years only to be eventually discovered in some cesspool or ditch. Nobody ever dared talk about *them*.

"But that's just it. I feel in my heart that it should be a police matter." This time she was certain she would never see Jack again. Suddenly, it all felt so futile.

She gently hung up. She felt duped, used and walked all over. It was now too late for her and Jack, she thought. It was definitely the end.

Andy had been right all along. Andy cared. And look what she had done in return: she had cruelly broken her friend's trust. *Stefano*. With a shout she picked up the phone and threw it into the opposite corner of the bedroom, where it smashed into pieces. She needed Andy. And dammit, she needed Stefano.

She ran downstairs, picked up the other phone and called Andy's number. It rang and rang. Anita let it ring a dozen times and then hung up. Andy didn't "do" answering machines.

She lay on her back watching the shadows on the ceiling from the trees swaying outside her bedroom windows. Suddenly, bright lights sliced through the shadows and a deep, rumbling noise made its way up the driveway, stopping at the front door. Anita stared wide-eyed as she heard a heavy door open and then slam shut.

Somebody was ringing the doorbell.

Anita jumped up and ran to the bedroom window. She looked out to see Stefano's truck right below it.

She scrambled down the stairs and slid over the ceramic tiles to the front door. With a flair, she threw the door open and jumped at Stefano. She straddled him as she clung to his sturdy neck and broad shoulders.

Stefano closed the door behind him and let Anita kiss his face and his neck. He could feel her tears against his own flushed cheeks. He gently lifted her away from himself and half carried, half dragged a clinging Anita. They made their way to the family room and flopped down on the cushy couch. He manoeuvred her onto his lap as he brushed her hair away from her eyes.

"Shhh," he whispered softly. "Shhhh." Anita's tears eventually stopped, and she played with Stefano's shirt collar.

"He's gone again," she said softly.

Stefano grunted quietly and patted her on her head and then on her shoulder.

"And he took my coat, my jewellery, what money I had to last this week. He wouldn't do that if he loved me, would he?"

Stefano grunted softly and shook his head. She felt good in his arms. Cuddled up, soft and sweet, gentle and sad. He wanted to take care of her, make her happy, watch her as she smiled and laughed at the animals, the chickens, the goats. She would appreciate all that he did—his hard work, his ability to make very good money. He still had enough energy in him to have half a dozen sons and still keep up with them. And Anita would be softer and kinder as a mother. Maria needed such a mother.

Eventually, Anita slipped off his lap and wiped her eyes and nose with her sleeve. "I'm sorry, I shouldn't be crying like this."

"I would-a cry-a, too. I cry tonight with Andy," he admitted.

Anita looked up at Stefano and felt sorry for him. "No," she said, concerned. She cradled his cheek. "Why did you cry tonight?"

He took a deep breath and looked at his socks as he gathered his thoughts together.

"Andy, she-a angry at me-a," he said softly. "She say she no happy wi' me-a."

"She said that to you?"

He nodded. "An' I say da same. To her-a."

"Then all three of us are hurting," Anita pointed out quietly.

"Maria, too. Tonight-a she-a cry. She never cry. Never."

"What happened?"

"Adriana, she-a tired of cooking-a. She kill-a my bird."

Anita's eyebrows raised high. "Tired of cooking for you? What bird?"

He motioned the long tail on demon rooster.

She gasped. "Your new rooster?"

He nodded at his feet.

She wanted to laugh, but with one look at him she realized he was very sad. In spite of herself, she slowly smiled and then grinned. She shook her head in awe and humour as she thought about Andy's audacious prank. She covered her face and pondered on how to tell him about Jack. Surely he would never hurt Jack—that is, if Jack had not been hurt already. She rested her hand on the cushion next to her and remembered their making love in the dark during his brief return.

"He was frightened, Stefano. Very frightened. He said he had a terrible time in Venezuela, that he was almost killed, and he insists that ..."

"Si?"

"Well, he believes that Peter is wanting him dead."

Stefano's mouth dropped open. The he shook his head. "No. Ma he has-a money, an' no' Peter's, is everybody-a money."

Anita frowned and shook her head. "He's penniless, Stefano. We have nothing now. We're losing this house, the car's gone, I don't know what I'm going to do if he doesn't come back."

Stefano looked surprised. "Where is he now-a?"

"Disappeared! Again." She threw up her hands and let them drop.

He reached out and brushed a blonde tendril from her eyes. He felt sorry for her and shook his head again in sadness. He sat back against the cushions and exhaled slowly. Then he turned his classical Roman profile towards her. He reached out and touched her cheek tenderly and then bent forward to kiss her slightly parted lips.

The electrical shock was felt by both, a shock of emotion that zapped through their beings, up and down, exploding in their brains. They threw themselves together, clinging and kissing. They felt and explored, hungry with passion. He gently laid her back and kept kissing as he loosened up her bra in one deft movement of his right hand. He pulled her pants down and tore off her panties. As he dug at his fly, the phone rang. They paused for a brief second and looked into each other's eyes.

"Let's not get that," she whispered into his grizzled chin. They resumed loving intensely, grabbing and sighing. Now skin on skin, sweat against sweat.

The ringing clicked into the answering machine.

"Yeah, hi Anita, it's Andy. You called but I was busy with Maria. We're home, so if you want to give us a call, go right ahead."

There was a long pause. "'N I hope you're doin' okay. You looked pretty sad tonight. Oh, well. Talk to you soon." And she hung up.

By the end of the message, Stefano and Anita had stopped groping and kissing. They leaned back away from each other, their mouths dropped open. Slowly they disentangled. Anita covered her breasts, and Stefano sat back and brushed his dark locks out of his eyes.

"She sure sounded … *happy*."

Stefano smiled sheepishly and shook his head. "Ha," he laughed. "She-a no sound-a like-a Adriana."

"No, not at all, ha."

They stared at each other and smiled sadly.

"She even sounded … *nice*."

"Andy, she-a not stupid."

"No, I guess not. Do you think she knows that you're here?"

"No," he sighed. "But she call-a at a good time-a, *si*?" He smiled and cocked his head. "Or bad-a," he laughed.

She nodded and looked down at her half-naked body. "I guess you can say she has impeccable timing." She sat smiling softy at Stefano. Then she frowned. "This isn't good, Stefano. This is selfish on both our sides. You're married to Andy, and you have a wonderful, delightful daughter."

He looked at her sideways and smiled. "*Si*," he grinned. "She-a wonderful and *bellisima!*" He kissed the tips of his fingers and grinned.

Anita laughed. "You should've heard her on the radio!" she laughed.

"She-a good?" he asked, glowing.

"Oh, she was a winner. No kidding! I thought I had lost my job after she did that trick on me, but a few days later, she was the queen of our station. She singlehandedly increased our advertising base by 300 per cent!"

They both laughed jovially.

"My-a *principressa*."

"*Si*," she smiled. "Your little princess."

Chapter 29

"JESUS WAS WALKING ALONG ONE day when He came upon a group of people surrounding a lady of ill repute," Andy was saying, smiling at Father Carl. "It was obvious that the crowd was preparing to stone her, so Jesus said, 'Let the person who has no sin cast the first stone.' They all felt ashamed, and one by one they turned away. All of a sudden, this little old lady walked to the front, and she tossed a pebble at the woman. Jesus looks over at her and says—" and Andy couldn't help but snicker, "—'Oh Mom, I really hate it when you do that!'"

Father Carl leaned back and howled. With tears streaming down his face, he said, "Where do you get these stupid jokes?"

"Oh, I find 'em. Here's another one." She poured some more wine into Father Carl's juice glass. "A nun asks her students what they want to be when they grow up. A little girl, Suzy, says, 'I want to be a prostitute.' 'What did you say?!' asks the nun. 'I said I want to be a prostitute,' little Suzy says. 'Oh, thank heavens,' says the nun. 'I thought you said a Protestant!'"

Father Carl howled.

"Here's another one," continued Andy, grinning.

Father Carl put up a hand. "No, no! Please! My guts ache already!"

Andy laughed while she watched Father Carl wipe his eyes. "Are ya sure?"

"Ho! I'm sure."

Andy's smile slowly vanished as she fiddled with a spoon. "So, thanks for coming. I needed to talk to you about something."

Father Carl stuck his handkerchief back into a pocket. "Andy," he sighed. "God never promised that life would be easy, but He's always here to help."

"Yeah, but you know that my life hasn't been easy."

He nodded slowly. "Yes, you've had your share."

Andy cocked her head and stared at her glass of watered-down wine. There was quiet in the house. She had asked a neighbour to take Maria off her hands for an hour or so. Maria loved it because their neighbour had a horse, and Maria would take any and every opportunity to go there. So Father Carl and Andy both allowed their thoughts to wander. They could hear the hens clucking amongst themselves at the back of the house.

"Oh, and I didn't tell you."

Father Carl looked up at her, questioningly.

"I killed Stefano's rooster."

He bent towards her. "Like in 'slaughter'? So that you could eat it for supper?"

"Yeah, but this bird wasn't raised to be supper. Stefano apparently paid a lot of money for it. He'd been trying to find this particular friggin' bird for over a year." She paused.

"How'd you kill it? Did you wring its neck?"

Andy shook her head and her auburn curls swished. "I shot it."

Father Carl blinked. "You shot it?"

"Yup."

"With a gun?"

"With a shotgun."

"A shotgun. Wasn't that a bit of overkill?"

"You better believe it! It took eight shells to finally put him out of my misery."

Father Carl leaned back in his chair and wiped his mouth. "So …?"

"So, I plucked it and cooked it up. He tasted very good, actually."

"And did he do something to deserve this?"

"Yeah, he was loud, opinionated, cocky—no pun intended—ugly and acted like he ruled the place."

"And that's why you killed him."

"No, I killed him because he shit on me for the second time."

Father Carl cleared his throat and didn't know if he should smile.

"The first time, I was at that window," she pointed to the kitchen window by the sink. "I took out a cig—"

"A cigarette?"

"Er, no. I was throwing away a … a syphilitic cucumber … that doesn't sound good either, does it."

Father Carl blushed.

"Anyway, it shit all over the sink, the counter, me, the cupboards!"
Father Carl howled. "Is this for real!? Hahahahah!"

"You bet your bottom dollar it is!" And she couldn't help but laugh
as well.

Again out came the handkerchief, and Father Carl wiped his face.
He grinned and said, "Okay, go on."

"Well, Stefano came home right when this bird did the deed and
saw me standing there, dripping, and that was when we got a call from
Ma about Dad being sick. I had to run off looking like a stinking statue
shit-upon all the way to Ma's. I got cleaned up as much as I could before
we all followed the ambulance to the hospital."

"Yes," Father Carl frowned. "How is your father? Is he still in
hospital? I came by once, but he was fast asleep."

"Thanks, Carl. Thanks for dropping by. But he's okay. He's at home
now, but in a wheelchair and hooked up with these tanks of oxygen
for now."

"Wasn't your mother also ill?"

"Ma? Maybe in the head. She broke her hip. The wheelchair that
Dad is sitting in? Well, it was for Ma, really. She refuses to sit in it, says
that she'll end up being an old woman within a day if she did."

"How old is your mother?"

"Ma? Oh, she's sixty-two goin' on twelve. She'll live forever unless
I get my way with her before old age." She sighed. "Anyhow, you want
to hear about what that demon bird did to me the second time?"

"Er, yeah!"

"Well, we're comin' home from visiting Dad—Maria and me."
She shifted on the chair. Hard chairs hurt her behind quite quickly—
mostly because, as even she would say, she didn't have much of an
ass. "And poor Maria, we were arguing. I have no idea what it was
we were arguing about, but I was pretty mouthy with her and vice
versa. Anyhow, she wouldn't push that button to open the garage.
I needed to drive the Caddy in. She kept her finger over it and
wouldn't push it. Just to push *my* buttons, see? Yes, pun intended.
Anyway, I put the car window down to yell at her, and up comes
this screaming devil and shits through the window onto the dash, on
the steering wheel, over the seat, on my hair—and you know that

Stef likes to get a new Caddy every year, so this is a new car we're talking about here!"

Father Carl nodded. "Yeah, I can see why you would've wanted to kill it."

"Well, yeah. But it was bad, Carl. I did it with anger. I got one of Stefano's shotguns and ran after it until I got it. *Bang!*" She motioned shooting and the kickback that occurred after pulling the trigger.

Father Carl frowned deeply.

Andy put up her hand. "I know, Carl. I could've hurt somebody. As it turned out, I ended up pumping some shot into the barn wall. Scared the bejesus out of the hens, I tell you. We'll probably never get any more eggs out of 'em." She hung her head. "Then I plucked it and cooked it and served it to Stefano. And he broke a tooth on one of the shot pellets."

Father Carl choked back a guffaw.

"That'll cost us, I tell you." And then she fell silent. Father Carl watched as she slumped into the chair and grew pale. Then she did something he had never seen her do before. She covered her face. She stopped breathing as she tried to control herself, but it didn't help. Years and years and years of sadness and heartbreak broke through. "Carl, I'm so ashamed. I'm so ashamed. So ashamed." She was rocking on the chair saying it over and over again as if it were a chant.

Father Carl put out a hand and touched her on her head. "Shhh. Shhh." He took away his hand and slumped towards her. "Shhh." It took many minutes before Andy found her voice, albeit a very sad and tiny one. "Carl. God forgive us. We've lived a bad and evil lie. And I don't know whose fault it is, but Stefano and I are major players here. Such a strange … oh I can't say! Oh, so terrible, just terrible." And then finally, like a soft little girl, she was able to cry.

❧

"Where were ya? We had that surveillance tape of Anita's break-in," said Peter as he looked up at Stefano entering the mortuary. Peter had just taken away a sign from a viewing room.

Stefano stopped and looked in at the coffin. "Who-a dat?"

Peter waved it away. "Oh, no one we knew."

Stefano nodded as his eyes lingered on the coffin and the rest of the room.

"Come with me," Peter said. "We can talk out back here. I need your help with somethin'." Peter led Stefano to the back of the building, through the lab, and out again into a holding area. In the middle of the floor, on a gurney on wheels, was a coffin. The lid was up, and in the coffin lay a middle-aged woman. She was heavily made up and wore a dress with large motifs of parrots; on her head was a black Hollywood wig. Stefano walked over and looked at her. He lifted up his hand and pointed at her.

"Das, ah …"

"Yup. Mrs. Santarini."

"How she-a die?" asked Stefano.

"She choked. On a sandwich. She was alone. Very sad. Family's terribly upset."

"Oh, *si*. She make-a the best gnocchi. Is-a too bad-a."

Peter nodded in agreement.

"She-a big."

Peter nodded again in agreement.

Stefano looked at his brother and the two of them locked eyes. Stefano looked over at Mrs. Santarini again and back at Peter. "She-a gain-a weight?"

Peter nodded.

Stefano looked again and then at Peter and held up his hands. "No!"

Peter sighed. "Oh, come on, Stef. The guys aren't here and I have to get this coffin closed. She's being buried tomorrow. This is the coffin they chose. I can't put her in another one—or at least I'm not going to put her in a more expensive one that's bigger. Aw, c'mon."

Stefano let his head nod slightly. He shrugged and then took off his lumberjack jacket. "How she grow so-a big-a?"

"They didn't find her until a day later. She was bloated up before …" Peter shook his head slowly as he stared at Mrs. Santarini's stomach.

"Okay. How we-a do this-a?"

Peter motioned for him to come around and lowered the gurney. "You sit on her, and I'll try to get the lid down."

"Sit-a? On-a Mrs. Santarini?" choked Stefano incredulously.

Peter motioned irritably. "Just sit, Stef."

So Stefano gently sat and lowered himself down on top of Mrs. Santarini. Foul air escaped despite the various plugs. Almost instantly, they desperately and frantically bolted from the incredible cloud of putrid death. They ran through the lab, past the viewing rooms and out through the large front door. They stood catching their breath out in the freezing cold, where passers-by might have looked over while driving along and wondered what it was they were doing, coughing and hacking outside a funeral home. But no one saw, and no one wondered.

Nancy rewound the surveillance tape again and then played it right from the beginning. She chewed on her nail as she watched Anita go to her desk for the umpteenth time, and again she watched Anita take that darn photograph away with her.

She figured there was no hiding it now. She sighed and clenched her jaw.

Outside an apartment building, Mario and Guido sat in the black Cadillac with the darkened windows and *ZIO* as a license plate. They were arguing over something in Italian and pushed each other around until one of them noticed something and told the other to shut up. The other looked around and followed his brother's gaze.

They saw a woman who had just walked out of the front of the building. She was carrying car keys, and she looked down at them as she walked towards a little red convertible.

Guido turned on the ignition, nodded at Mario, and then watched as his brother got out of the car. They had been given orders by Peter to keep an eye on Rose and to search her apartment. Guido saw Rose start her car, and he waited until she drove away. He then deftly turned into the traffic about four cars behind her. Down the street, another set of eyes patiently watched as, in the meantime, Mario ran into the apartment-building lobby. Once in, Mario pushed a bunch of buttons. Someone buzzed the door open and he slipped in. The front door locked behind him and the lobby echoed with a female voice calling, "Hello? Helloooo? Who's there? Ah, shit! Not again!"

❦

Father Carl was silent as he pondered on what Andy had just shared with him. Then he shook his head. "Are you sure, Andy? Perhaps it's a terrible misunderstanding! Even then, it's still no proof. These things do happen, even when there is absolutely no evidence of inbreeding."

Andy shook her head. "No, Carl. It's the goddamned awful truth. It has to be. I mean, look at me! I lost three babies, the third—poor little thing—deformed!" She sniffed and blew her nose and shook her head again. "I found *that* out by accident. I know all the nurses and, well …" She waved something away. Perhaps an image in her mind she couldn't shake.

"And you've lived with this belief all these years."

She nodded sadly.

"And Stefano? Does he believe this?"

"I, ah, tried to tell him, but I was so ashamed, Carl. Look at how long it took for me to talk to you. I mean, I'm sorry, I just couldn't face it. It was far easier to not *think* about it …"

"And your marriage …?"

She shook her head and bit her lip. "There hasn't really been a 'marriage' since the day we brought back Maria. If you know what I mean," she added.

"I tell you what, Andy. I still have no leads on Jack, but this is more up my alley. Leave it with me, and I'll do some research on your family myself and get to bottom of this. You can't go on punishing yourself and Stefano as well. Calabria, right?"

Andy nodded and dabbed at her nose again. Father Carl saw the nose and for the first time ever, he suddenly realized that Stefano had the same nose, Fabrizio had the same nose, Maria had inherited the same nose. He felt a sinking in his stomach. Could Andy be correct about she and Stefano being directly related?

"At least she is a healthy child, Andy."

Andy looked at him with an odd angelic look, a look he had never seen in Andy in all the years he'd known her. The look of someone who had gone through a soul-burning fire and come out the other end. There was a ray of golden light on her brow. "Yes, she is healthy, Carl. But she's *special*. And, oh, isn't she just so wonderful?" Her gaze fell across Father Carl and moved on towards the toys and colouring books by the TV. "Yes," she said again, "she's our very special angel."

Mario softly stepped out of the elevator and looked both ways down the hallway before turning left. He checked the apartment numbers on the doors. He stopped at one and gently pulled out a handgun from a holster under his arm. He put his ear to the door and listened for a moment. He heard nothing but wind blowing under the doorway. There was a door or a window open somewhere in the building, and as he stood there, he was aware of the suction of air and could tell when it stopped.

He stepped back and held up a hand. He shrugged as he debated whether he should try to get in or whether he should simply wait hidden in the stairwell. He made up his mind. He raised his hand and rapped at the door.

What he didn't know was that Jack was indeed inside the apartment, and that Jack was also debating to himself whether he should smash his way through or just remain where he was. Jack stepped quietly towards the door to look out the peephole. But as he bent forward, the floor squeaked. He winced.

On the other side, Mario heard the squeak and looked down at the bottom of the door. He could see a shadow.

With his heart pounding in his chest, Jack tiptoed to the back of the apartment, opened the bedroom window and climbed out onto a ledge wide enough—barely—for him to stand on. The ledge connected the lines of the building; it spread from the bottom of each balcony. Carefully he slid along the ledge until he reached the next-door balcony and climbed over. Fortunately, the balcony door was unlocked. He stepped into the apartment just as Mario picked his way into Rose's apartment and barrelled in. By the time Mario searched that apartment, Jack had run out of the other apartment and down the hall to the stairwell. He scurried down the stairwell until it ended in the basement. He hid under the last portion of the stairwell and stopped to catch his breath. Then he winced and slapped his forehead.

What Mario did not know was that as he searched through the apartment looking for Jack, he walked right by the keys that Anita had retrieved from the office.

Mario shrugged. He checked to see what was in the fridge. He looked into the cupboards and then into jars. He took out a couple of cookies from one and grabbed a box of Captain Crunch cereal. He walked as he munched and looked out the balcony door. He checked the lock on the door, and it was locked. He shrugged and then left the apartment, locking the doorknob after himself.

Mario took the elevator down and walked out the front door. As he continued to munch, he walked over and sat at the base of a large tree. There he could keep an eye on the front door and the road. He settled down to wait.

Across the road from behind another tree, a spent cigarette was tossed onto the ground, and the sole of a shoe pressed it into what was left of the dirty snow.

Chapter 30

PETER SAT TAPPING A PEN against the edge of his new desk. He was deep in thought. Things were going well in the final cleanup of construction in the Vindenza Village Mall, and the coming grand opening was thankfully a huge distraction to those who counted higher up. But he knew if he didn't get that money back, shit would hit the fan, and his life would be over. He groaned and threw the pen at the wall.

He hadn't exactly been honest with his brother and Fabrizio about the money he had invested in Jack and Jack's big ideas. And Jack didn't exactly run away with all the money. Peter was being honest when he said he had used his in-laws' money as well, including all that he and Sandra had. He had even remortgaged the house. Men still got away with doing that kind of thing in the eighties, especially in a small European-based community, and now he wished he'd never had the greed that made him fall into temptation to begin with. Ha! He'd wanted to be the richest man in his community, and it wasn't happening fast enough. He didn't like having to bow to the others. He was a one-man show, he always told himself. A poor youth without a future coming to the land of plenty and making it really, really big.

Now he had nothing, not even a good handle on his own life. Should he commit suicide? It would be better than what they would put him through once they knew what had happened to one whole shipment of dirty money. Cement boots were unfortunately still quite fashionable.

"It's Jack's fault," he said to the wall.

"What's Jack's fault?" asked Nancy. She had just arrived for the afternoon, having spent the morning at J & P Plastics and doing some special chores.

"Nothing," he announced. "Just thinking."

Nancy took off her coat. "Just thinking that it's all Jack's fault?"

"Whatever," he said as he straightened out and shuffled some papers on his desk.

Nancy hung up her coat in a closet within Peter's office. "Why do you always blame Jack for everything?"

"Because it's always Jack's fault," he muttered. He scrunched up some paper and tossed the paper ball at the corner, missing the garbage pail. Nancy stepped over and picked up the paper and threw it in for him. She gave him a dirty look as she turned to go to her own desk just outside Peter's door.

Peter sat thinking for a moment as he watched her through the door, pulling out her chair and flipping her beautiful hair over her shoulder. She sat so daintily, that lovely behind pressed against her clothes, that tight-butt look just before she finally settled into it. He sighed, stood up and stretched. "Well, I'm going to the funeral home."

"More dead bodies? Anyone we know?"

Peter grabbed his coat out of the closet but stopped and froze. "I know what you're thinking."

He could hear the creak of her chair as she swivelled towards the door.

"Oh, do you now."

"Yes, I do. Just because he could get it up." He palpated the collar of his coat.

There was a pause and he could hear her sigh. "It's sort of a big part of it, don't you think?"

He pulled at the tag at the neck, twisted it and tore it off in quiet anger. He swallowed hard. "Yup. So they say."

He walked past Nancy as he pulled his coat on, but Nancy grabbed at the sleeve of the coat and held him back. He turned to look down at her.

"What," he muttered.

She smiled brightly, her eyes sparkling. "Well, that's a major part of an affair, don't you think? Or were you wanting to join a bird-watching group with me, and we can get our thrills watching cardinals do their mating dances?"

He stood and looked at her with a sneer on his face.

Nancy threw up her hands. "Hey, wait! It's not my fault. Why be angry with me?" She sat back in her chair. "And so, is bird-watching enough for Sandra?"

"Shut the fuck up."

Nancy picked up a pen from her desk and fiddled with it.

"Is she a supportive wife, Peter?"

"Shut your fucking face."

Nancy smiled and sucked on the pen suggestively while studying his face intently.

Peter felt a sensation he hardly ever felt. He didn't know how to tell her that he really felt she was the one—that if only she were more patient, she would be able to get him to that point he so achingly thirsted for. He decided to act as if he was ignoring her and leave the office.

On the way out of the mall, Peter mulled over his little problem, with no pun intended on the *little* part, he thought to himself. As he walked, he thought back on his trip to Vegas.

Peter had gone on one of those freebie junket trips that Sandra got as a travel agent and it was Sandra's idea that he go with a few friends, as she was far too busy and felt he needed a break. She, too, was very concerned that Peter no longer had what it took. She thought he was working himself to death, and a little fun might bring him back renewed.

Yes, he went to Vegas. He took Mario and Guido. Stefano didn't want to go, so he asked Jack to come along and make it an even four.

Jack jumped at the chance to go to the city of sin. They had a riot, they drank the moment they got on the plane, and they didn't stop until they got off the plane home.

Well, they had too good a time, all right. It was Jack's idea to try out a formula he had heard about that made winning at gambling a cinch. Peter was impressed by Jack's ability to count the cards, and he seemed to be having a good run of winnings. So, with that in mind, Peter lent Jack money to win for himself. And yes, of course, it was for the final benefit of his wife, his children, his in-laws—who cares how you make money? He'd just borrow theirs, just for a little while. It's the end that justifies the means, right? Right, but only if the end is exactly what you wanted in the first place.

He lost more than he brought, and more again. And he had no choice. With threats of innuendo and fear tactics, it was made very clear to him that he better have the bucks or they were going to make him go through the legal mill or worse—the *not* so legal way.

There was one silver lining to this cloud called Vegas. The guys wanted to take part in the Nevada prostitution law, and yeah, they had a ball. More than that, Peter was able to have a ball. The woman was an animal. She knew tricks that he'd never heard of. He came away thinking that perhaps he could somehow teach Sandra a few new things and maybe, just maybe, if he didn't really look at her too closely (for she had steadily kept gaining an awful lot of weight since their wedding day), just maybe this stuff could work at home.

Actually putting it into practice was another matter, however. What was he going to say to Sandra? "Hey, Sandra, I learned this really neat trick in Vegas …"?

His whole world looked black now. He couldn't even share in the festive feeling of this great mall, he thought, looking around him as he walked out the door to the parking lot. He looked at his watch and then over at the construction shed. He saw that Stefano's truck was still there. He walked towards the shed, shivering in the icy cold air, watching his breath float by his face while he briefly wondered what death was like.

❧

Father Carl sat in his office at the church with the phone pressed against his ear. He was waiting for someone to answer. He was looking over at the window when a bit of hail pelted against it.

"Yes, hello? Professional Italian Geneology Research Institute? Yes, I … I'm Father Carloni calling from Our Holy Mary Mother of God Church in Vindenza. Quebec. Canada. Canada. No, we're north of the United States. Yes, Ca … Well, I'm calling concerning a dear parishioner of my church. We're wanting to sort out a gray area in her family tree, so to speak …"

❧

Anita sat at her desk at the station, doodling while she pondered on the mystery that was her Jack. From some of the snippets of conversations she had overheard from Peter at that party, it seemed that Jack might possibly be in real trouble or about to be killed. She wished it was all just a movie, or a book you could put down and never read again.

She sighed. She had been frightened for him, for herself, angry at the things he'd done, that other people said he'd done. She was an emotional wreck and felt sick over the whole thing. Should she even care anymore?

She had to make a move, any move. Anything was better than doing absolutely nothing. She was his wife, and a wife goes through thick and thin, for richer and for poorer. This thought had structure, and she found structure easy to follow when there was nothing else to go by.

She slapped her desk and said, "Okay!"

"Okay?"

She turned around to see Mike standing watching her. She smiled.

"Okay what?" he asked.

"Oh, I was just thinking …"

"Yeah, you're still thinking about Jack." He nodded.

She nodded.

"You look tired. Are you getting enough sleep?" he asked kindly.

"Oh, do I sound tired on-air?"

He put his hands up and let them fall by his sides. "No, it's just you look a bit tired, is all."

She pushed her chair under her desk and took her purse off the back of her chair. "I better get home."

"How's it going with the house, Anita? Are you going to be okay?"

"I have to be out by the end of this month." She stood looking down in shame.

Mike shook his head and wished he could tell her what he thought about her husband, but he was only her boss and it really wasn't his business. But he found it so unfair.

"So, where are you going to go?"

Anita slung her purse over her shoulder. She brightened up and said, "Well, I have a standing open invitation at Andy Giordani's."

He laughed.

"Yeah. She was upset with me for a while there, but it's almost as if she felt better for being proven right about Jack."

"Well, if you need another option of where to say, I know Darlene won't mind at all …"

Anita smiled. "Thanks, Mike. It's nice of you to say. And thank Darlene for me too."

Mike stepped aside to let her walk by to the elevator. She pushed the button and turned to face Mike. "When's Joe coming back?"

"Maybe next week," Mike said. "I know what you're thinking. The Jeep."

Anita nodded.

"Let's not worry about that yet. He may not be ready to do anything more than just sitting at the desk. He could do the press releases, write the news, whatever."

The elevator door opened with a ding. "That sounds fine with me. Thanks, Mike." She stepped into the elevator and smiled at Mike as the door shut.

Mike shook his head and looked at his watch. He went back to his office to clean up and call it a day.

Peter knocked on the construction shed door and opened it. He banged his feet against the edge of a step to loosen the snow and dirt off his soles. He walked in and slammed the door shut, making the whole shed vibrate.

Stefano was sitting at his banged-up desk, looked sideways at Peter. He wordlessly pointed at a sign that said, "Do Not Slam the Door." Peter waved it away while he pulled up another banged-up stool and sat facing Stefano. Peter leaned forward on his elbows and jiggled his legs as he looked around the shed.

"Stop-a da shaking," Stefano said without looking up from a ledger on his desk.

Peter jiggled harder and faster. He grinned as Stefano looked up at him. Then Peter stood up and spread his legs and arms and rocked side to side to really make the shed rock.

Stefano sat back and looked at his brother. Peter now snickered.

"Das no funny," said Stefano.

Peter flopped back on the chair. "Oh, come on now, Stef. Can't we have a bit of fun!?"

Stefano shook his head. Then he smiled.

Peter pointed at him. "See? You can do with a bit of fun!"

Stefano chuckled a little and then sat back and stretched. He debated whether he should tell Peter about what Anita had told him about Jack being back, but just like Peter had decided not to tell him, so Stefano decided not to tell Peter. Instead, he rubbed his eyes and looked at his watch. *"Due giorni."*

"Yup!" said Peter, clapping his hands. "Two more days to the big day!"

"Is-a jus' in time-a," mumbled Stefano. He looked up, his eyes shining. The edges of his lips curled upwards.

"Just in time? Why?"

Stefano threw over a copy of the Italian newspaper *Corriere Canadese* and pointed at the headline. Peter bent over and read.

"'Walmart *l'Andirivieni*'," Peter read. His mouth dropped open. "Walmart coming and now going?' Peter asked.

Stefano grinned and pointed at him to read further.

Peter sat back and straightened out the newspaper to read. From behind the paper, Peter said, "Holy shit!" He whacked the paper down onto his lap with his left hand. He looked amazed. "Since when was Walmart trying to move in?" He looked again at the paper and read some more.

> ... and for the first time in Walmart's history in its steady expansion across North America, our little town of Vindenza was the David to its Goliath. The council voted hands down against giving Walmart the permits needed to develop at a location just south of the town. Especially proud of the newly built soon-to-open Vindenza Village Mall, the town council proclaimed that the move against the onslaught of a large corporation saved all the Italian-Canadian mom-and-pop shops of Vindenza. As one citizen of this town of ours said, "[Walmart] promised new jobs and new business, but us Italian-Canadians don't need new jobs or new businesses. We already have perfectly good

businesses. The bakeries, meat shops, markets, dress shops, jewellery stores, morticians—you name it— they're all Italian owned and Italian run. We knew that if we allowed Walmart a foothold in our community, someone's son would lose a good deal of business at his jewellery store, or someone else's wife's dress shop would go belly-up. And those older citizens who never learned to speak English or French—how would they shop in stores where nobody spoke Italian? God forbid! Holy Mother of God! Our kids might have to get lower-paid summer jobs at Walmart and never learn to apprentice in anything useful!"

Peter looked up at Stefano. "Wow."

"*Si*, wow," smiled Stefano.

"We're the first town to do this? And you and me, Stef, we're here instead! Isn't that great!?"

Peter forgot all about his problems for the time being. At least *something* was going right. Maybe, just maybe, if he kept the dice rolling the way they were, he might recoup what he had lost, and his wife and in-laws might never be the wiser.

Or so he prayed.

At Pierre Elliott Trudeau International Airport in Montreal, Quebec, a short tanned man with a ruddy complexion stepped off the plane and thanked the stewardesses standing at the exit wishing the passengers goodnight. He felt the floor of the passageway rock under his feet, and he thought of the rocking café around him during the tornado down in Shellman's Bluff. Suddenly he was aware of a wall of cold air emanating from the corridor's walls. *Holy shit. I must be in the Arctic!* he thought.

Like most Americans, he thought of Canada as a combination of Aboriginal Indians and Eskimos skiing and eating pea soup, but he never really thought about the difference in weather until he felt that cold. He shivered and hoped it wasn't as cold outside as the inside implied. To onlookers, he appeared strangely underdressed, but his tan explained half the story, and those who cared to think further on the matter assumed he had more appropriate clothing with him.

Leo Mangiano spied a public phone on his way to luggage pickup and walked over. He wasn't interested in placing a call; he just wanted to look through the phone books. Unfortunately, he didn't see one that covered the town of Vindenza. He spied an information booth and walked over. When he arrived at the desk, he flipped his briefcase onto the surface of it, rested his elbows on the counter and leaned forward, waiting for one of two young women to help him. One pretty thing was busy with what looked like a family of Oriental background. The other, sitting at a desk, spied him and stood up.

"*Bonjour!*" she sang. "*Bienvenu à Montreal!*"

"Er, yeah! Thanks. I'm looking to find an address in Vindenza, Quebec." He pointed over to the public phones. "I don't see a phone book that covers that town. Do you know how I can go about finding an address there?"

The young girl frowned. In her delightful French-Canadian accent, she said, "Where, *monsieur?*"

"Vindenza."

"*Oui.* In Quebec?" She smiled.

Slowly he looked around and then patiently said, "Yes, in Quebec. I just said that."

"Ah, *oui, pardonez moi. Un moment, s'il vous plait.*" She walked away into the back through a doorway and came back almost instantly with a young gentleman in the same uniform as the young girls, though the young man didn't come close to making the uniform look so stylish, thought Leo.

"Sir, you are looking for an address in Vindenza? Would you like to take a taxi or an airplane limo?"

"Do you have any buses going there?"

"Well," the young man made a face, "it is a little far for a bus." He took out a paper map and, with a pencil, circled the town of Vindenza. It looked very far up the province. "Here is the town, sir," the young man said, and then he drew a line starting from the airport all the way up to the town.

"How long will that take?" asked Leo, wondering how far ahead of him Jorge was.

"With a bus, eight hours. However, if you take a limousine, just two hours."

Leo stared at him and blinked. "Where do I go to rent a car?"

The young man pointed wordlessy to a sign overhead that directed people to the rental cars.

"Thanks," Leo said as he hurried away.

"*De rien!*" said the young man.

Grumpily, Leo muttered, "Whatever."

Chapter 31

THE NEXT DAY, ALL WHO were in the fashion show had to come for a rehearsal at 7 p.m. sharp. Sharon had told everyone that the rehearsal should only take about an hour and that there would be lovely refreshments for those who would not have time for supper before arriving.

The mall, by this time, had that shine to it that new materials give their surroundings. The marble was polished, the new plants and flowers were freshly sprayed, and the statues were white and clean without a speck of dirt or plaster on them. The central pool and its waterfalls sparkled, and the lights below the surface made the turquoise colours of the water and the mosaic motifs of the lining of the pool and waterfalls shimmer like the Aegean sea. Not all the lights were on; a few of them, as could be expected, didn't work, and a team of electricians were busy correcting them or replacing them with new fixtures.

Volunteers from the Italian Canadian Club scurried around hanging up flags representing all the provinces of Italy. Others were carting in garment bags of clothing to organize and have ready for the models the next day.

Anita slammed the door of the Jeep shut as she briskly walked through what was an unseasonably crisp night. She shivered in her short jacket and quickened her pace through the deepening dusk to the brightly lit main entrance. As she approached, she heard a familiar little voice.

"Aaanniittaaaaaa!"

She stopped and looked over into the dark, where she could just make out the lighter clothing that Andy and Maria were wearing. "Hi baby!" cried Anita, and she held up her arms, ready to grab Maria. The girl ran and jumped up hard against Anita, and the two of them lost their balance and fell back on the cement walk.

Instead of yelling, Andy stopped and laughed. She watched patiently as Maria's and Anita's legs and arms unravelled. They scrambled up and brushed off each other's coats.

"Well, are you all ready for tomorrow?" laughed Anita.

"Nooooooo," drawled Maria.

Anita looked over to Andy. "Hi Andy! You look great!"

Andy looked her up and down and said with a laugh, "Well, you look like shit, but then what else is new?"

Anita smiled and nodded. She reached over to open the large glass doors for Andy and Maria to go ahead of her into the mall.

As they worked their way towards the large centre court, they noticed that some of the new stores were already open for business. Maria spied three little puppies in a store window.

"Oooooooh! Look Mom. Puppies!" She ran over to the window and smacked her palms and nose against it.

"Maria, keep your friggin' hands off that window!" But Andy did walk up to the window and looked at the three little balls of fur rolling over each other. One stopped and looked at the faces staring through the window, and he focussed so hard that he lost balance and fell backwards. "Isn't that cute?" laughed Andy. Anita looked over at Andy and saw that she indeed was looking down at the puppies grinning.

"I thought you hated all animals?" Anita reminded her.

"Well, I'm not the only one on this planet, I guess. Dogs have their reason for living, too." Andy tapped at the window and laughed again.

"Can I have one, Mom. Pleeeease!" Maria stood with her palms together begging and praying at her mother.

"Not on your life. I know it's going to be me cleaning up the poop." She turned to Anita. "What do they call it now, scoop and poop?"

"Nope, the other way around." Anita nodded at a puppy. "Cute, huh?"

"Nope. Not on your life!

They came in sight of the central court and took in the beautiful shimmering lights that danced on all surfaces.

"Beautiful, isn't it?"

"Yup, that's my Stefano at work. Not bad for an almost illiterate immigrant, huh?"

Anita smiled to herself. She already knew that Andy had come to terms with whatever demons she was forever running away from. She was a brand new person. Almost.

"Okay, where the frig do we go?" yelled Andy.

People milling around stopped to look at her.

"Mooom, don't!" Maria cried.

"Oops, I forgot. Sorry, precious. Are you going to tell on me?"

"Yes!" said Maria.

"Then I won't consider getting you that dog in the window!"

Maria stood as straight as a little soldier. Her eyes grew wide and her mouth fell open in amazement. "Really?"

"Try me. You tell, no puppy. You don't tell, maybe puppy."

Maria started skipping and chanting, "I'm gonna get a do-og, I'm gonna get a do-og!"

"You keep that up and you won't!"

Maria stood pondering the ever-changing rules laid down by her mother. She played halfway and silently whispered, "I'm gonna get a do-og!"

"That's better. Keep it up." Andy looked around and spied Sharon by the hallway leading to the mall offices and the washrooms.

"Hey, Shar!"

Sharon turned and spied them, and then waved them closer. She held up a dress that she had just taken out of a garment bag and looked at its tag. She turned to her seamstress and asked her to make a note that it was a backup for Anita if there was time.

As her seamstress was about to write a new tag, she spied Andy, Anita and Maria coming. Suddenly she dropped the tag and pen and begged to be excused. She ran to the washrooms while taking out a handkerchief and covering her mouth.

They walked up to Sharon, and Sharon shot Andy a look. "You have the most interesting effect on some people, Andy."

"That's their problem, not mine. Where can we get a drink around here?"

Sharon looked at Maria and nodded. Maria stared at her piercingly. She held up two fingers making a cross.

Sharon smiled and said, "That's very funny, Maria. Come here and try this on to make sure we actually resized it the way it should be after it was …" She gave up pointing out the obvious and then silently shrugged as she watched Maria take the dress and look back at her as she went into a makeshift dressing nook. Sharon wiped her hands on her skirt and turned to Andy. "Are you sure you won't consider modelling, Andy? You have the perfect body, you know that."

"Yeah, I know that, but I'm not about to flaunt it like other people I know," Andy said as she looked at Anita.

Anita took offense. "Andy, it was *you* who volunteered me for today."

"Yeah, I remember. You didn't have to do it." Andy was taunting Anita and Anita knew it, but the look on Andy's face was benign, and she realized there was no hidden message behind that big smile. So she playfully hit Andy's shoulder.

Andy grabbed her shoulder and winced. "Ooooow! Abuse! Friendly abuse!"

The seamstress came back with a paper cup of water. She kept her face hidden from Andy, grabbed a tag again, finished writing on it and hung it on the dress that was backup with a pin from between her lips. Then she went to hang it up in a change nook and opened the curtain. Maria stood in her underwear—panties and undershirt. She crossed her arms and screamed. "*Aaaaaaaaaaaaaahhhhhhhh!*"

Everyone stopped what they were doing and turned to look. Now everyone saw Maria in her panties and undershirt. With another howl, Maria reached up and pulled the curtain shut again.

The seamstress looked quite pale. She had accidentally swallowed the few pins that were between her lips. She gulped and shook her head, her eyes wide. She walked over to a work table, grabbed her bag and coat, and started leaving. Sharon looked up and frowned.

"Theresa? Where are you going?"

"I no-a take this-a girl. I now go-a to da hospital-a!" The seamstress hastened her exit, which ended up in a trot. She hadn't run in years, but it all came back, and she couldn't go fast enough. She would never return to Sharon's shop. As a matter of fact, while she was lying on the table waiting for an X-ray of her abdomen, she promised herself she would never, ever ever be a seamstress again. And this thought gave her some peace.

With a smile, she waited for the X-ray to do its job. It was while she was deep in thought on what the future had to offer her that she decided to learn to speak English properly, go back to school and learn to be an X-ray technician, and move out of Vindenza into the country and have an unlisted number. There might be more changes to come, but she felt it was enough to comfort herself that she really didn't *have* to deal with people like that anymore.

What she didn't know at the time was that yes, she would learn English, and even go as far as getting her Canadian citizenship, but she was going to lose her husband because he would feel threatened by the changes in her and claim he was no longer number one in her life and that a good wife should always hold a husband up as a semi-god. She didn't really mind the change.

A few years later, though, she would have no choice but to be around "people like that" because Andy would be coming in for regular X-rays while she remained under observation for spots on her lungs. But Theresa didn't know that as yet, and she felt rosy about such a productive plan for her future. Of course, after she spent a couple of months taking X-rays of Andy's lungs, she would again come to some life-changing decisions, but that was far into the future yet, and it would've been very cruel of fate to let her see so clearly so far into her own.

Meanwhile, in the moment, Sharon was without a seamstress for the fashion show.

Peter sat at his desk in the mall office and leaned back in his chair. He changed his mind and sat up straight. Mario and Guido faced him on the other side of the desk.

"You're telling me there was no sign of him," he asked incredulously.

Mario and Guido nodded.

"Well, what *did* you find?"

Mario and Guido looked at each other and shrugged. Suddenly, they could hear music with a quick beat in the main court. Mario and Guido again looked at each other, and then they both stood up to go see what all the excitement was about. A fashion show usually meant beautiful women walking in high heels with that "come unto me" look. Something akin to a striptease, but with more clothing. Of course, they had never been to a strip club, so their vision of the coming excitement was quite Hollywood compared to the middle-aged women in conservative clothes and elderly women traipsing in traditional costume that they would actually encounter. But they had yet to discover that, and so they were very anxious to get the meeting over and done with.

Peter sighed. "Sit down."

Mario and Guido slowly sat down.

"Well, where did you follow Rose to? Huh?" Peter rested his left leg over his right knee. He slumped into his chair and interlaced his fingers in front of him. "Hmm? Did anybody follow Rose?"

Mario and Guido both nodded and said, "*Si.*"

Peter threw up his hands. "Whoa. Wonders! So?"

Mario said, "*Che?*"

Peter stood up and yelled. "Where the *scopari* did she go?"

Guido shook his head. "Pietro, das-a bad word."

"Oh, pardon me! Then where the *fuck* did she go?"

Guido asked Mario something. Then Guido straightened up. "*Si, si*, is-a me go wid' Rose-a."

"Good. We're getting somewhere."

"To da bank-a"

"To the bank."

"*Si.*"

"How long was she in the bank?"

"*Che?*"

"I saaaaiidd, how long was she in the bank?"

"*Si.* Maybe-a …" He pondered on this for a bit. "Maybe-a half-a hour."

"Did she come out with anything?"

"Out?" Mario looked to Guido because, after all, it was Guido who followed Rose.

Peter smacked his hands on the desk and stood up. "For fuck's sake, did she have anything in her hands?"

"Oh! *Si!* Many, ah, many bags-a."

Peter sat down. Bags. Yeah, that made sense. Bags of money. Coming out of safety deposit boxes, the keys for which Anita took out of the office. That's it! Happy at last, Peter grabbed their hands and shook them. Mario and Guido laughed along and then pointed to where the music was coming from. Peter nodded and said, "Sure, go ahead, leave me with this shit to deal with. Go, I don't care." But he said it with a tight smile, and so the cousins were happy to go.

Peter slapped his forehead. He had forgotten to ask his cousins what they might have seen in Rose's apartment. But that would be a question for next time he could corner them. For now, he sat back and pondered on the bags of money. He figured it could be a combination of the money Jack was supposed to help launder from Venezuela and the money he had borrowed from everyone else to invest in his own business, which obviously wasn't getting off the ground. And maybe even …? No. There was no way around the money he lost that belonged to Peter's wife and in-laws. No. Nothing ever came that easy. Quickly he prayed that the mall would do wonders for the conglomerate, the other vendors, and especially him. He took a deep breath and decided that perhaps he would also go see what these women looked like. He would end up just as disappointed as his cousins.

Leo had spent the night at a motel near the airport. He had rented a car for his stay and drove to the motel, asking the manager for directions for his trip the next morning. Unfortunately, the manager, though the motel was close to an international hub of air traffic, could not apparently speak "American." So Leo bought a map in the office and decided to skip dinner and go straight to his motel room and study the map. He turned on the TV and looked desperately for an American station.

"What is wrong with this country?" he muttered, "Don't they know they're in North America?" In disgust, he gave up and decided to go to bed early. He had to catch up and find Jorge. He hoped it wasn't too late.

In the morning, his day was ruined when he got out and saw about six inches of that godawful white stuff all over his rental car. He felt his pulse race, and he had to consciously control his temper. He looked up at the clear blue sky and prayed briefly. "I know. No temper. Thank you. This I do for my Yvonne and another chance at a life in which you love me." He'd come to talking to Santa Maria as a close friend would. He reminded himself that Santa Maria would help him get to Jorge in time, before the man hurt another soul at his bidding. He made the cross and apologized and looked at the snow anew.

"Aaah. So white! And the sun is out. That's not so bad." He nodded at himself and was pleased with his progress. He dug out the car key and started humming *Ave Maria*.

"For Yvonne," he muttered as he drove. "For Yvonne."

Jorge sat outside at the base of a leafless oak tree across the street from Rose's apartment building. A police cruiser slowly drove into sight and then came directly to him. The window went down, and Constable Stan popped his head out and demanded to know what Jorge was doing there.

"I'm vaitink foh meine friend," he said in mock German.

"I'm sorry?" Stan saw the accent as sinister. Slowly he got out of the cruiser and put a hand on his holster out of habit. He always laid a comforting hand on his holster whenever he felt frightened, although he tried very hard not to look it. He raised his right eyebrow in an effort to look easygoing and fearless.

Jorge relaxed, drooped his shoulders and spoke normally. "Well, I'm really waiting for a relative of mine to come home. I thought I'd stay here and wait for her to drive by." Jorge smiled at Stan, who seemed to be quite the approachable guy. *These Canadians are simple but kind of nice*, he thought.

"What's your relative's name?"

Jorge only knew Jack Taylor and his girlfriend, Rose. "Ah, I'm waiting for Rose Taylor." He held out his hand for a shake. "Nice to meet you, officer, my name is Jack Taylor."

Stan stepped back and took another look at the guy. "So you think you're Jack Taylor, huh?"

"Uh oh," said Jorge, "did I say I *was* Jack Taylor. I meant to say I *know* Jack Taylor. I'm a friend." He motioned to Stan. "You're just such an imposing fellow, I got a little nervous." He tried to give an affable smile. His white teeth shone like a movie star's grin in the shade of the street light.

Stan grabbed at the guy's upper arm and pulled him directly into the light of the street lamp. He then put a fist on his hips and held out his hand. He blew up his chest and took a tough-guy stance. Jorge took the hand and shook. Stan shook his head and nonchalantly leaned on his right foot.

"No, I need some ID, if you please."

Jorge eyed him curiously and motioned to the corner of his own mouth and then pointed at Stan's. He mumbled a little. Stan frowned and then wiped his mouth with his fist. He found icing sugar and pulled out a tissue and wiped his mouth thoroughly, almost roughly. He nodded.

"Um, thanks."

Jorge nodded affably.

Stan froze for a moment trying to remember where he was. "Oh yeah! ID."

While he waited with his hand out, Stan did not tell Jorge that he knew Jack Taylor very well, and that according to Rose, Jorge might be spying on her to get to Jack. It seemed everyone was looking for Jack these days. Looking at the guy, though, Stan was sure it was also probably because of Rose. Sweet Rose. Over the years, he'd had to shoo a lot of guys away from her.

Rose was at home after all. She had watched Jorge from her apartment while he stood in the shadows smoking cigarette after cigarette. She was actually starting to worry about this gentleman's health. But more importantly, she knew in her heart he was what they called a "hit man." Jack had warned her this might happen. She told Stan so when she had contacted him through dispatch. Knowing her well for her expansive and almost innocent imagination, he didn't believe her at all, but he humoured her because she was so darn cute. He was forever wanting to impress her with his protective manliness anyway. It's what she brought out of a certain type of man. And he was one of them, through and through.

Anxious to impress her, Stan had left where he was enjoying his coffee and jelly doughnut at the neighbouring Tim Hortons and excitedly drove the two blocks to her place. And there he found the guy easily. He cast a quick glance up at her window now to make sure she was watching. Damn, she just made him want to protect her, that's all.

Jorge patted his shirt and then dipped into his pants pockets, then under his coat and back to his shirt pockets. Nothing. He shrugged.

Stan again raised that one eyebrow. He took out his flashlight and shone it on Jorge. "Who are you?"

"My name is Jorge. How do you do?"

"Hmm," hmmed Stan. "Come with me please, sir."

Jorge had no choice but to go and sit in the cruiser while Stan called Rose on his car phone. Rose answered the phone breathlessly.

Damn, he thought. "Hi Rose, it's me, how are ya?"

Rose was watching in her fluffy pink bathrobe from her window. Stan craned his neck to look up from the driver's seat. She waved from behind the window pane. He waved daintily with his fingers.

"Who is he, Stan?"

"Well, he says he's a 'Jorge.' Does that sound familiar?" He suddenly turned to Jorge. "Are you a Kraut?"

Jorge bobbed his head up and sideways. "I am from Venezuela."

"He's German but from Venezuela. Another one of your crazy admirers, Rose?" Stan chuckled. He watched that head of red hair. And he could just make out those eyes.

Rose ran to her kitchen window and opened it, leaning out onto the bit of snow along the window frame. She shook her curls down at him. "No," she said into the phone. "But maybe Jack knows him. He's been to Venezuela, I know that!"

Stan thought for a moment. Rose looked so darn pretty leaning out the window like that. He remembered back in the sixties a shot of Marilyn Munroe doing the same cute thing. So womanly. As if she read his mind, she looked down at her housecoat and realized she was partly falling out of her robe. She covered herself demurely.

"Well, I'm not goin' to ask if Jack would know this guy, 'cause Jack's not around, is he?" Stan wanted to say, *wink, wink, nudge, nudge*, but that would take his professional relationship with Rose a bit too far, especially when everyone knew that Jack was in hiding and Stan's own wife, who happened to be the chief of police, wouldn't like to think that her husband was becoming *that* familiar with one of the citizens of the town of Vindenza.

"Well, what do you want me to do with him, Rose?"

Rose bit her lip. She wished Jack was there, but he was out hiding just for a little bit longer. "Well, first ask him if he's going to hurt me," suggested Rose.

Officer Stan looked at Jorge. "Do you have, sir, any negative intent here with the lady?"

Jorge looked at him wide-eyed. He looked around the interior of the cruiser and didn't like sitting behind the screen. "Uh, no. I was only trying to get a hold of Jack Taylor," he said meekly. "That's all." He blushed in the shade of the cruiser, feeling a little hot under the collar.

Stan looked up at the window. "Did you hear that, Rose?"

Rose bit her lip again. "Okay, if he's only waiting for Jack, I don't mind if he's there. But you can tell him he won't see Jack for a few days."

Officer Stan went to pass that on to Jorge but then thought again and paused. He looked quizzically up at Rose and said into the phone. "You aren't really wanting me to tell him that Jack will be here in a few days, are you now?" He winced. "You said this guy might be an assassin!"

Jorge rolled his eyes but played dumb. He dropped his head into his hands.

"An ass what?" asked Rose.

"Assass … hit man!"

Rose frowned at the windowsill. "Well, all I know is, he can't hurt him if he's gone, can he?" she reasoned. "All I want is for him to be gone by the time Jack comes back."

"All right, I'll let him go."

Jorge choked and coughed. He couldn't believe his luck.

"And *are you sure Jack will not be returning?*"

"*Yes, Stan. I am sure!*"

"All right then." Stan turned to Jorge. "Well, she says she doesn't care if you want to freeze your butt off, but she knows Jack ain't coming back."

Jorge stepped out of the cruiser. He pulled up his pants and shot his sleeves before he turned to look at the window. He waved goodbye to Rose.

Rose waved goodbye with a gleaming smile. Jorge felt his heart skip a Venezuelan beat. Stan was about to take off when he caught that familiar lingering look. He didn't like it one bit. *If only Rose would turn off the charm sometimes*, he fretted.

Jorge turned to Stan and said, "I think I shall go then. Shall I?"

"Yup! I'd say that's not a bad idea. Hey, can I give you a lift somewhere?" Stan wanted him gone. *Vamoose!*

"Uh, yeah. All right. It is a bit cold, isn't it. Okay. If you don't mind, if you can drop me off in the centre of town, then I will just walk back to the motel."

"Well, which motel are you stayin' at then, eh?"

Jorge blinked. "At the Nova Vida Motel in town."

"In town, eh? Well, hop back in, and I'll take you there," said Stan.

Jorge nodded and went to sit in the front. Stan put up a hand and stopped him. If he was going to have someone in the cruiser, it had to look like he was doing real business. He motioned Jorge to the back.

Slowly Jorge nodded and got into the back seat, *again*.

"Say, I've never met a hit man before. I thought they were all Italian, but you sure don't sound like one."

Jorge cringed. "As I said, I'm from South America and … I'm not a hit man."

"Right," said Stan, tapping the side of his nose with a wink into the rear-view mirror. He clicked on his seat belt. He turned the ignition on and put the cruiser into drive. "Hold onto your hat, Yogi," he cried happily as he put the siren on.

In a whiz, they were in the centre of town, and Stan let Jorge out. Unfortunately, no one was around to either witness Officer Stan graciously give someone a good-will ride into town or catch a glimpse of someone potentially dangerous in the back seat. He just loved getting on the gossip trail. *Oh, shoot*, Stan said to himself. *Oh well. Maybe this Yogi guy might get out of hand.* So Stan gave Jorge an up-and-down warning gaze and then saluted.

"Stay out of trouble, Yogi."

"Yeah, thanks," said Jorge, and he waved as the cruiser pulled away, wailing with sirens on.

Jorge slapped his forehead and shook his head before turning and heading up the Nova Vida Motel's drive.

The ladies were wrapping up the rehearsal. Sharon had to rely on some of the elderly members of the club to help with the adjustments in the outfits, but apart from that, Sharon was feeling hopeful enough to rely on the old adage, "the show must go on." She'd done this fashion show for eleven years, though always at the Italian Canadian Club. She looked around at the new surroundings and thought they were quite an improvement. Better still, she was going to get a tremendous amount of free advertising with Anita promoting the mall and the show all day. That made her year!

She looked over at Maria asleep on Andy's lap and shook her head. *That girl*, she thought. *What will become of her*? Andy suddenly looked up at her and Sharon quickly looked away. "Um, Mrs. Carlesi," she said to cover. "Please, would you mind not stepping on Mrs. Palazzo's heels? Stay at least one arm's length away from whomever is in front of you!"

Anita was sitting beside Andy, drinking a coffee. Andy leaned over and whispered, "What do you think, Anita? Will this get off the ground?"

Anita looked around and nodded. "Somehow these things always tend to fall into place, don't you think?"

"I didn't want to think. That's why I asked you, silly." Andy looked down at the angel face on her lap. "But I think it's time to take this little monster home. She has a big day tomorrow." Andy stood and hefted the lanky Maria over her shoulder. She turned to Anita and grabbed her hand. "Are you going to be okay at the house, or do you want to stay with us?"

Anita thought quietly about Stefano and the unfair things she'd done behind Andy's back. She shook her head and smiled. "Thanks, Andy. I'll be okay. I won't be there too much longer, and I still have to pack this and that. I'll see you here tomorrow." She felt like a real jerk. She reached out and touched Maria's limp hands. "I think she'll really enjoy it tomorrow."

"Well, we can be forever hopeful, yes?" Andy turned and walked through the court towards the main doors. Anita then looked over to see Mrs. Carlesi stepping on Mrs. Palazzo's heels again.

"Mrs. *Carlesi!*" pleaded Sharon.

Chapter 32

EARLY THE NEXT MORNING, LEO Mangiano got up out of bed and slowly struggled to the bathroom. He was getting old. The long brutal drive through the snow to Vindenza was more tiring than waiting out a gale at sea. He looked in the mirror and groaned. "Now why would an angel face like Yvonne possibly love an asshole like you?" he asked himself out loud.

He stuck out his tongue and studied it. Then he picked up a soggy cigar butt he'd left on the edge of the little glass shelf under the mirror. He looked at it with disgust and threw it into the corner garbage pail with a hollow *plunk*. He picked up his toothbrush and started running the tap. He absentmindedly picked up the plastic cup with his soaking dentures and studied them as he brushed what little teeth he had left in his mouth.

Then he picked up a glass ashtray holding a book of matches off the other end of the glass shelf. He read the logo on both: "Nova Vida Motel, Vindenza, Quebec."

Next door, on the other side of the wall, Jorge slowly woke up. He passed a hand under his pillow, felt the gun and relaxed. He heard some grumbling in the unit next door and some banging but wrote it off as some old grumbling bastard. He didn't give it a second thought until suddenly he heard the old guy sing a tune off key: "*Bella* Yvonne, *mia bella* Yvonne, la la la la, di, la la la la!*"

Jorge held his hand to his head and groaned up at the ceiling. *What kind of people are these?* he asked himself. "Geez," he said aloud.

He really didn't want to go through with this assassination. It seemed like more trouble than it was worth, but he had no idea as to how to get out of it. Leo would simply follow the protocol and have him rubbed out as well. He thought maybe there was a way of disappearing, like this Jack guy. It was like looking for a pin in the proverbial haystack, but the haystack was impervious to penetration. And these people can't be for real. He wished for the umpteenth time that he could simply pick up the phone and call Leo. Damn that tornado or whatever it was. All the lines were still down.

He thought back on the night before. That Rose looked like a sweet gal. Dumb as a Venezuelan goat, though.

He sighed and looked at his watch. If what Rose and Stan the Man had said was true, Jack just might be back tomorrow. From wherever he was.

"Another day," he groaned as he covered his head with a pillow.

Anita hurried to the mall. She had to be there before 8:30 a.m., as she had to show up with the station's Jeep in time for Peter to let her drive through the main doors and park it a little ways away from the temporary runway that had been put up the night before.

The doors were still locked, so she rapped at them with her keys. She had to press her face against the glass to be able to see further into the mall. She stood back when she saw the cousins coming to let her in. They ran up and unlocked two of the doors so that a larger opening was created to allow her to drive the Jeep into the mall.

"Heydiho!" yelled Guido.

"Ah, da lady-a wid da focka fur!" yelled Mario.

Anita rolled her eyes and turned to go back to the Jeep. "I don't have that fucka fur no more!" she threw over her shoulder.

The cousins looked at each other. They mumbled in Italian. They shrugged and waited for the Jeep to drive through before closing the doors again and shutting out a terrible winter wind.

Anita slowly and carefully drove the Jeep to a taped mark on the marble floor. She parked it and jumped out. She was starting to take down the convertible top when the cousins came up and motioned to her that they would do it.

Anita nodded and smiled. "Gee, thanks! That's the nicest thing you've done for me!" She turned and walked towards the mall offices.

Mario looked at Guido. *"Che?"* Guido shrugged and continued to unbutton the top away from the frame of the roof. Mario shrugged, too, and started at the other end, humming to himself.

Anita knocked on the office door before trying it. It was open, so she sidled in. She could smell coffee brewing somewhere, and her stomach growled to remind her she had just gotten up, dressed and took her big bag of curlers and makeup, knowing that she would have loads of time to do that once at the mall. Still, she regretted not picking something up at Tim's.

"Hello?" She followed the smell of coffee. She came up to a tiny kitchen where she found Nancy standing by the counter, staring down at her cup.

Anita rapped against the door frame. "Good morning, Nancy."

Nancy was startled and scratched at her hair suddenly. "Oh, hi, Anita, good morning."

"Are you okay?"

"Yeah, I'm just not a morning person."

Anita stood reminding herself that this woman had gone to Italy with her husband, though she wasn't able to prove it was anything more than a business trip. She had been able to at least zero in on what year that trip was. It was the same year that she and Jack got together. So it could've been something more, but obviously not enough. *I'm the one that Jack married*, she said to herself. She stepped in to look for a mug for coffee.

"Do you mind if I pour myself a cup? I figure I'm here on mall business, right?"

Nancy didn't smile. She nodded and said, "Be my guest."

Nancy had grown to hate Anita. *She has no backbone*, Nancy thought. *She's an idiot, and I don't know what Jack saw in her*. Nancy didn't even bother saying anything else. She simply took her cup and went to her desk.

Anita poured a cup and was soon joined by Peter.

"Well, top of the morning to you, Anita!" Peter said gaily.

"The same to you! You don't mind, do you?' She held up her cup and the coffee pot.

"Fill your boots! After all, you are here to promote this wonderful mall and all our vendors. Not only that, you're sacrificing yourself by having volunteered to do the fashion show with all our venerable old ladies from the old country. So Italian of you."

"I didn't volunteer. Andy volunteered me."

"Ah. I should've known. Hey," he said, suddenly turning towards her. "Have you noticed a change somewhat for the better with our Andy?"

Anita looked up at him with eyebrows raised. "Yes, isn't that nice? What happened?"

"Lord knows, but it makes me a believer in miracles."

Anita sipped at her coffee. "Yeah, it does, doesn't it?"

Peter looked over at her, sensing an odd sadness in her voice. "I know what you're thinking," he said.

Anita looked up at him startled, "What do you mean?" *Does he know about her and Stefano? He might as well. The whole community seems to know everything she didn't know.* "What am I thinking, oh partner of my husband, who, by the way, is still missing and may be presumed dead." She then froze, staring down into her cup.

Peter turned to face her. "You think he's dead?"

She looked up. "Don't you?"

Peter took a sip of his coffee. "No, I don't think he's dead."

Suddenly Anita snapped. "What is it about you Italians!? You think that life is a game? That you can just up and run away from your wife? I *wish* him to be dead. You know why? Because if he was dead, at least I could believe he loved me and someone prevented him from fighting to get back to me. If he's alive, it means he's deserted me! *Deserted me!* We're losing the house, we lost our cars, I lost the apple of my eye, my darling Jack! If he's still alive, then I'll, I'll, I'll … kill him myself!" She angrily tossed the mug of coffee at him and then grabbed a roll of paper towels and threw that at him too. Then she reached over for a tea towel off a hook on the wall and threw *that* at him. Then she looked around frantically for something else to throw at him. She spied the garbage pail and put it upside down over his head before she stomped away.

Peter slowly took off the pail and looked down at his shirt and his five-hundred-dollar suit. Italian. With matching calf-leather shoes, also from Italy, and *also* ruined.

Nancy poked her head around the corner. She eyed him up and down and snickered. Then she, too, stomped away.

"Maria, get down this minute!" Andy stood for a moment at the bottom of the stairs and listened. She could hear rustling in Maria's bedroom. Instead of yelling more, she turned and walked into the kitchen. Stefano was sitting in his usual place going over the Italian-Canadian newspaper of the previous week again. "You hear-a about Walmart?" he asked Andy.

Andy did a double take and frowned. "What about Walmart?"

"We-a tell Walmart to get-a lost."

Andy walked over and looked at the story upside down. "Let's see."

Stefano slid the paper towards her and let her read. Her lips moved as she slowly read the Italian story. "Wow. No kidding!"

Stefano looked at his wife's face. He cocked his head and studied it. Andy looked up and locked eyes with him. Stefano smiled. "Is good-a, no?"

Andy moved closer to Stefano and silently put a hand on his shoulder and nodded. He looked down at it and then patted it with his other hand. "*Si*, is good."

Andy took her hand away and nervously readjusted a lock of hair. She walked to the hallway again, and this time she almost sang to Maria. "Mariiiiiiiiiaaaa. Yoo hoo!"

This time, there wasn't a sound coming out of Maria's room. Slowly the door squeaked open, and Maria poked her head out and looked down the hall. Andy waved at her with her fingers. "Remember, you do the fashion show and we *might* get that puppy."

Stefano looked up frowning. "Andy, no make-a da deal if you no get-a dog."

"Well, Stefano, I have learned something recently that I figure is a pretty good idea. I never wanted to make plea bargains with a kid of mine, but I have come to realize that sometimes it's okay to bribe a kid. I really mean it now when I bribe. Listen."

Stefano cocked an ear and listened. A moment later, he heard something crawling on all fours along the hallway. Andy poked her nose out of the kitchen in time to see Maria crawl head first down the stairs.

"Why on earth are you crawling down the stairs like that?" asked Andy softly.

"So that I can understand what the dog will feel when he goes down these stairs."

Andy mutely looked into the kitchen and over at Stefano. Stefano silently laughed and shook his head.

And Andy smiled.

～

Rose looked into her closet and couldn't make up her mind what to wear to the grand opening. It was the fashion show she was excited about, and she wanted to look like a million bucks.

She pulled out a black dress, and then she pulled out a red dress. She wanted to wear her new coat, so the dress had to go with it. Her microwave beeped at her, and she slipped into the kitchen to retrieve a reheated cup of tea. As she sipped at it, she looked into a wall mirror in the hallway of her apartment. With one hand she pressed up the skin at her temple for an instant estimation of what she would look like with a facelift.

Jack suddenly appeared and stood behind her. "You don't need any work, Rose. You're beautiful the way you are." Jack bent over her and held her in his arms. "You're so cute it hurts," said Jack.

"Oh come on now, Jack. I look terrible! I just got out of bed, for crying out loud!"

"Yeah, but morning sex makes you look even better. Is it true what they say about a good screw does wonders for a woman?"

Rose turned around and slapped him lamely with her right hand. "I don't know! Go. Eat your eggs and leave me alone. I'm trying to think of what to wear."

"Where are you going again?" Jack asked, almost pouting.

"The grand opening of the mall, silly. It's too bad you can't come!"

"Yeah, too bad." He made a gagging sound, and she slapped him again in jest. Then she wrapped her freckled arms around Jack's neck. "Oh, I can't wait till we go, Jack. I hate not being able to go around with you. I want everybody to know that you love me." She smiled and looked up at him with those lovely sparkling eyes.

"Yeah, one more day, Rose. Just one more day, and this will all be behind us."

She planted a big wet kiss on his lips. "I can't wait!" With that, she took her reheated cup of tea and went back into the bedroom. "Now you have to behave yourself while I'm gone. Don't answer the phone or the door."

"You better believe that I won't!" He looked over at the coffee table, on which sat six lumpy medium-sized canvas bags. More than enough for them to live off of nicely.

❦

Jorge stood with his ear at the base of one of the motel's plastic cups pressed to Rose's apartment door. He quickly pulled back and looked up and down the hallway for the hundredth time, it seemed, before resuming his stance of intense concentration. He was extremely glad and relieved to have finally cornered the guy, and he was just buying time now as he listened for the sake of his own entertainment. He was also getting another glimpse into this cute gal's life and her way of thinking.

❦

Fabrizio sat in his favourite chair watching Saturday morning cartoons. He was hooked up to a pair of oxygen tanks strapped to a mini dolly. Claudia limped into the room in her traditional costume for Calabria, even though the fashion show was still four hours away. Claudia couldn't wait. Besides, this way last-minute details wouldn't detain her.

For the fifth time that day, Claudia walked up to Fabrizio and asked if he was very, very sure that he wanted to go to the mall.

"*Si!*" he said irritably.

"Okaaay. Good Fabrizio. You will like-a da show."

If there was one thing Fabrizio loved to do, it was watch women. He couldn't wait to see the show. But most importantly and surprisingly of all, he had to be there for his Claudia.

His brush with death had left him more aware of the sweeter things in his wife—Claudia's smile, her eyes, her zest for life, the way she took such good care of him. It was as if he had been blind for many, many years and now he could see. Thinking about her brought a tear to his eye.

He was also very proud of Stefano and Peter. Building the mall was an amazing thing for them to do. Two poor little boys from a poor part of Calabria, two brothers who had graced his and Claudia's lives with so much happiness, two … His heart skipped a beat. He clasped his chest with a small cough and frowned.

Suddenly it was very important that he carefully visualize the members of their family and his. It was hard for him to concentrate, as he hadn't used his brain for anything more than just years and years of watching TV. It was no use—he lost the train of thought he was on, and he couldn't remember what he was thinking about. But it was very important. He shook his head and sighed. His inner musings were interrupted by Claudia.

"Fabrizio. Before we-a go, you go-a to da washroom, *si?*"

He suddenly lost what little breath he had and coughed and wheezed. He rasped and coughed and wheezed, but he couldn't catch his breath.

Claudia, wide-eyed, jumped at Fabrizio and pounded him on the back. "Fabrizio! Fabrizio! Breathe-a!" she screeched.

Slowly he regained his breath and sat back, spent of what little energy he'd had. Claudia stopped pounding and now just rubbed his back.

"See, Fabrizio, you are-a a bambino. You no can do anything!"

'N-now I no can-a breath, thought a frightened Fabrizio.

Claudia stood gazing at him and, with a sickening awakening, thought exactly the same thing.

❧

Leo pulled up in front of Anita's house. He looked around at the neighbouring houses and felt certain that it was pretty safe to drive up the driveway. *Even if a neighbour did happen to see me drive up, who's to say I couldn't be the meter reader or something?* So Leo backed up a little and then pulled into the driveway. He parked the car in front of the garage and got out.

There was enough snow on the ground to see Anita's footsteps leaving from the front door. He looked around and then followed her footsteps to the door.

First he pushed the button for the doorbell. He could hear a chime play in the house somewhere and waited. Nothing. Exactly as he expected. Then he tried the doorknob. Surprisingly, the door was unlocked.

He opened the door and knocked on it as he stepped into the house. "Hello?" he called. Nothing.

Leo put his car keys into his pocket and closed the door behind him. He searched the house and realized that this Jack must've moved out, as half of the master bedroom walk-in closet was bereft of most of his clothes. Leo was concerned. He was tempted to think that he had been too late. *Jorge must've gotten to him before I could stop him.* He shook his head. *Ah, mamma mia.* He felt very sad.

He looked around the master bedroom and saw the photo in the broken frame on the chest of drawers. He picked it up and studied it. *A nice young couple.* He sighed.

He went back down and walked through the kitchen. He'd been in such a hurry the last few days that he hadn't eaten very much, and he was suddenly starving. He wondered what there could be that he could swipe and nibble on. He stepped to the fridge and opened the door. He searched and found a gallon jug of milk. He took it out, and as he closed the fridge door, his eye caught the calendar hung up on the door with a magnet. There was writing on it. He looked closer and read the various activities Anita had written. He saw that for today, she had gone at 8:30 a.m. to a place called Vindenza Village Mall. He tipped the bottle up and drank his fill. Then he wiped the neck of the bottle and put the cap back on before putting it back into the fridge.

He was sad for the wife. She looked so innocent and sweet, and he hoped to God that Jorge hadn't beaten him to them.

He reached up and took the calendar and left the house, carefully making sure that he left the door unlocked.

First thing's first, he thought. *Find out where that mall is.*

❧

In the tent set up in back of the runway, eight women and one child were frantically getting ready for the fashion show. Anita was still at the

Jeep, reporting and interviewing people for the station live. She looked at her watch briefly and decided she had better get ready herself.

"And Roger, as you know, I am also a part of this special grand opening of the Vindenza Village Mall, and it looks like I've run out of time!" Anita smiled brightly at the people who had gathered in the court and were watching her as she sat on a small stage beside the Jeep. She had set up promotional displays of the call letters, CHJX-AM, and had been handing out free bottles of Basilio soda drinks to the onlookers.

"Yes, Anita, I'll take over while you go off and get glamorous for the show. I have an entire lineup of requested songs for the next half hour, and our listeners will also hear Sharon Fazzolari of Fazzolari Fashions, which by the way is one of our many sponsors for today's show and the grand opening celebrations of Vindenza Village Mall."

"You are right," Anita replied, "but I have to say first that I don't know about me getting glamorous, Roger. I'm sure the other women taking part in this wonderful fashion show are already lovely enough, and they don't need a lot of work to look glamorous, I tell you! Roger, I'd like to also remind listeners that this is a live broadcast and the full show will be aired, including Sharon's real-time commentary during the show so that listeners can easily visualize the look of the outfits. Of course, they will also hear traditional folk songs, as many of the fine lady members of the Italian Canadian Club come out dressed in their traditional costumes. I would also like to point out, Roger, that this fashion show is an annual affair normally held at the club, and that the wonderful luncheon of favourite Italian dishes served for the duration of the show is provided by many of the same lady members of the club."

"Yes, I am certainly aware of the long list of sponsors helping out with the grand opening," added Roger.

"Yes, I can list them off for you, Roger, if you like."

"Go ahead there, Anita."

"Well, as you say, you can find Alessi's House of Style in the Vindenza Village Mall where you get your hair, makeup, pedicures and manicures done—you name it, she's got it and gives it. Then there is Stefano Giordani & Sons Contractors, Prediletto Pet Shop, Torbay Travel, J & P Plastics, Pietro's Trattoria, Lorenzo's Electronics, Bella Bellisima Jewellery, Mario's Shoe and Tailor Shop, Capone Shoes,

Gregori Men's Wear, Vindenza Bakery, Genova Children's Wear, Paola's House of Toys, and last but not least, Lisoni Florists. Well, I'm on my way, Roger. I'm handing the mic to you for the duration of the fashion show, which will begin in about twenty minutes."

"Break a leg, Anita."

"Thanks, Roger," she laughed. "I hope not!" Spectators around her chuckled loudly, hoping they could be heard and recognized on live radio.

Over at the runway, people who had already arrived and taken seats at the tables clapped politely as Anita walked away from the Jeep. Some teenagers around the periphery of the court whistled. Anita smiled brightly and waved goodbye as she stepped into the dress tent at the back of the runway.

"And now that I have the mic, I will be playing your requested favourite songs until the fashion show begins, which as Anita said, will be in about twenty minutes," Roger took over. "We have a lineup of music carefully chosen by our hostess, Sharon Fazzolari of Fazzolari's Fashions. So, at the new Vindenza Village Mall, we begin with our first request, called, 'Maria, Bela Maria,' about a man in love with another man's wife and he tells her to, ah, kill her husband so that he could marry her."

Immediately, the folk song started: *"O Maria, bella Maria piermi mi, Maria, bella Maria piermi mi ..."*

Leo drove around looking for the Vindenza Village Mall. He had been listening to the radio and followed the live on-air program as he drove. He hit the steering wheel in frustration but then suddenly caught sight of a massive collection of different-coloured helium balloons floating in the slight breeze. He turned onto the next road and saw the mall.

Jorge decided to continue to stake out Rose's apartment from the same tree across the road as the day before. He looked both ways and reminded himself to watch out for that damn police constable Stan the Man.

The weather wasn't too bad. The sun shone brilliantly, and the sky was a clear blue. Jorge looked up and watched a jet fly overhead and leave a long, straight contrail. He looked over at the branches on the trees and could tell there were tiny buds forming. The beginning of March. He'd come to realize that he really didn't mind this cooler weather and wondered if perhaps his posting in Venezuela could be shortened. Then he realized that the conglomerate would not be too happy if he up and left his position. *Oh, well*, he said. *One day.*

He walked over to another tree and sat on a bench below its branches. The green paint on the bench felt cozy and warm, and he leaned back against it and raised his face to the sun. He closed his eyes and hummed.

Stefano—wearing dress pants, a striped shirt and a tie underneath his dress coat—walked into the mall and made his way to where all the noise and music was coming from. As he approached the gathered crowd, he looked with pride at the design and detailing of the massive court under the glass dome. He followed the length of the mature maple tree they had planted in the middle of the surrounding fountain pool. It cost a bomb, but it was worth every penny.

He looked at the Jeep and then around the crowd to see if Anita or Andy were still out front. They were both gone, so he looked over to the curtained entrance to the change tent and noticed his little Maria with her head stuck out between the curtains. She saw him and stuck a hand out to wave frantically. She then jumped up and down and accidentally pulled a hook out of the track holding up the curtain. She looked up and saw what she had done and covered her mouth while she giggled.

Stefano shook his head, smiled and waved her away. She popped her head back in.

He looked around and saw that he knew most of the people there. He nodded at some, waved at others and nodded at some more.

Peter stepped out of the hallway leading to the offices and stood with his hands in the pockets of the fresh suit he had just put on. He saw Stefano and waved at him, but Stefano didn't see him. So Peter stuck his fingers in his mouth and whistled.

Stefano recognized the old call and looked over. He hurried through the crowd towards his brother.

Peter reached out to Stefano's tie and straightened it. "No woman to do your tie, I see."

Stefano grinned and shook his head.

"So, what do you think?"

Stefano raised his eyebrows. "Yeah, is no bad-a." He was surprised and impressed by the turnout.

"Well, the radio station's been great, I mean, they know what they're doing, you can tell. You know, Anita and all. And the people keep coming in. Obviously they've been listening to the radio out there."

"*Si*, where is-a 'Nita now?" asked Stefano, looking around. They were standing off to the left of the change tent, and he could hear a cacophony of female voices from inside.

"Yeah, she must be inside getting ready for the show." Peter slowly turned and then looked at his brother. He smiled. "You got the hots for her?"

Stefano whipped his head around and stared at his brother. He couldn't hide the wave of crimsom spreading up his face.

Peter nodded once. "'Thought so."

Stefano made a small growl and waved his brother away. He turned towards where the main mall doors were and watched to see who he would recognize amongst the new arrivals.

Leo finally parked the car. The parking lot was full, and he'd had a hard time finding a spot, but he did. He didn't like the fact that he had to walk from the edge of the main road right across the lot. He felt pretty miserable; by now, he had come to believe that he was too late anyway.

He had specifically come to see if he could find this Jack's wife, Anita, even if just to look at her. He toyed with the idea of talking to her and perhaps somehow make amends, but he couldn't think of anything that would not seem too strange or too familiar coming from a stranger.

As he neared the mall, he could hear traces of an old Italian love song his *nonna* used to sing to him. *How odd*, he thought. As he moved through the main door, following other newcomers, he walked into a festive atmosphere. He looked around and was impressed by the freshness and originality of the design. Somehow it made him feel at home, but he couldn't figure out why at first. Then he spotted a number of Italian provincial flags amongst the red and white Canadian flag and the blue Quebec fleur-de-lis.

As he watched the marble floor go by his feet, it suddenly occurred to him that the materials used in the mall were reminiscent of his home in Calabria as well. Then he looked around with renewed interest and spied a mural on one of the walls. It looked very much like his mother's home where he grew up. The same rolling hills, the same type of farmhouse.

He shook his head in amazement. *What a coincidence*, he thought. But then he reminded himself that he was actually on a heavenly mission, and that all of these amazingly familiar surroundings must have been Santa Maria's way of showing him he was on the right track. Santa Maria knew how to make him happy, and the memories that flooded in of his homeland in Calabria almost overwhelmed him. His step quickened and his heart sang as he looked at other familiar details in this Vindenza Village Mall.

Leo turned a corner and saw the most exquisite central court he had ever seen in North America. There was a massive tree, the kind of which he wasn't sure, that stretched up its branches towards an impressive glass cupola that allowed the sun to pour in. Fountains sparkled and sang and danced, and the colours were a feast for the eyes. Off to the side he spied the radio station's Jeep, but he didn't see anyone near it.

As he walked further, he realized that there were a large number of round tables covered in white tablecloths, each topped with a small vase of fresh flowers bearing a little tag saying, "With the Compliments of Lisone Florists." He stopped to stare at the people. They looked familiar. He searched their faces and saw elderly men with their shirts and ties, elderly women in black or other conservative dresses. There were women finely dressed. There was gold everywhere you looked. Little children were playing on the marble floor while parents chatted away. What was it that made him feel so at home …?

It finally dawned on him.

They were all shouting in Italian.

I think I like this place, Leo said to himself. He gave the area another sweeping glance before he spied a vacant spot along the water fountain wall. He carefully manoeuvred through the bodies, over legs, around feet and bags, and over little tots. Finally at the fountain ledge, he went to wipe at the marble but noticed it was quite clean. He nodded at the person on the right and on the left and then sat down between them. He crossed his arms and settled himself into simply enjoying the music. He even started singing softly to himself along with the music.

He frowned and closed his eyes. "Let me see," he whispered. "O Maria … O Maria …"

"You-a right-a!" said the man next to him. "Is '*O Maria Bela Maria piermi mi …*'"

Leo held up a finger and grinned, "Yes! It's that silly little song about killing a woman's husband!"

The other man nodded and held out his hand. They shook, and the man said, "My name is-a Guido, this man-a on you other side-a is-a my cousin, Mario."

"Hi, I'm Leo." He smiled and let the gentlemen chat away at him. He nodded and absently answered their simple questions … and then suddenly the meaning of the song's words dawned on him. He felt extremely ill. He broke out in a sweat and pulled out a tissue to wipe his brow. He felt a new urgency. He turned, smiled politely at Guido, and asked, "Excuse me, but when does this show start?"

"Da show-a?" asked Guido, "Oh, is in minutes-a only." He elbowed Leo and grinned. "Some-a nice women in show. I go every year-a *ma* is first-a time-a no at-a club."

"Club?" asked Leo.

"Si, Italiano Canadian Club-a. You come-a sometime-a." The man took a closer look at Leo and his eyes widened. "You have-a face I know-a."

"Me?" Leo asked, pointing to himself. "No, couldn't have. I only got here the other day. I'm from Georgia."

"Georgia. *Europa?*"

"No. USA."

"Oh, you *Americano*."

"*Si*."

"Ma, you look-a like … ah, *si!* Peter 'n-a Stefano Giordani."

Leo's heart did a gigantic flip. Giordani was his mother's maiden name. He shot up on his feet and stood over Guido and Mario. "I look like who? Where? Where are these guys?"

Guido beamed while he tapped on Mario's shoulder. "Where-a is Pietro?"

Mario looked over at his cousin and then up at this stranger. He, himself, thought Leo looked rather familiar. It was the nose and the eyes. He then searched over to the entrance to the hallway to the offices and pointed at Peter and Stefano.

"*Si*, dere!" Guido pointed out Peter and Stefano to Leo.

Leo bent over and shook Guido's hand. "*Grazie*," he said, happy as an Italian lark, which felt funny because it had been a long, long time since he'd spoken a single word of Italian, though he'd been working with a lot of his fellow countrymen in his particular line of dirty work for decades.

Leo made his way around the fountain wall, but just as he was debating as to the best way to navigate through the tables, the introductory music began and a beautiful woman in her mid-thirties stood up on the side of the stage and welcomed everyone.

Everyone whistled and clapped, making it impossible for Leo to get around, so he stood still for a moment and decided to watch the show while keeping an eye on the men standing at the back. Every once in a while, he would look over at Peter and Stefano with intense curiosity and compare their features and mannerisms with relatives he remembered from his youth. Then his gaze followed Peter and Stefano as they moved amongst the tables, finally reaching one at which a man about Leo's own age sat hooked up to two unwieldy oxygen tanks on a large cumbersome dolly. Leo guffawed and started to laugh like a young boy. No one heard him through all the noise.

He could swear this was his older brother, Fabrizio. And now it dawned on him why Stefano looked so familiar. He remembered him as a little boy playing with goats around the time Leo had emigrated to the States. They were cousins. Leo shook his head in disbelief. What a ride this experience was becoming! "Santa Maria!" he exclaimed.

"Ladies and gentlemen ..."

"And kids!" yelled a little girl somewhere in the audience. People laughed and clapped.

"And kids," Sharon smiled. "*Benvenuto!*"

Everyone clapped and whistled.

"*Benvenuto* to our annual Italian Canadian Fazzolari Fashions Fashion Show in the beautiful new Vindenza Village Mall!" Sharon waited for the clapping to die down. "Today we are on the radio, live, and we thank CHJX-AM for coming out and not only covering the fashion show but also to help celebrate the grand opening of this fabulous mall by being *in* it."

As people clapped again, Sharon looked at a stack of cards in her hand and switched the front to the back. She looked back up at the audience, brilliantly smiling again.

"We also celebrate the many provinces of a beautiful country where most of you have come from. *Italia!*"

Clapping. Smiling. Nodding.

"In celebration of these provinces, we have members of the Italian Canadian Club come out in full traditional women's costumes, and I'm sure many of you will recognize the provinces as they come out. Now, Mr. Maestro, please!"

An arrangement of old and popular Italian folk songs played full blast, and the audience clapped to the beat as a line of middle-aged to elderly women began to traipse along the runway that ringed the waterfall walls. Some of the women modelling waved at relatives, grandchildren and neighbours. As each woman walked onto the runway, Sharon would tell the audience from what province the costume came from. Some of the women were too slow, so there was a bunched-up mess around the middle of the runway.

"Come now, ladies," Sharon cooed. "Keep it moving please." And to the audience, "Oh, they're such beautiful hams, aren't they?"

Some people laughed while others looked around, asking others what Sharon meant by "hams." Did she mean they looked like pigs? Many finally understood, and there was a beat in time before they laughed as well.

Finally, Claudia came out onto the runway. She was by far the most outgoing of the bunch, and everyone could hear her screeching over the music quite clearly. "Heeeey, Theresaaaaaa!" She looked over at a nearby table where Fabrizio was sitting. She raised her arms and grinned. "Heeey, Fabriziooooooo!"

Fabrizio looked up at her and tried to laugh, but it made him cough. Claudia walked by close to him and pointed at Stefano to help Fabrizio. "Stefano, you-a help-a!" she screeched. Stefano looked over and started to pound Fabrizio's back. He then bent over to look up at Fabrizio's face while he was doubled over. He mumbled something comforting and then sat up again along with Fabrizio.

Claudia had stopped on the runway and caused a traffic jam. The runway was not wide enough for anyone to pass, so it was a little while before they all got going again. Claudia looked back at her husband one more time before she disappeared behind the back of the stage. She just caught sight of Stefano raising the thumb. *He's okay*, he motioned.

Claudia turned, stepped off the runway and headed back into the models' tent to change.

❧

Jorge yawned and then hugged himself. The day was getting on, and the temperature had dropped considerably. However, it was just a moment later that his long wait paid off when he saw Rose's car drive out of the parking lot at the back of the building. He stood up and nonchalantly walked towards his rental—but as Rose was passing him, she leaned over, opened her passenger-side window and called out, "Helloo?"

Jorge tried very hard to pretend he hadn't noticed. He quickened his pace, but she adjusted and cruised at his speed.

"Sir? Hellooo?"

He ignored her a little longer.

She honked on the horn and then yelled, "Hey you! Hey stalker!"

Jorge stopped and dropped his head. *This is ridiculous*, he said to himself. Slowly he turned and looked into the car. Rose motioned for him to come closer. He sighed and looked around. Then he obediently stepped to the side of the car.

"Yes?" he said dully.

"I'm going to a fashion show. You wanna come with me? I mean, you're following me anyways."

Jorge took a long look back at the apartment building.

"You might as well forget it. He's not there," she lied. She smiled brightly and said, "Maybe he'll be at the fashion show."

Jorge looked over to his rental car and sighed. He opened the passenger door and got in beside her.

Rose held out her hand and said, "Hi, I'm Rose. Nice to meet ya."

In the models' change tent, women were frantically putting on a variety of outfits. The Traditional Italian Provinces Costume part of the show was over, and they were now ready to strut the stuff from Sharon's shop.

Maria was whining about her shoes. "They're too big, Mom. I'll trip over them, see?" She showed Andy by walking and then tripping and falling. She reached out and caught hold of another lady's dress, which then ripped along where the skirt was attached to the bodice.

Back at the runway and stage, screams and swearing distracted Sharon briefly before she continued commenting on the outfits as her friends strutted along the runway. The lady whose dress had ripped was supposed to go on next, but she didn't as she tried to figure out how to fix the dress before going on.

Of course, Sharon described the outfit that should've been there. To accurately describe the outfit on the runway, she should have given the details of a "two-piece vanilla-coloured linen outfit of jacket and matching culottes over a satin lavender sport's style blouse, topped by a wide-brimmed vanilla-coloured summer hat and matching purse, good for daytime and, if one wished to, a walk along the boulevard by the sea. Shoes also lavender and of fine Italian kid leather, and the whole outfit beautifully finished off with mother of pearl button earrings and matching necklace." Instead, she recited, "A lovely peach-coloured T-line summer dress with a hidden bodice and short sleeves, peach- and salamander-coloured leather pumps and matching handbag, and turquoise crystal cluster earrings with a turquoise cluster choker."

People looked at the vanilla and lavender culotte outfit and noted that it was obviously not peach-coloured. Unfortunately, because

Sharon was looking down as she read, every single outfit commented on afterwards was incorrect.

In the meantime, the wearer of the actual peach-coloured T-line summer dress with hidden bodice and short sleeves still stood backstage having a nervous breakdown. Andy, standing nearby, looked around and saw a massive paisley shawl. She threw it over the crying woman and then physically turned her around and almost threw her onto the runway, giving her a good smack on the behind to get her going.

Unfortunately, the woman wasn't ready to go, so she stayed at the opening with her back to the audience. Andy hissed at her to go, but the woman suddenly had stage fright.

"Oh for fuck's sake," yelled Andy, and she went up the stairs and entered the runway herself. She grabbed the woman's arm and dragged her along, pretending they were walking along enjoying a stroll. Andy hammed it up and pretended to point at wonderful things out in the distance, all the time keeping a tight hold on the frightened woman. She hissed through her tight smile, "Look, is it a bird? Look over there, you idiot, is it a plane? Now over here. It's—" Suddenly, Andy stopped hissing. Off at the back of the crowd she noticed a stranger who looked disturbingly like her father—and in fact, he was looking over at her father, Peter and Stefano. She stopped without meaning to and inadvertently tripped Peach Lady, who did a flying leap and landed in enfolding arms of a large palm.

Sharon looked up as the audience whooped and hollered and she smiled brightly, her eyes twinkling with pleasure over the edge of her three-hundred-dollar Italian bifocals. She thought it was her performance that was so nicely appreciated.

Stefano whooped and grinned. Peter howled at Andy as she helped Peach Lady out of the palm, and the two women resumed their stroll along the runway. As they went by the table, Andy grinned and gave Peter the finger, which made Stefano turn beet red and choke. Her father innocently and happily continued to beam at the ladies, though out of breath once again.

Rose and Jorge parked in the "Do Not Park, Fire Zone" area of the mall. Jorge looked over at her expectantly, but she simply turned off the engine and started stepping out of the car, wrapping her fur coat tightly around herself against the cold.

Jorge shrugged and rolled his eyes. He dutifully followed Rose through the front mall doors. As they walked, he watched her shapely calves. He had always been a leg man. The walls resonated with music, and Sharon's voice echoed clearly over the sound of a mob, even though the center court was still out of sight around a bend.

Jorge looked around feeling very out of place, but he didn't know what else to do but follow her. Obviously, this woman did not realize that he had been sent to kill her boyfriend, Jack. Or did she? It was hard to tell whether she was very clever or very dumb. It was part of her mounting attraction.

He coughed and patted the gun in his holster to bring himself back to reality.

They rounded a corner and came into view of the show. Rose clicked her way along, keeping her coat on but taking off her gloves as she made her way along the back of the crowd. She passed right in front of Leo, who was still watching the table by the runway. Jorge passed right in front of him as well, distracted enough to not even notice that the man whose toes he was stepping on was Leo. He excused himself to Leo over his shoulder, and Leo distractedly grumbled back. The two ships passed in the night.

Rose stood up on her toes at one point to find a couple of vacant chairs. Miraculously, as she watched, two men stood up at one of the front tables, and she rushed forward through the crowd, excusing herself as she went along, to grab them.

Anita was waiting to go out on the runway with the second of her three outfits. She waited for the woman ahead of her to reach the midway point that marked the beginning of her stroll. She stepped up onto the steps leading to the opening of the runway. She felt ill, and she hadn't slept or eaten well for days, but in spite of it all, she stood straight and tall. She took a deep breath before she paused at the opening and posed before walking along the runway.

She listened as Sharon described, incorrectly, her outfit. She did a quick little turn at the first corner and then stepped towards the other corner. She looked towards the table that Stefano had sat at and noticed that he and Peter had left and were making their way to the back, so she smiled brightly at Fabrizio, who loved every second of it. She did a little turn and then started towards the corner closest to the table.

Leo looked over from where he stood behind the wall of people along the edge of the seating area. A beautiful woman with a head of red locks in white mink caught his eye, and he watched her for a moment weaving her way between packed tables, obviously heading towards the two seats Stefano and Peter had just left. He was about to see if he could beat her to the table so he could speak with Fabrizio, but then he noticed the man who was accompanying her.

"Holy fucking crap!" he exclaimed loudly. *"Jorge!"*

Jorge jolted to a stop and looked around. His jaw dropped at the sight of Leo waving at him. "Holy fuck," he whispered to himself.

A heavy, perspiring woman next to Leo glared at him. He quickly apologized as he bodily forced her aside. He held up an arm and waved. Then he cupped his hands and shouted again. "Jorge!"

Jorge quickly retraced his steps back to the edge of the crowd and met Leo halfway. Leo gratefully slapped Jorge's back and, with a laugh and a grin, gratefully pumped his hand.

"My God, Jorge. I've been trying to catch up to you!" He leaned into Jorge. "Did you, you know ..."

Jorge apologized. "No, not yet. I'm sorry, boss. But I'm, like, *this* close." He held up his hand showing a small space between the thumb and forefinger on his right hand. "What are you doing here?" For a moment, he was deathly afraid. *Was he being questioned? Did he screw up?* "What's up?" he asked with a slightly trembling voice.

Leo, relieved as hell, was about to explain when suddenly they both heard, *"That's my fuck fur!"*

They swung around in time to see Anita flying off the runway and flattening Rose with a full body slam. Both landed on Fabrizio, knocking him back in his chair, oxygen tanks and all. Rose landed full-breasted onto his face, while Anita landed face-first in his groin. People jumped up screaming all around them. Stefano jumped up and scrambled over to pull both women off Fabrizio. But he was too late.

Fabrizio lay there quite contentedly it seemed. He had died of a heart attack with a frozen grin on his face, his eyes wide with excitement.

Leo and Jorge finally made it to scene of the crime. "Holy crap!" cried Leo as he stood staring down at his older brother's face.

Out back, Andy heard Anita's expletive and then the screams. She opened the curtain separating the change area from the runway just in time to see Stefano pull Anita and a redhead off a body. In horror, she saw that the body was her father.

Maria ran out from the change room and clutched at her mother's hand.

"What's happening, Mom? Mom?"

Andy's blood had frozen in her veins. What she thought she saw was her father in spirit staring down at his own comatose figure. Whatever it meant, she knew he had died.

Nancy was watching from the hallway when Anita hurtled herself at Rose. She had recognized the coat as Anita's, for she had looked at that coat jealously many times before. Her first thought intuitively was that someone was going to die here.

She had always suspected that Jack was fooling around with someone else, but there had never been any proof. Like Anita, she had refused to believe it—until now. That mink was the giveaway. It had Jack's slimy, weaselly fingerprints all over it.

Nancy turned and ran into her office to grab her red woollen coat off the back of her door. As she looked for her purse, she could hear the screams on her radio echoing those out in the hall. She left it on as she hurried out, her heels clicking as she raced through the pressing crowd towards the mall's main exit.

Chapter 33

I T WAS VERY QUIET IN the viewing room, though all the walls had been removed to allow the use of the entire length of the funeral home. It was open to the public for Fabrizio's viewing. Hundreds of well wishers squeezed in.

Claudia quietly cried into a well-wrung embroidered handkerchief off to the side of an open, huge, gleaming white casket detailed heavily in brass. Fabrizio had been very tastefully done, but Peter had been in a quandary. He either had to straighten out Fabrizio's face or keep the uncanny look of ecstasy in that smile. He decided to keep the smile. It was too beautiful to take away.

It was perhaps precisely because of the smile and the way Fabrizio had died that there was more mirth than grief in the hearts of the gathering. To a man, they all thought it was the best way for Fabrizio to have given up the ghost. However, if Andy had heard any of their jokes, she would've strangled them in the blink of an eye, and they knew that. So the men were careful to maintain a sorrowful look as they stared down into the open coffin and then went over to offer their condolences. Once in a while, a gentleman would appear to be racked with sobs, but the others knew it was mirth and suppressed laughter. Claudia only thought they were overwhelmed with grief and cried and howled anew every time it happened. The rest hung at the back, every once in a while sneaking out for a release of bubbling humour.

Anita saw and heard it all as she sat in the back—way in the back. Andy was in the front beside Claudia. She was the one who thanked everybody for coming. She was the one who held it together. At one point, Maria, who was in the first row as well, looked back and waved at Anita. Anita sadly waved back. She knew intuitively that she was being written off. After that day, she would never see Maria or Andy again. Or Stefano.

Peter stood behind Anita. He fidgeted nervously and kept straightening out his jacket and tie, hiking his pants up, shooting his sleeves and straightening his jacket again. Stefano stepped up beside Peter from the lobby. From where they stood, the two brothers could see everything and everybody.

Stefano watched as Andy very capably handled the guests and comforted Claudia. Then he looked over and saw his daughter fidgeting quietly. He looked at the many friends who were sitting and standing, whispering amongst themselves. Eventually the whole Italian-Canadian community would come out, and Peter had to extend the viewing by two more days. In the end, eighty-six cars would snake slowly through the centre of the town of Vindenza on their way to the Mary Holy Mother of God Vendenza Cemetery on the other side of town. Constable Stan's wife, the police chief, would have to set up extra officers to direct the resulting heavy influx of traffic.

In the meantime, Peter kept looking over at a strange man who looked slightly familiar. Peter didn't trust him, thinking he was sent from higher up to poke his nose into the missing money. Or maybe to get at *him*. He thought of those cement boots. It never occurred to him to run. It really didn't matter anymore.

His insides were churning wildly. He hated this emotional roller coaster ride that he'd been on since he lost all that money gambling and then stupidly trusted Jack with the rest. Two deadly boo-boos.

Peter now also harboured a very bad and awful secret. He now knew for certain that Jack was dead. Only two other people knew: Rose and Nancy. Two redheads. He promised himself never to get turned on by a redhead again, *ever!*

Back at Rose's apartment, Nancy and Rose were scrubbing the floors and walls. Rose was still sniffling and crying. But Nancy was cool, though she had a stronge urge to kill Rose too.

Peter had been a massive help. In fact, Nancy was very impressed with how Peter took immediate control of the situation. Not only that, it had turned her on in a creepy way.

"Whoooey!" Nancy said to herself.

"What?" sniffed Rose.

Nancy, on all fours, looked up at Rose from beneath her left underarm. "None of your business, bitch."

"It *was* my business! You, you, you ... whatever," Rose pouted. "Jack was my business, my love, my life, my—"

"*Shut up!*"

"—cuddly Pooh bear! Because of you, I'm all alone again!"

Nancy grunted angrily and scrubbed harder. "Please! Pooh bear!"

After Nancy had seen Rose wearing the white mink, which she knew damn well Jack had given to Anita, she knew for a certainty that Jack was back. It infuriated her that Jack didn't even bother letting her know. And the ultimate insult was that he preferred this bimbo Rose over her.

After leaving the mall, she had driven to Rose's apartment and knocked on the door. Just as she had expected, he pretended he wasn't there until she whispered that it was Nancy and that she missed him so very much. "Please, Jack. Please. I miss you so much. Let me in."

She hadn't actually planned *how* she was going to kill him. In fact, she hadn't remembered anything until Peter stood in front of her, shaking her awake. She had looked around at all that blood, still holding the lamp in her quivering hand. He had made her clean up the blood. Rose came by a little later, screaming high heaven. Peter had to calm her down and then threaten her to get her quiet. It was while on all fours in a daze that Nancy came across a loose board in the floor and found a bloody canvas bag full of money—in dirty US bills.

When Peter got the call from her in his office, he had ordered her to stay right where she was. He knew exactly what to do. He'd done it before for others. Very clever.

To his amazement and massive relief, Rose broke down and showed where the other six massive canvas money bags were in the apartment. It was as if his life had been given back to him. *Boom bada bang!* Just like that. He had blubbered like a baby, he was so happy.

So Rose and Nancy scrubbed the last bit of blood away. While Nancy cleaned herself in Rose's shower, Rose stuck a thumbtack up through the bottom of Nancy's boot. She also went through Nancy's purse and stole the photo of Nancy and Jack that Nancy had in her wallet. Then, while she was there, she stole one of Nancy's credit cards. Then she opened up a bottle of makeup and spit in it. Then she wrote a note to Nancy ordering her to leave and never come back again. Then she slipped out and joined Jorge across the road where he waited for her. The two sat side by side, she in Anita's fur coat, he with his hands clasped on his lap. He was going with the flow. Besides, he thought Rose was cuter than cute and secretly wondered if she would like the idea of returning with him to Venezuela.

He redirected his attention to Nancy's shadow moving back and forth in Rose's apartment. They heard when Nancy pulled on her boot, and Rose watched in delight as Nancy finally appeared at the front door of the building and started limping out to her car.

After Nancy drove away, Rose very sweetly invited Jorge to come up for a cup of hot chocolate. As they walked across the road back to her apartment, she asked, "So, Jorge, where do you live?"

His heart flipped. "Venezuela."

"What's in Venezuela?"

"Jungles, coffee beans."

"Ooo, that sounds nice. Monkeys? I love monkeys."

"If you like," he beamed at her.

❦

Leo was standing in a phone booth in a parking lot, waiting for an answer at the other end of the line. He shivered in his light coat and stamped his feet.

"Hiyall, Navy Café."

"Yvonne! It's me, Leo. *Bellisima*, how are you?"

"Leo, chil', where are you?"

"I'm at the North Pole. It's freeeeezing here. What's it like there?"

"Well, apart from things being topsy-turvy, the weather's beautiful. Sun shinin' every day straight since you left."

Leo smiled and leaned into the phone. "Do you miss me, *Bellisima*?"

"Oh, now, you are so fresh!"

Leo giggled. "So, do you?"

"Now you just hurry home. Did you stop that man from hurtin' the young man you were talkin' about?"

Leo grinned. "Yeah! I stopped him! My man hadn't touched a hair on his beautiful head. You won't believe what happened, my *Bella*. This has been a week of such beautiful miracles!"

"Thank you, Jesus!" cried Yvonne. "And was he a nice young man?" she asked.

"I couldn't tell you, my angel. I never got to meet him, but let's just say he is now safe from me."

"Hallelujah!"

"You could say that again!"

"Well, praise the Lord!"

"So I'm comin' home, babe. Keep those hush puppies warm for me!"

"Oh, you are baaaad!"

Leo hung up with great joy and high spirits. He pushed the phone booth bifold door open and walked towards the shuttle bus that was waiting for him at the Jet Park near Pierre Elliott Trudeau International Airport. In his hand was a timetable of flights to Italy from Georgia. He was excited, because he was going to take his very own Venus back to the land of romantic love to meet some of his long-lost relatives. *Thank Santa Maria!*

As visitors started leaving the viewing room of the funeral parlour in Vindenza, Anita kept her seat in the back row. She wanted to run away screaming, but she knew she was responsible for the whole scene at the show. Tears streamed down her cheeks every once in a while, and she was determined to stay and apologize to both Andy and Claudia. And to poor Maria.

She was well aware that Fabrizio was dead because of her.

She waited until the room cleared out for the evening before she walked up to the front. Andy looked over, and Anita couldn't keep it together. Her face caved in remorse. She tried to talk but couldn't. Andy looked at her coldly, but Claudia raised her arms and ran to Anita.

"Anita! Oh, *mio* Fabrizio, he-a die!" Anita bent her head over Claudia's and cried with her. Maria sidled up and held both her *nonna* and Anita, and Anita put out an arm and drew her in tightly.

Andy just stood and watched. She watched her mother actually hug that woman. And Maria! Andy rolled her eyes and walked over to the front row to sit down and give her feet a break. She kicked off her shoes and rubbed her feet as she looked once again at her father.

Smiling, Andy shook her head. As she did, something caught her attention. She frowned and stood up. She cocked her head and walked to the foot of the coffin. She moved a large floral arrangement from Peter's florist shop and bent over to study something.

Anita and Claudia finally parted and moved to sit down together in the front row. Maria walked up to look at her mom before sitting down. As Anita bent over to hold little Maria close to herself, she noticed that Maria was distracted by what her mother was doing. She looked over at Andy as well. Then she cocked her head as well and looked to where Andy had removed the flower arrangement.

She saw a portion of a very familiar-looking tie sticking out from between one of the seams of the coffin.

Somebody screamed. And she thought it was her.

Chapter 34

ANITA SAT WITH A VERY long face. Stan sat opposite her at his desk in the police station. He was leaning back in his chair, fiddling around with an empty Tim Horton's coffee cup.

"So, you've gone through the mill, haven't you?"

Anita nodded and sniffed. "Yeah, it's been a long time since life had some semblance of balance." She looked down at the single remaining piece of jewellery she'd gotten when she married Jack—the plain and elegant gold wedding ring. She squeezed at her finger and tugged it off. She looked at it and laid it gently on Stan's desk. She took in a long breath. "Now what?"

"Well, our pretty friend Nancy is charged with the first degree murder of your husband."

Anita kept staring down at her hands.

Stan sat up straight, and his chair squeaked under his shifting weight. "Our Peter ..." he said, shaking his head. "Oh, I liked Peter." He stretched out his arms to the side and jiggled them. "Yup, you know, you just never know. You think you know someone. A good businessman, a good father, and then ..." Stan clicked his tongue and winked. "First thing you know, you find out he's been workin' for the Mob."

Stan winced. He leaned back again and looked at his coffee cup. He rolled up the rim to check to see if he'd won anything. He had. "Hey! I won a cupcake!" He looked at Anita, who looked back and blinked. "Ah, yes," he said, and he placed the cup on his desk and proceeded to tear the rim off the paper coffee cup. He threw the remainder of the cup into a wastebasket in the far corner of his cluttered office. "It also

~ 354 ~

didn't help that he was caught with almost a million U.S. dollars of drug money."

Anita sat up straighter. "Well, I hope for Sandra and the boys' sake, he will be safer in jail?" she asked hopefully.

"Oh, I don't know, Anita. Those mobster arms reach pretty far," Stan quipped, as if he was some sort of expert.

This saddened Anita. She hadn't liked Peter, but she certainly would never wish him harm. Nor Sandra and their boys. She sighed sadly, "Poor Peter."

Stan sat back and interlaced his fingers. "Yup, poor Peter," he repeated.

"Poor Sandra and the boys."

Stan shrugged and picked at a tooth.

"So, do you need any more statements from me?" asked Anita.

"No, Anita. You're good to go. And I'm sorry about your loss, Anita."

"Thank you, Stan. So am I. In more ways than one."

She stood up, pulled her coat off her chair and started to put it on. Stan stepped over to see her out. As they walked to the door, he rubbed his nose and took a deep breath.

"Anita, you look pretty beat up. Take care of yourself," he said—and then, wanting to end on an upbeat note, he blurted, "At least your insurance policy is coming in. I know it doesn't replace—"

Anita turned around to face him. "It doesn't. It doesn't make up for the fact that my husband fooled around, it doesn't make up for the fact that he dealt in crime and drug money, and it doesn't make up for the fact that I've not only lost my home and car but also my job."

Stan did a double take. "How'd you lose your job, Anita?"

"Because I said a bad word while live, on air."

"You did? What on earth did you say?"

She cocked her head but couldn't help but let a tiny smile curl around the edges of her lips. "I said, 'That's my fuck fur.'"

Stan blinked and then guffawed loudly. He continued laughing as he watched Anita walk out the door and down the sidewalk towards the little car she had rented. She looked back at him and blew him a kiss before getting in.

She flopped into the car seat, turned on the ignition, tilted the rear-view mirror so as to see her own face and grinned at herself before pulling out of the parking space.

Chapter 35

2005—Pearson International Airport, Toronto, Ontario

ANITA GRABBED THE HANDLE OF her carry-on suitcase and shifted her heavy coat a little higher onto her shoulder. She looked around, up the hallway at the terminal, and then down the other way. She spied a few extra seats. There was time yet for a tea and a Tim Hortons Boston cream. She had sent Steven to get them, but she couldn't see where he'd gone.

She sat down with a sigh and organized her coat, heavy purse and suitcase. She sat back, spied a newspaper on the opposite side on one of the side tables and hopped over to grab it. She looked over and saw a young man next to it.

"Oh, I'm sorry. Are you reading this?" she asked.

The young man looked over and shook his head pleasantly enough, shaking what curls he had along the rim of an otherwise bald head. "No, go right ahead." But he gave her a double take and studied her more closely.

"Thank you," smiled Anita and she settled into the chair and shook the paper straight. She started reading the front page headlines but stopped and bent over to get a pair of bifocals, check that they weren't dirty and perch them on her nose. She raised the paper and gave it another shake.

"Excuse me?"

Anita lowered the paper and peered over the top of it. "Yes?"

The young man leaned forward. His eyes seemed to twinkle at the sight of her. "Aren't you Anita Taylor?"

Anita was surprised and yet not. She lowered the paper and took off her glasses. "Yes, I am," she said with a smile.

"Wow," he said.

"I've listened to your show on CBC. I found your interrogative journalism style amazing. Your insight into the history of Canadian Mafia is fascinating and though you don't skip the raw reality of the organization, you talk as if you really understand the culture itself. As if you know the very fabric of just the day to day kind of stuff."

Anita sat back in surprise. "Now, why would you want to listen to my show? Are you a student of investigative journalism?"

"Well, no, but my family is Italian and in the past, I think some of my family were quite involved. Actually, my parents knew you." He grinned.

"No kidding? Who are your parents?"

He looked around and leaned forward. "Do you remember Andy and Stefano Giordani?"

Anita felt as if the world stopped turning. She covered her mouth and stared at the young man. "Oh, my!" She shook her head and raised a finger at him. "Yes, I can see the similarity." She smiled broadly and wanted to cry. *Oh, how wonderful that they finally had a son,* she thought.

There was a lot of good to remember, but there was also a lot of sad. "If you don't mind, what exactly did they talk about?"

The young man straightened up and looked at the ceiling thirty feet above them. "Oh no," he laughed, "good stuff." He grinned. "For the most part!"

Anita's mind went reeling. So much to remember. "Oh my God. How are they? Are they still at that farm in Vindenza?"

"Well, yeah, still in Vindenza. At least, my dad's doing okay. He's retired now. Just."

"No kidding!" said Anita, omitting the fact that she never went through a day without thinking about him. She bit her lip. "How wonderful. And your mother? Is she the same old firecracker she used to be? I've never known a more intelligent and, well, bossy woman!"

She laughed at the thought of Andy's knack at telling jokes. "Well, at least you always knew where you stood with Andy!"

The young man looked down at his hands. "Well, Mom died just last year, as a matter of fact."

Anita sat back in shock. "Oh!" She didn't know what to say at first. "Oh, I'm so sorry. My God!" Anita leaned over and grabbed his hand. "I'm truly sorry to hear that. The world is a far sadder place without your mother in it."

He frowned and nodded. "Yes, I agree, the world has lost a star."

"Yes. Totally. The world has indeed lost a star. Do you mind me asking, how did your mother die? I mean, she was far too young to die of natural causes. What was she, sixty?"

"Just. She died helping Dad. She drove the lawnmower into the pond. Nobody was around. The machine fell sideways and pinned her down."

Anita sat back and covered her mouth. Her eyes watered quickly, and though she tried very hard, she could not hold back the tears and she whimpered into her hand. He jumped up and sat beside her, putting an arm around her to comfort her.

After a few moments, Anita searched her purse for a tissue, but the man quickly drew out a handkerchief and gave it to her. She looked at it and held it back towards him, but he put a hand on it and shook his head.

"No, I know. It's old-fashioned, isn't it. But no, you keep it. By all means."

"But your Mom used to hate everything to do with the farm—"

"Oh, I know. Ha, don't I know it. She only went so far as to mow the lawn, and sometimes she helped him with the weeding." He leaned in conspiratorially, "But she still hated the chickens."

Anita laughed aloud, her laughter echoing gaily through the terminal, but she had to wipe away some tears again.

"Mom?"

Anita twirled around to face another tall young man of about twenty-five years old. The man looked suspiciously down at the stranger.

"Mom, are you all right?"

Anita lifted her arms and took her son's hand.

"Yes!" she said, beaming. She pointed to the man but couldn't seem to find the words. Instead, he stood up and held up his hand.

"Hi. I'm Mario Giordani. My family knew your mother."

The younger man shook his hand and then pointed at him.

"Yeah, Mom always talked about the Giordanis. Your mother and father were Andy and Stefano! Oh! I'm sorry. I'm Steve, son to this lovely lady," he said, smiling down at his mother. He spied her tears. "Oh, Mom," he said teasingly. "My mom has a big heart, as you can tell."

"Nice to meet you, Steve."

Steven looked behind him up the hallway and pointed to another man coming towards them. "And that gorilla there is my brother, Pat. Hey Pat, you'll never guess!" he called out.

Pat took a couple of big strides and held out his hand. Mario shook his hand grinning and then pointed from one brother to the other.

"Twins!"

"Yup," said Pat and Steven in unison.

By now, Anita had settled down enough to join in the conversation.

"I'm so glad to know you," she said to Mario. "You're father always wanted a son! Not that he didn't worship Maria!" she laughed. "How is your sister? I tell you, I love that kid! I'm surprised she isn't prime minister by now! I don't know how often I would talk about her to these guys." She turned to her sons. "Do you remember me mentioning her to you over the years?"

Steven rolled his eyes in jest and laughed. Anita grinned and waited for Mario to talk. Then Anita frowned and her heart skipped a beat. Mario looked so, so sad.

"Oh, my. Is she all right? What happened to Maria?"

Mario cocked his head and looked at Anita and then at the two young men who looked strangely like himself. Like his father. He then gave a half smile to Anita and leaned forward.

"I *am* Maria. You see …" He looked at Anita when he said this. "Do you remember that Mom always described me as being *special*?"

Anita nodded.

"Well, I am. I am what they call a hermaphrodite, or what I would prefer to use, intersex. When I reached puberty, it was easier just to go on as a male—ergo, Mario."

Mario watched Anita's face intently. At first he thought he had stepped over a line, but when Anita stood up and held up her arms, he jumped up gratefully and hugged her close to himself. He stepped back smiling.

Anita was speechless. Pat and Steven exchanged confused glances.

"I never told you this," said Mario, "but there was a day when I was with you on the radio trip, d'you remember?"

"Ha! I've never forgotten that!" Steven and Pat laughed along with their mother. It was one of their favourite Maria stories.

"We must've heard that story a million times!" laughed Pat.

"Well, I remember you were very, very sad because your husband—" He looked at the guys and said, "I guess he was missing, and I saw you cry, and you were looking out the windshield. You had tears running down your face? I thought I saw what I had envisioned to be, well, what a saint must look like. And I wanted so much to do this."

Mario reached out and cradled Anita's face in his hands. He gently kissed her forehead.

Anita looked up at him in a curious way. Then she looked at her sons, eyes widened. She was moved, as she only saw herself as having been cruel to Andy for her brief affair with Stefano. And for her hand in Fabrizio's death. Just because of a mink coat. And the thought that perhaps she was only doing her human best under such stressful times had not occurred to her. *Could I actually be forgiven?* Suddenly a massive weight seemed to lift off her shoulders, and her heart expanded with a new sensation of joy.

Mario followed her gaze over to them.

Suddenly a ray of sunshine burst through the clouds and shone through the massive windows, releasing the brilliant aqua blue in their eyes. He looked again at Anita. Anita smiled shyly in return. He stepped back and pointed at Steven and Pat. His mouth fell open.

Anita nodded and sighed. "Yes, your father wanted so much to have sons." She blushed and stood happily looking at the three handsome men with the aqua eyes and manly profiles. "Well, he's got three, I guess. Too bad he retired. He finally is Stefano Giordani & Sons Contractors!"

Suddenly an announcement calling for boarding caught Anita's attention. She looked around and then up at her boys. They looked at each other and shrugged. Mario caught the motion.

"This is your flight? To where …?" Mario asked, suddenly flustered and looking up at the flight schedules over their heads.

"Well, we *were* going back to Vancouver," Anita said slowly.

"You're going back to Quebec?" asked Pat.

Mario nodded.

Steven looked at Anita. "Mom, why don't we …?"

"Yeah," Mario piped up. "Why don't you …?" he asked hopefully.

Anita took a deep breath. "Steven, could you please go and see if there are any vacant seats going to Pierre Elliott International Airport? I think it's time you met your father!"

Steven motioned to Pat, and they both hurried away to find the ticket counter. She turned happily to Mario and pulled him down onto the seats. "Oh, tell me more. Will your father be all right if we come visit?"

Mario grinned. "He'd love it! Do you remember how Mom was always full of the neatest jokes?"

Anita laughed with glee. "Oh my God, I have no idea how she could remember them all!"

Mario's aqua eyes twinkled. "Have you heard this one? An Irish priest is driving to New York and gets stopped for speeding. The cop smells alcohol on the priest's breath and then sees an empty wine bottle on the floor of the car. He says, 'Sir, have you been drinking?' 'Just water,' says the priest. The cop says, 'Then why do I smell wine?' The priest looks at the bottle and says, 'Good Lord! He's done it again!'"

Anita slapped Mario's shoulder and laughed loudly, her laughter echoing throughout the Gates.

Then gleefully she leaned in and asked, "So, how come you're not prime minister yet?"

Fini